MADNESS INCENDIARY

Lady Lust gone, you'd have thought Janna Somata would die. If you were a dispossessed mortal with a Brainrock trident driven through your chest you'd die, too. Would have already, I'd have thought. I know I did. But I'm still alive and watching in sick fascination as Janna writhes about like a skewered dolphin at the end of a harpoon; dolphins being Shiva as well as Apollo's pet psychopomps, you mythology duffs, unless it's buffs, might recall.

The Crimson Corona was still wrapped around his forehead. I've never seen it glow so brightly, not before nor since, and I've seen it a few times since. Something came out of it. Abe was free to finish the job at hand. Janna burst into flames. Leaving only the fang-fingered glove smouldering on the oversized bed to mark her passage, she blew away into so much smoke in the breeze of his brutality.

That was enough for me. My boy, my Squiggly incarnation of the day, may not have been the swashbuckling sort, not in comparison to his, then mine, best buddy, Janna's Sraddha of a twin bro, but he was relatively fit for his years and liabilities, meaning me. Even though I lived there, in keeping with our procreative imperative, he, me, we, had a secret way into and out of the palace, an upper floor window.

Unfortunately, the vines broke and so did my leg when I landed. I wasn't done yet, though; not half. I knew I had to get away, no dummy me, and I knew both how and where to get away to, so long as I could first get to the tavern where – through no fault of my own, you'll no doubt recall since I just described how Uncle Abe hauled my most desirous ass to the Masters Palace – I'd left my cap, quill stuck in it. I was in unbelievable pain. It was so bad I couldn't concentrate enough to will it back to me.

Dying always hurts, but I'd died lots of burial plots over the centuries, so pain and I went way back. I persevered. At the point of exhaustion and at times beyond it – I kept passing out, only to have the incessant if not quite incandescent throbbing in my leg jolt me back to consciousness – I hopped and hobbled and, in the end, crawled and slithered toward my getaway.

I made it too, to boot, albeit what must have been hours later. Whereupon I discovered firsthand what Janna had just experienced.

Phantacea Publications presents:

Jim McPherson's

PHANTACEA MYTHOS

- *PHANTACEA* **One to Six**
(A series of comic books with artwork by various artists)

- **Forever & 40 Days – The Genesis of *PHANTACEA***
(A graphic novel with artwork by Ian Fry as well as
background material and a short story featuring the
Damnation Brigade, the Death Dodgers & Signal System)

- **Feeling Theocidal**
(Book One of *'The Thrice-Cursed Godly Glories'* Trilogy)

- **The War of the Apocalyptics**
(The first entry in the *'Launch 1980'* story cycle)

- **The 1000 Days of Disbelief**
(Book Two of *'The Thrice-Cursed Godly Glories'* Trilogy
consisting of three mini-novels complete unto themselves)
- **The Death's Head Hellion**
- **Contagion Collectors**
- **Janna Fangfingers**

- **Goddess Gambit**
(Book Three of *'The Thrice-Cursed Godly Glories'* Trilogy
and the second entry in the *'Launch 1980'* story cycle)

In one form or another, all are available for ordering through:
www.phantacea.com

The Thousand Days of Disbelief

- Book Two of 'The Thrice-Cursed Godly Glories' Trilogy -

Jim McPherson

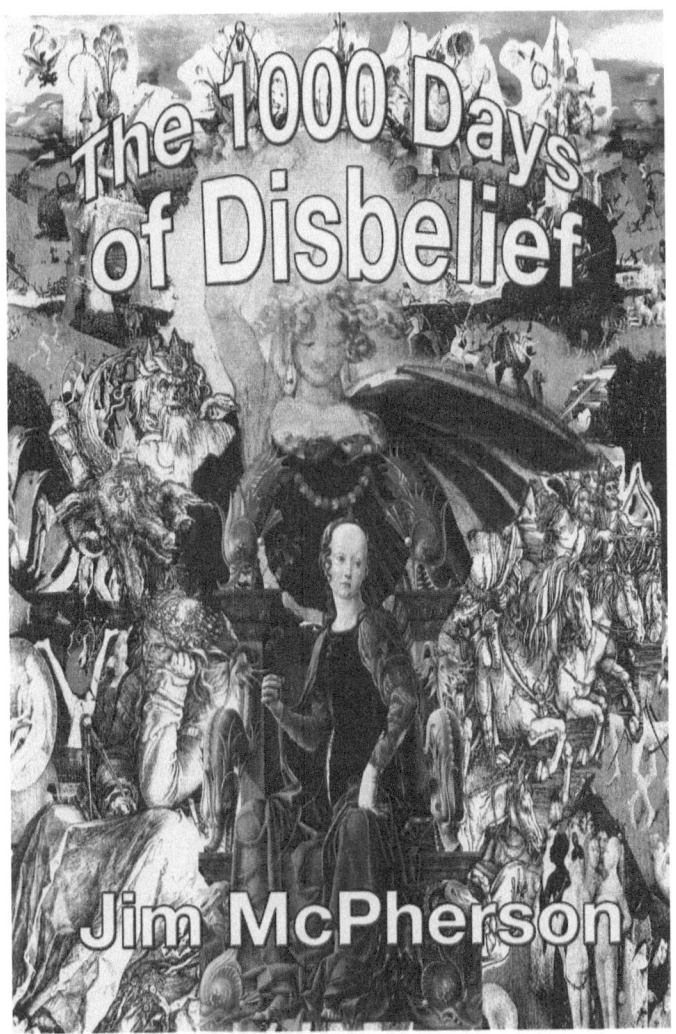

A **PHANTACEA** Mythos Mosaic Novel
published by James H McPherson

ISBN 978-0-9781342-1-1

JANNA FANGFINGERS

Copyright © James H McPherson

A *PHANTACEA* MYTHOS MOSAIC NOVEL

Conceived, written and produced by Jim McPherson
Cover by Jim McPherson
Interior collages prepared by Jim McPherson

Phantacea Publications
(James H McPherson, Publisher)
74689 Kitsilano RPO
2768 West Broadway
Vancouver BC
V6K 4P4 Canada

www.phantacea.com

Auctorial Prefatory

Unlike the first two mini-novels extracted from "The 1000 Days of Disbelief" (henceforth 1000-DAZE), Book Two of '*The Thrice-Cursed Godly Glories*' trilogy, namely "The Death's Head Hellion" (HELLION) and "Contagion Collectors" (CONTAGION), "Janna Fangfingers" (FANGERS) doubles as a prequel to the '*Launch 1980*' story sequences.

It therefore doubles as a prequel to both "The War of the Apocalyptics" (WAR-POX), which came out in 2009, and the upcoming "Goddess Gambit" (GAMBIT), which in many respects picks up from whence the comparatively modern aspect of FANGERS leaves off. This will come as no surprise to readers who followed web-serials presented on *pH-Webworld* (which is officially known as the *PHANTACEA* **Mythos online** these days) since its storyline was first presented therein.

As for one of its most significant episodes, for readers who realized the true identity of Freespirit Nihila when she made her startling appearance in the Faerie Garden during the latter stages of WAR-POX, well, there's no surprise there either. That its narrator is none other than the Legendarian, a recurring deviant perhaps better recalled as Jordan '*Q for Quill*' Tethys, at the end of Djerridam 5980 YD (October 1980) is, admittedly, a change.

What isn't a change is that a certain almost never-remembered, ever-smiling, judgelike character (who I tend to call Smiler rather than either Judge Druj or the Smiling Fiend) haunts the edges – glimpsed, briefly; even heard, perhaps; but never, seemingly, irreplaceable.

Stuff happens. Stuff doesn't need him to happen. Except ... um, sorry but in terms of the *PHANTACEA* **Mythos** it probably does.

Smiler was around, explicitly, in "Feeling Theocidal" (FEEL THEO), which was partially set in the Imperial City of Rome in 376 AD (4376 Year of the Dome). He was only maybe around in HELLION (824/5 AD or 4824/5 YD). That was when

Thrygragos Everyman (Lazareme – the Helios lookalike in Harmony's eyes) contends Tomcat Tattletail was Dusted Daemonicus back for more intolerably disruptive merriment at everyone else's expense.

He was definitely around again in CONTAGION (5454-5476 YD). That's because, on a couple of occasions, someone was quoted as talking highly distinctively, *in both bold and italics* (just like that). That's the reader's cue. Outward appearance notwithstanding, someone quoted as talking in *bold-italics* either has or is a very specific internal infernal, to quote a green-eyed putto spotted fluttering about the Nuremburg Free City of early 1476 our time.

(In case you missed it, CONTAGION's putto, the daemonic offspring of Tomcat Tattletail and Herta Heartthrob, was referring to something devilishly shining that he'd eaten relatively recently. Although never confirmed, it's probably safe to presume that whomever, rather than whatever, he ate wasn't smiling at the time. Being something of a Cheshire tomcat, Tattletail may have been, however.)

No one in his alternative universe realizes Smiler exists unless he's manifested himself right there beside him, her or them. Thus, whenever a storyteller who is in his reality, such as Biblio Drek (Lazareme's Librarian) or Jordy himself (who also told us about the Death's Head Hellion, albeit in CONTAGION's timeline, and even though he wasn't around for most of HELLION's dramatics), comes to Smiler he draws a blank (as in doesn't realize it).

I mention this prefatorily since there will be times in the book you are about to embark upon reading where you will see someone quoted *like this* when it appears the words are emanating from someone entirely different. And if this leads you to conclude that the Launching of the Cosmic Express resulted in a stellar prison break masterminded by our friend, the Smiling Fiend, award yourself bonus points.

Of course from a Byronic standpoint (not that Great Byron has any legs left to stand on), it didn't start out that way. But, hey, that's as they say, another story.

========

THE THRICE-CURSED GODLY GLORIES TRILOGY

- A Capsulated Character Companion
    Book One: "Feeling Theocidal" (FEEL THEO)
    Book Two: "Thousand Days of Disbelief" (1000-DAZE)
    Book Three: "Goddess Gambit" (GAMBIT)

Many of the characters featured in the mini-novels extracted from 1000-DAZE are immortal or seemingly immortal. Their influence is thus felt throughout the ages covered by the overall trilogy. Indeed, some of those listed on the reference pages counted with Roman numerals hardly ever appear in the mini-novel at hand, whereas a few others are only mentioned in it.

"Janna Fangfingers" commences on page 1. PREGAME-GAMBIT 1, the first chapter of "Goddess Gambit", the final book in '*The Thrice-Cursed Godly Glories*' trilogy, is provided as a bonus. It begins on page 191.

========

Sedon Purge 5476-5495
(as told in 5980)

– "JANNA FANGFINGERS" –

(Extracted and adapted specifically for this book from a capsulated character companion for *'The Thrice-Cursed Godly Glories'* trilogy)

INDEX

- Demogorgon, the Conglomerate Deva

3. Mortal Descendants of Original Extraterrestrials

- Utopians of Weir on Earth
- Pure U-Bloods (Cabby the Daddy, Melina born Sarpedon become Zeross, Demios Sarpedon)
- Hybrid Utopians (Melina born Tethys become Somata, Johann & George Somata, Morgianna born Nauroz become Somata then Sarpedon, Saladin called Devason Nauroz)

4. Norman & Norma Notables

- 55th Century of the Dome (Hierophant Koatyl)
- 15th Century beyond the Dome (Tomas de Torquemada, Queen Isabella of Castile, King Ferdinand of Aragon)
- 60th Century of the Dome (Alpha Centauri, Janna St Peche-Montressor, Gottfried Kenton, Achigan Auranja, Governor Ferdinand Niarchos, Ambassador Gomez Niarchos, Sraddhite High Priest Holgat, Barsine born Mandam Holgat-wife, Sraddhite High Priest Thartarre Sraddha Holgatson)
- 20th Century beyond the Dome (Angelo & Aristotle *'Harry'* Zeross, Yataghan Montressor, Hiyati Samarand, George Hannibal, Romaine Kinesis)

========

1. Shining Ones: First, Second and Third Generation Devils

- The Moloch Sedon
  - the seemingly immortal, but nowhere-near-almighty, All-Father of Devazurkind; the Devil Himself, capitalized;
  - although his star is absent from the night's sky throughout the 55th century sequences, Cathonia (the Cathonic Zone or Dome, also the Sedon Sphere) shows no indication of imminent collapse.

- The Six Great Gods and Goddesses
  - the Thrygragos Brothers and Trigregos Sisters comprise the entirety of the second generation of devakind;
  - the Three Great Gods are Thrygragos **Lazareme** (aka sometimes the Lackland Libertine, but most commonly Thrygragos Everyman), Thrygragos **Byron** (aka both Bodiless Byron and the Unmoving One due to that fact that he's all head, with his facial features frozen in the same expression, not because he can't transport himself wherever he wants on the Inner Earth), and Thrygragos Varuna **Mithras;**
  - though perhaps not explicitly, both Byron and Mithras appear in the 60th century aspect of the mini-novel: the former in possession of Alpha Centauri; the latter as a (perhaps too) lifelike bust being sculpted by yellow-skinned Sedunihas (qv) on Frozen Lathakra, where dwell his parents, the Thanatoid Death Gods (Heat and Cold);
  - during his tale-telling in the 60th century, the Legendarian speculates on

the existence of an eminently forgettable, but possibly not apocryphal, individual known as the **VAM Entity** – Thrygragos Varuna Ahriman Mithras;

- Smiler, the ostensible *'A'* in the VAM Entity, plays a mean panpipe; someone hearing it may suggest to the reader that he's around, possibly between-space; though when he's acting as narrator the Legendarian won't be able to confirm that since he can't remember he even exists.

- the often three-in-one Great Goddesses are Trigregos **Devaura** (the Spirit or Soul), Trigregos **Demeter** (the Body), and Trigregos **Sapiendev** (the Mind or Consciousness); they do not appear in the mini-novel;

- their terrible talismans do, however; hence why "Janna Fangfingers" is an integral part of *'The Thrice-Cursed Godly Glories'* trilogy.

- Master Devas
  - dictionaries often define *'devas'* or *'daevas'* as *'the shining ones'*; hence also the English word *'devils'*, meaning *'little gods'*;
  - Master Devas compose the third generation of devazurkind; the Trigregos Sisters always bore them simultaneously, in threesomes;
  - they believe their fathers are one or another of the Thrygragos Brothers; hence why it's accepted that there are only three devic tribes: the Lazaremists, the Byronics and the Mithradites;
  - when Master Devas, whose bodies are debrained daemons, interact sexually, without possessing anyone, all they can produce are azuras;
  - a fourth generation of devakind (as opposed to devazurkind) began coming into existence during the second, third and fifth decade of the Dome's 60th Century; as of late Maruta 5980 YD, every known member of the 4th generation has been born as a twin instead of a triplet;
  - when Sedon, Great Gods and/or Master Devas possess sentient beings for procreative purposes, their resultant offspring are often long-lived and, once in a while, unnaturally gifted mortals known as deviants;
  - it seems likely that many of the Outer Earth's so-called supranormals or supras also had devic half-parents; this is especially true of supras born as a result of the Simultaneous Summonings of 59/1920.

- The Firstborn Unities of Lazareme
  — **Harmony**, called Datong Harmonia by bygone Illuminaries of Weir on Earth; the Unity of Balance as well as Panharmonium (her pet project, a planetary panacea for beneficial devils and their worshipful multitudes alike);
  - reputedly, by a matter of a few seconds, the first Master Deva ever born; beauty incarnate as well as loveliness personified;
  - her power focus or Tvasitar talisman is a golden torc, the so-called Necklace of, as you might expect, Harmony; from it she conjures her golden, chain-mail gowns and the broken chains often manifested manacled to her wrists; from them she sometimes shoots, what else?, chain lightning.
  — **Chaos**, called Unholy Abaddon by bygone Illuminaries of Weir (after the Biblical Angel of Apollyon, the Bottomless Pit); the Unity of just that, Chaos;

- his power focus or Tvasitar talisman is the Chaos Blade, which he keeps forever-sheathed out of fear of causing a chain reaction that would bring irreversible carnage to the world, if not the cosmos.

— **Order**, called Thunder and Lightning Lord Yajur, or variations thereof, by bygone Illuminaries of Weir; the Unity of just that, Order;

- from his power focus or Tvasitar talisman he shoots vajra bolts – white lightning of the non-alcoholic variety;

- goes by Sparky when he's in altogether human form;

- Chaos and Order hate each other passionately; they'd seek to annihilate each other, and all that stands between them, if Harmony didn't always do just that, stand between them mollifyingly.

- Significant Additional Lazaremists

— **Fangfingers**, called First Fangs in 60th century sequences;

- a comparatively lowborn Lazaremist called by bygone Illuminaries Faustus Vladuca after a combination of Dacian, Carpathian, Gothic and/or Slavonic deities, folk legends or heroes;

- devils tend to refer to him as the Fop because he fancies himself something of a fashion plate, one with a penchant for wearing a black opera cape with red lining;

- has, for a power focus, a Brainrock glove with fangs rather than claws on its fingertips;

- a Black Godling with an unsavoury and perhaps undeserved reputation for sadism in that he welcomes animal sacrifice.

— **Metisophia**, aka Titanic Metis and Wisdom of Lazareme;

- second-born brood sister of the Grey Lady (Krepusyl Evenstar) and the devic Anthea, who vanished not long after becoming a solid entity circa 2000 YD;

- devic half-mother of the first Legendarian by younger brother Rumour;

- power focus or Tvasitar talisman is a cauldron that bubbles up all-seeing fumes; mainly during her Outer Earth years as a major participant in its Goddess Culture (the so-called Mad Goddesses' Middle Sea Matriarchy, which lasted from roughly 2000 to 1500 BCE), she wore it à la the Olympian Athena as a breast plate;

- Methandra Thanatos confiscated her cauldron during the expansion of the Empire of Lathakra; as a result of this, Metis lost her demonic body and promptly vanished from sight.

— **Irisiel** Mercherm, Lazareme's preferred Heliodromus or sun-runner; called Speedy by devils for reasons irrefutable.

- Significant Mithradites

— **Belialma**, Sinistral Lust of Satanwyck (Hell on Earth, Pandemonium, Sedon's Temple on a map of the Hidden Headworld); Hell's Belle, also sometimes called the luscious or lascivious Lady Lust as well as Bouncing, Beguiling or Bedazzling Belialma and variations thereof;

- a second-born Mithradite whose power focus or Tvasitar talisman is the Ruby Red Apple of Concupiscence; like her fellow Apple Goddesses, Concord and Discord (who are mentioned in the mini-novel but don't appear), she carries it as the pupil of her third eye;

- always an object of desire, her reciprocal interests cross tribal boundaries to include not just Unholy Abaddon, the Unity of Chaos, and his brood brother, Lord Order, but their father, Thrygragos Lazareme;

- Bouncing Belle resides in her bastion of bliss overlooking Pandemonium, the capital of Satanwyck (Hell on Earth), where she entertains her paramours, who also number Zuvem *'Gravedigger'* Nergalis and, centuries earlier, King Cold (Tantal Thanatos) and the Bull of Mithras (Cruel Plathon);

- her affinity, arguably even affection, for Janna Somata from a very early age triggers much of the tragedy that unfolds on the Hidden Continent of Sedon's Head in the latter half of its 55th Century.

— **Gravedigger**, a fourth-born called Zuvem Nergalis by bygone Illuminaries of Weir; generally manifests himself black-skinned, like a male Utopian of Weir;

- name in part derives from his power focus or Tvasitar talisman, which is a Brainrock spade with a razor-sharp edge, and in part because he's sometimes called the Nergalids' Planter even though he actually alternates planting duties (of Vetala-Fecundity) with King Harvest;

- among his other love interests include bedazzling Belialma (Hell's Belle, still Sinistral Lust of Satanwyck in 5476);

- figures he should *'occupy'* Sraddha Somata when the latter gets married and whenever he fathers children; that way his deviant offspring would be as impressive as Zuvem is and always has been, at least in his mind;

- Lord Order was attempting to cathonitize, ill-star or catasterize Gravedigger, whom he (**wrongly**) reckoned was occupying the Legendarian of 5476, when he accidentally cathonitized Dame Chance (who was occupying Janna Somata) and consequently drove Star Sedon out of the night's sky;

- becomes forever-after known as Devil Doom for the accuracy of his prophecies regarding Janna still Somata in 5480.

— **King Harvest**, Underlord Yama Nergal, a fifth-born, so-called Earthling;

- when the Lathakran Empire conquered the Penile Peninsula (better known as Iraxas, Sedon's Mutton Chop on a map of the Hidden Headworld), he helped cathonitize Vanthysces Vastness (Scarecrow), the Byronics' Grim Reaper;

- he thereafter fused the latter's power focus, a scythe, with his own, a miner's pickaxe; hence King Harvest, the Mithradites' Reaper or Harvester;

- for millennia alternated, on a lunar basis, fecundating duties of much younger sister Nergal Vetala with brood-older brother Gravedigger;

- unchallenged devic ruler of the radioactive Ghostlands since circa 4825 YD; as such, Death's Angels, whose touch can kill but, being animated by Nergalazurs, bodily dissolve in rain or running water, are his to command;

- more so than the Thanatoids of Lathakra or the Apocalyptics' Mother Murder (the Medusa, Mater Matare), he's considered the devils' primary Death God.

— **Vetala**, Nergal Vetala, more commonly addressed as Fecundity by her fellow Master Devas until events described in FANGERS;

- also called the Nergalids' Grower; the Legendarian sometimes refers to her, when she was Fecundity, as Vulva-Vetala;

- though only a twelfth-born Mithradite, she's a Moon Goddess like Lunar Uma, a Byronic firstborn; her power focus or Tvasitar talisman is considered a moon-sickle in that its blade is shaped like a crescent moon;

- until events described in FANGERS, Vetala became pregnant by one or the other male Nergalid come the New Moon and gave birth every Full Moon;

- her azuras, who number in the thousands – more like tens of thousands – are called Vetalazurs or Nergalazurs (albeit only if their fathers were either Zuvem or Yama);

- Vetalazurs seem to be only good for animating Dead Things, thus in effect rendering them zombies; the bodies they animate dissolve in rain or running water;

- when the Lathakran Empire conquered the Penile Peninsula (thereafter once again better known as Iraxas, Sedon's Mutton Chop on a map of the Hidden Headworld), thus displacing the Byronics who'd ruled it (as El Dorado, the Golden Land of mostly Outer Earth legend) for millennia previously, she stayed behind to oversee its affairs on their behalf;

- despite, as first described in FEEL THEO, commonly having vaguely greenish skin, blood-red lips and too-sharp teeth, when not pregnant, considered something of a mouth-wateringly beautiful temptress;

- by tradition vetalas (lower case) manifest themselves with their hands on the wrong wrists; Vetala, though, seldom remembers to adopt this affectation;

- resides in the former Weirdom of Manoa, called the Gleaming City due to its golden walls, throughout most of 1000-DAZE; as described in HELLION, her azuras were the main reason the Dead rose during the Infernal Equinox of 4824/5 in Grand Elysium;

- Byronic forces led by the firstborn Silverclouds, as well as the Great God's second- and third-born Nucleoids, are invading her domain, what had been their golden land until the Dome's 48th Century, at the start of FANGERS.

- The Thanatoids of Lathakra
   — **Methandra** Thanatos, a firstborn Mithradite also known, accurately, if perhaps somewhat disrespectfully, as Hot Stuff;

- until Antheal 5933, a red-skinned, almost always masked and thoroughly covered (in fabrics invariably coloured different shades of red) giantess whose power focus is a firebrand or matchstick (cane); thereafter, thanks to Sedona's Spell of Disproportionment, often only 6 inches tall;

- the mother, while being subsumed by a be-brained daemon or demon pre-Genesea (the Great Flood of Genesis) of Klannit, the world's first azura;

- considered the devic patron of the Athenan War Witch sisterhood (to which Janna St Peche-Montressor, Fisherwoman and Superior Sarpedon, among many others, belong in the mid-to-late 60th Century of the Dome);

- a self-proclaimed death goddess, that of heat and fire, who nonetheless became the conceptive and birthmother of the first members of a fourth generation of devakind (not to be confused with devazurkind) sometime after waking up from a thousand year sleep in 5908 Year of the Dome.

— **Tantal** Thanatos, firstborn Mithradite most commonly known as King Cold;

- a gigantic, blue-skinned, icicle-bearded, archetypal-Viking whose power focus or Tvasitar talisman is a labrys (a double-headed war axe);

- pre-Dome father, while being subsumed by a be-brained daemon or demon pre-Genesea (the Great Flood of Genesis) of Klannit, the world's first azura;

- besides his thought-father, Thrygragos Varuna Mithras, probably the most prolific male Master Deva in terms of having azura offspring;

- self-proclaimed death god, that of cold and ice, who nonetheless became the conceptive and birthfather of the first members of a fourth generation of devakind (not to be confused with devazurkind) sometime after waking up from a thousand year sleep in 5908 Year of the Dome.

— **Sedunihas**, evidently the last non-cathonitized, or otherwise unaccounted for, devic offspring of Tantal and Methandra Thanatos;

- one definite brother (Demon Land) appeared in "The War of the Apocalyptics", which came out in 2009; another brother and two sisters seem somehow connected to Airealist, Sea Goddess and Rainbow Rider, three members of the Damnation Brigade who also appeared in War-Pox; the Launching of the Cosmic Express is not scheduled to take place until November 30, 1980 (the 60ᵗʰ Century events described in Fangers occur just before it's supposed to take off from the Outer Earth's Centauri Island);

- a yellow-skinned artist who specializes in exceeding lifelike statuary;

- for reasons not as yet detailed, was not given birth until 5955; like all ten of his 4ᵗʰ generational brothers and sisters, born a twin, not a triplet; also unlike Master Devas, all twelve were born with possibly daemonic bodies; there is, however, thus far no indication he's a metamorph like they were;

- as yet inexplicably, his twin brother, named Motan, was born (and remains) altogether dead; also for reasons not yet detailed, Sedunihas only ages one year in five; consequently appears to be only 5-years-old in 5980.

- Moderately Significant Byronics
— **APM** All-Eyes, lone daughter born in Bodiless Byron's third brood; as such a member of his secondary Nucleus (along with her triplet brothers, Damon Goldenrod and Nevair Neverknight);

- a love goddess, Byron's Venus, bygone Illuminaries of Weir named her Aphropsyche Morningstar, hence APM;

- likes to appear as if composed entirely of eyes, hence All-Eyes;

- her witch-followers, who aren't just confined to the Byronics' territory of Aka Godbad at the time of the mini-novel, are known as love-loving Afrites;

- Janna St Peche-Montressor (qv) is a love-loving Afrite as well as an Athenan War Witch; she is also APM's most frequent host-shell in 5980.

— Rufous **Rudra** Silvercloud, Bodiless Byron's firstborn son, his Beast Master, also his Storm Lord;

- as per Hellion, a onetime friend and ally of the Thanatoids of Lathakra who, along with sister-wife Umashakti, led Byronic forces during the First War between the Living and the Dead.

— **Umashakti** Silvercloud, Unmoving Byron's remaining firstborn daughter;
- a Moon Goddess, she waxes and wanes with its phases; consequently sometimes called Lunar Uma;
- her attribute is gravity; hence why devils usually address her as just that, Gravity;
- as per HELLION, a onetime friend and ally of the Thanatoids of Lathakra who, along with brother-husband Rudra, led Byronic forces during the First War between the Living and the Dead;
- the Silverclouds' brood sister, whom much later Illuminaries of Weir eventually named Serathrone Hallow, never made it out of the Celestial Sphere (which devils aboard the Sedonshem barely escaped, howsoever long ago preEarth — hence perhaps the myth, legend or belief in Fallen Angels).

- More Lazaremists
— **Rumour** of Lazareme: devic half-father of the first Legendarian;
- probably does not appear in 1000-DAZE, but is mentioned in it fairly frequently because his power focus or Tvasitar talisman, a multipurpose Brainrock quill, transfers to the Legendarian, a recurring deviant who, whenever he returns to life, does so in his dying son or daughter, grandson or granddaughter.
— **Librarian**, Biblio Drek, sometimes called Specks due to the fact that his power focus or Tvasitar talisman is a pair of three-lens eyeglasses.
— **Chance**, called Wintry Moira by bygone Illuminaries of Weir; a fifthborn also known variously as Lazareme's Luck, Fata Fortuna and, most commonly among devils, Dame Chance;
- because of her dangerously unpredictable attribute, coupled with her nevertheless undeniable attractiveness, some refer to her as the luscious Lady Luck;
- her azuras are called Fatazurs;
- her power focus or Tvasitar talisman is the 3-spoke wheel of fortune traditionally known as the Triskelion;
- as per CONTAGION, became a star in the night's sky above the Hidden Continent of Sedon's Head on 5574's summer solstice when Lord Order accidentally cathonitized her while attempting do away with Gravedigger, whom he thought (*mistakenly*) was occupying the Quidnunc Legendarian of the day.
— **Skinless**, the Skinless Rasp, or variations thereof; a comparatively lowborn Lazaremist called by bygone Illuminaries Rastha Aragon;
- a White Godling flagellant with a flail for a power focus;
- confined within All the Invincible on the Prison Beach of Incain at the start of FANGERS and as such is only mentioned a few times in the mini-novel.
— **Krepusyl Evenstar**, **Tvasitar** Smithmonger, **Amal-Althea**, **Azkeecyoos** the Healer, Ursine **Bardol**, Black Zenit **Suryad**, Rapith **Nauroz**, Icy **Miros**, Mercurial **Kometes**, and Battle Babe (the Morrigu **Badhbh**) are among the other Lazaremists who are either mentioned or appear, howsoever briefly, in the mini-novel.

More Byronics

— **Chimaera** Glimmenmare, along with triplet siblings, **Sedona** Spellbinder and **Devil Wind** (the Whirling Deva, aka Vayu Maelstrom), are Byron's Primary Nucleoids;

- all three once frequented Iraxas (the Penile Peninsula, Sedon's Mutton Chop on a map of the Hidden Headworld);

- they are among the many Byronics seeking to drive Nergal Vetala out of what they called the Golden Land (El Dorado), which she has been ruling since the 48ᵗʰ Century of the Dome, at the beginning of FANGERS;

- all three featured in WAR-POX.

— **Draconic Yati**, Byron's Dragon (beware his burps);

- a highborn Byronic somehow in tune with scientific developments on the Outer Earth during both eras described in FANGERS.

— **Djerrid** Ruin, **Pyçonja** Volant, **Camorva** Freeflight, **Vanthysces** Vastness (called Scarecrow by devils), Damon **Goldenrod**, Nevair **Neverknight**, **Qosgod** and **Petrogod** are among the other named Byronics who appear, howsoever briefly, in the mini-novel.

- More Mithradites

— **Phantast** Thanatos, the third of the firstborn Thanatoid Death Gods; called Dream or Dreamweaver by devils;

- carbonitized circa 4000 YD for masterminding the Crimson Conspiracy on the Outer Earth along with Strife (Mithras's Ewe for Aries, aka Kore-Eris, Discord, Kanin Marut, Fitna Marutia, among many other names);

- does not appear in "Janna Fangfingers" but is mentioned occasionally.

— Sinistral **Envy**, a lower-born called Bobby Badboy or, less frequently, Robin Goodfellow by bygone Illuminaries of Weir;

- generally manifests himself as a cupid or putto, which is why devils, somewhat incorrectly, tend to refer to him as Cupidity; the Legendarian also refers to him as Sinistral Spiteful;

- seemingly for perpetuity has been waiting in the daemonic wings to replace his much higher born sister, Prime Sinistral Lust, whom he senses, quite rightly, has been bored of acting as Demon King Sedon's surrogate when it comes to ruling Satanwyck (Sedon's Temple, Hell on Earth) for a very long time;

- figures he's in line to succeed her when Bouncing Belle moves to take over the Mastery of Marutia via Janna Somata, which may still be a possibility at the start of FANGERS;

- like virtually everyone else, possibly including Sedon himself, Envy has no recollection that someone else has a far greater claim to the throne of Hell until he manifests himself visually in front of him and starts being quoted in ***bold-italics***.

— **Domdaniel-Pride** and most of the other former or eventual Prime Sinistrals of Satanwyck are mentioned by name;

- in 5980, for example, Demon King Sedon's surrogate is Prime Sinistral Sloth (Baaloch **Hellblob**), a vaguely egg-shaped, surprisingly gourmet-calibre cook perhaps even better known as Lord Lazy.

— **Pyrame Silverstar**, the Pauper Priestess, the fabulously female (adult) Perpetual Presence; sometimes called Providence, among many another name or title;

- unless programmed otherwise, All of Incain obeys her; hence why she can often be found occupying the She-Sphinx on the Prison Beach of Incain, at the bottom of the Cattail Peninsula (Sedon's Ponytail on a map of the Hidden Headworld), about as far south as one can go on the Head without having to swim or ride in a boat;

- for reasons left unexplained in the mini-novel, she was cathonitized in 5950; that suggests she somehow lost her formerly (and perhaps still) be-brained, daemonic body, that of Primeval Lilith, the Demon Queen of the Night, much like she did in 4824 YD when they were jointly occupying the Death's Head Hellion;

- devic half-mother of Saladin born Nauroz Devason (qv), the Master of the Weirdom of Cabalarkon since 5950; (half-father: the Moloch Sedon — it may therefore be that Saladin is the last Sed-son or sedon, small case, left alive beneath the Cathonic Dome).

— **Tammuz** and **Osiraq**, Mithras's onetime torchbearers;

- not just devils nowadays think of them as either the Idiot or Atomic Twins; this after their perhaps inadvertent, but unquestionably cataclysmic, rendering of the Ghostlands lethally radioactive in 4825 YD;

- among the many who help compose Demogorgon, the Conglomerate Deva, on Incain Day (the 5495 conclusion of the 1000 Days of Disbelief).

— various **Apocalyptics** including the Primary Four (**War**, **Death**, **Plague** and **Catastrophe**), **Drought** (Cathune Bubastis) and **Flood** (Diluvia Ran) make howsoever fleeting appearances in Fangers.

— so does at least one of the two surviving **Reptilians** from Mithras's Eighth: namely, the **Emperor Chameleon**, Deva-Dand of the Floodlands, Lord of Lizarados and the mutually despised brood brother of Saur Lord **Klizarod Rex**, Devil-Dand of the neighbouring Lake Lands (together they make up Sedon's Sweat Glands on a map of the Hidden Headworld).

— the entirety of Mithras's Sixth are among the many mentioned in literal conjunction with Demogorgon, the Conglomerate Deva; Dandset **Typhon** and Geld **Neargon** have only then recently come to grief (as in become All of Incain's guest) whereas their brood brother, Abdullah Ziderite (**Magnetism**), is but one of the many devils who've been stuck in the She-Sphinx for hundreds, even thousands of years, prior to Incain Day.

========

2. Deviants, Demons, Faeries and Mandroid Monstrosities

• Deviants

- When Great Gods and/or Master Devas possess sentient beings for procreative purposes, their resultant offspring are often long-lived and occasionally unnaturally gifted mortals known as deviants.

— the **Legendarian**, aka always Jordan *'Q for Quill'* Tethys, the legendary 30-Year Man or Woman, as well as 30-Beers;

- 5980's narrator and a central character in much of the 55th Century storyline;
- a multitalented musician, painter and recurring tail- as well as taleteller who, whenever he (as he prefers) returns to life, does so in his son or daughter, grandson or granddaughter;
- when he comes back he keeps the memories of whomever he was previously; additionally brings with him his own memories, which date back to his first incarnation circa 4000 YD;
- for reasons never explained (other than as an aspect of his deviancy), cannot come back into anyone who hasn't already turned 20 before apparently dying the first time; equally oddly, can never stay in anyone longer than 30 years; hence the 30-Year Man or Woman;
- evidently, when he comes back he revitalizes the body that either died a first time or, more feasibly, was irreversibly dying a first time; if that body makes it to the full allotment of 30 years, Quill returns to Limbo but the original son, daughter, grandson or granddaughter lives on (albeit without any of the Legendarian's memories of other lives, just memories of his or her lifetime both pre-Legendarian and as the Legendarian);
- such exceedingly rare individuals are referred to as Quit-Quills; Quidnunc's white-skinned, red-headed father, Quibble Tethys, became Quit-Quill in CONTAGION;
- Rumour's quill, what Tethys sometimes calls his power pen (as opposed to power focus), follows him from lifetime to lifetime;
- among many other purposes, he uses it to draw himself and others betweenspace (the Weird, the dark-grey universal substance of Samsara, mundane reality), provided they've previously given him permission to do so;
- he can draw on anything, even the air itself, but generally draws on a pad of paper or parchment that he splotches out of the nib of his quill; he naturally calls it his splotch pad;
- Rumour's quill being Brainrock, its ink is too; as such, it never runs out;
- anyone can use his quill while he's dancing the legless limbo between lives but it always comes back to him whenever and wherever he reincarnates;
- count among the named characters who eventually became Legendarians in the 55th century: a young swordsman whose Q-name was Quidnunc; his birthfather, Quibble become Quit-Quill; Queer become Quoits (before she became Quill), an extremely long-lived hybrid Utopian who, albeit mostly behind-the-scenes, played a nevertheless highly significant role in both CONTAGION and FANGERS; and Squiggly Tethys, Sraddha Somata's best buddy and sister Janna's beloved before things got seriously crazy for all three of them;
- count among the named characters who eventually became Legendarians in the 60th century: Sister Jordan, originally of Subterranean Temporis, and George Taurson, originally of Apple Isle;
- we also learn that Gordon 'G for Glee' Tethys, the Valkyrie novitiate, Ute Tethys's younger brother, became a Legendarian in the late 44th or early 45th Century of the Dome (both Ute and Glee appeared during FEEL THEO).
— **Quoits** Tethys, originally a (very white-skinned) hybrid-Utopian daugh-

ter or granddaughter of Quill Tethys (the Legendarian);

- a millennial child, meaning she was born in the Year of the Dome 5000;

- chances are Dame Chance (the Master Deva bygone Illuminaries named Wintry Moira) is her devic half-mother, which at least partially accounts for her extremely extended lifetime (even by the longevity-standards of a full-blooded Utopian, which she's not since pure U-bloods can't be possessed);

- before she became one herself, faithfully served an unspecified number of Masters of the Weirdom of Cabalarkon over the nearly five centuries of her life;

- given Jordan for a first name, her initial Q-name was Queer (possibly because, despite being a hybrid, she looked very much like a pure-blooded Utopian woman); gave herself the Q-name of Quoits when she rediscovered ringots in the Weirdom of Cabalarkon;

- Melina nee Tethys Somata, the Trigregos Titaness, called her Granny Jordy even though many generations separate them;

- briefly became Master of Cabalarkon in 5476; remained such after she died, or virtually died, presumably of old age, since the Legendarian came back inside her;

- died (or virtually died) a second time when, according to 5980's Legendarian (George Taurson), he (as her) drank her into a tub of Cathonic Fluid (wherein he, as she, inexplicably drowned) on the cow-swill Cabalarkon's version of First Weir's Mother Machine manufactures and dares call beer;

- voluntarily gave up her Mastery by passing it on to Zalman Somata on the 4th of Kamor (July) 5476 (1476 AD).

— **Zalman** Somata, black-skinned, once very popular Master of the Weirdom of Kanin City and, with it, the Mastery of Marutia (Sedon's Cheek);

- an acknowledged deviant whose devic half-father was Thunder and Lightning Lord Yajur, the Unity of Order;

- (possibly) possessed by Thrygragos Lazareme when he impregnated wife Melina (definitely possessed by Harmony, the Unity of Balance as well as Panharmonium) with result being the Terrible Twins, Sraddha and Janna Somata;

- became the Master of the Weirdom of Cabalarkon in 5476 after its then-current Master (Quoits Tethys) resigned in his favour.

— **Sraddha** Somata, deviant son of Zalman (possibly possessed by Thrygragos Lazareme) and Melina nee Tethys Somata (definitely possessed by Harmony, the Unity of Balance as well as Panharmonium), respectively the Master and High Illuminary of the Weirdom of Kanin City, when conceived;

- staff-half of the Terrible Twins; on their 18th birthdays (celebrated on the summer solstice of 5474, the night Star Sedon disappeared from Cathonia) their parents and the Unities of Lazareme agreed that he would be occupied by Fangfingers (Faustus Vladuca) when he married and conceived children;

- black-skinned like his father; best buddy of Squiggly Tethys, son of Quidnunc, who also had black skin;

- banished beyond the Dome by Thrygragos Lazareme for his damn near direful deeds in the so-called Garden of Earthy Delights (the Hoodoo Hamlet) in the Spring of 5476;

- after visiting Torquemada (whom he knew as Twisted Tommy in the Hoodoo Hamlet of 5476), in the Outer Earth court of Ferdinand and Isabel, became a veritable *smiling fiend of a master swordsman*;

- as such, fought in the second naval battle of Otranto in 1481, during which his cartographer, chronicler, lifelong friend and until-then-inseparable travelling companion, Squiggly Tethys, was killed only to arise anew – as the Legendarian;

- Squigs thereupon used his miraculously restored quill (once Rumour of Lazareme's Tvasitar talisman) to whisk them both to the Egyptian Sphinx and thence back to the Inner Earth of Sedon's Head.

— **Janna** Somata, deviant daughter of Zalman (possibly possessed by Thrygragos Lazareme) and Melina nee Tethys Somata (definitely possessed by Harmony, the Unity of Balance as well as Panharmonium), respectively the Master and High Illuminary of the Weirdom of Kanin City, when conceived;

- distaff-half of the Terrible Twins; on their 18th birthdays (celebrated on the summer solstice of 5474, the night Star Sedon disappeared from Cathonia) their parents and the Unities of Lazareme agreed that she would be occupied by the Skinless Rasp (Rastha Aragon) when she married and conceived children;

- very white skinned, like her mother Melina (and many times removed great-grandmother Quoits Tethys), and silver-haired, like her lookalike ancestor, the Valkyrie novitiate Ute Tethys (whom the Moloch Sedon fancied in Feel Theo); beloved of Squiggly Tethys, son of Quidnunc;

- became the Master of the Weirdom of Kanin City in 5476 when Abe Chaos finally learned the truth of her Hellion of a mother's Hate-Sedon double-dealing as early as 5454 and ever-onwards;

- acquires the Susasword (from Faustus Vladuca) upon the occasion of the birth of her presumably deviant son by Abe Chaos in 5480.

— **Johann-George** Somata-Faust, so named by his mother, Janna Somata, upon the occasion of his birth in 5480;

- as a newborn, sliced to the Outer Earth (via the Susasword) in order to prevent Mithradites capturing him;

- aspects of his subsequent life beyond the Dome may have inspired the calumny of Faust (in which case Smiler probably played the role of Mephistopheles).

- Probable Deviants

— the Molech **Xibalba**, a Black King or Vampire Maker born as a result of the Simultaneous Summonings of 59/1920;

- a long-thought dead Irache shaman believed thoroughly sliced and diced (killed both decisively and irretrievably) by Second Fangs (Janna Fangfingers) sometime prior to 5980 YD;

- possibly has a twin brother or sister who became an Outer Earth supranormal during its Secret War or Wars thereof;

- more than likely doesn't appear in Fangers; though a panpipe-playing someone who *looks identical* to him definitely does.

— **Night Owl**, otherwise unnamed, presumed Inner Earth Irache who became a vampire during the Simultaneous Summonings of 59/1920;

- most likely Xibalba's father;

- somehow associated with Metisophia (Titanic Metis, Wisdom of Lazareme, devic half-mother of the Legendarian);

- as such, becomes an owl rather than a bat when he transforms into anything non-human other than smoke.

— **Saladin** born Nauroz called Devason;

- Master of the Weirdom of Cabalarkon as of 5950 YD, when he beat Demios Sarpedon and Fisherwoman (Scylla Nereid) in the Challenge of Weir;

- mother and father (as the devil-transformed faerie tricksters, Young Life & Young Death) appeared in Sister-Grandmother, a short story published in "Forever & 40 Days – the Genesis of *PHANTACEA*" (Phantacea Publications, 1990);

- has an abiding hatred of witches;

- presumed devic half-mother: Pyrame Silverstar; presumed devic half-father: none other than the Moloch Sedon himself;

- may yet prove to be that Saladin is the last Sed-son or sedon, small case, left alive beneath the Cathonic Dome;

- mentioned often, but does not appear in mini-novel.

— **Morgianna** born Nauroz become Somata then Sarpedon, an Inner Earth Summoning Child, Saladin Devason's year-younger sister;

- probable devic half-mother: Pyrame Silverstar;

- mother and father (as the devil-transformed faerie tricksters, Young Life & Young Death) appeared in Sister-Grandmother, a short story published in "Forever & 40 Days – the Genesis of *PHANTACEA*" (Phantacea Publications, 1990);

- husband of Demios; mother of Andaemyn by Demios; mother of Tsishah Twilight by the faerie-human hybrid, Tom-Tiddly Taddletale (think both Lazareme and the Male Entity);

- codenamed the White Witch on the Outer Earth; called Superior Sarpedon by Wilderwitch (who seemingly distrusts her intensely) during War-Pox;

- mentioned in mini-novel as a latter-day ally of Alpha Centauri, CE and Greater Godbad; sympathetic to their plans re the Inner Earth in general and the Weirdom of Cabalarkon, with its still somewhat-functioning, originally extraterrestrial science and technology, in particular;

- the Hecate-Hellion's Morrigan, an Anthean Nightingale and the Athenan War Witches' Mother Superior;

- does not actually appear in mini-novel.

- • Outer Earth Supranormals

  - arguably the same as Inner Earth deviants in that one or both of their birth-parents may have been possessed by a devic spirit being when they were conceived.

    — **Emeralda** Plantagenet, beloved wife of Alfredo Sentalli (Alpha Centauri), mother of his only son, Yataghan raised Montressor;

- can trace her ancestry back to Barbara and Wooden Tethys, the Deadly Dryads who appeared in FEEL THEO;
- one of a number of Plantagenets to figure in the Outer Earth's Secret War (or Wars) of Supranormals; as such, would have been familiar with Barsine born Mandam become Holgat-wife, Fisherwoman and various members of the eventual Damnation Brigade, WAR-POX's predominant protagonists;
- apparently died well prior to events described in the mini-novel.

- Mandroids
    — **All** the (self-proclaimed) Invincible She-Sphinx of Incain; as per FEEL THEO, once Ginny the Gynosphinx;
    - Mandroid Mother Machine as well as occasional monster maker;
    - more often than not huge and winged; a therefore perhaps surprisingly mobile psychopomp;
    - as such, can travel at will through the Weird (between-space, the dark-grey universal substance of Samsara, mundane reality), though always leaves a root of herself behind on the Prison Beach of Incain;
    - used by devils, especially Unmoving Byron and the Unities of Lazareme, as both a temporary holding cell or a long-term prison for their transgressing fellows;
    - in addition to highborn devils, though not to the Moloch Sedon, whom she's designed to eat, All tends to be responsive to Pyrame Silverstar (qv);
    - All, whose human head resembles the Female Entity (think Harmony), tongue-tugs Pyrame and non-devils she favours (notably Chrysaor Attis, from FEEL THEO, and the Legendarian) through the Dome to her otherwise moribund male equivalent out there, the Egyptian Sphinx, whose head resembles the Male Entity (think Lazareme);
    - although possessed of a modicum of sentience, if not much in the way of actual intelligence, still a machine; as per HELLION, can be turned off and on as well as reprogrammed.
    — **Demogorgon**, the much-feared conglomerate devil, a version of whom may have appeared in FEEL THEO speaking *like this*;
    - comes out of All, Incain's (self-proclaimed) Invincible Mandroid Monster Maker (qv);
    - is in fact composed of the multitude of Master Devas still imprisoned within All either FANGERS-recently or over the course of her millennial existence.

========

3. Mortal Descendants of Original Extraterrestrials

- Utopians of Weir on Earth
    - **Utopians** living in the Weirdom of Cabalarkon are brought up to hate the Moloch Sedon and his devic progeny;
    - oddly, as if to prove their non-Earth heritage, pureblood U-men are always

black whereas pureblood U-women are invariably white;
- pure U-bloods can't be possessed;
- the be-all and end-all of most U-bloods, pure or hybrid, stuck on the Whole Earth (either beneath the Cathonic Dome or, due only in part to an absence of functional spacecraft, beyond it) remains the destruction of their ancient enemies.
- **Illuminaries** of Weir, Utopian polymaths, supposedly learned in a wide variety of not-necessarily-related matters;
- the highest educated class in Cabalarkon, Illuminaries could also be found in former or decrepit Weirdoms like Godbad City, Manoa and Kanin City;
- often act as advisors to the reigning Master, who's usually elevated from their rank; very seldom are they not pure U-bloods;
- both Zalman and Melina Somata were at one-time High Illuminaries of the Weirdom of Kanin City;
- Quoits Tethys, who was a Millennium Child born in the Year of the Dome 5000, was the High Illuminary of Cabalarkon for a very long time;
- Melina nee Sarpedon Zeross, an Inner Earth Summoning Child codenamed Illuminatus in the Thirties, Forties and Fifties, became the High Illuminary of Cabalarkon during the reign of by-then brother-in-law Saladin Devason (which began in 5950).
- **Imbeciles** of Weir, also the idiots of Weir; inbred and therefore very much low functioning Utopians; almost always purebloods, hence the inbreeding.
- **Trinondevs** of Weir, Weir's Warrior Elite, almost always purebloods who manage to overcome their inbreeding in order to function as soldiers;
- their main weapons operate by willpower channelled though extraterrestrial devices such as Mother Machines and eye-staves;
- eyeorbs placed atop eye-staves double as prison pods in that they can suck devic and azura spirit being out of the shells they're occupying and into them, thus incarcerating them;
- once an eyeorb is full it ceases to function as anything except a prison pod; if it's not replaced, the eye-stave becomes useless;
- eye-staves, like all their other anti-devil weaponry, never functioned in the Weirdom of Kanin City during the reigns of Zalman then Melina or Janna Somata;
- since Saladin Devason began his reign as Master in the Weirdom of Cabalarkon in 5950, its Trinondevs are exclusively male.
— **Cabalarkon**, Cabby the Daddy, the Undying Utopian; a biogeneticist when he lived and worked on, or travelled off of, the First Weirworld;
- when he was a wholly alive Utopian Scientocrat the Dual Entities used his right eye to jumpstart the process that resulted in the Moloch Sedon, hence Cabby the Daddy;
- currently subsists in a tub of life-preserving but animation-suspending Cathonic Fluid beneath the Citadel of the Thinkers in Cabalarkon City;
- it, like the rest of the territory composing the Weirdom of Cabalarkon (Sedon's Devic Eye-Land on a map of the Hidden Continent of Sedon's Head), is named after him.

— **Melina nee Tethys Somata**, the High Illuminary of the Weirdom of Kanin City throughout most of "Contagion Collectors"; became a one-day wonder (a sort of Queen for a Day), when Abe Chaos deposed her for daughter Janna as Master of Kanin City, in 5476;
- thereafter relocated to a Hellion Witch Shelter in the Forever Forest of Wildwyck (in the Head's Occipital regions, southeast of Ophir-Moorset and north of Samarand, once Sedon's Tongue) until she reunited with Zalman sometime after he attained the Mastery of Cabalarkon, also in 5476;
- as both a Hellion Morrigan and an Ant Nightingale she spent her years after turning 50 as a Mother Superior of the two oldest sisterhoods on the Whole Earth;
- her parents were distantly related to the same Jordan Q Tethys who fathered or mothered the eventual Quoits Tethys (or one of Quoits' parents); both claimed they could trace their ancestry back to George Masterson and Ute Tethys, who married sometime after the conclusion of FEEL THEO;
- at least one of their parents or grandparents was the Tethys who fled the Weirdom of Cabalarkon some centuries earlier and eventually settled in the rededicated Weirdom of Kanin City;
- probably not a deviant, Melina's skin is so white that many consider her a throwback to pure U-bloods such as the Sarpedon underclass and the Imbeciles of Weir;
  be that as it may, she's still a hybrid Utopian, one possessed by Harmony, the Unity of Balance as well as Panharmonium, when she and Zalman conceived the Terrible Twins, Janna and Sraddha Somata;
- late in her lifetime came to be called the Trigregos Titaness (Trigregos as in the long-lost three Great Goddesses and Titanism, capitalized, in the sense of a fancy word for rebelliousness).
— **Melina born Sarpedon** become Zeross, twin sister of Demios; may have been named after the Trigregos Titaness of the Dome's 55th Century;
- an Inner Earth Summoning Child who first came to the Outer Earth in 1938;
- there, during its Secret War (or Wars) in the Thirties, Forties and Fifties, codenamed Illuminatus;
- became the High Illuminary of Cabalarkon during the reign of (deeply disapproving) brother-in-law Saladin (born Nauroz but called Devason), which began in 5950; Sal, who hates Demios, seems to have been enamoured of her but she rejected him for reasons as yet only implied;
- the mother by much younger Aristotle (Ringleader) Zeross of three daughters;
- does not appear in mini-novel but mentioned in it; suggestion is she's sympathetic to Alpha Centauri, CE and Greater Godbad's plans for the Inner Earth;
- directly descended from the Sarpedon underclass who, as revealed in HELLION, are inclined to worship Thrygragos Lazareme since they see him as the Male Entity.
— **Demios Sarpedon**, twin brother of Melina become Zeross;

- an Inner Earth Summoning Child who first came to the Outer Earth in 1938;
- there, during its Secret War (or Wars) in the Thirties, Forties and Fifties, codenamed Blackguard then the Ace of Spades;
- exiled, along with wife Morgianna, from the Weirdom of Cabalarkon once Saladin (born Nauroz but called Devason) won the Challenge of Weir in 5950 and became its Master;
- considered Saladin Devason's chief rival for what passes as Cabalarkon's throne and the Weirdom's Mastery;
- does not appear in mini-novel but mentioned in it; suggestion is he's sympathetic to Alpha Centauri, CE and Greater Godbad's plans for the Inner Earth;
- wife Morgianna is Sal's year-younger sister, another Inner Earth Summoning Child (the Hecate-Hellion's Morrigan, an Anthean Nightingale and the Athenan War Witches' Mother Superior);
- reputedly possesses the oldest eye-stave in the world (Morgan Abyss, the Death's Head Hellion, had it in HELLION);
- directly descended from the Sarpedon underclass who, as revealed in HELLION, are inclined to worship Thrygragos Lazareme since they see him as the Male Entity.

========

4. Norman & Norma Notables

- Inner Earthlings active during the 55th Century of the Dome
    — Hierophant **Koatyl** (later Bat-Koatyl), in life, Vetala's High Priest both before and after the Byronics drove her out of Iraxas (their El Dorado) and into exile in Marutia (though probably didn't follow her to Satanwyck, where she accumulated what came to be called the Baby Bomb);
    - performed much the same function even after he was turned.

- Outer Earthlings active during the 15th Century beyond the Dome
    — Tomas de **Torquemada**, a Black Friar Dominican (sometimes thought of as *'Domini canes'* or *'Hound of the Lord'*, albeit in Latin, for the order's lead role in spearheading the terrifying Spanish Inquisition of the day);
    - eventual, under Ferdinand and Isabella, Grand Inquisitor of Spain;
    - both Sraddha *'Shreds'* Somata and Squiggly *'Squigs'* Tethys knew him as Twisted Tommy in the Garden of Earthy Delights;
    - it was through Torquemada (who was by then talking **like this**) that Shreds (who thereupon started talking **like this**) and Squigs joined Aragon's armed forces (this after Thrygragos Lazareme banished them from the Head in 5476);
    - like Queen **Isabella** of Castile & King **Ferdinand** of Aragon only mentioned in mini-novel.

- Inner Earthlings featured in the 60th century story segments
    — Alpha Centauri, called the Fatman for reasons immediately obvious to anyone who sees him;

- founder and head of Centauri Enterprises (CE), the de facto government of supposedly democratic Godbad;
- CE, as it's often called, is why the subcontinent and territories neighbouring it in Goatwood, the Gulf of Aka and Sedon's Underlip, as well as Krachla, the tip of the Penile Peninsula, and on the Akadan coast of the near-western Cattail Peninsula, is best known as the Corporate State of Greater Godbad;
- an Outer Earthling born Alfredo Sentalli, the Fatman is grotesquely obese; so much so he's confined to an automated wheelchair for most of his waking hours;
- evidently the only way he can survive being so massively overweight is because he's often the very willing shell of none other than Thrygragos Byron himself — proof, as he, despite his Roman Catholic background and persistent faith, very much begrudgingly acknowledges, that devic possession can be beneficial.

— **Janna** St Peche-Montressor, wife of Yataghan raised Montressor, daughter-in-law of Alpha Centauri, evidently the most common host of APM All-Eyes in 5980 YD;
- a Lovely Lady Afrite as well as an Athenan War Witch;
- effectively the Fatman's nursemaid as well as his chief bodyguard in Aka Godbad City, where he lives in same Outer-Earth-modern building that houses the headquarters of Centauri Enterprises.

— **Gottfried** Kenton, a *'prip'* (Public Relations Professional), who desires to become president of the Godbadian republic;
- actually doesn't appear in the mini-novel, though someone who purports to be him does – that someone, as one might expect, speaks in ***bold-italics***.

— **Achigan** Auranja, former King of Greater Godbad; deposed during the Godbadian Civil War of the Fifties by (at first) anti-devil, Republican forces supplied with Utopian weaponry by a then-nascent Centauri Enterprises;
- an orange-skinned and orange-textured Bandradin, Fisherwoman's estranged husband (**Fisherwoman**, born Scylla Nereid, is a major – perhaps even the major – non-devic character in the upcoming "Goddess Gambit"; about her much can and will be written);
- in 5980, lives in exile on Godbad's far, north-westernmost shore: namely, the lower-lip-tip-principality of Achigan (named after him);
- Byronics invited his royal forbearers to Godbad proper, from their ancestral homeland in the Cattail highlands, at an unspecified time in the past (probably sometime in the previous century);
- apparently has had considerable dealings with faerie tricksters from Twilight (Sedon's Outer Nose on a map of the Hidden Headworld).

— **Ferdinand** Niarchos, the Legendarian calls him *'Weird Ferd'* or, perhaps even more rudely, plain *'Weirdo'*;
- the son of Gomez Niarchos, Godbad's dead but Sangazur-animated ambassador to the Bloodlands (Sedon's Inner Nose), he's the Centauri-appointed governor of New Iraxas, Godbad's petroleum-belching, north-easternmost province;
- New Iraxas is so polluted its workforce is largely composed of Haddazur-

animated zombies supervised by Janna Fangfingers' vampire elite;

- since the vampires are mostly Marutian, like Janna Fangfingers, and the zombies are mostly Irache aboriginals (natives of Hadd, old Iraxas) racial tensions are high;

- Weird Ferd has many children; the Legendarian suspects a number of them are actually Gomez's children;

- Ferd has come to Aka Godbad City to seek instructions from Alpha Centauri re contract talks with the zombie union and the continuing greening of New Iraxas;

- the Byronic Master Deva known as Petrogod may be possessing Ferd.

— **Gomez** Niarchos, Godbad's dead but Sangazur-animated ambassador to the Bloodlands (Sedon's Inner Nose);

- a friend of the Legendarian, albeit from an earlier incarnation, Gomez is charged with negotiating the neutrality of Bloodlanders (Valhallans, the Glorious Dead of FEEL THEO, who once worshipped Mars Bellona, the long-cathonitized Apocalyptic of War; are all dead and are currently led by Guardian Angel Tyrtod, an ambulant leftover from the Outer Earth's Secret War of Supranormals);

- Gomez is one key to Centauri's plans to render Hadd once again a fertile land of the Altogether Alive, albeit subject to Centauri Enterprises, the government of Greater Godbad and its Byronic devil-gods.

— among the Hidden Headworld's other notable, presumed mortals that are mentioned fairly often in the mini-novel include **Holgat** Sraddha and **Barsine** born Mandam Holgat-wife (both of whom were Summoning Children).

— their son, **Thartarre** Sraddha Holgatson, is the current High Priest of the Brown-Robed Sraddhites;

- supported by the Godbadian military, Sraddhites are once again attempting to wrest control of Hadd (formerly both Iraxas and El Dorado) from its Irache natives, alive or otherwise, as well as Janna Fangfingers and her Dead Things Walking (and Biting);

- the Ambulant Dead desperately want to keep Iraxas-Hadd as it has been since the cessation of first War between the Living and the Dead in the Dome's 56th Century.

- Outer Earth Notables in the 20th Century beyond the Dome

 — among non-Head, presumed mortals mentioned fairly often in the mini-novel include **Angelo** & Aristotle *'Harry'* Zeross (father and son Ringleaders), Alfredo **Sentalli** (Alpha Centauri's real name), his son by Emeralda nee Plantagenet **Yataghan** (Sentalli) Montressor, Hiyati **Samarand**, George **Hannibal** and Professor Romaine **Kinesis**.

****

Janna Fangfingers

- Years of the Dome 5476-5495, 5980 -

Jim McPherson

A *PHANTACEA* **Mythos** Mini-Novel

published by James H McPherson

ISBN 978-0-9781342-7-3

1: Back Alley Preamble

"Bat attack, bat attack!"
So shrieked the rat with a long, squiggly tail.

========

Thanks in large measure to monotheistic religions, the demons, the monsters, the gods and the goddesses of antique mythologies have been trivialized, their worship proscribed and the entities themselves confined to another realm. This realm is known by various names. In some traditions it is called the *'Otherworld'*, in others *'Shadowland'*, and in certain places on the Outer Earth, including parts of modern day Tibet, it is known as the Inner Earth.

When he's beyond the Cathonic Dome – or Sedon Sphere, as it's just as correctly called – the legendary 30-Year Man often prefaces the stories he's about to tell with suchlike preliminary commentary. He then goes on to remark that there are many supernatural entities. He further makes a distinction between *'cathonic'*, or skyborn, and *'chthonic'*, or earthborn.

Count chthonic such familiar creatures of folklore as faeries, demons, werecreatures, vampires and zombies. Count cathonic the fallen angels or devils of the Bible. Because devils are described as fallen that implies they are extraterrestrial in origin, which in his estimation amounts to a tautology.

Dictionaries regularly have you believe that the Sanskrit word for god is *'deva'*. In actuality – in that ancient tongue, make that – the word simply means bright or shining one. Be that as it may, he opines, as part of the show, it's difficult to deny that it's the root for English words such as devil, deity, deviant, divine and diva, as well as the Indian honorific *'devi'*.

At least, he'll qualify, if too many in attendance have brought said pocket- or backpack-sized reference books to whatever gathering he's yapping at, it is according to better dictionaries – he, conveniently, having forgotten his at what passes for his home howsoever faraway from his present severely diminished circumstances. It's too big to cart around, don't you know, especially when you're living on the street like he is, poor boy. So please give generously.

He'll further note that the Latin word for God is *'Deus'*. He contends it's just a variation of *'dev'*. This appears self-evident, he'll add gratis, when you consider that in English the plural of *'dev'* would be *'devs'* and Imperial Romans wrote *'Deus'* as *'devs'*. Ipso facto, he babbles on, to state that today's devils were the gods and goddesses of pagan faiths is to restate the bleeding obvious.

Naturally, he only babbles in universally understood, pre-Babel Sedon-speak when he's telling stories out there. When he's recounting tales in here, there's no need to preface anything. Some of the gods and goddesses of antique mythologies might be in attendance. As for the demons and monsters, since they were more or less mortal their descendants might be there.

Although, being for the most part subtle matter shape-shifters, they could be there in one form or another; the forms they take rarely inspire puking. Nonetheless, he'd been doing a lot of that in the last few moments. Ergo, he must have exceeded his 30-beer daily limit last night. That happened, he generally got disgustingly drunk and despicably disorderly. That being the case, or six pack of six packs, well, Fata Fortuna, to spout some genuine Latin, always seemed to favour his survival.

One form or another also probably explained why he'd woken up in the rubbish heap behind the bar where he'd downed his last beer. He might have, over the incessant chatter and amplified din of the pub's inexcusably shrill rock music, started shouting a tale about a devil that didn't appreciate his or her story being shouted, let alone told. He couldn't remember.

He could remember how much he hated getting drunk. It approximated how much he hated coming back as his daughter or granddaughter. Hangovers hurt. So did giving birth. Neither hurt as much as getting killed, though, and third generational devils, who by Sedonic decree weren't allowed to kill lesser beings, didn't count killing him as murder.

They counted him as one of them, an immortal, one who couldn't be put away permanently.

========

The only thing chiropters had in common with helicopters, besides the fact the two words vaguely rhymed, was both could fly. Bats were no more basically blind, winged and mostly night-flying rats than they were rodents. Strictly speaking, while there were chiropteran tee-tees, ones whose wings allowed them to be read like open books (so long as you could decipher the squiggly lingo), regular tee-tees weren't rats either. They were rodents, though.

On the Outer Earth neither bats nor rats could be deemed sentient beings. That didn't necessarily hold true on the Inner Earth of Sedon's Head. Sooth said, which the better storytellers swore they always did, within reason, on the Hidden Headworld there were heaps, if perhaps not hillocks, of different sorts of sentient species. However, even though tee-tees could speak, no one declared them smarter than your everyday or every night average, wires-munching, household rat or belfry bat.

Indeed, most agreed the only reason they could speak was because they were low-grade demons and, intelligence-wise, most demons – be they harmless, sometimes even beneficent agathodaemons or genuinely nasty cacodemons – came in at or near the bottom of the Head's totem pole in terms of sentience. Contrarily, one phylum of demon could and sometimes did possess intelligence approaching the top of said totem pole, where also perched humans, Utopians and devils themselves.

Of course most of these last started out as a different species. The airborne bat pursuing the ground-bound tee-tee was one of them.

Clang! That was the sound the bat made when she swooped in for the kill and instead collided with a big, commercial garbage bin. Seeking howsoever short-lived safety in a back alley, the tee-tee had scampered underneath just that. Crash! That wasn't so much the sound it made as the reality of what happened when the enraged bloodsucker, next to instantaneously transformed, effortlessly flipped the dumpster and hurled it into the concrete wall of the nearest building.

The tee-tee squeaked a terrified yelp when the vampire, impossibly fast by ordinary human standards, impossibly clothed by any logical standards as well, snatched it up.

========

Short, at maybe 5'5 or 5'6, and with a noticeable beer belly, Jordan Q Tethys was a hard-living man evidently in his forties. A street person by choice, he claimed to prefer living outdoors. When he couldn't take over a squat or a cave or even an empty dumpster for himself, he'd sleep under cardboard boxes before paying for a room at an inn or boarding house.

Given what he could do, it wasn't that he couldn't readily acquire the where-withal to fork over for much better than merely decent accommodations. He also had plenty of patrons situated in very comfortable circumstances throughout the Head. Some of them were exceedingly well off. In that regard you couldn't ask for a richer or more generous fellow than Alpha Centauri, who generally resided right here, in Aka Godbad City.

However, Tethys didn't enjoy being beholding to others for much the same reason. Too often others wanted him to do what he could do for them. To live outside the law, he'd heard said as well as sung, in a variety of tongues, you must be honest.

No freeloader, in return for his pilsners, of which he drank copiously, and food, of which he ate as if every meal was his last, Tethys would tell a tale or two. When no one wanted to listen to his stories, he'd go into busker mode in order to earn his beer and eats. The trouble with that was, although he could play just about any instrument there was, and many there hadn't been for long centuries, he could no more sing than he could dance, except at the end of a rope.

Plus, he'd finally remembered, last night's past-last-call, heavy metal band did not feel like jamming with a flautist; especially not with a flautist who flaunted his deviancy. He really shouldn't have drawn his own personal amplifier and speaker system beneath his table. Either that or he should have first thought to draw himself with big pink hair.

He hadn't, which was another indication he'd surpassed his thirty beer limit. He didn't think he had anything to do with the state of his pre-selected townhouse, though. He did wonder how a normal-looking sewing needle could stick a note, along with a severed tee-tee-tail, into a freshly painted and therefore non-rusty, metallic dumpster, however.

The note, he read, said: *'I want to see you.'* It was signed *'Janna'*. The *'j'* was in lower case. Always dot your *'eyes'*, he thought to himself. He looked closer at the dot. It was rendered like a disembodied eyeball. *'Oh, aren't you ever so clever, Janna?'* He was about to pluck the note off the garbage bin when he noticed the needle holding it on was glowing ever so faintly. *'Eye of the needle, Janna? Hmm. Me-thinks now you're going out of your way to be funny.'*

"Bat whack, bat whack," squealed a near-rat no longer with a long, squiggly tail.

It lay sputtering its life away across the alley from the overturned dumpster. Tethys was fond of tee-tees. He wasn't at all pleased to see one that looked as if it had been discarded like so much inconsequential trash. Someone must have just missed hitting the bin and really didn't give a good or bad gods-damn it was only three-quarters dead.

Without touching it any more than he'd touched the needle, he bent down to examine the sorry beastie. Most of its throat had been ripped out. 'Oh, that Janna,' he muttered to no one in particular, not even to the hoot-owl perched on a fire escape railing above the alley. For his part, the owl didn't bother hooting a hello.

Mercifully Tethys quickly made sure the tee-tee was four-quarters dead.

========

"Nice crate, Janna," Jordan Tethys said in all genuineness.

It was too. Properly fumigated, it would make for a splendid, even spacious shelter in a back alley somewhere.

========

At 27, married, with one child and another one rumoured to be on the way, Janna St Peche-Montressor remained one of those women about whom it could be said that, when she walked into a room, all eyes were instantly upon her. Cut-short dark hair, shapely, extremely fit and trim without being skinny, everything about her said athlete.

Very little about her said witch, however. Yet that was what she was: two very different sorts of witches, a love-loving Afrite and an Athenan War Witch. The latter was the main reason you didn't want to describe her as drop-dead gorgeous. She probably wouldn't dropkick you dead for it but she could, in the blink of an eye.

As for the former, Lovely Lady Afrites offered up their lovemaking to the goddess and, yes, some of them were fairly free with their favours. It was theirs to give, and yours to receive, but only if they chose to bestow it. You didn't want to whisper, as she passed, that you wouldn't kick her out of bed. You did; you probably wouldn't get out of bed for a month afterwards, let alone out of traction.

You didn't want to *'presume'* upon Lovely Ladies either. While very few were War Witches like St Peche-Montressor, for multiple centuries rape of an Afrite was punishable by castration in the subcontinent of Aka Godbad. That hadn't been the case since the overthrow of the imported, Bandradin aristocracy back in the Fifties and its supposedly democracy-espousing successor, Centauri Enterprises, established the Corporate State of Greater Godbad.

Nonetheless, that's why there remained in the Godbadian vernacular an ancient saying. It went: *'Old traditions die hard – or not!'*

========

He wasn't admiring her backside, though he made sure he was standing well back of her when he opened his mouth just in case she took it the wrong way. She did whirl.

Maybe she did so with malicious intent. Fortunately she smiled the moment she spotted him, 10-feet behind her in the newly built museum's foyer.
Smiling was good; it certainly beat being knackered.

========

"Jordy! I see you got my message."

That was another thing about this Janna. You didn't want to merely think, as she passed by, that you wouldn't kick her out of bed. All eyes sometimes weren't just on her when she entered a room. Sometimes APM All-Eyes was within SPM and APM's ilk had more than five senses. They may even have had substantially more than five senses. (Then again, the way some of them acted it was more like they didn't have any sense whatsoever, especially not of the common garden snake variety.)

Antique Illuminaries of Weir, whose ancestors were pureblood Utopians and therefore originally extraterrestrial, named this particular, third generational Master Deva Aphropsyche Morningstar, hence APM. A third-born Byronic, the very devil-goddess to whom Lovely Lady Afrites offered up their lovemaking, she most often manifested herself in the form of a human-shaped woman composed entirely of eyeballs, hence All-Eyes.

"I had a dream I should come here. I hope that isn't the message you mean."

"I don't do dreams and neither does APM."

Dream was another Master Deva, a firstborn Mithradite: Phantast Thanatos, as well-travelled Illuminaries from centuries easily 2000 years bygone by now named him. Although officially unbound – at least in Godbadian territories – Athenan War Witches originally swore adherence to the devic Dream Weaver's triplet sister, Heat.

Whereas some disrespectful, as well as foolhardy, devils called her Hot Stuff, those selfsame Illuminaries named her Methandra, after Mediterranean Athena. Her still inviolate protectorate, Mythland, which she abandoned more than 1200 years ago, was once the jewel of Sedon's Crown.

(These days the Mithradite Dream was merely a relatively bright star in the night's sky. The brightest, the Moloch Sedon himself, did not appreciate bad dreams. They made for dreadful ideas and worse repercussions. So, after narrowly avoiding perhaps the worst consequence imaginable – namely the sinking of his precious Headworld – most of 2000 years earlier, he cathonitized Phantast and his allies in the ill-fated Crimson Conspiracy.

(While the vast majority of stars shining out of the Sedon Sphere were devils that directly caused the death of lesser beings, you shouldn't screw with the approaching almighty Eye-Mouth upstairs in the heavens. He didn't need an excuse to cathonitize, catasterize or ill-star, devils that annoyed him. And if he ill-starred an innocent devil, tough two-by-fours. He was beyond punishment. He had to be. No one could cathonitize him. He was Cathonia.)

Jordan 'Quill' Tethys was white but his skin was richly tanned and prematurely lined, like old parchment. Regardless of his manifest humanity, many devils believed he was a devic suicide, Rumour of Lazareme. Furthermore, most of those believed he was driven to cutting out his third eye by this Phantast-Dream. He wasn't, he asserted. He was a deviant; albeit, he would allow, one with stacks of knacks.

Among them he included occasionally having weird dreams indicating precisely where he should draw himself to such that he'd be in position to accurately report on what occurred there and then. Tethys had had one of his occasional dreams a couple of nights ago, which was why he'd drawn himself to Aka Godbad City.

"But she could."

"Sure she could, if she knew or cared where you were. She's a devil. But I don't see why she'd bother. So long as you weren't in Cabalarkon she'd just go and visit you in person. I don't have the time or ability to do that. So, on the off chance you were in town, I sent a tee-tee to find you. You're their pied piper, aren't you? Attracting tee-tees is one of your whatnot stacked full of bric-a-brac knickknacks, isn't it? What message did you think I meant?"

Puke-spattered as they were – and lacking both the inclination and requisite coinage for a morning at the laundrette – he'd replaced last night's rain slicker, sweats and running shoes. He now wore a scruffy, checked jacket; an oft repaired, though seldom cleaned and therefore not-quite-white-anymore, woollen sweater; an open-necked tee shirt, blue jeans, socks and, despite the wet, chilly weather, sandals. However, he still wore his familiar, peaked, tweed cap, pin-cushioned as it was with feathers like an Irache war chief's headdress.

Multicoloured strands reminiscent of knotted rat-tails wormed out from underneath it. They were the severed tails of tee-tees. As if somehow akin to Incan quipus, Tethys could read their Braille-like nodes, ridges, gaps and depressions. Consequently, he could weave tales out of tee-tee-tails. So could any devil and most witches, even ones like St Peche-Montressor, who weren't as thoroughly well trained as Antheans or Korants, the two main rivals for the title of Superior Sisterhood.

He doffed his trademark cap, indicating his latest acquisition. "I got this and I got the message that went with it. It said: *'I want to see you'*. Except, I'm thinking it's the other way around. Shall we go somewhere private?"

She didn't say anything about his thinning hair. Neither did she boot him where it wasn't thinning. Instead she frowned disapprovingly. "Don't be obtuse. Every tee-tee has two tales to tell. I meant the tee-tee itself, not its tail. I told it to tell you I wanted to see you here. Which it must have, otherwise why would you be here, right? I've something to show you. It's in that crate, not in private."

"Perhaps I should have said *'read'*, not *'said'*. The message I got was written on a strip of lined paper ripped out of an ordinary notepad. It was signed *'Janna'*, which I realize is the middle name of every Sraddhite woman over in Hadd. But its *'j'* was dotted with an eyeball, which is highly suggestive. It was attached to a metallic dumpster with a sewing needle. And, unless I'm more mistaken than usual, that's one of APM's more quirky calling cards."

Her frown of disapproval changed into one of concern. "You didn't touch it, did you?"

"Not the needle, just the tee-tee-tail. I decided I'd be better off waiting until I had a friendly devil beside me. So I drew the needle into a lead box in my satchel, then I drew you, a friend indeed, as well as both in need and sometimes in deed, whereupon I drew myself to you. That's why I'm here, not what the tee-tee said."

"One of these days I'll get a simple yes or no out of you. And that's all you'll ever get out of me, make no mistake about that."

"Heaven forefend I dare dream such a Phantast-folly. More pertinently, heaven forefend I dare tell you about it. Put it this way, I get feelings. It's one of my bevy of bric-a-brac bents and some of them, you might be shocked to learn, aren't at all bent. The one I got first thing this morning told me that, if I touched the needle then, I wouldn't be here now – though where I would be, well, like I said, I never got that far."

"Lady Luck was on my side once again, it seems. So was the tee-tee itself. Its last words were '*bat whack, bat whack*', which …"

Something in the nature of relief etched her lips. "As good as identifies the writer as the Janna every Sraddhite woman is named after, I got you. Where is it?"

"Someplace private," Tethys repeated, cap in hand. He tapped one of the feathers stuck in it. The quill glinted a split second, for their eyes only. It was why his initial was a '*q*'. "Last night I blundered big time showing off my deviancy in public. Mind you, that's probably another reason I'm not three nights away from turning in my grave and rising again. I didn't come to until after dawn."

"She'd do that to you? Weren't you once lovers?"

"I was her lover twice, father and son. Actually I was her lover thrice, now that I think about it, but the third time doesn't really count because she was possessed."

"By that other lady, the former Sinistral Lust?"

Tethys nodded confirmatively. "May her star shine forever brightly."

He must have told Janna the tale before. Or someone else had. He was hardly the only yarn-spinner around; just the only one who'd been a recurring deviant for coming up to two millennia. Unless, that is, her inner spirit self (as opposed to her inner soul-self) had been there then, which she may well have been. All three tribes had their own versions of Venus.

"At any crate, we haven't really seen eye to eye since."

"Can the crate cracks, Jordy. And save the eye jokes for APM."

"I thought I had."

"You thought wrong. She's busy beyond the Dome."

"Then I better dispose of it myself. No point inviting Janna Fangfingers to come through without a devil around to protect me, is there?"

"On the contrary, there would be at least two points; one at the end of each of her fangs. Let me call the Fatman first, before you do anything drastic. He might have a better idea."

"Damn it, Janna. I know almost everyone else does it, sometimes to his face, but must you call your father-in-law the Fatman?"

"Oh, I don't mind, Jordy," came a voice from behind them. "Not when it comes from my Janna. Sooth said, I don't mind anything that comes from my Janna, especially grandchildren."

Evidently, calling would not be required. Evidently also, Janna had seen him coming — because he was smiling at their exchange not unlike a bloated Silenus in the entourage of Dionysus.

========

Alpha Centauri had a new wheelchair. Electronic, hence electric, and, hence also, silent running, what will Centauri Enterprises come up with next?

He'd find out soon enough.

****

2: The Portentous Piper of Aka Godbad City

"As for me, in some respects unfortunately, I'm currently as vacant as she is."
"Guess that makes three of us," Tethys muttered, absently scratching his itchy scar more in perplexity than disappointment.

========

Situated in the lower part of his forehead, just about where his eyebrows would have met if they'd kept growing, it always itched when devils were nearby. Too often regrettably it never itched indicatively. That meant he had no idea where they were, if he couldn't see them, or who they were possessing, if they weren't here either between-space or in an irregular guise.

He never talked about his scar, which only he, not any of his children or grand-children, ever had. More than anything else it looked like an incision whose scab had never quite healed over. The scar and the fact his quill was a devic power focus contributed to the notion he may well be a third generational Master Deva; that he was none other than Rumour of Lazareme.

(The Thrygragos brothers and the Trigregos sisters – who never got as far as the Whole Earth – made up the second generation of devazurkind. Aka Thrygragos Everyman, because he somehow looked to be the very ideal of godhood for every member of any sentient species save pureblood Utopians of Weir, reputedly Laz-areme was the first of the six more like brought into being than born as such.

(Even though he was hardly ever seen, due to the fact that he spent virtually all his time asleep on Tympani, the Isle of the Undying One, in the Aural Sea, Sedon's Ear, Lazareme along with Bodiless Byron were the Hidden Headworld's last two Great Gods. Its onetime third, Thrygragos Varuna Mithras, whose tribe nevertheless remained the most numerous by far, didn't survive Thrygragon, which occurred in excess of 1500 years earlier.

(Quill Tethys considered Lazareme his half-grandfather twice over. In other words, the Lackland Libertine was his devic grandfather on both sides of the bed. Assuming Tethys's rendition of his own origins could be relied upon then Rumour, a seventh-born, possessed his human father when he was conceived, whereas a second-born, Metisophia, Wisdom of Lazareme, possessed his conceptive mother, who was also human.

(Titanic Metis didn't deny it. Since, reputedly anyhow, the Mithradites' dastardly Dream force-fed him to faeries circa 4000 Year of the Dome, Rumour couldn't deny it. Undeniably, some two millennia pre-force-feeding, the god-devils' Lazaremist of a Prometheus, Tvasitar Smithmonger, first forged Tethys's Brainrock quill to become Rumour's talisman.)

Deviants were hardly rare on the Hidden Headworld. While they were always mortal, only he had lived, as well as remembered, a series of never more than 30-year lifetimes. And he'd had perhaps as many as sixty of them, going back close to two thousand years. However, he was not the only one who had a Tvasitar Talisman adhere to him lifetime after lifetime.

Even so, truth told – which he always strove to do, even if he occasionally exaggerated his importance as more than just a nosy bystander – he knew of only two other deviants who had a history of coming back cognitively. Although both wielded devic power foci that returned with them, only one remained extant and that one, the famous fauna or satyress, Pusan Wanderlust, always came back female.

In sum therefore, the Legendarian, as his business card identified him, was essentially unique in terms of cumulative deviancies.

========

"Now, what about this exemplar of utter exquisiteness?"

========

While he wasn't a deviant, at least not that anyone could prove, Alpha Centauri was almost as unique as Jordan *'Quill'* Tethys, particularly when it came to accumulations. Fifty-three years old and balding, what he'd lost up top, in terms of hair, he had gained approaching exponentially down below, in terms of girth.

At slightly over six feet tall, swarthy, pink-faced and artistically goateed – though that tuft of fur was largely lost in his fleshy jowls and sunken chin – he could walk. But, since he weighed more than four hundred pounds, he much preferred to be pushed around or use an automated wheelchair. Took less effort that way. Besides, as by far the richest man on or under the subcontinent, if not, counting devils, the entire Inner Earth, he could afford his extravagances.

Having founded Centauri Enterprises in the late Forties, the Fatman prospered as it did. As a result, they'd attained a hugeness unheard of for man or corporation on either side of the Cathonic Dome. In (very) large measure, Centauri would admit, with a grin, both owed their enormity to Thrygragos Byron, the Great God whose age it had been on the Hidden Headworld for hundreds of years.

Tethys wasn't one of them – purely because he didn't know for sure – but there were those who said theirs was a reciprocal debt. Three and a half decades ago, the Unmoving One, who was all head and no body, was the apparent target of an assassination attempt. He only survived by possessing the then teenage, then slim man.

Whatever the truth of the matter, the date was the 9th of Hektor 5945 YD. Today was Sapienda the 28th of Maruta 5980. For the past hour or so they'd been watching, quietly but nervously, as CE's professional preservationists removed the carefully segmented, but still impressively large stonework from the crate and ensconced it in its pre-constructed position within the museum's walls.

"Like I told you, Al, we found this bitty bit of brilliancy covered by rubble in what was left of one of the last extensions to the megaron, rotunda or Great Hall of

Kanin City's Masters Palace. Like I also told you, years before I got killed again, the city-state's so ages-ancient it predates the arrival of devils upon the Whole Earth by hundreds of years.

"Starting way, way pre-Flood then, when Kanin probably wasn't a Weirdom and its rulers or overseers therefore weren't called Masters, almost everyone running the place added to this aspect of the ever-enlarging edifice. So what you've got here is merely a fraction of what was once an absolutely massive mosaic. It was so huge; it wound underground, through multiple centuries worth of covered-over wings of the palace, almost like a kind of backwards timeline."

"Or, put more poetically, like the world snake with tattoos." (The Fatman had earned his reputation for cracking unfunny puns.)

In advance of its public unveiling tomorrow, they were enjoying a privileged viewing of the astonishing mosaic ex of the crate the Legendarian, perhaps not facetiously, coveted as a future domicile. Centauri spent massive quantities of CE's Godbucks transporting it, and its contents, to Aka Godbad City's spanking new Headworld Museum, which he'd also financed from start to finish, so both better be worth the expense, the danger and the effort. Clearly they were, all there agreed.

"If its tattoos lined its stomach, not its skin. Ipso facto, when I first saw it the earliest stuff was already long, long, multi-millennia-long locked in what amounted to a subway tunnel."

When you've consciously lived as many as maybe five dozen lifetimes, you collect much more than mere memories and the no mater how bent stories that go with them. When you're a multitalented deviant who has, by and large, lived those lifetimes on the Hidden Continent of Sedon's Head, the main domain of the demons, the monsters, the gods and the goddesses of antique mythologies since the Great Flood of Genesis, hence the Genesea, you amass quite a history – along with more than a few her-stories – of your own.

As well as a musician and a beer-guzzling storyteller, in most of his incarnations he also found time to excel as a painter and sculptor. Consequently, just about every sentient species displayed, in their homeland galleries or museums, arguable masterpieces, in pigment or stone, tinted tesserae or crystalline rock shards, by two or three different Jordan Tethyses in one place. True, human societies held the majority. But that was mostly because he'd been wholly human much more often than he'd been, say, Saur, myrmidon, mer-creature or, yes, a hybrid Utopian like some of those depicted in what they were looking at.

While, in his almost non-stop wanderings, he'd seen some incorrectly ascribed Tethyses, very few genuine ones weren't his doing. This borderline minutiae of Kanin's once incredibly extensive mosaic was one of these rarities. Although a genuine Tethys, credit for it didn't belong to him. Rather, it did and it didn't belong to him. The tile-master didn't become this Tethys until he had a near-death experience, one that for him turned out to be terminal.

This Tethys, the Legendarian, had been among those who ventured to what was left of Kanin City back in the mid Sixties. Once there he helped unearth it. Of course, bodily anyhow, that was a different Tethys; albeit one who, notwithstanding that, remembered where this pre-specified aspect of the mosaic was buried to start with, which presumably was why the Fatman hired him in the first place.

For most of their acquaintanceship before then, this Tethys was yet another different Tethys's daughter, which was something else the Fatman knew. As for why, a decade and a half after its rediscovery, he'd evidently funded its ever-so-risky retrieval – by no less means than an obviously heavy-duty helicopter, probably of Outer Earth design, that was eminently capable of long distance cartage – that this Tethys remained desirous of discovering.

Curiosity was one of the many things that ended up killing him in the past. Yet, along with beer, it was one of the many things that always kept him going.

"In fact," he goaded, regardless of previous denials, "The Sedonshem landed atop Kanin City some 669 years pre-Flood, which makes it, you know, over 7,000 years old."

"Vacant, Jordy," St Peche-Montressor's pretence-prone, wheelchair-bound father-in-law repeated.

"Me, too," Janna reconfirmed. (Thrygragos Byron, being a second generational devil, had been around for stacks more than well over 150-thousand years pre-Earth. By contrast, third generational so-called Master Devas like APM All-Eyes had been around a paltry aeon or two less than their six progenitors.)

"Fair enough," said Tethys, scar still itching. "On the Outer Earth, you say," he further cogitated. "It's pissing rain outside but we're indoors and Janna Fangfingers is as big a wig bloodsucker as there is left. She may well dare to venture here via between-space even during the day. Then again," he concluded dubiously, "I suppose a topnotch security team like yours doesn't need devils to handle super-vamps of the non-shoe variety."

"I said APM was beyond the Dome," the Janna there reminded him. "I didn't say Great Byron was out there."

"But he might be."

"As much as he might be in your head, sure. But, hey, you're right. Even if you don't really believe it, you've nothing to worry about."

"I better not." Chances were he didn't; chances that had nothing, or very little (since she could be one of those around one way or another), to do with Dame Chance. "After all, I could come back to haunt you."

"Oh I don't doubt that. You've a very talented quill."

"Now who's teasing who?" As he'd just remarked, simply because Janna and the Fatman's usual occupants were elsewhere that didn't mean there weren't plenty of other Byronics – or non-Byronics in Chance's case – present. Indeed, it could be they had other devils possessing them. It could even be he had a devil possessing him. It was impossible to be sure.

Since Centauri wasn't volunteering Byron's whereabouts, Tethys felt obliged to forge ahead. "Anyhow, all I'm saying is that, as extremely well-preserved as most of this fragment is, even after transportation, and indeed, as most of what we unearthed back in the Sixties was, parts of it are literally thousands of years old. That makes it the not-so-light work of many hands.

"And, hey, I've only been around 2,000 years or so, so I couldn't possibly identify all of them, let alone everyone depicted in it."

"It isn't everyone I'm interest in," said Centauri. "Otherwise I'd have had a whole lot more of it brought back. You do recall them, don't you."

"All too painfully, in some of my worst nightmares as well," Tethys acknowledged. "And so do you, on account of when I first told you about it, all those years ago, you taped me then had it transcribed and published. Called it *'Feeling Theocidal'*, too, the same as I did. Sooth said, which I always strive to do, I haven't seen any royalty cheques lately."

"Probably because there haven't been any," said Janna. "It may have caused a minor sensation when it first came out but, for a supposedly firsthand testament of events 1500 years in the past, it didn't sell very well. The critics thought it was fictional and as such missing some rather important ingredients – a genuine bad guy, for one. Other than you, that is."

"Hey, this is the Head. When the Devil's above us all, we don't need villains."

The section of fancy stonework the Fatman had gone to such lengths to retrieve depicted a wedding party posing underneath a Branstock Oak. It captured a happy lull in the turbulent life (and death) of a highly significant character in the annals of not just Outer-Earth-born Roman Catholics like Centauri, or opera lovers like all three of them. (Though, to be fair, her significance for the former came long before the group gathering shown, whereas that for the latter came well after it.)

Arguably, if her firstborn son, whom she had when she lived beyond the Dome, hadn't asserted imperial authority, and thereafter begun to coordinate the not-just-theological struggles of Europeans and Near-Easterners that so dominated the so-called Dark Ages out there, the Whole Earth might now be devic.

No wonder the Outer Earth's all-male Xuthrodite brotherhood (whom devils scathingly referred to as Horrites in here) still revered Helena Augusta. Which begged a couple of fairly crucial questions. When not possessed, was Alpha Centauri a closet Horrite? Was that why he'd brought this specific portion of the mosaic here – to help win the same battle for the hearts and minds of wafflers and disenchanted former devil worshippers beneath the Dome?

"Or maybe we don't remember them," Centauri speculated oddly. "So, just in case my memory's more leaky than yours, kindly refresh it." (Tethys had discovered some time ago that the Fatman, using Outer Earth technology, taped many of their conversations. That was how, when he went back home for a visit, or whatever he really did beyond the Dome, he could recollect there was a Hidden Continent of Sedon's Head.)

"The bridegroom's George Masterson," the 30-Year Man obliged, "So-called because his mother stopped using her married name after I wandered off in pursuit of more fertile fields, as in fillies, to plough. The bride's name was Ute. And, yes, she was a Tethys too: my daughter in fact; the daughter of the same Legendarian circa the mid-44th Century, if you prefer.

"Her younger brother – his name was Gordon, but everyone called him Glee – was quite a talented fellow, even if I do say so myself."

"He did the scene," Janna anticipated.

"He did indeed."

"Before you got hold of him."

"And ruined his voice, yes; not to mention his terpsichorean prowess. I see you read my report too."

"So I did, with all my eyes as well."

"All two of them."

"Precisely." Only APM was all eyes. Rather, only APM generally chose to disport herself with a body seemingly made up of nothing but enticing eyeballs.

(With the exception of a couple of disagreeable cyclopses he could think of, most devil-gods manifested three. They did it so commonly Tethys often pointed to his forehead as proof he wasn't a devil. It was no such a thing of course. Debrained demonic bodies were mainly composed of a form of subtle matter known as Stopstone or Solidium. That gave them approximately incalculable advantages. Comparative ease of metamorphosis was just the one cited most often.

(While, on a day-to-day basis, a few devils took perverse delight in rendering themselves truly monstrous to behold, many only needed to suppress their extra eye, and occasionally their most frequent skin texture or tint, in order to appear wholly human. That meant any devil could appear to be all eyes. APM had thought of it first, though, and whatever else they might be, unlike storytellers devils were seldom plagiarists.)

"Ute and her Swan Maiden of a mother were choosers of the slain," Tethys enlightened his hosts perhaps unnecessarily. "By that I don't mean her mother was a maiden when this was done, though she might have been when I first met her – hence Jotan, Ute and Glee's older brother. No, by that I mean they were Valkyries back in the days when Valhalla was still in the Upper Head, just below the Mystic Mountains, Sedon's Crown."

Shortly after 4825 (the year the Atomic as well as consequential Idiot Twins – actually, as always with Master Devas, the remnants of a set of triplets – so catastrophically reduced Sedon's Forehead to the still impassable, due to rampant radioactivity, Ghostlands), the Apocalyptic of War's Valhalla in effect reincorporated itself within the Bloodlands.

(Then as now the Bloodlands were situated within Sedon's Inner Nose. That the Head had an Inner Nose suggested there was an Outer Nose. And there was – Crepuscule, the non-oceanic, mist and fog-shrouded, westernmost territory on the entire Inner Earth, which also made it aka the Grey Land of Twilight.)

"That's Volsanga there, a regular Nordic beauty even though she'll have been getting on in years by the time Glee made his artistic contribution to the city-state's miles-meandering mosaic. Ute and her both went by Volsanga's maiden name, Nibelung. Yes, that Nibelung. In fact, the owl-masked woman there is wearing the renowned ring thereof."

"And you're sure that's Helena Somata?" Centauri asked of the owl-masked woman uncertainly. "Kanin City's Master of Weir throughout the latter half of the 44th Century?"

"That's her," Tethys verified. "That's my matricidal mama. She swore by the sanctity of matrimony. Then she proved her insanity not so much by marrying me as by expecting me to think the same way. You can't tell it because of the mask but she'd be around a hundred and thirty when Glee portrayed her. Which suggests pretty strongly Helena was mostly Utopian."

"Only mostly," Janna supplied, "Because Pyrame Silverstar got hold of her."

"And then the Devil Sedon got hold of them fused," Centauri finished for her. "And we all know what that made her first born boy."

"So we do," Tethys agreed. "A sed-son, one that turned on Sed-dad when he embraced the Illuminated Faith of Xuthros Hor, the Biblical Noah. Whereupon he made the badly fractured Church he took over, for practical purposes, the vanguard in its ever-ongoing fight against the forces of pagan polytheism – read your usual occupiers and my devic parents.

"But that was way before I came along. The malicious Master didn't give the ring to Volsanga but she eventually acquired it, which was when it came to be called Volsanga's Nut. I trust you can appreciate why." Janna certainly did. Its oversized gemstone was shaped just like a golden acorn. She said as much.

"Because that's what it is," Tethys concurred. "Although I suppose it'd be more accurate to describe it as a gilded acorn. You've one guess who gave it to hellacious honey Hel."

"The oak tree does look distinctly feminine," said Centauri.

"That's a dryad," realized Janna, whose late, still much-missed mother-in-law, Emeralda nee Plantagenet become Centauri, had related forbearers.

"More than that, that's an Acorn Ant."

"The ring's a soul sink?"

"Chalk another one up to the lovely lady. You'll note it isn't cracked – yet."

"Yes, yes, Jordy," interjected Centauri, growing impatient. He'd finally appreciated that Tethys had nothing new to add to what he did remember.

"The bride and the groom were half-brother and half-sister. Ergo, even though they didn't use it, the Valkyries and the mosaic master-craftsman, Master Helena, her final child and even the dryad, all shared the same last name at one point in time; that of the deviant whose soul the Acorn Ant sucked into her oak-nut. Lorna, the Master's adopted daughter, the little black kid with the two-toned hair, didn't. But it turned out she wasn't a hybrid Utopian either."

"And the crow-headed mule she's shown riding," Janna contributed, "The thing with the stunted wings on its back and the vestigial facsimiles of same on both sides of its upper hooves, it's an intentional hybrid – a hinny-bird, I'd guess they called it. Her fur's feathers – that of a ravendeer, right?"

"As if you didn't know that already, SPM." Even though it was moderately better than 'Spam', Tethys knew Janna hated it when he called her SPM. It sounded so much like APM she felt it was almost as if he was intentionally trying to rob her of her own individuality. (About the best that could be said about her attitude was that perceived transgressions of it weren't punishable by well-placed boots to wherever it hurt the most.)

"We realize what Helena was trying to accomplish when she crossbred it," said Centauri, reasserting himself testily. (Before devils sought to exterminate the species circa 2500 YD, very nearly successfully, certain sorts of ravendeer, the ones that could telescope deadly unicorn horns, were proven cathonitizers.)

"But how can you be so sure that's Helena Somata? For one thing, why is she wearing an owl-mask? She was an Anthean Mother Superior, not a Hellion Matron Inferior, as in hellish."

"Stealing my jokes, eh, Al," Tethys responded. He was not pleased at being questioned so sceptically. "But Volsanga was a Hellion as well as a Valkyrie – most probably they all are. Her and horrid Hel became the tightest buddies after

Thrygragon. So maybe she altered the talisman she's wearing into an owl mask as a tribute to Ute's maiden mom. After all, to this day Hellions regard owls as one of their most sacred totems after crows or ravens."

(He didn't make stuff up. Not without telling anyone he was filling in blanks, howsoever speculatively, he didn't.)

"Hellions are anti-devil," said Janna. "So that fits."

"They're also pro-demon," frowned the Fatman, his sad excuse for a goatee all but disappearing into his mound of chins as he did so. "So that doesn't."

Tethys silently noted their exchange. Notwithstanding that, instead of poking further into their differences, he drew their attention to something the owl-masked woman had round her neck. "Look, that's the standard chain of office for a Master of Weir. Saladin Devason wears exactly the same thing to this day. Mind you, he wears it up north in Cabalarkon."

An all-red, bloodstone necklace from which dangled a mirrored medallion, triangular in shape and out of which stared a solitary eyeball, with a curved blade underneath it like a cedilla, was indeed the standard chain of office for a Master of Weir; had been since, for Utopians of Weir on Earth, the halcyon days of Morgan Abyss, the Death's Head Hellion, who may well have inherited the fullness of Helena Somata's Hate-Sedon spirit.

"Mind you again, Sal's is just a facsimile. That's the real thing. So is the Cloak of Many Colours. As I found out once I got Glee more so than he got me, poor soul, horrendous Hel somehow acquired the original six, anything-but-sacred objects from friend Mithras and the Attis in the immediate aftermath of Thrygragon."

Even though the Legendarian was descended from Lazaremists, the Great God Mithras (which did mean *'friend'* in some Outer Earth tongues) actually appreciated his story-telling. As for Chrysaor Attis, Mithras's deviant son via Strife-Marutia, his Ewe for Aries, they were actual drinking buddies for a few centuries worth of mutual reoccurrences. (Neither Mithras nor Attis had been seen since Thrygragon, at least not that Tethys could confirm.)

"And you've no idea where any of them are anymore," Centauri wondered, not very subtly.

In doing so he all but bore out Tethys's therefore no longer nascent suspicions that he was a closet Horrite. It certainly fit his background. The moon-faced, massively overweight Fatman was a devout Christian; a devout papist fatso, to be absolutely accurate. Even in its 60th Century, fully faithful Christians, like pureblood Utopians of Weir for more than four millennia longer, remained barely tolerated outsiders on the Hidden Headworld.

When you're anti-devil on an Inner Earth where initially just as extraterrestrial devils were worshipped as gods and goddesses, that was to be expected. As Tethys was well-aware, though, what was now wasn't necessarily forever. Maybe that was the real reason Unmoving Byron kept taking over the Fatman – to keep him under control.

"Best thank your Almightiest Ubiquity I don't, Al. The real Female Three in particular are not just anti-devil. They're positively virulent, anti-anyone. And, before you ask, that's why I refuse to draw anyone to them – or vice versa. It'd be tantamount to murder either way; probably suicide for me, too. I don't do dot nor ditto."

"Neither do we," Janna insisted. Her father-in-law's mind must have been else-where because he acted as if he'd altogether missed their exchange.

"Then the crutch your Glee portrays Kanin's Helena leaning on can't be the True Cross."

Not just Centauri believed Helena Somata was Helena Augusta, the suppos-edly British-born mother of the Roman Emperor Constantine I – aka Augustus, meaning *'the Great'*. He further believed she was the Church-anointed saint who found the True Cross of the Crucifixion just before her reported death, circa 428 or 429 AD, at the age of seventy or eighty or somewhere in between.

Although reports of her death were, as they say, greatly exaggerated, Tethys could verify he was right on the other two counts. That she actually lasted – hale and hardy, except for an infirmity evidently requiring the support of a cross-shaped crutch – well into her second century didn't faze the Fatman. So long as they died of natural causes, Utopians of that era, even hybrid Utopians (which, again if Pyrame got hold of her, she had to be), usually lasted much more than 130 years.

Pure U-bloods up north in the Weirdom of Cabalarkon, Sedon's Devic Eye-Land, where Saladin born Nauroz had been reigning as its Master of Weir for thirty years, still did. Wretchedly, especially for everyone who had to look after them, the price a high majority paid for suchlike unprecedented longevity was congenital idiocy.

"Not unless the True Cross was a Great Godly Glory."

"And you don't think that too likely."

Tethys made a policy of avoiding religious hornets' nests, So he removed his cap and not so much scratched his head, as rummaged through the forest of tee-tee-tails stuck to it by their own ichors. As if by Braille, he plucked one out. "I think that's the Cross of Mithras. So, no, I don't think it too likely."

"Because there's no doubt about it. Got you."

"Better yet, got any pills?"

"Dumb question."

"So it is. Tell you what, once we leave here, we'll go to your place and I'll read you this here tee-tee-tale for free. Or at least as free as you opening your fridge to my semi-unlimited indulgence for the duration. You might want to play Herr Wagner's Ring on your fancy, Outer Earth sound system while I'm doing so, though. You'll be surprised how bang on he was right up until the end."

"Actually I wouldn't. I realize you're not so much losing your memory as it's already full, but you have read it to me before. I even recorded it. Still haven't had it printed, though. Like Janna said, a best seller, you're not."

"That's okay, I've plenty more. And what I don't have attached, I might have inside," he tapped his skull tellingly, "Up here, in my noggin noodle. Unless it's my noodle noggin. I know just the one too, buckle my shoe. As I was saying to Janna awhile back, I got another keepsake from her just this morning."

"Poor tee-tee."

"At least it wasn't plural. Back then more than half the Headworld didn't make it – and not just reproductively either."

========

A painfully high-pitched note abruptly snapped through the gallery. All eyes went all over the place, questing for its source. Even well afterwards it was impossible to determine who appeared first, the piper or the piped.
    "*Rats!*"
    "*Xibalba!*"
    "*Haddeus!*"

========

Doors and windows slammed open as if parted by squalling poltergeists. Into the CE-built and financed edifice scurried demented dozens of jaws-snapping, teeth-gnashing rodents. Far and away most were familiar urban nuisances: mice and rats, squirrels and chipmunks; burbling bustles of long-tailed tee-tees, no doubt with tales to tell and their tails to tell more, noticeable amongst them.

Since this arm of the Headworld Museum was brand new they must have spewed out of sewers, parks, derelict houses and warehouses, dockside businesses and marketplaces city wide. Whereupon, somehow unnoticed by passersby, they collected in its basement bowels, older wings, or outside the monumental structure until they were musically compelled inside. Even worse, some moved so slowly, and were already in such a deteriorated, often half-eaten state, they must have been dead already.

Zombie filth – how that could that be? Easily solved, that most minute of mysteries: had to be the devils' Spirit Being offspring. On the Hidden Headworld, where to this day the Dead did occasionally walk, how so many of the ambulatory horrors got here was much more relevant, albeit not immediately. Like the clearly alive ones, the solution would have to wait until the inevitable after-the-fact investigations concluded.

The Molech Xibalba – who had indeed first gained notoriety in Godbad under the ultimately terrifying, but initially mocking name of Reilly Haddeus – was dead, and not buried, years ago. Janna Fangfingers herself tore him apart. Her hatred was so strong she didn't turn or otherwise revitalize him. Nor did she let anyone else do so. His body had been cremated, his ashes scattered to the winds. Tethys knew this. Rather, having been dancing the legless limbo when she slew the reddish-skinned mage, he'd been told this.

Yet there he stood, seemingly on the air itself, a congenitally irrational Irache as far as Tethys had been concerned even before he got himself killed the last time he came across the madman. Equally as far as Tethys, a prototypical pacifist if ever there was one, was concerned, the Second Fangs Janna did everybody on the Head a big favour when she did away with him so painstaking maximally.

The ever-unwelcome newcomer was – or had been, at least nominally – a bona fide Irache shaman or medicine man. (Ever-unwelcome in Godbad, where he may have been born near the end of Tantalar 5920, that is to say.) A rabblerousing revolutionary disinclined to take prisoners, let alone negotiate with Godbadian authorities, he had also been a Summoning Child, as knowledgeable folks on both sides of the Dome came to call the mostly humanoid, presumed deviants born within six weeks of that year's Mithramas.

(Even though they didn't come into their own until they reached maturity in the late Thirties or early Forties, there had been literally hundreds of those. Because one of his eventual incarnations was one of them, Tethys could recollect what they were most commonly called, especially beyond the Dome – supranormals or, put more simply, supras.

(Fortunately for the Whole Earth, their heightened, at times approaching god-devil-calibre abilities proved short-lasting. By the mid-Fifties virtually every onetime supra to survive that long was once again just a Normie or Norma Normalman. As might be expected, the arguably ancillary devastation they were responsible for provided material for, yes, bestselling volumes of hence non-fictional biographies more so than made-up stories in here. Astonishingly, though, most of it was kept out of the ordinarily sensation-seeking mass media out there.)

The spiteful Geronimo had just appeared, in all his carefully cultivated spookiness, as if out of nowhere not twenty feet away from them. A crazed pied piper if ever there was one, the bloody-minded *'Holy Man'* was riotously tooting on his musical peace pipe. And, by God or the Devil above, that had to be what was making the typically contagion-contaminated creatures act as crazy as he'd always been.

That bespoke azuras in more ways than one. It also bespoke devilishness. Xibalba was neither. An Inner Earthling with an Outer Earth name (Mayans gave the same name to their underworld), he self-declared himself a Molech, magician or Magus back in those selfsame late Thirties, early Forties when he first came to prominence in Hadd (old Iraxas, the shaft of the Penile Peninsula, which cartographers also called Sedon's Mutton Chop as much for purposes of prudery as metaphor).

But, did he ever have the abilities he was now demonstrating before? Was he a self-psychopomp like some of them undeniably were? More grist for the post-mortem mill – and there would be plenty of mortems to post, the Legendarian would have remarked had he not been so pants-pissing terrified by what was transpiring right that minute.

Tethys, St Peche-Montressor and Centauri may or may not be possessed. Many members of the Fatman's security team definitely were, however. So were some of CE's preservationists. Devic eyefire can instantly burn anything, even vamps of the non-shoe variety. So long as there's anything there to burn, devic eyefire can burn it, put even better.

A dozen or more Master Devas manifested third eyes in their shells' foreheads. They blasted him. It wasn't him they blasted, though. It was the expensive drapery on the museum's walls, the tiles on its floor and the wooden beams of its ceiling. Those things were real. So were the rats and suchlike likely rabid, bite-anything vermin, most of them.

The insubstantial illusionist sullenly ceased tooting – unless it was an illusion the Molech Xibalba cast of himself or, if it wasn't him, which was far more likely, an illusion cast of the Molech Xibalba. The silence was deafening but much shorter lived than many of the suddenly squealing, ghastly invaders, both mobile deceased and altogether alive, that the devil-occupied men and women in the museum had commenced incinerating as rapidly as their eyefire allowed.

Desperately, but dutifully, the non-possessed bodyguards huddled, facing outwards, around Tethys and their real charges, Janna and her father-in-law. They'd unholstered their guns reflexively but, for fear of shooting their occupied fellows, had not yet pulled any triggers. There wasn't much point. Unaffected by anything and everything fired his way, the Xibalba eidolon, or whatever-it-was, began laughing characteristically maniacally.

Third eyes kept blazing regardless. Xibalba found their efforts hilarious; must have because he just kept on laughing and laughing and laughing the more. Finally he spoke, didn't boom, evidently addressing Alpha Centauri but loud enough for everybody to hear: **"Back off Iraxas, you greedy tub of ludicrous lard. It's ours, ever has been ours. As soon shall be the whole of the planet – again!"**

That voice, flashed Tethys, whereupon he suddenly recalled the Fatman's odd words about villains. He yanked Rumour's Brainrock quill out of his cap, sluiced out his splotch pad and started squiggling essentially unconsciously. (He did that sort of thing regularly; so did anyone who used Rumour's Tvasitar-trinket. That was how it worked.)

Not quite as flashingly fast, it was all over. Xibalba vanished abruptly. The creatures that weren't real did ditto, unless it was dot, dick or dildo. The ones that were real – and mobile – more like scampered, or squelched, back the way they came, devils in pursuit. Rather, their shells pursued; guns, though not rodents, drawn. Calm returning, a selection of those possessed as well as apparently not possessed ushered Centauri elsewhere.

"I'm a mite flustered, Jordy, so take a rain cheque. Tomorrow will have to be story time."

========

"I still need a beer," For a welcome change, his scar no longer itched.

"What'd you draw?" Janna had lingered, her with her still only two eyes.

Equally intrigued, both regarded his splotch pad without being able to come up with any analysis other than what was staring out of the page in front of them. He'd hadn't done the Molech Xibalba, or whomever had either been manifesting or masquerading as him.

He'd done the letter 'D' at an angle of 90 degrees clockwise. Just as weirdly, he'd done it with pronounced horns at the corners of the rotated 'D' and, albeit without actually having any, gleefully grinning ear to ear ever-so-proverbially. They had just enough time to register the recognizable yet inexplicable scrawl when the entire pad burst into flames.

He dropped it with barely an ouch. "Better make that thirty," he obliged.

Anyone for roasted rats?

****

3: Withstanding Distractions and Asides

The launching of the Cosmic Express from the Outer Earth's Centauri Island was scheduled for the 30ᵗʰ of November 1980.

========

The day before its scheduled launch, the 29ᵗʰ of Maruta, Year of the Dome 5980, was the day after the Molech Xibalba's startling reappearance and just as un-expected vanishing act. As was their wont, Alpha Centauri's daughter-in-law, Janna St Peche-Montressor, got him up early. After bathing him thoroughly, then bathing him again, she helped him get dressed and into an ordinary wheelchair. That done, she pushed him into the elevator that carried them to his top floor solarium.

The glass-enclosed conservatory-cum-solarium, with its fabulous view of Aka Godbad City and the warm-water Gulf of Aka itself, doubled as his unofficial office. It was his favourite place in the veritable fortress complex where they both lived and often worked. A genuinely welcome sight greeted them by Centauri's name.

"Morning, Al. Want a pill?"

"Not quite yet, Jordy." The Fatman glanced at the huge raindrops splattering on the transparent ceiling of the conservatory. "Lousy weather we're having."

"Lousy weather? You should have been around five hundred years ago. That wasn't just lousy weather. That was lousy life! Great time to be dead, though."

After he transferred himself into his fancy, automated wheelchair, Janna left him there with his houseguest as of yesterday. It could well be the start of a very long day. Throughout most of it his presence wouldn't be required. He was the boss, though, the boss had to be kept amused, and no one was better at that than the renowned Legendarian, who had already cracked his first six-pack of pilsners.

"Dead, huh? After yesterday I'm not sure I want to hear anything more about Haddit Zombies but, hey, I can bite at least as well as them so pray tell."

"Don't mind if I do," segued Tethys, not needing a second invite. "It was the twenty-second of Azky, 5456, the summer solstice and the longest day of the year. Throughout most of the Headworld it was a day of sadness. Being the last of the long days and the start of the long nights, the solstice marked the end of hope and the beginning of despair.

"Appropriately for the day, mortal twins were born. Deviants like me, meaning they had devic half-parents, these twins would prove the catalysts for some of the most momentous events in the entire six thousand year history of Sedon's Head. This then is the story I call: *'Janna Fangfingers – The Disunition of the Unities of Lazareme'.*

"Zalman Somata was the Master of Kanin City, southeast of Sedon's Mole. His wife, whose name was Melina, was his successor as High Illuminary. Something of a genetic throwback – I was hardly the only one to believe she was born a *'reverso'*, a somehow borderline reverted, and thus resultantly near-pure U-Blood – she was pregnant.

"Zalman hoped there would be no complications. You see, his wife was possessed of a devil by the name of Datong Harmonia just as she was giving birth."

"You've told me of those particular Somatas before, Jordy," recalled Centauri somewhat rudely. "For hundreds of years, since before Thrygragon as a matter of fact, Somatas were the ruling family of a onetime Weirdom, that of Kanin City. The Mastery of Marutia, Sedon's Cheek, which they led, came into being a few hundred years past it, not all that long after the Era of Empires ended in the Upper Head with the genesis of the Ghostlands.

"Zalman's father was also possessed of a devil, Lord Yajur, the Unity of Order, but we're not absolutely sure about Zal's mother or Melina's parents. We do know, as I'm sure you were about to note, proudly if not precisely paternally, her maiden name was Tethys, meaning she was descended from one of your earlier incarnations; either that or one of his and/or her descendents.

"Datong Harmonia was, as you'd expect, Harmony, the Balance between her immediate siblings, Abe Chaos, aka Unholy Abaddon, being the other triplet. The Unities were the firstborn of Thrygragos Lazareme, Thrygragos Everyman; Abaddon by Demeter, Yajur by Sapiendev, and Harmony by Devaura. When Mel conceived the terrible twins Lazareme possessed Zal, in effect making Harm a father-fucker, not that there was anything new about that."

"Just so," admitted Tethys, sucking back another beer. The Fatman was obviously distracted, in no mood to listen, but the Legendarian knew his friend and long-time patron (in, for him, a variety of incarnations) needed to relax. It would take time but he'd get to his tale eventually. Centauri would listen and be soothed by his voice.

"Harmony," Centauri persisted as if by rote, "Rather, the woman she possessed, Zal's Mel, gave birth to these twins. Once Janna and Sraddha Somata reached puberty, actually a few years later I imagine, they hooked up with Chaos and the Grower, Nergal Vetala, respectively. Which annoyed the hell out of literal viceregent Belialma, who had designs on Abaddon, and the other two Nergalids, the Planter and the Harvester, Zuvem Nergalis and Yama Nergal, both of whom had been Vetala's bi-lunar mates for approximately forever."

"Hell's the appropriate word," Tethys agreed, "When you're talking about beguiling Belialma. Lady Lust was on her second go-round as the Prime Sinistral of Satanwyck by then."

"And Abaddon had no business getting involved with Janna in the first place," added Centauri, presumably still intent upon saving time. "She was the elder twin and Thrygragos Lazareme had promised her to one of the Black Godlings, Faustus

Vladuca, called Fangfingers. He'd also promised Sraddha, nickname Shreds, to one of the so-called White Godlings, Rastha Aragon, the Skinless Rasp."

"Who has virtually nothing to do with this story." interjected Tethys, becoming frustrated despite his better nature.

"Neither do Bouncing Belle and First Fangs," suggested Centauri disputatiously.

"Now there's where we differ," Tethys stated. "Shall we begin again?"

"By all means."

"Good. Just let me tell the story this time, okay."

========

A Tethys Tale – JANNA FANGFINGERS: THE DISUNITION OF THE UNITIES OF LAZAREME – Part One: THE WEIRDOM OF KANIN CITY

========

In 5456, the year the twins were born, Kanin City was one of the last Weirdoms left on the Headworld still occupied by a majority of Utopians. Although these Utopians were no longer purebloods, otherwise devils couldn't have possessed them, their genetic integrity remained strong. That is to say they were still more Utopian than human.

Without getting into a great deal of detail, Kanin had lasted so long after the disasters of Thrygragon, and its aftermath, because of its thousand-year tradition of allowing devils to occupy – not that they could do much to prevent it – the ruling couples and thereby parent successive Masters.

Its main purpose for persistence, besides being the then capital of the Utopians' Cheek-wide Mastery, a kind of essentially non-devic, hence secular empire, was the Moloch Sedon's charge to its Masters to preserve the Gregarian Fields, evidently better known to you as Sedon's Mole, as a place of perpetual peace. In some respects this was only fitting.

Pacifica, the Places of Peace, was the original name of the Whole Earth archipelago that became the hidden continent we know today as Sedon's Head. I say that provisionally, hereby adding that it did so only after the floodwaters of the Genesea raged outwards, to help swamp the rest of the planet, and the land between what had been Pacifica's islands dried up.

As such, as a place of peace, the Gregarian Fields were the only area in the entire Inner Earth where neither devils, for fear of instant cathonitization, nor anyone else, initially for fear of destruction via the Utopians' undeniably extraterrestrial weaponry, were allowed to do physical violence to each other.

I said initially, note. Due to inviolate Sedonic decree, devils didn't dare breach its sanctity. But it was supposed to be the Master of the Weirdom of Kanin's duty to see to it that the Fields remained a violence-free territory for non-devils. Harsh Reality, however, pays heed to no man. Nor to any god or devil, not that's there's any difference between gods and devils beneath the Dome – especially not if Dark Sedon's the Devil Himself, which he may be.

Harsh Reality, Kanin's Utopians interbreeding with indigent humans, no matter how insignificantly slowly they did so, continued to dilute the purity of their bloodline. By an admittedly difficult to fathom psychic link between the Utopians' bloodline and the functionality of the Weirdom's extraterrestrial technology, its weaponry was consequently rendered more and more irreparably useless.

Notwithstanding Thrygragon, which I shouldn't have remind you took place there, what?, around 1100 years before the stories I'm about to relate, the burden of keeping the Gregarian Fields a peaceful place for everyone venturing inside them, be they expecting sanctuary or just some degree of safe passage, more inevitably than eventually fell to devils exclusively. As I said, our story takes place in the latter half of the 55th Century of the Dome. That means the devils in charge of doing just that were Lazaremists, more specifically Everyman's firstborn triplets.

Further to that, Bodiless Byron had relinquished control of Kanin at the end of the 50th Century. He didn't, or doesn't, expect to have his tribe's turn again until a thousand years later, at the beginning of the 61st Century; in other words, if a habitable city's re-established, twenty years from now. Back then though, the transitional period between Lazareme Spawn and Mithras Spawn should have already been well underway.

It's important to remember that each of the Thrygragos Brothers had – has, two out three – his own attitude with respect to being a Great God. Backtracking to before Thrygragon, Mithras ruled by coercion. Which goes a long way to explain why most of his offspring eventually turned against him. By contrast, Byron rules by law and Lazareme doesn't like ruling at all.

As is commonly said about humans, Master Devas, third generational devils, are very much like-father, like-son. Or daughter, I hasten to add. Like sperm-sprung like sperm-spring might be the best way to put it. When you think about it, that's hardly surprisingly. All devazurs are genetically bound to obey their fathers.

It was becoming the Mithradites' turn to influence events in the Weirdom of Kanin City, but their father was dead. Lazaremists, anarchists virtually to a one, Jack or Jill, saw no reason to relinquish their hegemony over the Weirdom. And, as one would expect, their father could see no reason to hedge them in.

========

"That's a pun, by the way. A series of them; in a hedgerow, as it happily hop-happens."

Although tempted, Centauri didn't even chuckle. Given what else he may have to attend to today, succumbing to spontaneous mirth was not high on his agenda of things-to-do. Plus, he hated fay-saying almost as much as he was wary of fays themselves – the feeorin of Twilight especially.

Fucking faeries had caused him a whole whack of botheration over the course of his thirty-five years on this side of the Dome; his 35-years of awareness there were two sides to the Whole Earth, put better. Besides again, even for him, it was too early in the day to be popping pills, as in pilsners, the same as Tethys did most any time of the day or night.

Having no need to worry about heart attacks was one thing. Making sure you remained your own man was another. When you were oft-times possessed of a Great God, sobriety had both its necessities and its rewards. All the more so when it was All-Eyes, APM, Aphropsyche Morningstar, occupying his daughter-in-law, who rewarded it.

Like beer, Lovely Lady Afrites proved God wanted folks like him to be happy.

=========

At that time, as I may or may not need to tell you, the tribe of Byron was having enough problems of its own trying to wrest back control of the Penile Peninsula – Sedon's Mutton Chop, Iraxas and Krachla – from what remained of the once nearly Headworld-encompassing empire of Lathakra, to risk becoming involved with what was happening in the Cheek Lands. So it came to pass the Weirdom, and the Mastery of Marutia that went with it, became a battleground between Lazaremist extremists on one side and Mithradite malcontents on the other.

Truth be known being my motto, one of them, highborn from the tribe of Varuna Mithras had never been overly pleased the Age of Mithras had, in their estimation, devolved into the enduring Age of Lazareme. Needless to say, being a naturally disputatious batch they were even less thrilled that it had evolved into a peaceable, almost friendly, panacea: the dreamtime Age of Panharmonium become reality, with the irresistibly delightful Datong Harmonia as good as – as very good as – running the nonetheless never precisely serene show.

Needles to slay, to pun afresh, the Byronics were perfectly content to let the two other tribes go at each other tooth and flail. Or dental floss, if you prefer.

The twins upbringing proceeded normally enough. Zalman Somata shared with the devils who had possessed his wife, father and, yes, he himself, a distaste for Mithras Spawn. However, like the drop-pants gorgeous Harmony, Lord Order, and their Great God of a sybaritic sire, he was prepared to accept tradition and allow the Weirdom be turned over to them on New Year's Day 5500. What he wasn't prepared to do was serve under a Mithradic hegemony.

As a deviant, the quarter- or half-son of a devil or devils, Zalman could expect to lead an extended, yet active and healthy life. Most deviants did, myself being a radical exception – the extraordinarily ancient Quoits Tethys didn't acquire me until her first death in 5476, so she isn't even the exception that proves the rad-rule. His family having retained a surfeit of Utopian blood, Utopians being naturally as hale and hardy as they were very long lived in mortal terms, Zal was doubly blessed in that regard.

Although as I recall it, it was mostly his much younger wife's idea, he amassed a splendid army of likeminded followers – in terms of Hate-Sedon fanaticism in nothing else. Then, to mark his hundredth birthday, he led them out of Kanin City, leaving its rulership to Melina. And, before you seek to remind me, even though I was dancing the legless limbo at the time, I'm well aware Mel's Mastery lasted barely a day.

Abandoning Kanin City to the prematurely slavering Mithradites and their forces, the Utopians, if I can call non-purebloods that, marched far to the Cheek's west, beset by Time Quakes all the way. Upon reaching the Gulf of Corona, Sedon's Human Eye, they took to the sea in brigs built by Zal-Mel's son Shreds and his oddly worshipful cohort over the course of the previous year to eighteen months or more.

(And, yes yet again, when you consider the lifetime of another me – or pre-me, put better – by the aforementioned nickname of first Queer then Quoits Tethys, therein lies awfully close to half a millennium worth of stories that might collectively be called the, um, *'Contagion Collectors'*. None of which, since I'm no more a devil than you are, and therefore don't have 500 years to spare, I'm inclined to dip into right this minute.

(Suffice it to say, the god his worshipful cohort came to revere was none other than Shreds himself. Which is also the main reason he ended up stranded on the Outer Earth with a later me, Second Fangs Janna's beloved Squiggly. Him, whom dear old, pre-too-toothy Janna once declared the *'most handsome and desirous of men'*, and them, post-godhood for Sraddha, I will get into eventually. Promise)

Dodging Apple-Apis Isle, where to this day Mithrant Legionnaires and their Korant womenfolk venerate Mithradite gods and goddesses; where at least one of them, Kind Plathon, Ap Isle's Apis, still strides about openly, in all his naked bull-ishness; they sailed into the Head's western ocean, that of Fearsome Fobbiat.

They thereupon beaded north, skirting the Floodlands, Sedon's Eyebrow, where dinosaurs yet roam (as overruled by Eden-mutated Saur Tsars and Tsarinas, and they in turn by another Mithradite Master Deva, Klizarod Rex, whose devic protectorate is the Floods). They were heading to Sedon's Devic Eye-Land, the one place on the Whole Earth where, howsoever ironically given its geographical location, Utopian bloodlines remained largely undiluted.

If Star Sedon had still been shining downstairs in the night's sky, which he (as opposed to it) wasn't thanks mostly to Lord Order murdering me – the Quidnunc Tethys version of me if you're keeping score – eighteen years, to the day, after the twins' birth, the mighty Eye-Mouth when upstairs might have spotted a vicious cyclone whipping itself into a truly colossal fury some miles off the coast of Floods.

Moving rapidly northwards, as if chomping at their butt-ends – ergo, as if it wasn't a natural phenomenon at all, which it may not have been considering how good devils are when it comes to witching weather – it caught up to the laggard of the re-consecrated Utopians' warships some days later. Named the Kanin, it was the flagship of four barques built under the also aforementioned supervision of Sraddha Somata, possibly at least partially pre-godhood.

Nautically speaking, by a really long and comparatively fat pole, it wasn't a barquentine. It was a brigantine, a two-pole (or mast) vessel square-rigged on the foremast, and fore-and-aft rigged on the mainmast. Although he wasn't on it, when it was being built Squiggly was fond of calling it a hermaphrodite brig. Strangely enough, he'd learned from the actual shipwrights that that term was a legitimate categorization for such a boat, unless it was a ship. (Not that I consider myself a ship-disturber when it comes to distinguishing the difference.)

Flash of lightning, slash of whipping wind, crack-of-doom thunder, this and much, much more Zalman Somata registered the moment he was blasted off the warship-cum-troop-transporter into the near-freezing froth of Fearsome Fobbiat. For Zal it was all over but the false light at the end of the tunnel and thence its darkness. He was inhaling water; drinking drowning and dead save for the gone bit; that and the narwhal, who was as Knotty as he was nautical.

Moments later he was being offered a beer by none other than Jordan *'Quill'* Tethys, the 30-Year Master of the Weirdom of Cabalarkon.

========

"This would be, as correctly, the 500-year-old you alluded to previously?"

"Mel's grandmother twenty-odd generations removed, yes, though to be absolutely accurate she came nowhere near attaining 30 years as me."

"Best to call her the 30-Beer Master then."

"Too true, if you want to get technical – though that's what killed her the second time. The beer's swill up there."

"What killed her the first time?"

"Ah, as to that ..."

========

Born Queer, therefore not always Quoits, yet nonetheless always Tethys, that Jordan or Jordy was four hundred and seventy-six years old. As stunning an age as it was for a humanoid mortal, even a pureblood Utopian, which she wasn't, to the best any of Cabalarkon's scientocrats or her fellow Illuminaries could determine her genes were not anything special. She had to be a deviant of some sort to have lasted so long and since she'd always been lucky, there wasn't much doubt as to who her devic half-mom had to be – Wintry Moira, Dame Chance, Fata Fortuna or, most commonly, Lady Luck.

A millennial child, one whose mixed blood was apparent from her last name, Quoits had next to no chance to make it to the upcoming millennium. She figured she had a realistic one of making it to the half-millennium, however. (That'd be 5500 YD, the year the ever-fractious tribe of Mithradites were scheduled to take over rulership of Kanin City and, with it, the Mastery of Marutia).

Even though it was only a quarter-century away, she remained hopeful that, by then, there would be no one left for them to rule bar demons, devils and maybe a few deviants like her, assuming she did have a devic half-mother, a devic half-father (the Legendarian was as easy to possess as anyone except a total U-blood) or both. Oh, yes – and that the Weirdom of Cabalarkon would have a new ruling family.

Which makes it all the more improbable, synchronicity-wise, that she died the first time within a few days of the imbeciles of Weir anointing her Cabalarkon's Master. Evidently the stress of replacing the equally mass-murderous old man she'd served under for so long almost immediately proved too much for her. Evidently also, me reincarnating both inside her and, as a strategic necessity, as her – something most everyone up there failed to realize until it was your elephant ...

========

"Your elephant?"

"Irrelevant. Haven't I used that one on you before?"

"Evidently not, though maybe you have. I'm feeling a mite distracted."

"You must be, otherwise you would never have thought she was 500-years-old. As a millennial child, she was a mere 476 years old at the time of her first death."

"Thus dispelling the notion you're always bodily between 20 and 60."

"There's no such a notion; not one you could prove by me at any rate."

"As a strategic necessity?"

"The new ruling family, rather its paternal progenitor, hadn't arrived yet."

"So she had to pretend being herself even though she was actually you."

"Assuredly. And her first death left Squiggles, and with him banished pal Shreds, in quite a quandary beyond the Dome, that I can equally assure you."

"Squiggles? Shreds?"

"*Also Squigs and Sraddha, other Janna's twin. In case you missed it, Squiggly was the Q-name of the Janna's sweetheart. He was the fine fellow who had my quill both before once Queer, then Quoits, then Quill died the first time, and again after she died the second time, as me – albeit not until he died the first time and thereby got hold of it on the rebound, as me, also as it were. We clear on that?*"

"*As a bell of bitumen. But no doubt thou shalt illuminate me further in due course.*"

"*Consider yourself dittoed on that ringtone assuredly.*"

========

Although Quoits was undoubtedly a trained Hellion, like the infamous Morgan Abyss of centuries earlier, the narwhal of the moment was that eventual Master's ally more so than pet or familiar. As I believe I've already noted, his name was Knotty, as in nautical miles, not Naughty, as in misbehaving, though almost everybody assumed it was the latter on account of his pokey-playful nature – except, being poked by a narwhal, no matter how playfully, can be painful.

Knotty the Narwhal was also somewhat like Hinny the Hippy, whom we made mention of yesterday, in that he was bred by Weir's Eden-like biomages of the era to be, theoretically anyhow, a cathonitizer. Quoits had assigned him to follow Zal's fleet of four, which he had done faithfully ever since it left the mainland coast of Corona, Sedon's Human Eye.

Good thing, too, as it happened. Him psychically alerting her, the Quoits-Quill, of Zal's plight was how he got to Cabalarkon. As for why Kanin's absentee Master didn't drown like his younger brothers, Johann and George, and the rest of those on Zal's ill-fated flagship, that was down to the narwhal too. Quoits rescued him, via her long ago rediscovered ringots. Hence her calling herself Quoits in the first place; hence so much more as well; but I said I wasn't going to get into any of that.

Providentially – albeit not Providence as in much missed, and not just by me, Pyrame Silverstar, who's been a silver star shining out of the night's sky for the last thirty years – the other three ships in Zal's armada made it through the storm in basically one piece. So it was, on Kamor the 4th, in the Year of the Dome 5476, a date that continues to be celebrated as Independence Day in Cabalarkon, Zalman Somata and his adventurers took over the only partially antediluvian Weirdom.

I say took over out of respect for my one-man audience. I could say took control. I could also spout propaganda, should you so desire. Truth told though, they didn't so much conquer the megalithic city and its splendidly green and bountiful environs, what makes it naturally self-sustaining. They walked into it; more to cheers than jeers, it should also be said, and very little in the way of resistance.

I'll stick to conquered henceforth, if you don't mind, because that's how the history books record it. And I should know. I helped write some of them.

It would have been an easy task regardless of Quoits rolling out the welcome mat anyhow. Again, that was due mostly to me – and the necessity of her not appearing to be anyone other than herself until she eased Zal into her position. Quoits being me, she much preferred popping pilsners to popping pills in prisons – or whatever Masters did besides funnelling their Utopians' self-preservative willpower into its version of pre-Earth Weir's Mother Machine.

Cabby's idiots had paid a steep price to retain the purity of their bloodlines. Still do. As its ambassadors to Godbad will begrudgingly attest, if pressed; as Morgianna and Demios Sarpedon will verify, even if they haven't been allowed anywhere near it for the selfsame last thirty years that Pyrame's been upstairs; as I myself will confirm, for the price of another pilsner, having been there many a time since their exile, albeit in a variety of different incarnations, one of whom was all too sadly, for all concerned, daughter Ukemoshi, Sister Jordan; Utopians there, in Zal's time, as now, were akin to inmates trying to protect Bedlam.

Except, as we'll get to shortly, these imbeciles still had extraterrestrial weaponry.

=========

"In his wake Zal, whom you will have already gathered I knew personally, in a somewhat disturbing as well as bewildering number of successions, left Kanin City to wife Melina. Imagine his surprise when, not long after being acclaimed Cabalarkon's Master, he went to bed only to wake up with Mel not only climbing in with him but telling him she was going to stay."

"Not only? She was a witch. Couldn't she have got to Cabalarkon on her agates?"

=========

"Contagion Collectors, Al, not going to get into them. But to answer your question without sliding into too much detail, once Zal took over, sure, but not previously."

"Jordy ..."

"Oh, very well. You see, Quoits's Hate-Sedon Masters had allowed her, pre-me, to bring infectious carriers of all noxious sorts in from the Outer Earth for a couple of hundred years. While neither shy nor, like your Centauri Enterprises, averse to advertising, they nevertheless didn't want her, um, sickening successes bruited about beyond those in the know up there. As a result they were especially anxious not to let anyone into Cabalarkon who, once they learned what they were up to, could get out next to effortlessly and start doing just that."

"In other words – you. Though I guess *'you'* is only one word."

"Nor witches of any kind, not even sympathetic Hellions on account of, no matter what sisterhood you belong to, stepping stones are virtually identical."

"All this for fear of retaliation," appreciated the Fatman, who as a teenager had been through World War Two on the Outer Earth, hence also his hatred of propaganda and reluctance to let CE advertise its advancements except to flaccidly further sales.

"Like the Lazaremists did the Death's Head Hellion. Or tried to, put consequentially ghostly and/or radioactively."

"Understandably. Directly or indirectly they were responsible for hundreds upon thousands, if not millions, of deaths or near-deaths Headworld-wide. Me, Ghostlands or no Ghostlands, stone cudgels or extraterrestrial weaponry, I found that out, I'd organize a strike force capable of destroying the whole unspeakable nation. Yet you did the moment you became Quoits. And you didn't do anything to stop them."

"I said she drank herself to death. She wouldn't have done that without me."

"Still, you're friends with devils, always have been. You consider Thrygragos Everyman your grandfather. You could have alerted him or his Unities years before you got hold of her."

"If I knew about it, which I didn't, mostly because I rarely wanted to go there during most of that time."

"Surely your suspicions were aroused. Or is the beer really that bad?"

"It really is, hence how torturous her second death truly was, her being me. But there was more to it than that. For one, you're right. Ever since the time of another mass murderous Master, much-mentioned Morgan Abyss, circa the early part of the 49th Century, Masters of Weir have been wary of me for just that reason.

"For another, with the exception of Dark Sedon, most devils enjoy my company. I like most of them back. I also like Sed's Daddy Cabby and that's another reciprocal ditto, if not a dildo. But to this day some of Weir's most influential Illuminaries reckon I'm a devic suicide. And, socially needy sort that I am, I tend to avoid places where I'm not welcome. Or at least where it's unlikely I'll get any decent brew gratis.

"Further to that, while they can't block me drawing their Weirdoms, Masters can block access to it between-space. They can therefore prevent me drawing myself there the same as they can witches on their stepping stones, psychopomps like Garudas, Chimaera's pterippi, the Valkyries' psycho-swans, and even the gaily gallivanting Goat, Pusan Wanderlust. It all depends on how they choose to concentrate their peoples' psychical puissance."

"Psychical nonsense more like, if they can't dome the entire land, over under sideways down. Which they can't according our, um, aforementioned pals, Demios and Morgianna."

Wars, even the talk of wars, disagreed with Centauri. Nonetheless, as the Molech Xibalba, whoever or whatever it was, attested howsoever fleetingly yesterday, he was in the process of spearheading one against Janna Fangfingers and her Haddit supporters, be they living Iraches or the walking dead.

Was that just for starters? Was he really thinking of mounting an invasion, so many thousands of miles far to the north, of the Weirdom of Cabalarkon? It was what the husband and wife Sarpedons – former enemies, but long ago thoroughly co-opted allies – wanted. And favours earned were often returned, with interest, on the Inner Earth of Sedon's Head.

Sixty year old Summoning Children like Xibalba, and so many, many others, Centauri's Godbadian-based conglomerate had surreptitiously acquired much of the technology that went into the Cosmic Express from them and their Hate-Sedon Utopian loyalists. Just as significantly, both Dem and Morg – whom Tethys had known, as the saying goes, since before they were born – had legitimate claims to the Cabalarkon Mastery.

Was seeking to replace Saladin Devason, Morg's year-older brother, by establishing them, individually or together, on its throne, such as it was, appropriate payback? All the more so given their bellicose back-story, Centauri spent many sleepless night fretting about just that. In all likelihood, he'd concluded, his ultimate decision would be predicated on Hadd's outcome.

Be that as it may, regardless of whether they stayed down or rose up (perhaps on the other side), folks died in wars. Unlike Tethys, if the Fatman did in this one or the next one or the one after that, he doubted he'd be coming back.

Especially after tomorrow's successful launching of the Cosmic Express – the first step in Thrygragos Byron's grand scheme to depart this dead-end planet, hopefully taking every still extant member of the devazur race, including the Moloch Sedon and his Daddy Cabby, the Undying Utopian, with him – that was certain.

========

"Ah well," he said, thereby signalling Tethys to carry on, "Maybe it is time for a beer after all."

========

As I've alluded to already, Unholy Abaddon, the Unity of Chaos, forced Melina Somata to abdicate her caretaker Mastery the day, or day after, Zalman left it to her. It may or may not be relevant where she went to in the months between her resignation and her dramatic return, unexpectedly crawling into the sack with her husband up in Cabalarkon, but it probably is worth noting why Uncle Abe kicked her out of Kanin City in the first place.

He did so after he gleaned – mind-mined more so than mind-reamed – her involvement in the cynical subterfuge aimed at getting his much-loved, as opposed to much-hated, immediate sibling, the Unity of Harmony as well as Panharmonium, to self-cathonitize. It may also be he'd learned, through her, of the Utopians-supported, Quoits-led, anti-devil, anti-Head, conspiracy to contaminate and thereby kill off countless thousands of devil-sustaining worshippers.

Understand, I'm not saying Mama Mel was a contagion collector herself. It's certainly conceivable she didn't know what they were up with their disease-carrying imports from the Outer Earth. And by they I mean great, great, dot-dot-dot, but not dotty, great-grandmother Quoits, her fellow Utopians and the Hellion sisterhood, via such intermediaries as the Pied Piper of Hamelin, initially; Tomcat Tattletail, who I maintain is really what became of Rumour of Lazareme; and Herta Heartthrob, the daemonic simulacrum of Datong Harmonia.

As a result, governance of Kanin City, the city-state at the centre of the Marutian Mastery, at least nominally fell to Zal-Mel's as yet not even twenty year old daughter Janna. It's at this point that the whole affair gets very, very interesting indeed. For you see, much to the annoyance of just about everybody, including his immediate siblings and, howsoever hypocritically, his libertine of a full-father (the terrible twins' devic half-father, don't forget), Abe was already having a torrid dick-dildo with the silver-haired teenager.

Only now I'm talking dick-dildo (or dot-ditto, if you're coming to feel sensitive to suchlike salacious silliness) in the sense of him having an affair of the heart with her, and not having her take over affairs of state. With respect to the latter, though, I have to admit it actually proved quite a good choice for a few precious years. Janna was pretty, and far more popular than intelligent, but she had enough commonsense to leave most of the unpleasant, nitty-gritty bits of quotidian administration to Zal-Mel's remaining functionaries.

That allowed her to concentrate on her strengths: the happy smiley-face-first, public appearances and castanets-clacking assurances, more so than tub-thumping exhortations, that all was well. And it largely was, again thanks in no small measure to her once perhaps betrayed, devic half-mother, Datong Harmonia, and the good fellowship endemic to her ongoing Age of Panharmonium. To put it in rally-round-the-black-flag terms: Anarchism Ruled! Which is just the way Lazaremists prefer it.

The wild card in all this was of course Unholy Abaddon. I still called him Uncle Abe Chaos even as I was drinking Quoits-Quill-me to an overdue, for her, second death on all that horrible beer. Abe was a ferocious iconoclast, a predictably unpredictable specimen of humanoid deviltry. Like Byron's Stallion, Chimaera Glimmenmare, he often seemed to change on an hourly basis, sometimes minute by minute. Could be he'd be a good-looking, standard six-footer with the body of a swimmer, slender and tightly-muscled. Could be he wouldn't be.

Could be he was clean-shaven and short-haired. Could be he'd have a tangled, lava flow of rats-nest hair stretching down to his buttocks-bare barrel-butt on one side and a big red beard, like Grim Thordin's, rolling over a beer-keg-gut on the other side. Could be he was wearing the foppish fineries of Kanin's court, go to the privy, and come back in tatters, like a man a year submerged in the bottom of the sea, or a nearby lake, and reeking of it as well.

The one constant was his trident, his Brainrock power focus, although even that changed occasionally. Plus, there were times he didn't carry a focus at all. Devils can keep their talismans inside their bodies, you'll have heard, and not just from me.

(For example, the Apple Goddesses, Divine Coueranna, Marut Kanin and bedazzling Belialma, had their different coloured, apple talismans shining out of their third eyes. Had, as in past tense; although other than Lady Lust who, like Pyrame, is a star in the night's sky nowadays, no one knows for sure what's become of either Concord or Discord.)

Perhaps that's logical since there are those who say that a devic talisman is the devil's body. As you may recall, if you were paying attention, I'm not one of them. I hold to the notion, oft-repeated, just in cast you do pay attention to what I'm saying once in a while, that devils gain and keep solidity by occupying the subtle matter bodies of debrained demons.

As to how demons could allow themselves to get to a point where they could be debrained in the first place, well, that's another story, one that goes back to roughly 2000 YD. Capsulated bluntly, they aren't overly endowed in that department to start with, are they?

========

"That's a rhetorical question, by the way. Take it from me, Al, they aren't. They do, however, have voracious appetites. Aren't much for cooking, though."

"Because they're so stupid it's usually them who get cooked."

"Oh, you've heard that before. Sorry, I should have remembered. Try this one instead: 'It is, however, one of their few saving graces.'"

"That they cook so easily?"

"That they go up in smoke so easily, yes."

========

Abe Chaos was definitely a loose cannon, probably the loosest cannon of all the loose cannons Lazareme sired. As we'll quickly see, he didn't have the same restrictions every other substantial devil on the Whole Earth had. I reckon that's why he's Chaos. Regular rules, even Sedonic decrees, don't seem to apply to him.

Just as he changed his appearances according to his whim of the moment; just as his unforeseeable mood changes were far and away his most dangerous aspect; apparently he could also change his genetic code. Yes, he still obeyed his father, howsoever begrudgingly. Yes, he couldn't lie and was still bound by his oaths. But there was something else about him.

He had something no other devil had. While devils, by virtue of the fact they can transmogrify, to use a fancy word, can render themselves coitally compatible with humans, or any other species, even non-sentient ones, they can't render themselves conceptively so, if you can appreciate the distinction. That's why devils have to possess humans, or whomever, in order to half-have non-azura deviant offspring like me. Chaos, though, had somehow achieved cross-species fertility without any need for a shell, daemonic or otherwise.

Here's where Beguiling Belialma, Satanwyck's Prime Sinistral, for the second time, and the Mithradite quintessence of concupiscence, to fay-say some, enters our narrative big bad she-wolf time. By virtue of her own shape-shifting abilities, a formidable series of lures and allures, an insatiable and highly refined desire for sex, not to mention a biologically experimental bent, she masqueraded as Janna Somata and seduced Abaddon on her behalf.

On both their behalves, better make that, since it turned out Janna Somata was more like Bouncing Belle than Datong Harmonia, her gorgeous but selective and moderately prudish devic half-mother, in this regard. Abe may have fallen for Lady Lust in Janna's guise but, when he finally bedded the real Janna, he probably didn't notice any difference.

On the 31st of Djerridam, 5480 YD – 31 October 1480, in your terms out there – Janna gave birth to Abe's son. Howsoever significantly, in for me 20-20 hindsight, and for devils in 20-20-20 ditto, it was precisely six hundred and fifty-five years to the day since the Atomic Twins, freed from All of Incain but unable to contain themselves any longer, blew up on the northernmost Gates of Cabalarkon. (In doing so they thereby finished off the utter ruination of the Laughing Lands of the Upper Head that the Death's Head Hellion had started a few months earlier with her horrifyingly destructive empyrean vessels.)

No sooner had Azkeecyoos, another Lazaremist, the devic god of medicine (whom his feebly funny father called Surgeon the Sturgeon), cut the child's umbilical cord than King Harvest (Yama Nergal, a highborn Mithradite) appeared in the palace's birth room; whereupon he laid claim to the boy on behalf of his family.

Underlord Yama was born in the fifth litter of Thrygragos Mithras and, hence, had considerable power. By then he was a classical Grim Reaper, dressed more in shadows that black cloaks, with a skinless skull for a head and three eye-holes instead of three eyes. He also had at his disposal an army of radioactive Dead Things, a legacy of the aforementioned Idiot Twins and multitudes of his own azuras, whose touch could kill.

Because of their vulnerability to ordinary rainfall, and indeed to plain old running water, Yama's army, Death's Angels or the Inglorious Dead, as they were and still are called, could never leave the Ghostlands long enough to engage anyone in battle. (The Ghosts being what had become of said Laughing Lands, the Elysian Fields of Outer Earth myth and Inner Earth reality.) In other words, while their touch could kill, you could rot them on the spot with a squirt gun.

All right, I exaggerate, but only somewhat. Point is, unless there was a drought – which there has been in the Cheeks for over a quarter century, I understand, despite the fact that the Apocalyptic thereof, Cathune Bubastis, has been upstairs as long as Pyrame, her often silver-haired brood sister – they could never venture far from the Ghosts without running the risk of decomposing mid-step. Although, being a devil, Yama Nergal did not share any of his army's weaknesses, his power focus, a miner's pick become a more-acceptable farmer's scythe, wasn't much of a fighting weapon.

All of which is to say the Nergalid didn't present much of a threat, not to someone like Abe Chaos anyhow. Appropriately for a god of death, Yama's major attribute was patience. And that's probably what annoyed Abaddon so much. His son was presumably mortal but, if he was like the offspring of possessing devils and possessed humans, which was by no means certain, he could expect to live a long time; perhaps as many as two or three hundred years, more if he was like Quoits Tethys and could subsist on the slop churned out by Utopian replicators.

How dare Yama show up on the day his son was born? How dare the Nergalid claim his son was Mithradite property when Mithras Spawn had no right to Kanin City until the turn of the half-millennium, twenty years thereafter? Moreover, even if Sinistral Lust was occupying Janna when the boy was conceived, which admittedly was remotely possible, Belialma had always been the bouncing, or beguiling, or bedazzling, not the birthing, type.

The Unity didn't just refuse to turn over his son. He was so incensed he drove the Nergalid out of Kanin City and didn't stop there. He pursued him through the universal substance of Samsara, what witches and most devils call the Weird or the Grey. They fought intermittently for three days. Yama put up only as much resistance as was necessary to keep Abaddon occupied as he purposely fled north.

They clashed all the way to the Ghostlands, which lay between the Lake Lands (Sedon's Sweat Glands) in the South, the Mystic Mountains (Sedon's Crown or Headband) in the North, Satanwyck (Sedon's Temple) in the East, and the Weirdom of Cabalarkon (Sedon's Devic Eye-Land) to the West. In the absence of anything actually alive save his Yamazurs animating Death's Angels, the Ghosts were, and still are, the Underlord's effective protectorate.

As enraged as he was, Abaddon wasn't irrationally so. He knew a trap when he was about to spring one – on himself. Still, only four years earlier, in 5476, intent upon saving the Hidden Headworld from too often aforementioned contagion carriers, he, his father and his immediate siblings had overthrown a devic Dand in his own territory.

That the Dand was a deviant, none other than Sraddha Somata, in control of the Fop, First Fangs, Vladuca Fangfingers by Illuminary-given name, a Lazaremist Master Deva who couldn't disobey their mutual father, had a lot to do with that of course. Nonetheless, not to mention even more importantly in terms of his personal perpetuation, as a Mithradite Yama was a totally different matter.

The Nergalid's powers would increase exponentially once he was fighting in his own realm. Chances were, Abe no doubt reckoned, he could take him out, cathonitize or perhaps even kill him. However, as mighty as he was, the Ghostlands were so imbued with Atomic Radiation that entering them might prove as – pun-time – devastating, as debilitating, as they invariably proved fatal to any non-immortal foolish enough to spend much of any time inside them.

"Next time I catch you outside your protectorate," the Unholy One promised the Reaper, "I'll unsheathe the Chaos Blade and you'll be one dead Death."

Yama Nergal scoffed at the Unity. "When you unsheathe the Chaos Blade, you'll be mine to claim. For surely Grandfather Sedon will kill you for it." And he might have too, considering what Abe's black lightning purportedly could do.

========

"Good Shit Lollipop time," decided Centauri, who hadn't quite got to the laziest length of obese laxness where he peed or crapped into colostomy bags.

"Thought you'd never ask," said Tethys, who had begun to fear he was about to go the way of Zalman's fellows on the Kanin, except he'd drown in his own urine, not Mother Earth's.

And without any Hellion's Sangazurs handy to reanimate him either.

****

4: Devil Doomsayers

The Janna who wasn't the subject of Tethys's tale brought the Fatman his mid-morning snack, not that he needed one; that and a preliminary report on yesterday's verminous invasion.

========

Cleaning up the Headworld Museum – it wasn't just humans who had been scared shitless – was progressing apace. Unfortunately, thoroughly scrubbing down and disinfecting the intentionally megalithic structure wouldn't be completed in time for this afternoon's planned unveiling of the magnificent new wing and it's even more marvellous mosaic.

None of them needed reminding that he had longstanding commitments for tomorrow, Devauray-Saturday. That understood – and kindly bear in mind all the professional celebs and/or otherwise distinguished personages he'd invited to Aka Godbad City for the prestigious event-slash-photo-op – she wanted to know when to reschedule it.

Although presently unforeseeable circumstances wouldn't allow him to commit to attending it as yet, he instructed her to set up the museum's official reopening for Sedonda-Sunday, as he habitually referred to what was to everyone else in Godbad plain old Sedonda.

(Being a practising Roman Catholic, someone who made a point of attending high mass once a week even though there were no churches in Godbad, he continued to think of it as the Lord's Day. As he also put it, come hell or high water, delayed for damn near six thousand years as it may be, he refused to call it the Devil's Day, even if that's what it was.)

There hadn't been any Utopian ambassadors, let alone rogue Trinondevs loyal to the Sarpedons, at the museum yesterday. Without anyone armed with eye-staves, especially not ones topped with eyeorbs, none of the offending azuras got captured. As predicted therefore, she had not been able to ascertain what kind were animating the dead rodents.

She wasn't prepared to accept prevailing wisdom that they were Haddazurs – some of whom were Yamazurs akin to those who motivated, to use the word properly, Death's Angels in Tethys's tale – for the simple reason that any azura could make the dead walk. As well, in the absence of any of the Nergalids, didn't Haddazurs do the other Janna's bidding?

The Legendarian didn't believe that the case but couldn't be absolutely certain one way or the other. He also couldn't prove or disprove the notion that the Molech Xibalba had that ability. Then again, he was no more persuaded that yesterday's phantasmal piper was the Irache maniac somehow reborn, or otherwise returned, than any of the others there were, including the Fatman and his Lovely Lady daughter-in-law.

He was intrigued when Centauri asked Janna if any of the old-timers who'd been around when Xibalba was causing Godbad so many problems, and/or any of the Byronics there then or consulted since, had recognized the voice he recorded. Until that moment Tethys hadn't recalled the Xibalba manifestation spoke. The other two confessed they hadn't either, not until yesterday night when Centauri decided to review what he'd taped at the museum.

She said she hadn't heard whereupon, on the off-chance it triggered something for him, Tethys asked to hear it again, albeit on tape. He might not be a devil but, notwithstanding short term beer blockages, he did have a near devic calibre memory. Pudding proof patently, it was one of his stacks of knacks.

That the tape hadn't gone up in flames like his splotch pad had was almost as amazing, Centauri remarked somewhat snidely for him. His sudden outbreak of high and mightiness made Tethys wonder, hardly for the first time that day, if he was back in the possessive presence of Thrygragos Byron. In which case, might Janna be APM as well as SPM again?

The Janna in question left to fetch a copy of the tape from CE's techies. Tethys took that as his cue to get back to what he did better – hearing his own voice tell tales.

========

A Tethys Tale - JANNA FANGFINGERS: THE DISUNITION OF THE UNITIES OF LAZAREME – Part Two: SECOND FAUSTUS

========

Janna Somata hugged the newborn to her breast. In the three hours since giving birth, she had no time to savour the joy of being a first-time mother. Her bedroom had become a battle zone. First, the shadowy Reaper appeared and laid claim to the baby. No sooner had her devic lover driven him through the wall and followed him into the sky, where they'd presumably been duelling ever since, than two dozen more devils appeared.

With only Azkeecyoos, lover Unity's brother in Lazareme, to protect her, she knew she was in serious trouble. Then, as a three-eyed, multi-horned Minotaur and a black-skinned devil waving some kind of glowing shovel grappled Azkeecyoos to the floor, a bare-breasted woman with four arms, snakes for hair and horrid, filed-sharp teeth, yanked her baby out of her arms.

Two of her undying progenitors materialized. These were Datong Harmonia (on her side, that is to say her mother's insides) and Lightning Lord Yajur (in terms of her paternal grandfather). With them came twelve of their lower-born siblings, very few of whom she'd seen before. More devils came out of the air. Curses, glowing weaponry, and more blood than she thought possible followed as much as flowed. Some of it was even red, not black like most demons reputedly bled.

One exception to the premature, never-seen-before statement was Ursine Bardol. At her fate-fraught, ever-after-traumatizing 18th birthday party, so-called (it being also the day their impending marriages were announced), he'd occupied her twin brother, a position subsequently taken over, until somewhat more than four years ago now, by the very devil betrothed to her that day. That would be the Fop, one Faustus Vladuca by Illuminary-given name, but most commonly called Fangfingers by devils and non-devils alike.

Fate-fraught because that was the day Lord Yajur got suckered into, um, non-culpably catasterizing Fata Fortuna, Dame Chance, whose Illuminary-given name was Wintry Moira. In the process of doing just that, he simultaneously killed the me born Quidnunc Tethys. And Quid's the poor guy who acquired me after Melina, also born Tethys, set Harmony up to kill him precisely eighteen year earlier, on the very day the Terrible Twins were born.

(Just to doubly or trebly complicate comprehension, the moment he did the dreadful, very much pivotal deed, Order was occupying Janna's also affianced true love, Squiggly again Tethys, a future me. At her insistence, Squiggles was going to be her human hubby. But that got scotched when, once the public outcry rose much too vociferously to be ignored, Master Zalman felt obligated to banish the popularly perceived patricide from Kanin City.

(Which, in case you care, explains why he ended up in the Hoodoo Hamlet as Sraddha's cartographer and thereafter got banished all over again, this time by Thrygragos Lazareme, to the Outer Earth. And that, hopefully, concludes my regrettable references to the unspeakably genocidal Contagion Collectors for today's presentation.)

A gigantic bear-man, wielding a huge tree branch with what appeared to be a hardened beehive at one end, Bardol thrust her son back into her arms just before he was cleaved, almost in twain, by a pestiferous devil, all covered in pus-drenched bandages, swinging a pendulum-like blade on a long, skull-carved shaft.

For more than ten minutes, as the ferocious struggle raged around her bed, the bear-man's body lay on the floor. Then the corpse got up, completely healed, and rejoined the fight. With Yajur and Harmony leading the Lazareme Spawn, they cleared the room, but she could hear the destructive, even earth-shattering battle continuing throughout Kanin.

Although devils were proscribed from personally killing lesser beings, their private war was causing tremendous damage. Dozens of Kanin's locals would die that day, mostly from collapsing buildings and erratic discharges of devic energy. Wise people would be hunkering down in their cellars or fleeing the city. She wished she could do the same but was too weak to move. The Unities had left just one of their own to guard her and, not that she was in any position to protest, she wasn't too happy about their choice.

As aforesaid, Vladuca Fangfingers had been betrothed to her on her 18th birthday. Over the intervening years, both before and after he occupied brother Sraddha,

she had met the devil many times and neither liked his appearance nor his personality. Highly strung is a term that comes to mind. To which Janna, who, against her
better nature, could still be quite petulant and had a nasty sense of humour, might
have added: *'from a scaffold'*.

He had pale, waxen skin, three bloodshot eyes and thick red lips. He was
incredibly skinny, always dressed in whatever courtly finery was fashionable in the
Weirdom at the time, and was particularly fond of black capes with red lining. In
short, he was a fop in a flap. So much so that, when Unholy Abaddon – Abe as he let
her call him – started to woo her, Janna dumped Vlad as fast as she would a chamber
pot if there weren't any servants around to do it for her.

Sperm-daddy Zalman Somata, who had never relinquished his claim to
Kanin's Mastery and kept in touch with her via his wife's witch-stones once they
both made it to the Weirdom of Cabalarkon, devic half-mother Harmony and devic half-grandfather Yajur weren't persuaded this was an appropriate thing to do.
However, being Lazareme Spawn, to whom freewill meant everything, they did not
overly object to their dalliance. For one thing Abaddon was not known for taking
possession of shells. Which meant there'd be no deviant offspring.

Mindful of the scheduled succession come 5000 YD, they insisted that, if Abe
did decide to take over a human shell and impregnate the Utopian hybrid, any offspring half-he and Janna had could not take over the Mastery of Marutia. This was
fine with Janna. She thought her twin, if he ever made it back for the Outer Earth
and settled down, would make a better ruler than her in any case. It was also fine
with Chaos, who hated rules and rulers of any kind.

Then, without him possessing anyone, entirely unheard of genetics conspired
to allow Janna to have Abaddon's child. Whereupon all bets were off.

========

Understandably, even if he didn't resent her because she'd opted for Chaos over
him, Janna didn't think Vladuca would be any good as her protector. His power
focus, a glove, which he wore on his right hand, with sharp talons on its fingertips,
was neither as grand as Abaddon's trident nor as effective. You couldn't scratch a
Master Deva to death. In fact, as far as she knew, Mithras being the exception, you
couldn't even kill a devil-god.

Human beings, however, even if they were mostly Utopian beings, ones descended from very long lived extraterrestrials, were an entirely different matter. Even
though, what with Abe Chaos on the scene, she reckoned she'd never have to marry
anyone possessed by Vladuca any more, she'd nevertheless had six years worth of
nightmares about being caressed by that devil with that loathsome glove. In most of
those nightmares she'd ended up being shredded into flesh and blood confetti solely
suitable for sprinkling over bride and groom ghouls.

Vladuca Fangfingers, obviously exhausted, sat on the edge of her bed. He
pulled something out of his waist band and tossed it at her side. She picked it up,
still holding the baby boy tight to her chest. It was a rectangular-shaped block made
of what she later learned was Stopstone, what devils sometimes also called Solidium,
the underground stuff of tellurian Mandroids and the Mantels of Temporis. Grabbing both ends of it she pulled it open.

The block was a sheathe or scabbard of some sort, just like Abe's trident was actually the sheathe of the Chaos Blade. Inside it was a short curved sword or a long curve-bladed knife with a razor-sharp edge. It glowed crimson, with the intensity of a devil's Brainrock power focus. For that was what it was – and not just any devil either. Tvasitar Smithmonger made it for one of the pre-Earth-lost Trigregos Sisters, none other than Demeter, Abaddon's reputed birthmother.

"I love you, Janna," swore Vladuca. "By rights you should have been mine. Despite what you might think, I can't blame you for choosing Chaos over me. He's an egocentric jerk, though, too easily lured away by the Nergalid. I'm not much compared to him but at least I'm loyal. I'll stay by your side.

"If the Mithras Spawn come back, I'll fight as best I can but I won't be able to stop all of them. Your mother knew that, so she sent better weapons to me between-space, via some of her Ant friends. They were of no use to me, so I sent them back to her. Only she sent this thing back yet again; said it's for you, not for me. And I guess now I know why.

"Make no mistake, it's the boy they're after so you can use it one of two ways. The easiest is to kill yourself and your child. The smarter way is to slash it into the Weird, slash it through the Cathonic Dome, it'll do that, and send him, your baby, to the Outer Earth. First name him, though. For in names reside power and with names, once it's safe to do so, we can track down and retrieve him."

Janna Somata was too terrified to think clearly. All she could come up with were the names of Johann and George Somata, her father's non-deviant brothers, who had gone off with Zalman four years earlier in search of the thence-proven not-at-all-semi-mythical Weirdom of Cabalarkon. Since both had drowned the day Zal's flagship, the Kanin, went down just off the Devic Eye-Land, it snapped sentimental sense to her to memorialize them hereafter.

"I'll call him Johann-George."

"Give him a surname as well," urged Vladuca. "The more names the more power. The more names the harder it is for a sorcerer to learn them all."

"How is Abaddon called?"

"We don't have names as such. To us he's just Chaos. Illuminaries named him after the bottomless pit of the Outer Earth's Biblical Book of Revelations and, to my knowledge, they only gave him the one name."

"But you've two names, don't you. I mean another one besides Fangfingers. What is it?"

"Faustus."

Janna Somata silently gave her boy-baby a multitude of names.

=======

"Don't ask me what they all were," said Jordan Tethys, interrupting himself. "The only ones I know are Johann-George Somata-Faust.

And, even though he had quite the life, one worthy of more than a few stories of his own – and even though some of them actually got turned into operas, song settings or, as I'm sure you could pull out and play for us as background music, an overture by our perennial pal Richard Wagner – his involvement in this saga is about to end."

========

No sooner had she named her child than four of the Apocalyptics suddenly emerged out of the air. They were, to call them by their attributes: War, whose body was a living arsenal; Death, one of a number of devils so particularized, her being a snake-haired gorgon with four arms and filed teeth; Plague, he with the tick-tock, time's-running-out, pendulum-blade; and Catastrophe, Sudden Disaster.

For reasons I've never quite been able to fathom, Illuminaries named this last Nakba Ramazar. His power focus, at least originally, was a blowgun. Which, when you think about it, is kind of funny since he lost his head, quite literally, not long after he attained solidity. I mean, how can you properly blow a gun, or anything else for that matter, without a mouth?

Valiant twit that he was, Faustus Vladuca leapt at them. As he himself had predicted, he was nowhere near a match for even one of them. They overwhelmed him almost instantly, took turns battering him nigh unto senselessness. Scratching and clawing at them desperately Vladuca struggled on, which only made the Apocalyptics angrier.

"Rip off his head!" cried War, whom Illuminaries named Mars Bellona after a couple of Outer Earth Roman deities of just that, War. His spike-crested skull had no skin, nor any internal constituents, but he nevertheless somehow managed to grow a full beard.

"It's too ugly!" came Ramazar's response. "Besides, we haven't enough time to dispose of it properly. The Unities will be here in a second."

He was holding Vladuca in a vice-like grip. The Lazaremist was swiping at his skull; was therefore swiping futilely at the air itself since the Apocalyptic had no skull of his own, let alone a mouth out of which either to form words or shoot off his blowgun of a Tvasitar-talisman. It would have been funny, except there was nothing funny about either Fop or Apocalyptics.

"Grab the baby, Murder," ordered their consensus leader, Disease, Plague, Carcinogen the Leper as Illuminaries named him. "Grab the mother as well. I'll open a gash to Satanwyck."

The Medusa, Mater Matare, Mother Murder, the devic deity of deliberate death, that caused by routine homicide and/or suicide, whom assassins and executioners invoked when they were in the mood to pray as well as slay, moved swiftly. Janna Somata moved even quicker. She unsheathed the blade Vladuca gave her, cut an opening through Samsara and thence the Cathonic Dome, then stuffed her baby through it. Even if the Apocalyptics killed her at least her child had a chance to live, albeit on the Outer Earth.

Black Zenit Suryad, he of Midnight, Krepusyl of crepuscular Twilight, her long time lover, Rapith Nauroz, he of Starlight, Irisiel Mercherm, Icy Miros, and Mercurial Kometes, Lazareme Spawn the lot of them, came into the bedroom. The four Apocalyptics – their target, Abaddon's son, lost thanks to the mysterious power focus Vladuca gave Janna and which the fearsome Medusa, presumably having recognized it, shied away from in evident terror – disappeared, presumably back to their protectorates in the western parts of Sedon's Cheek.

Janna re-sheathed the thrice-cursed blade and, presumably before any of the Lazaremists realized what she had, tucked it underneath her pillow. Immediately behind her rescuers, the Unities, Yajur-Order and Balance-Harmony, came out of the Universal Substance, the dark grey matter of between-space.

Ensnared by the latter's Brainrock chains, which grew out of the neck-torc that was her Tvasitar-talisman and covered her neck-to-toe in glowingly golden mail, they brought with them a Mithradite. This was Zuvem Nergalis, the devil with the black skin of a full-blooded Utopian male (though not of a female pureblood, who are as white as snow).

Within a matter of minutes all the victorious sons and daughters of Lazareme joined or rejoined them. They commiserated with Janna at the loss of her newborn baby but most agreed an uncertain survival on the Outer Earth was better than Johann-George being enslaved by Mithras Spawn like the Nergalids or Apocalyptics.

Or, though they didn't voice it, being raised as the Son of Chaos.

========

Zuvem Nergalis was the only Mithradite to be captured. He was bleeding profusely. His power focus, as one would expect from the Nergalid who epitomized the planting season, as opposed to the reaping season, a Brainrock spade, was in the hands of Ursine Bardol, the animal god whose own power focus was a bludgeon-like, Brainrock branch with a beehive-shaped burl at one end. (Tvasitar Smithmonger was a funny guy.)

Without a talisman to give them solidity devils would discorporate in short order; become spirit beings once again. That was just the start of the humiliation the Lazaremists inflicted on the Mithradite, though. As partial compensation for all he'd endured before they got there, Vladuca was allowed to gouge the third or devic eye out of the Nergalid's skull. Which he promptly swallowed. Selective dismemberment followed, much to the delight of Janna's hunting hounds, whom she should never have kept out of her bedroom cum nativity ward.

Given that kind of treatment most other creatures would at least pass out, before they bled to death. But Zuvem was from Thrygragos Varuna Mithras' fourth litter. That made him one of the mightiest of all Mithras Spawn left loose on the Inner Earth. Truth told, with the Thanatoids of Lathakra still lying moribund on the Frozen Isle, only the two second-born Apple Goddesses, Divine Coueranna and Bedazzling Belialma, and third-born Cruel Plathon, the Minotaur who'd popped by the birth-room earlier, were the Planter's elders.

With Janna, Harmony and some of his fellow Lazaremists looking on, Lord Yajur interrogated him in the Weirdom's Megaron or Great Hall, the very place where we unearthed Glee's mosaic from over a thousand years earlier by then. The full measure of the Mithradites' perfidy was thus revealed.

In twenty years time, Mithradites would assume half-parenting rights in the Weirdom of Kanin City and, therefore, the entire Mastery of Marutia. No matter what sex the heir-apparent was, he, Zuvem, was to possess her male of the pair while the unappealing but powerful Medusa, Mater Matare, Mother Murder, was to take over his wife.

Furthermore, even if they could only do so in a second-hand sort of way, they did not want to mingle their genes with that of the half-offspring of low-level Lazareme Spawn such as the still imprisoned flagellant Rastha Aragon, aka the Skinless

Rasp, who was promised to Sraddha, or Vladuca-Fangfingers, who was supposed to be given to Janna. They had great plans for Marutia.

Which, until their father, Thrygragos Varuna Mithras, was killed on Thrygragon those selfsame thousand-plus years earlier, had for far longer been ruled by Mithrant legionnaires based on Apple Isle. Those days were about to return.

Mithradites led by their crafty first lady – aforesaid, as well as afore-bedded, Bouncing Belle, Sinistral Lust of Satanwyck, a long-time lover of Plathon, Zuvem and, yes, Unholy Abaddon himself – had quite deliberately manipulated events such that Uncle Abe fell in love with Janna Somata.

(First Lady, I hasten to add, just in case our Lovely Lady War Witch Janna is listening in, only in the absence of moribund firstborn Methandra Thanatos. Hot Stuff, as not just devils sometimes referred to her, was still commonly thought of as Mithras Virgin even though Abe laid her beside brother Tantal in the king's bed-room at the pinnacle of one of the volcanic Frozen Isle's highest peaks.

(He did so after borderline-heroically hauling them both out of the atomic wasteland now called the Ghostlands. Had he not, had he left where they'd fallen already unconscious, even they may have perished. This notwithstanding the notion still prevalent in Cabalarkon, among other places and other peoples, that Tantal and Methandra ended up as they did, because they absorbed into themselves most of the radiation expelled by the Idiot Twins.

(Doing so, they thus saved Cabby the Daddy, and with him their Grandfather Eye-Mouthy Moloch, from that which the Death's Head Hellion wished to wrought – the up-until-then proper, but perennially postponed, sinking of the Hidden Continent of Sedon's Head. Abe, though, did so additionally in a highly suggestive pose.

(Being who he was, something of a perverse trickster at heart, and they being in a state of insentient stasis, he laid them together side by side, not to mention naked, as if anticipating what a horny old bugger like King Cold would do if he awoke first. As if, put less lecherously, they were man and wife as well as immediate brother and sister.

(And it must have worked because that, of course, is what they are now and have been since the tail-end of this century's first decade.)

Then something absolutely unexpected occurred. That Janna had the son, not the half-son, of Chaos. The Unholy Unity had not needed to possess anyone to fully father the boy.

========

"Imagine what a son like that will grow to become?" Tethys asked rhetorically. "Another Attis at the minimum."

Thankfully for concentration's sake, for once the Fatman didn't respond.

========

"But why snatch a newborn?" demanded Harmony, whose sense of balance made it imperative she hear all sides of the story before she passed judgement. "None of us, not even Grandfather Sedon, is prescient. You have no idea what he might grow to become. Or even that he will grow at all."

"We couldn't take the chance," admitted the Nergalid. "Once we realized Chaos needed no intermediary to have him or her, we determined to raise him or her as one of us. He or she was a child of the Weirdom, he or she might have become its Master by the time we took it over. He was ours, not yours, to do with as we needs be, not as you needs be.

"Ask yourself this: Would either you or Order have ever let us have a child of Chaos? No, never. You'd have taken him away from his parents yourselves; probably to Tympani, where sleeps your debauched father and where even Chaos dare not attack. Either that or you'd have had the baby killed well before it was our turn to rule Kanin."

"Tell us your real reasons," Yajur demanded. Then, not waiting for a response, he told them to the Nergalid and his, Order's, siblings instead. "You know my brother Unity never possesses humans, nor any other sentient lifeforms, as far as that goes, which is nowhere. He hasn't done so since he attained independent solidity and probably never will. Neither, as an obvious consequence, has he ever had a mortal child.

"You reckoned that with your tribe holding his son he'd switch sides, fight alongside you Mithradites against his own kind, like he did when he joined the non-Dream Thanatoids, King Cold and his Scarlet Empress, and thereafter aided them expand their Empire of Lathakra. That's what you want, isn't it? Another Lathakra. Only this time with someone more amicable to the designs of you lower born Mithradites than they, your superiors in every way, ever were."

"That cannot be allowed," stated Harmony, her judgement thus made.

The expansion of the Lathakran Empire culminated with the Idiot Twins going Novadev-nuclear on the Upper Head's ass as much as assholes. That resulted in the deaths of hundreds of thousands of genuine, much less so than speculative or potential, devil worshippers. Indeed, the entire Era of Empires represented the antithesis of Panharmonium, the then ongoing time-period she considered more her own Epoch or Age than that of her father. She refused to countenance anything approximating a repeat performance.

"It may yet happen," the already savagely mutilated captive warned them, perhaps hoping one or the other Unity would finally put an end to his suffering. "The girl's young. She's at least as special as her twin brother, who became a god, briefly, and she will have other children."

Harmony was the likelier to show mercy but, given his ugly history with Lightning Lord Yajur, cathonitization was more liable to be today's endgame than her preferred form of long term punishment: namely, imprisonment within All of Incain. (And, just in case I haven't mentioned it recently, an unresolved and hence still festering instance of their mutual antagonism had to be Order killing the Quill-Quidnunc I-he-me after mistakenly thinking Zuvem had taken wee-we-me over for some reason, on the night Star Sedon disappeared in 5474.)

Janna was sitting on her throne, wrapped for warmth as well as comfort after her ordeals of the day thus far – not least of which included giving birth. She chose that moment to speak up. As subsequent events transpired, her doing so was not only ill-advised; it may well have been Headworld-critically, as in cataclysmically.

"Your heart's blacker than your skin, Nergalid, but I've Witchie ways. How else could I spirit my boy beyond the Dome to safety? I'll see to it no child of mine will ever be possessed by, or make love to, someone possessed by a Spawn of Mithras. Mark me on that."

"Then mate as you please, mortal." the devil cursed her. "Have a thousand children. Defy us and everyone of them will be born dead."

Life inevitably led to death, to termination. Therefore, like the two other Nergalids, Yama and Vetala, death was as much Zuvem's province as life itself. Originally a god of agriculture, of the cycle of fertility, plant it, grow it, harvest it, not for nothing was he also called Gravedigger. Yet, from this moment forth he earned an additional appellative, that of Devil Doom, because his angry proclamation proved a dire prophecy indeed.

"Whatever happens," proclaimed Yajur-Order, "You'll not be around to enjoy its fruits, no matter how bitter they may be."

He gave him three choices. Zuvem could accept interminable imprisonment on Incain, ill-starring – catasterization or, more commonly beneath the Dome, cathonitization – or he would execute him the same way his brood brother delivered the death-stroke to Zuvem's Great Godly father at Thrygragon over a thousand years earlier.

Given Zuvem's condition, he could have offered a fourth choice, the favourite method of devic disposal during the Lathakran expansion – having his spirit self sucked into a ringot. Regardless of whichever way he went, Yajur promised him, chances were it would be the last time he went anywhere.

"Then do as thou wilt, Unity," laughed the Nergalid, realizing the truth of this. "But know that whatever you do to me, your end is nigh."

Yajur cut off Zuvem's head; had Irisiel bury it exactly a thousand miles away. First though, using his Lightning Sword, he immolated the rest of Zuvem's body.

That's the way to kill devils.

========

"Perhaps he should have immolated Janna's not-so-hungry-anymore hounds. Or done a dick-dildo to Vladuca Fangfingers. At the very least he should have seen to it Bardol went to Sedon's Peak, Tvasitar's protectorate, and in its caldera, its lava lake, filled as it remains with molten Brainrock, melted the Nergalid's spade back into so much slag."

"Aren't you supposed to preface a statement like that with 'spoiler alert'?"

"Why bother, when you can do it for me?"

"Not possessed, Jordy."

"Just checking. One other thing I should stipulate about the three Unities of Lazareme, Yajur and Abaddon only minutely more so than Harmony. They were so damned powerful they rarely relied on intelligence. Me having much the same heritage, on both sides of the half-bed-mates damn near two thousand years ago, perhaps that applies to me too."

"You said it, not me."

========

When Uncle Abe Chaos returned to Kanin City two days later – on the 2nd of Maruta 5480, your November 1480, if you're keeping track – Janna refused to see him. Presumably thanks to remedial devic possession, she was fully recovered physically; altogether back off her back and onto her feet, as it were. But his son was lost forevermore. When he tried to force his way in to see her, Harmony and Yajur stood in his way.

He still wasn't insane enough to tangle with his sister and brother Unities so he left the Weirdom. Later that same year, which doesn't end in Tantalar-December as yours does, he found himself in Satanwyck. There, occasional lovers that they'd long been, he became Sinistral Lust's most constant companion. Howsoever ironically, he therefore replaced Zuvem, aka Devil Doom by now, in terms of acting as the double-dealing dazzler's consort. He spent the next almost half a decade at her side.

Thrygragos Lazareme and his offspring gave up on him, considered he'd gone over to the Mithras Spawn – the Dark Side according to Star Wars, that silly movie you showed me last year – and thereby made all of Zuvem's fatal predictions redundant. Foolishly, as it turned out, they also lost interest in Janna Somata; just left her alone to do as she pleased. Which, more oddly than suspiciously, was mostly what they'd planned for her from the get-go.

Her parents were safely out of the way in Cabalarkon, out of communication as well it seemed. Assuming they were still alive, no one down south knew or apparently cared what they were up to in Sedon's Devic Eye-Land. No one other than me, that is; not that I was down south at the time. As matter of fact, I was more down and out, as in lying drunk on the floor in a pool of my own making, than anywhere else.

Talk about conflicted, which we were earlier, I had Quoits' memories as well as 1500 years of my own. I knew precisely what she'd done. I also knew that Zal-Mel and their fellow Marutian transplants had bought into it on behalf of Utopians, Hellions and Mother-Earth-loving, but demonically disposed, devotees of the do-bad-for-the-sake-of-good school of stomach-churning thought everywhere.

I couldn't do anything to stop them. You see, ordinarily my persona doesn't just dominate that of those I incarnate inside of; it completely supplants them. For all intents and purposes, they've not just lost their individuality. They've died and moved on, never to return so long as I still hold onto their former bodies.

Yet, whenever I tried to draw myself away from Cabalarkon, Quoits would reassert herself. She'd do a ditto whenever I tried to send faraway warnings wherever, via what some savants call spirit writing, which is another terrific talent I keep on my shelves of whatnot knick-knacks. She was approaching devil-level domineering in that department.

Sure I'd fight back. And when, knowing my loyalties, Zal-Mel sought to confiscate my quill like the Death's Head Hellion once did, I still had enough willpower to draw it back. Quoits prevented me from doing much of anything else, though. Is at any wonder I/we compromised? Is it any wonder the only time I/we found comparative peace was when we were guzzling often much more my 30 beer daily allotment of Weir's Mother-Machine-made swill?

Finally, as healthy as I usually am even when I do drink to such extreme excess, is it any wonder Quoits slipped into a life-threatening coma?

========

"And died."
"Telling the story again, Al?"
"Sorry."
"No."
"I said I'm sorry."

"And I said 'no'; not no, you're not sorry."
"She didn't die?"
"Not yet."

=========

To this day in Cabalarkon, when someone slips into a coma, or comes down with a severely debilitating, as yet incurable, and/or diagnosed shortly-to-become-terminal illness, even if they haven't quite gone comatose, Utopians seldom, if ever, resort to palliative care such that a person dies quietly, with his or her dignity intact and without much pain. That's too much like giving up for them – and, as witness the Hate-Sedon ethos of even its inbred imbeciles, giving up is simply not part of their genetic makeup.

When all else fails they'll submerge you in a vat of life-preserving, but animation-suspending Cathonic Fluid until, at least theoretically, they come up with a cure. Since even the non-idiot scientocrats and biomages up there have deteriorated so badly that rarely happens, being thus immersed amounts to a near-death sentence, as opposed to a near-death experience. And that's what happened to the me who once was Quoits Tethys, Mel's Granny Jordy.

Had the Death's Head Hellion thought of it when I took over Quick Tethys in 4825, she might never have lost control of my quill. As it was, Mel held onto it during the months I languished immobile in a tub of Cathonic Fluid beneath the Citadel of the Thinkers. And guess whose tub Zal placed mine beside? Wait for it. None other than Dark Sedon's thought-father, Cabalarkon himself, that's who.

And who, Star Sedon still being missing from the night's sky, as he had been, at the risk of repeating myself again, since the night of the Terrible Twins 18th birthday-slash-bequeathal-slash-betrothal party, has nothing further to add to this story. Except, that is, to note the curious fact that I may have may have died on or about that year's Mithramas. And of course we both know who comes to visit his Daddy Cabby every Mithramas Day.

That's right. I'm referring to the satanic fellow whose star no longer shone in the night's sky above Sedon's Devic Eye-Land.

=========

"You reckon the Moloch Sedon was faking his disappearance."
"I didn't say that."
"No, you didn't, did you. Might you deign to say how you did die that time, officially?"
"One day Zal or Mel or someone else lifted the lid on my tub and found me dead and deigned. Sorry, damned. Comatose or not, I officially couldn't stop drinking. If you'll pardon the song, minus the dance, the river wasn't whisky, or beer, it was Cathonic Fluid. I swam to the bottom and never, ever, came up. In other words, I drowned. Told you those were lousy days."
"What you told me," the Fatman, Alpha Centauri, told the taleteller, Jordan Tethys, "Was that those were lousy days to be alive; that they were great days to be dead."
"I sit corrected."

****

5: Fat Head Facilitates Fat Belly

"Did an azura get hold of you? Was your Quoits corpse animated?"

"In Cabalarkon? Not too likely. Months before devils or, more probably, the Devil Himself lit up the sky by zapping her out of this life and into the next, if that's what happens to deviated or non-deviated mortals not named Quill Tethys, the Death's Head Hellion insisted her Trinondev Warrior Elite begin using their eyeorbs to sweep the city for azuras on a near daily basis. Her Masterly successors are no different in that regard. So, no, not that corpse."

"But another one was, right?"

"Story, Al."

"Right."

========

A Tethys Tale - JANNA FANGFINGERS: THE DISUNI-TION OF THE UNITIES OF LAZAREME – Part Three: SECOND FANGS

========

Recall Squiggly, Janna Somata's *'most handsome and desirous of men'*, as I'm so fond of quoting her since she's referring to me. On her eighteenth birthday-slash-etcetera, she made Zal-Mel and the Unities agree that whenever Vladuca, her fang-fingered, devilish betrothed, took her to bed, he would only do so inside her actual husband. That was no longer an, um, operable precondition due to the fact that Thrygragos Lazareme banished him to Outer Earth in 5476.

(Rather, Lazareme banished twin brother Shreds and Squigs went with him – at first, that is to say until Quoits died the first time, with my quill.)

Pass forward five years to 5480-81. Not that she ever did much with it but, like Master Morgan Abyss hundreds of years earlier, Melina took control of my quill the day Zal-Mel placed the Quoits-me in the tub of Cathonic Fluid near the beginning of the Mithradic Ternary of 5480. Rather again, if you want to get all anal about it, which I'm sure you don't, she takes possession of Rumour's Tvasitar talisman.

At some point later on, possibly in Tantalar, possibly as late as Yamana or the beginning of Belialmam, the reprehensible Quoits-me *'officially'* gurgles her last glug of Cathonic Fluid and croaks, non-froglike. Her passing leaves me dancing the leg-less limbo, as I tend to describe my state of being whenever I'm between lives.

5481 in here is, mostly, 1481 out there. And 1481 is something like 30 years after the fall of Constantinople, the city founded by, or at least named after, Con-stantine the Great – Zal's sainted, hybrid-Utopian ancestor Helena Somata, alleged-ly the locator of the True Cross, was his mother, you'll no doubt recall from not just yesterday.

Via their odd acquaintanceship, more so than friendship, with Tomas de Tor-quemada, imminently of Spanish Inquisition fame, and his association with Queen Isabella of Castile, who'd married King Ferdinand of Aragon in 1469, Shreds and Sraddha had joined the Crown of said Aragon in its efforts to prevent Rome going the way of Constantinople.

Which, when you think about it, was sort of strange. After all our heroes, the ever-adventurous, if perhaps not overly fearsome twosome, were at least partially, but very much visibly, black-skinned. By contrast, even in their own time both the primo Spanish royals had a well-deserved reputation for being intolerant racists.

Anyhow, I said I wasn't going to get into the series of synchronicities, more so than serendipities, that led to their connection with Twisted Tommy, as Squigs called him, and I won't. Suffice it to say that both our heroes had by now thoroughly forgotten all about the Inner Earth, let alone that they'd been born there. They thought themselves – and, therefore, for all intents and purposes were – Moriscos the dreaded Dominican Hound of the Lord had converted to Christianity a few years earlier.

Sraddha was still a fabulous fighter, though, whereas Squiggly continued to ply the map-making trade a former me, a Quit Quill by then named Squib, taught him while he was growing up in and around Kanin City. Circumstances as well as circumcisions involved them in the Crown of Aragon's attempt to retake the prized port of Otranto, the most easterly town in Italy, from the Muslim infidels. On the very day the Aragonese seemed about to claim victory, the cartographic non-com-batant of the pair took an Ottoman Turk's sword-thrust in the chest.

The thrust damn near killed him. Rather yet again, to put it perfectly precisely, even though he was rapidly on his feet again – and not so miraculously no longer bleeding either – it did kill him. Which is a convoluted way of saying I was no longer dancing the legless limbo. Unfortunately, now I was the one in the thick of things severely sharp, not to mention seriously severing.

(For me, if not him, it was lucky Squigs took a straight blade in the chest and wasn't hacked dead with a scimitar. I can revitalize my shells but I can't knit them back together again.)

You know that bit about the pen being mightier than the sword? For a guy like me, caught in a big, fat melon of a melee alongside Sraddha Somata, it's more a matter of which is speedier, my pen or the other guy's sword. Ordinarily it's no contest. I'm as fast to dot a preprepared drawing, and thereby take myself away to a safe destination, as I'm usually smart enough to avoid situations where I have to make a quick getaway in the first place.

In large measure that's why I occasionally do make it all the way through my 30-year per body timeshare. Should also say that, because of just that, my offspring are like son or daughter, like father or mother. As a general rule of pricking thumbs then, we're more circumspect than Squiggly was when we die the first time.

Except at a sensible distance we tend to avoid battlefields, even if they are naval skirmishes, as this one was, like the proverbial plague. Which, admittedly, sometimes can't be avoided due to breathing. But Squigs and Shreds were the best of buddies. They had been tight as leotards even before Lazareme sent them from the hoodoo hamlet, on the coast of the Gulf of Corona, to the Outer Earth some six weeks prior to the Terrible Twins turning twenty. I could no more change that than I could completely dominate Quoits in my then most recent lifetime.

Like I said, Shreds was a warrior. Sooth said, he was veritable smiling fiend when it came to wielding that curved Saracen blade of his. Like I shouldn't have to say, Squigs wasn't. He was a devoted sidekick much better at fawning than fussing, as in fighting. That goes double for me, as him.

So here's my predicament. I can't draw anyone conscious anywhere against their will and Shreds, with that gruesome grin he'd affected for afflictions, to fay-say some more, is still too intent upon battling the Turk ferociously, not to mention foolishly, to even notice that I'd not only dropped down dead and gored, I'd got up again – and with only a hole in my jerkin, not in my chest anymore.

What am I to do? Not much except take another Turkish blade in the vitals, I reckon. Getting killed always hurts, so I'm not looking forward to ending one my shortest lives since Thrygragon. Hmm, that cracked or broken beam above his head does look dangerously dangly. And, oh yes, one of the escape-routes I always have prepared in advance, just in case I'm feeling homesick on the Outer Earth like now, is the Egyptian Sphinx.

Squigs being me, I don't think therefore I draw; I think and my quill does the drawing for me. So I hunker into the equivalent of duck and cover mode for that day and age, then …

========

"Draw the beam down on Sraddha's head, thus knocking him out, whereupon you draw both of you to the Giza Plateau. There, you having all your memories back again, you hook into providential pal Pyrame's ages-old link-way through Cathonia between out there's Andy the Androsphinx and in here's Ginny the Gynosphinx, All the Invincible."

"Hers, close to Dome-long pre-cathonitization; the Attis's, nowhere near as long prior to Thrygragon; and mine, though not yours, to this day; that's very good, Al. Except, it's All of Incain. As she discovered on Thrygragon, the She-Sphinx never was invincible. Just conceited. One guess as to where I drew us as soon as we emerged on this side."

"Don't need it, do I."

"Guess not."

========

We're expecting to see John Barleycorn and Pusan Wanderlust at the Dinq Doinq Danq Tavern Cavern, and we do. But we're not expecting to see its proprietor, as drop dead gorgeous as ever, but we do that too. Fortunately, Harmony's in a forgiving mood. She always liked me and Squiggly pretty much worshipped her before I came along. Unfortunately, the Goat wasn't disposed anywhere near so generously.

Seems, even though technically speaking it wasn't me, nor even Squiggly, not by himself, I had left quite the unpaid bar bill behind. Neither Pusan nor JB appreciated being paid in sand dollars, of the sea urchin variety, and no one had thought to ask still acting Master Janna Somata to repay it out of the Mastery's treasury.

You see, Squiggly's father, an ex Quill by the Q-name of Quidnunc, meaning busybody, had been a Sangazur-animated corpse for a couple of years prior to crossing Lord Yajur, who for his troubles charcoaled him crispy critter and blowing in the wind, circa mid-Spring 5476. And, along with Sraddha and, yes, son Squiggles, he consumed easily the greatest quantity of the purloined pilsners Pusan subsequently charged to my account.

Because of that, and because Squigs and his Deadnunk of a deadbeat dad were under the depilated deviant Dand's aegis at the time, most of the suds were, shall we say, liberated (yes, we shall), Shreds offered to recompense the Danq, with maximal interest. Of course, before he could do that, he'd have to go up to Kanin City and prevail upon his twin to open that selfsame treasury. He couldn't very well do that if Harmony, her father or her immediate brothers were just going to banish him anew, now could he.

Ah, as to that, said Harmony, half-daughter Janna has become so infatuated with Faustus Fangfingers over the last few years of their absence, she's decided to marry him in the raw as it were, as in without Vladuca possessing anyone. Her, their, half-father Lazareme couldn't say no to the silver-haired vixen so he rehabilitated the Fop.

Furthermore, since Shreds overwhelming Fangs was what, besides shaving his skull, allowed him to become the depilated Dand, Harmony couldn't see Everyman refusing to do a dick-dildo for him, banishment-rescindment-wise. She could foresee some other problems, though.

For one, I might be me but I still looked like Squiggly: Janna Somata's *'most handsome and desirous of men'*.

========

"Enough of that, Jordy."
"Sorry, Al. Stick to the story, Jordy."

========

Truth told, I didn't foresee any such difficulties. I was sure Janna would dump First Fangs the instant I returned to Kanin City as Squiggly – her, well … you know. Doubly personally persuasively, I was also her de facto deflowerer. Furthermore, I was as prepared as Janna and Squiggles had been, at the time they good-as-signed a prenuptial agreement seven years earlier, to let the Fop take me over on our wedding night pre-bed-bagging.

Much to my disgust, Janna was nowhere near so magnanimously inclined. The moment I presented myself to her – happily with Shreds standing right there beside me – she angrily claimed that I had raped her on the night of her 18th birthday. That I was bodily the Quidnunc-Quill made no never mind to her. And nor should it, since I am always me regardless of whosever's body I've been reincarnated inside.

Now, as a man, and even as a woman, I may be a perfidious philanderer when it comes to pursuing my procreative imperative. But I would ever rape, nor attempt to rape, anyone.

Needless to therefore say, I was deeply hurt by the allegation. One can sort of see her point, though. She might never have gone with Quid-Quill if Dame Chance hadn't been occupying her. So I suppose that what I took to be consensual sex with an adult could be misconstrued as anything but by said adult. Still, even on the Head, the devil made me do it is rarely recognized as a valid defence for misconduct.

As well, devic possession is seldom deleterious. Other than in egregious situations, such as for example you having really pissed off the devil who thereafter takes you over for purposes punitive, it almost never comes at the cost of losing one's freewill. Yet it can't be denied that Chance always had an irresistible itch in need of scratching, over and over again, when it came to her younger brother, Rumour of Lazareme.

Too true also, that transferred to me, lifetime after lifetime, after he got eaten; hence the abominable faerie fart, Tomcat Tattletail, you may have heard me mention, between choking gags and bardic barfs, in the past. So, yeah, at a stretch maybe Chance did force Janna to act against her will, but I definitely didn't. As a result, I didn't then, and still don't to this day, almost 500 years to the date, buy her attitude.

While, admittedly, events only verified the Terrible Twins ability to overwhelm devils stupid enough to posses either he or her subsequent to Quill-Quid's second death, as me, on the night at issue, as far as I'm concerned Janna's motivations have always been her own. That said unqualified, not being much of a mind-reader, it isn't really my place to impugn them. Sooth said serially, I'd rather impugn Sedon's – for I reckoned we were somehow pawns in a Sedonplay. And you know who always wins those.

At any rate, even more irrationally she felt just as positive I'd somehow arranged for deviant darling Squiggly's death such that I could escape Limbo and have a proper body again. In other words, shades of Helena Somata and more than a few of my wives from a lifetime, make that lifetimes, over a thousand years earlier, she'd persuaded herself that the Legendarian was about the worst possible creature in creation.

Happily again, Shreds regarded me as his best buddy, or at least the best replacement buddy he could have given our deviancies. Janna allowed me to stay in Kanin City as a member of his staff and it was in that capacity that I, very much against my wishes, 'drew', in quotation marks, myself back to Cabby's Weirdom, wedding invitations to deliver.

To the surprise of some of those left behind in Kanin City, Zal and Mel were alive and together again. Some of those doesn't mean devils; they've their far-sight. At least it didn't mean devils – or even me on the ricochet. As for what they were doing up there, I pried of course. I was dismissed, also of course. And very forcibly, I might add.

Slash, unless swish sounds better to your ears, that'd be Zal striving to swipe off my stupid skull with the Susasword or its facsimile, presumably the Cross of Mithras transformed accordingly. Slurp, though fortuitously not burp, that'd be Mel trying to suck me into the Amateramirror.

As for a crimson crown forming around my no doubt laurel-leaves-worthy cranial externality, well, to say I'd been expecting it, or something like it, would be to imply I really am as thick as almost everybody reckons I am to this day; hence the quotation marks I drew around that very word, 'drew', a second ago. Beer is the incredible thinking fluid; not the incredible drinking yourself dim dot-ditto, I'm sure you'll agree.

In other words, they made it quite clear they didn't approve of me, let alone whom I'd come back as, Janna's truelove. For my part, howsoever reluctantly, I'd merely demonstrated that drawing myself in the flesh was just something I didn't do regularly enough to avoid foreshortened 30-Year-lifetimes. Notwithstanding your third death, skewered by fishhook then incinerated by lightning blade, thank you for the reminder, Sang-Deadnunk.

As for her twin brother, I wasn't so much back in Kanin City as I'd never really left it, when shaven-bald-again pal Sraddha Somata publicly disavowed any interest in either becoming its Master or sharing it with his silver-haired sister. Who, I also shouldn't have to mention, in her late twenties was still as stunningly pretty as she must have been pretty gods-cursed crazy, not even in retrospect, by then.

So it was, all the more so with Zal-Mel remaining such unremittingly anti-devil jerks up in Cabalarkon, Janna finally succumbed to pressure as much from her devic advisers – read Harmony and the Librarian primarily – as from the Weirdom's populace. She, to fay-say some – which, no doubt to your abiding disappointment, I haven't been doing enough of lately – bowing to bowdlerized boulders bowled at her burdensomely, allowed herself to be acclaimed just that, the Master of the Weirdom of Kanin City.

She even went ahead and married Vladuca Fangfingers in the formerly fright-ful flesh. Foppish-he was in his own body, complete with opera cape and fang-fingered glove, whereas I, in mine, my latest incarnation's, was his best man; a sop to the Fop, as it were. Subbing for Zalman, who'd turned down the invitation I didn't so much deliver as sort of far-sent to him, was his half-grandfather, Lightning Lord Yajur. Mother Melina not surprisingly having turned down the same scionic sum-mons, Harmony was there acting in Mel's stead.

Zal-Mel were done with devic doings. So they, as a euphemistic excuse for not coming, informed their daughter via their angelic messengers. (Angelyc, as in the cannibalistic species of winged primitives, I hasten to add.) Much more important were what they were doing up north in Cabalarkon, whatever that was, other than planning devic undoings. (I hadn't been able to discover its extent when I went there, weightily if non-corporally, and the Angelycs were too busy sharpening their teeth to say much of anything.)

By the way, once these non-celestial angels got beyond the near-space of the Ghostlands and its still radioactive between-space, it turned out they could use Hellstones. That meant they had to be Hellions. Which should have told the devils down here, in Janna's Weirdom, that something wasn't right up there, in Cabby's Headworld original.

Which of course I'd already warned them about. That they brought a couple of presents for their daughter, ostensibly just to show her there were no ill-feelings, should have emphasized their true feelings even more strongly. And, you know what, maybe it did. That, minus their ministrations, Zal-Mel had gone all Death's Head Hellion on them didn't seem to spook the devils I spoke to, that's for sure.

Janna opened the parcels at the reception after the marriage ceremony, weird as it was given her grandiose gorgeousness and his depraved devilishness. Having far-seen her parents seek to put them to use firsthand, on me, only a few weeks earlier – frustratingly futilely for Zal-Mel, I don't doubt – I recognized them immediately. Except they weren't glowing.

She strapped more than put them on anyhow. They still weren't glowing. I gawped gape-mouthed at Harmony and Yajur. Have I mentioned how charming she can be, ever incomparably beautiful to behold by everyone? And Thunder & Lightning, well, you can guess what he said to me when I buttonholed him on them; not that he had anything on with either buttons or holes in it at the time as I recall.

Yep, he said they weren't glowing. In other words, no worries; either that or nay probs – my memory isn't what it might be when it comes to verbatim-exact-itude. And if Herr Odorous was obtuse then, incredibly, Her Harmoniousness was obverse. They were two sides of the same credulous coin. And its third side, if coins can have three sides – which they don't 'can' but definitely do 'do', once you consider their side as a third side – was about to re-enter the frame.

Look out Headworld.

========

For whatever reason, on the last day of Djerridam 5485, five years to the extraordinary day of the even more extraordinary birth of his sole son, whom in his absence Janna had named Johann-George, Unholy Abaddon returned to the Weirdom of Kanin City. (I say 'for whatever reason' even though, being Chaos, Uncle Abe never needed a reason to do anything.)

He found Janna wandering in the very rose garden where, in that then still – and for many millennia before then – splendid city, he first seduced her. (Unless it was the other way around, which it may have been.)

She had been with Vladuca Fangfingers for three of those years and, testament to her talented womb when it came to trapping devilishly daemonic seed, been impregnated twice. As an aside, scandalmongers claimed the Fop had gone back to occupying Sraddha, this time outwardly. That'd mean it was twin impregnating twin. Be that as it may, I saw no evidence of it. Nor was there any need for it.

For one thing, First Fangs had his own subtle matter body so he didn't have to, um, appropriate anyone else's equipment, as it were, to bed-bag Janna in the Biblical sense. Plus, Janna had already demonstrated that a devil, highborn or otherwise, could give her a beautiful baby-bellyful. At any rate, both times their devil-deviant child had been born dead, never to rise let alone teethe, cry hellacious havoc and/or fill up noodles of nipper-nappies.

Appreciably, that left Janna in a near-constant state of despondency. So it was, presumably just because he could, or perhaps because it was Samhain, Halloween, when disturbingly diabolical detritus is supposed to go down, on both sides of the Cathonic Zone, our Uncle Abe wooed her anew.

When the Fop found out about their brazen affair, he apishly appealed to their mutual father for justice, a censorious rebuke or, I would imagine to his mind best of all options, an inviolable order to cease and desist on the re-wooing-anew front.

Regardless of whether he was any more appalled about the resumption of their always reprehensible relationship than he had been when it first began back in 5475/76, the Libertine as usual couldn't be bothered to intervene. Being jilted must have unhinged him because – unless it was in a fit of induced insanity – First Fangs, as I shall henceforth refer to Faustus Vladuca, attacked their distressingly double-dealing deviant darling in the Unity's presence.

As you might imagine, once Chaos intervened on her behalf, it wasn't much of a contest. He knocked First Fangs across the room ass over teakettle, unless it was the other way around, balls and spout over buttocks and tailbone, then pinned him to the floor with his trident. He might have asked Janna what she wanted him to with the Fop. He might not have. He would have been astounded what happened next, though, of that I am sure.

She'd done it again, the scarily supranormal madwoman. She'd turned her wedding ring into a facsimile thereof. Now she turned it back to what it had been five years earlier – the selfsame Brainrock blade she'd used to send their baby to the Outer Earth. Ergo, Thunder & Lightning Lord Yajur had been right about the Susasword her parents had sent her as a wedding present. It was a fake.

What had been a wedding ring in appearance was, and conceivably still is somewhere, in actuality, the real thrice-cursed Godly Glory kept transmogrified by Janna's incredible force of will for years now. And that's why, its constant presence on his hybrid-human – or, if you prefer, hybrid-Utopian – wife's ring-finger ever since, I ventured that First Fangs attacking his first born and, hence, infinitely superior eldest brother might have been due to a fit of induced insanity.

Handing it, aka officially the Body of Demeter, to the startled Unity, thus in my opinion crazing him forevermore, Uncle Abe promptly used it to cut off Vladuca's power focus, the devil's daemonic right hand yet inside it. After sending suddenly simply First Fangs on his miserable way, shells momentarily in grave need of possessing, he gave the fang-fingered glove back to the terrible twin – as a keepsake.

Allow me to introduce Second Fangs. Or, as I prefer, Janna hereafter Fangfingers.

========

"We've met," said Centauri. "I've also heard all about Thrygragon."

"Of course you have," said the Legendarian, mentally pressing his personal pause button yet again. "Wasn't meaning to imply otherwise. Blame it on the beer if I did."

========

"It's a poor workman who blames his lubricant, Jordy."

"Point taken. Maybe I need another break." Tethys drained the last of his pilsner and, resolutely, didn't get up in order to snag another bottle of the beneficent brew. "The Susasword is one-third of the three Sacred Objects, the Trigregos Talismans. It's one of the first talismans ever forged by Tvasitar Smithmonger, the devic Prometheus."

"My Rings, Harry Zeross," nodded Centauri, evidently not afraid of telling tales out of school, "Is attempting to acquire all three as we speak. After your Rings, his late father Angelo, whom I met and you've told me was your friend, in a couple of incarnations earlier on this century, he's like Janna Fangfingers in that he's the second Ringleader so called.

"Having met her way more often than I have, you're well aware that Harry's wife is Melina Zeross. She might even be named after the Melina in your story, Sraddha and Janna's mother. Except there's apparently no question she's a pureblood, Demios Sarpedon's twin sister as a matter of easily verifiable reality if not skin colour.

"They're Summoning Children, the same as one of your predecessors, Dem's wife Morgianna, and my endlessly lamented, dearly departed, Yataghan's mother and therefore my Janna's mother-in-law. It also makes her about twenty years older than Harry. Then again, Utopians don't age anywhere near as quickly as we do, so I suppose that's fine. After all, Emeralda was my senior by seven years and no one complained when we got married."

(Officially Yataghan's surname wasn't Centauri or Sentalli. It was Montressor, after the family that raised him once royalist forces painted big bull's-eye targets on his parents' backs during the lead-up to the Godbadian Civil War. Needless to say, the Fatman wasn't a fat man in those days. Scrambling to stay alive, even when you've got an infernal for an internal, as Tethys referred to Centauri's relationship with Bodiless Byron, is a great way to stay in shape.)

"Like the Melina of your story, Melina Zeross is also a High Illuminary, that of the Weirdom of Cabalarkon, and claims Morg's year older brother, Saladin Devason, the Master of Weir up there, needs it to attain his full Hate-Sedon destiny; that it's the perfect weapon to wipe out devazurs. I'm gathering Zalman felt the same way five hundred years ago."

"You're gathering correctly," Tethys confirmed. "For good reason too, though I don't see how it could be. Not unless it can be replicated hundreds of times over. Yet the Morrigan, Superior Sarpedon, Sal's seditious sister, wants it too. Wants all three of them, it goes without saying. So she can use them to leverage either her or Demios onto the throne of Weir more so than to help the Master fulfil their peoples' racial dharma, that too goes without saying."

"I've never understood how a brother and sister can turn against each other over a pine chair," said the Fatman. "Even if it is extraterrestrial. Mind you history, on both sides of the Dome, is rife with dynastic intrigues." Utopians were no more native to the Whole Earth than devils were. They had, however, been here, more or less trapped beneath the Sedon Sphere, for precisely as long as devazurs had - since the Genesea, the Great Flood of Genesis.

"I've sat in it," Tethys reminded Centauri unnecessarily. "I've also fallen out of it, drunk as the proverbial Sed-skunk, as mass murderous Quoits Tethys. I'm pretty sure the Master's throne isn't extraterrestrial but lots of other things up there are. Its Mother Machine, what manufactures the foul concoction they insist on passing off as beer whenever I dare visit Cabby's Weirdom, came out of one of their biggest generational ships, brought to ground, then buried underneath it, up-there in the Slopes of the Sleepers for, what?, a decade shy of 6,000 years.

"The Master's Mace might be as old as the second Weir World, the one wherein Cabby served as old King Kad's grand vizier, and the eye-stave Demios carries with him might be even older, from the first Weirsystem, the one that got consumed when Weir Star went all supernova on that galaxy's ass. Not that he's up there anymore of course."

"And not that much of anything that is up there works anymore either." There was, when Centauri said that, a glint in the Fatman's eye. It was, in the Legendarian's estimation, the glint of covetousness or cupidity. (Capitalized, devils sometimes addressed the Cupid, Sinistral Envy, a character who played a minor role in the story he was relating, as just that.)

"Of course that's mostly because Sal rules a bunch of inbred idiots."

"Oh, I wouldn't be so sure that, Al. What I am sure is that Morg and Sal should learn to get along with each other. It's a form of neither induced nor inbred idiocy that they don't.

"Yet, when it comes to any one of the Trigregos Talismans, idiocy, unless it's madness, is the operative term. Merely wielding the thrice-cursed blade led Susal, a very late born Mithradite, to go after her own father and therefore good as cathonitize herself. Forgetting for the moment where the other two sisterly talismans were at that time, in Devic Eye-Land, just being around it, the Susasword, could indeed have been sufficient to drive Vladuca insane.

"Inducement or no inducement, he was already so far gone as to think nothing of going after Abe Chaos. Ask me he went nuts the moment Melina Somata sent it from Cabby's Weirdom and had her witches give it to him. Otherwise he would never have attempted to stand up to the four primary Apocalyptics the day Johann-George was born.

"Here's what that Mel, that High Illuminary, didn't realize: Being in possession of it for five years had also maddened her daughter, Janna Somata. She went crazier than Morg's hoot-owl did years ago now. I mean, all else aside, what sane person would accept a Brainrock glove with Vladuca's severed hand still inside it?"

Centauri winced at the mere mention of Morg's hoot-owl, whose name was Metowl but whom she, more tauntingly than incongruously, referred to as '*My Towel*'. Now was hardly the time to dredge up that old horror story again. Especially not when Jordy was referring to a much older one; a horror story that in many respects was still being written, on a daily basis, in both Hadd, old Iraxas, and in New Iraxas, Godbad's most north-easternmost province, just below the Forbidden Forest of Kala Tal.

"Hey," he sidetracked, "It wasn't all that long ago, not even two centuries, that folks on the Outer Earth collected shrunken skulls just because they had nice tattoos. That some of the skulls were neither shrunken nor even detached when they were, um, first acquired didn't bother some of the eventual buyers."

"Bingo-bongo-bang-on, Al. Madness is contagious."

Having spent considerable time beyond the Dome over the course of two thousand years worth of previous incarnations, Tethys had no real affection for Outer Earthlings, especially modern day ones like some of the Fatman's cronies. Overall he found them innately self-centred, complacent and exceedingly gullible. As far as he was concerned they were only getting worse – and far, far more dangerous.

His increasing sense of despair had a lot to do with their development of atomic power and the subsequent proliferation of nuclear weapons. You people don't do something to stop it damn soon, he often lectured Centauri, you'll be buying waterfront property in the Rocky Mountains. The Moloch Sedon didn't erect Cathonia to withstand Atomics, just the Great Flood of Genesis – though the Bible was wrong about who caused it, men not God.

His fears were justifiable. One need only be sitting where he was to have proof of that. The Fatman's link through the Cathonic Zone – which only he and his chosen ones, many of whom were possessed of Byronic Master Devas, could access – was called the Nag Gap, after Nagasaki, a city situated in the Outer Earth islands of Japan. That was where, on the 9th of August 1945 out there, the Americans dropped the second atomic bomb used in warfare.

The Nagasaki A-bomb going off didn't collapse Cathonia. Nor did it rend it altogether asunder. It did, however, slit it slightly. No one knew that better than Alpha Centauri. It was on that date, albeit as the 9th of Hektoris, Year of the Dome 5945, that he, born Alfredo Sentalli in Toronto, Canada, who'd lied about his age in order to join the American navy two years earlier, at the age of 16, slipped underneath the Dome.

Whereupon Great Byron promptly possessed him; possibly saving both their lives.

========

"Anyhow," said Tethys, "Getting back to my tale, Unholy Abaddon had to hold the Susasword in order to cut off Vladuca's hand. Without his power focus, Former Fangs became just a spirit being again, little more than a simple azura. From then on, he had to occupy sentient shells in order to keep himself relatively intact.

"Neither of them having any interest in what had become of him, Janna Somata's long time consort recall, Abe brazenly moved in with Janna in Kanin City. Meanwhile, travelling in a succession of shells, Vladuca eventually ended up in Pandemonium, the Abode of All Demons, the capital of what's also known as Satanwyck. So it was the two sons of Lazareme, highest born and among the lowest born, in effect reversed positions."

Tethys paused then, eerily, switched voices. "*I've been expecting you, Faustus,*' said Lady Lust, as you might expect, ever so seductively. *I'd like you to meet some of my subjects. They'll be easy to possess and I'm sure you share similar tastes.*' (Black Godlings, you'll recall – or if you don't, I'll recall it for you – were all in favour of blood sacrifices.)

"Those subjects, you won't need to have guessed, were vampires."

========

Elsewhere, not all that far away from where the two acquaintances more so than friends were telling, and being told, not-at-all-tall tales, when they weren't just chatting, someone was contemplating a menu in a cafeteria. Can't call him a man because he wasn't; he just looked like a man at that moment. He was also smiling, but not necessarily because he was happy.

Like a condemned man hoping for a last minute reprieve, better yet, a successful jailbreak, smiling was just something he did.

"I'll order a Cathy for starters, miss."

****

6: Contacting the Stars

Before the current Quill Tethys could recommence storytelling in earnest, a buzzer went off in Alpha Centauri's inner sanctum. Good thing too, in some respects.
It was around noon – lunchtime.

========

After apologizing for yet another interruption, one that for once wasn't his fault, the Fatman gunned his automated wheelchair to his desk, whereupon he flipped a switch on the rotary telephone and commence balling out whoever was on the other end. "Listen, Yataghan, I told you never to contact me here. This is the only place I ever get any privacy."

"Sorry, Fatman." Son Yataghan's strangely accented, yet rich, golden baritone broadcast out of the intercom. "But we got problems."

"If they're technical, tell Samarand. If they're security, tell Maxwell or Dulles. If they're financial and Hannibal doesn't want to fork over, send me the bill. Monday. Better yet Tuesday. Understood?"

"Wish it were that simple, boss. I'm afraid you better get out here. Otherwise your whole bloody island might sink."

"What are you talking about?" Jowls jiggling, Centauri yelled into the intercom. "Are we under attack? Sound the alarm."

"Can't! No electricity. No power. Nothing's working."

"Damnation, man, I've got power!"

"You're on a different system, Fatman. I'm on Centauri Island and you're..."

"I know exactly where I am. And stop calling me Fatman. I'm your fucking father." Centauri flipped the switch and looked at his guest in exasperation. "Should have listened to my wife. *'Spare the rod and spoil the child,'* she was always saying. Then again, being a Plantagenet, she was fond of switches. Me, I read Dr Spock, the paediatrician, not the Vulcan."

Tethys caught the reference. The first was an Outer Earth author whose bestselling book, *'The Common Sense Book of Baby and Child Care'*, advocated permissiveness. The second was a character in a short-lived, but endlessly rerun, television series called *'Star Trek'* that was shown throughout Greater Godbad on CETV – Centauri Enterprises being the megalithic conglomeration of businesses Centauri himself set up in the late Forties and had run ever since.

It paid lip-service to the notion of tolerance while ending almost every episode with a big, lips-fattening fight scene. Centauri hadn't been too pleased with the movie version of it he imported from the Outer Earth last year and was considering reviving it as a television series, albeit in here and, as a result, probably with different actors. (Emphasis on probably – his kind of cash came with considerable clout, one of whom was named Thrygragos Byron.)

Claiming he wanted more realism he'd even offered special advisers' contracts to some of Cabalarkon's ambassadorial staff. Their ancestors had trekked the stars, hadn't they. So had devazurs of course, albeit minus azuras, since even way, way back then Utopians were trying to eradicate devils. Saladin's people turned him down flat. They knew what he was really after, the Weirdom's extraterrestrial technology. Not that much of it worked anymore and especially not outside of Cabby's Weirdom.

"Maybe you better go, Al. Sounds like all hell's breaking loose."

The Fatman wiggled pudgy fingers contemplatively then, decision made, clicked the intercom back on. "All right, Yataghan. Come and get me."

"Can't, sir," came the response, "Can barely move. Nobody can."

"Look, if things are that bad, get hold of Kinesis. He can do damn near anything he wants with that Godstuff of his."

"That's just it, sir. He's the bastard responsible for all this."

========

Angrily, Centauri snapped off the intercom. Grabbing a towel from the back of his wheelchair, he used it to wipe his brow. "What do you make of this, Jordy?"

"From what you've told me of the Cosmic Express, and everything else you've been doing out there since you finished building the island, I find it a little hard to believe one man could shut everything down."

"It isn't just Romaine Kinesis; it's that Godstuff of his, what he's being calling Gypsium for as long as he's known about it. Which is since '48; either '48. Even Rom doesn't know everything there is to know about it, though. Says you can't. Says Gypsium's unknowable. Says he wouldn't know anything about it at all if Gypsium didn't teach him itself. Imagine that, an inanimate substance telling one of the most brilliant minds of the late Twentieth Century, his time, what it can and can't do."

"Nothing shocking about that. What he calls always Gypsium, we call Brain-rock or both interchangeably. It's what makes up devic power foci. It's the main component of Cathonic Fluid, both the kind you drink and the kind you use to suspend animation. And it is the stuff of Godhood. When the Big Bang blew, what blew was the primordial Godhead. You can ask any physicist about that. They'll agree."

"I did – and that's precisely what I've been telling him. What he's hearing, what's teaching him, is the voice of God. But, thanks mostly to his parents and their Etocretan crew, your pal Angelo Zeross philosophizing at the top of the class, he's such an out and out anarchist he doesn't believe in any higher authority."

"Sounds to me," said Tethys, somewhat disrespectfully given Centauri considered himself a practising Roman Catholic, "Like your man's one of the most brilliant minds of the Sixtieth Century as well. You sure he isn't a closet Lazaremist?"

"I'm fairly sure he's a closet queen but that's as far as I'm willing to go on that score. And you shouldn't talk. A couple of lifetimes ago, you were a chanting a different mantra." The Fatman was right about that. Back in the Fifties, when he spent most of a decade as one of his most headstrong daughters, a nun inclined toward Outer Earth style monotheism no less, Tethys had leaned religious himself.

Hadn't stuck. For refreshment beer beat holy water every time. Besides, it was difficult to put much in the way of faith in a never-seen Ineffable God, especially one with pretensions to being both omnipotent and omnipresent, when just as immortal, if not quite so eternal, devils might pop by his cardboard-box domicile for a benighted brew at any hour.

"And, as much as I'd love to renew our debate on that, or any other topic you'd care to bring up, I better get out there. Yataghan's never been one for exaggeration."

"I can speed you up." Tethys withdrew a quill from his cap. It looked like a glowing feather. Monks of yore dipped similar things in ink and used them to write scrolls. He opened his sketchpad and, even though he didn't have any evident inkwell, prepared to go to work. "You'll have to describe where you want to go in detail. Otherwise I can't guarantee drawing you there."

"Thanks for the offer. But I'm perfectly capable of finding my own way."

"In other words, it's not that you don't trust me; it's just that you don't trust me."

"Your other words, not mine." Fingering his chair's arm controls, the Fatman rolled behind his oversized desk and pressed a sequence of numbers on the data keypad. A drawer sprang open. From it he took out a fat Havana cigar, a Montecristo #3 at the minimum, removed its band, bit off its end-nib and lit it. Sucking in deeply, he seemed immediately calmer.

"Emeralda thought smoking was the worst habit a man could have. She would, wouldn't she. As a Plantagenet, she must've thought I was burning up one of her cousins."

Tethys didn't laugh. He knew from firsthand experience Centauri was telling the truth. He'd been a plant person himself, more than once. It took him generations, and the 30-year lifetimes that went with them (at the maximum), before he started coming back wholly human again. Been fucking fun getting to that point, though, it had to be said, even by him. Been fucking fun even when he was female, sooth said. Giving birth was what hurt and what he dreaded going through again.

The Fatman handed him the cigar band. "Do me a favour and go find my Janna. You know, Yataghan's woman. Give her this."

"I'd gladly give a lot more than just this to a Lovely Lady Afrite like her. Only trouble is she's also a War Witch. She might cut it off."

(Athenan War Witches were named after Mediterranean Athena, the Virgin Goddess of War and Wisdom. Ancient Illuminaries believed she was actually a first-born Mithradite and thus, mixing Mediterranean with Athena, they came up with Methandra. Being Godbadian, Janna probably worshipped APM All-Eyes, who was named after a different Olympian, Aphrodite, she of the foaming waves and clamshell-contraceptive.

(She wouldn't worship Methandra Thanatos, the Scarlet Empress of Lathakra, Heat to husband-brood-brother Tantal's Cold, but she didn't need to in order to become, and remain, a War Witch. She just needed to be as fit as she was relentless in the defence of life, especially when it came to her own and that of her father-in-law.)

"I'll have her cut it off if you don't get the hell out of here."

"So, what is it – a signal for Janna to destroy the island?"

"Hardly. It's a signal for Janna to start sealing everything up. I started the de-struct sequence when I opened the drawer. If I don't cancel it in half an hour it's all going to go poof."

"I'm on my way."

Tethys rose not-too-unsteadily to his feet. As he made to leave the conservatory, Centauri had a final request: "Don't forget where you left off."

"I won't."

========

The Legendarian left the glass-enclosed, effective solarium by the same way he came in and Janna St. Peche-Montressor went out, via its main door. Janna was in the almost as bright outer chamber, within sight of both the door into the Fatman's inner sanctum and the public elevator up to the complex's top floor. He casually handed her the cigar band. They exchanged grim glances but there was no need to say anything to each other.

Once in the elevator he flipped through the pages of his sketchpad – a more so-cially acceptable alternative to his splotch pad, which he nevertheless still concealed within the between-space of Rumour's Brainrock quill. From the sounds of things there were any number of places he could draw himself to that might be infinitely safer than this building, or even this subcontinent, in the immediate short term.

He settled on the DDD, the same cavern tavern he, as the Squiggly Legendarian, drew both he and Sraddha Somata to immediately after their return to the Inner Earth, via the pre-Flood Sphinxes, all those centuries ago. Even though it had changed management more than a few times over the intervening half-millennium, it still made the best pilsner on the entire planet.

The Dinq Doinq Danq lay Cheek-side of the Diluvian Mountain Range, on its north-easternmost slopes. Since Diluvia was the wettest area of the Whole Earth, some said a better name for the Danq would be the Din Drab Damp. Tethys didn't disagree. Sooth said, he'd coined the phrase shortly after the incomparable Harmony, the Unity of Balance as well as, all-too-tragically according to her, Panharmonium, ceased being its proprietor.

Having left his rain slicker in the sumptuously appointed bedroom suite allocated him whenever he was staying at Centauri's modern day fortress, he took the elevator down a couple of floors. Getting off it, he nodded pleasantly at a couple of the Fatman's grumpy, rudely officious guardsmen, then made his way down the hall to his rooms. Once inside the suite he latched the door, stuffed the few personal belongings he'd left in the bathroom back into his banged-up suitcase and put on his overcoat. Whereupon there came a knock.

The immediate temptation was to disappear, to quite literally draw himself directly to the Danq. However, if whoever was at the door had seen him enter, which the hall guards had, and could get into the room, which both the guards and any chambermaid could, then he better be here. He wasn't, the secret of his deviancy would be out and Centauri's super-security-conscious minders might never let him back in.

He didn't dare take the risk. He liked visiting the Fatman. So, keeping his Brainrock quill at the ready, he peaked through peephole into the hallway. His sudden urge to scratch his forehead should have told him to bolt bodily instead of unbolting the chain. Cat-curiously, he cracked the door open. Didn't die yet again either.

"Good day to you, Mr Tethys. Hope I haven't caught you at an inopportune moment."

The suit was straight-backed and straight-laced, white-skinned, clean-shaven and manicured. He had short black hair, looked like he popped laxatives rather than after-dinner wafers, and probably considered rumpled or ruffled capital crimes – not that there were capital crimes on the Hidden Headworld anymore.

Suits, and the folks who wore them, were one of Centauri's innovations. Progress was a kind of plague, figured Tethys; suits an epidemiological symptom.

"Not at all, Mr Kenton. I've already had my morning shit."

It was meant to be an insult. Kenton merely smiled. Tethys shook involuntarily. There was something disconcertingly familiar about that smile and it had nothing to do with the fact that, as a political hack, his smile was as practised, as insincere, as it was commonplace. No, what disturbed him was there was something distinctly not commonplace about that smile.

Even though his mouth made it, there was something not Kenton about it; something, dare he think it, of yesterday's Molech Xibalba about it. And what had Janna said about that? Much the same that he said, wasn't it – that it couldn't be Xibalba? Or was it something else? He couldn't quite recall.

"Let's not be so formal, friend. Call me Gottfried. And what shall I call you?"

"Mr Tethys sounds fine, friend. Last person who called me that was an enforcement officer busting me for vagrancy."

"I trust that hasn't happened again, Mr Tethys."

"Hasn't and better not. Laws are made to protect people, not create victims."

"Quite so. Mr Centauri was very specific about that. Now, shall I come in or would you prefer meeting some place else, the bar perhaps?"

"The latter sounds fine to me, Gottfried. One with big, bright windows and lots of people around. Not rats either, present company excepted."

Kenton didn't rise to the bait. Didn't stop smiling either. What bait? Why was he smiling anyhow? Was that a panpipe in his pocket or was he just glad to see me? Tethys was getting giddy. Must be going through withdrawal already. Speaking of which, withdrawing, whatever else, mustn't forget the quill.

"Excellent, though it's a bit early for me."

"Too bad. It's never too late for me."

"Exactly what I wanted to talk to you about."

========

Tethys had no use for Gottfried-Kenton-types. They were all smiles and no soul. Facile, understanding, sympathetic, most things to most people, not so much ingratiating as wormy, he was the kind of person who spent more time flossing his teeth than using them to eat. In another time or place he would have been a confidence trickster. Still was, Tethys was sure. They just had another word for it these days: public relations professional. PRP, pronounced prip, as in prick. Sounded like something made up for a crossword puzzle.

Like him, Kenton told stories but, unlike he himself, he rarely listened to them. Unlike him also, Kenton was paid big Godbucks; not room, board, and a sack or two of pilsners per tale or tee-tee-tail told. Kenton's idea of job satisfaction was another assignment. Centauri used him as a spokesperson.

Since, like demons, the man had no concept of right or wrong, he was ideal for that task. Given enough information and clear instructions as to what message was required, he'd leave the most hardened cynic convinced life was a bed of roses and that thorns only added to its attractiveness. Pillows were for rock heads – and everybody must get stoned.

Consequently, hardly for the first time, inquisitiveness got the better of him. Thoughts of fleeing the building – let alone the subcontinent – forgotten, the Legendarian determined to discover what Kenton's mission was today. And, more specifically, what it had to do with him. He soon didn't find out. The beer was good, though.

"So, what can I do for you, Gottfried?" he asked after the waitress brought him a cold pilsner and Kenton a cup of anything but cold coffee.

"Immortality, my friend. Not for me, you understand. If I knew I was going to live forever I'd never get anything done. For you."

"You mean a recording contract? Sorry, mate, not my style. If people could just turn on my stories, who'd want to hear me tale-tell them in person?"

"Not your stories, your drawings. Hell's Teeth, Gottfried, talk truth: maybe a bit of both. Here's the idea. You go around Godbad recounting legends and picking up more, right? You specialize in devils, though I believe the term Illuminaries of Weir use for them is Master Devas and/or devazurs."

"The Shining Ones and/or the devazur race, yeah. So?"

"Well, Mr Centauri says you pass the time when you're not busy guzzling bleary booze by sketching. He says you're very good at it as well. What we'd commission you to do is a series of portraits of devils. We'd dedicate a special wing of the new National Gallery in Godbad City for your pictures, add some placards for a few of their better known myths, maybe a voice box, a slide show.

"You know what I'm talking about, multimedia spice. We'd call it *'Immortals Immortalized'*, or some such inspirational fluff predetermined to maximize ticket sales – and, I might add, your bonuses, kickbacks, royalties, call them what you will, your percentages of the return. What do you think so far?"

"Sorry, pal. Sounds too much like work to me. Want to pay for the pills I'm popping or shall I put it on the tab?"

"I pay, you pay, comes from the same source, doesn't it? Mr Centauri's generous if not quite bottomless pockets. Don't think I'm beaten. Don't know the meaning of the word, if you didn't already know. Here ..." Kenton reached into his suit pocket – only a guy like Kenton would wear a suit on a Devauray morning – and pulled out a list of names.

"Be a goose and have a gander at these goslings; I mean godlings. Bet you could do a damn fine series of portraits of this loathsome load, as Mr Centauri reckons most of them."

Tethys obliged. The list had over fifty names on it. Some weren't names real devils used, not that devils used names as such, just called each other by their attributes, but he had no trouble visualizing each and every one of them. Kenton's smile was unwavering and the scar in the middle of Tethys's forehead hadn't stopped itching since he first beheld the glad-handing bastard through the peephole upstairs. That only ever happened when …

"You know your stuff, mate," he granted, mentally trying, and failing, to identify who might be possessing the prick. "Problem is Mr Centauri's as usual right as rain for the plains, Unless it's for the horse, if your spelling's off by an '*e*' instead of an '*a*'. Or the king and queen, if it's really off. Not that Godbad has royalty anymore; just your aforementioned personage-percentages.

"Most of them are Mithras Spawn. And, from what I can recall, once I stop babbling inanely and start speaking sanely again, every Jack and Jill jollity of them has been cathonitized, some multiple centuries ago. Your Illuminary pals probably have the location of their stars plotted out on one of their maps of the night's sky. And this last bunch aren't even Mithradites. They're Thanatoids, speculative devils at best."

"You mean you made them up? Very unlike you, that. A violation of your craft I'd have thought. Their short lives and glorious demise is one of your most famous stories."

"What I meant was, if they're devils, they're fourth generational devils and surely your Illuminaries have told you there's no such thing. More likely they're deviants, the offspring of regular men and women possessed by Tantal Thanatos and his sister-wife Methandra, Mithras's Virgin obviously no longer. For one thing, they were born in pairs, not triplets, and something else everyone knows is Master Devas are born in litters of three."

"Yet Illuminaries have a Constellation Thanatos, don't they. As it happens, I've one of those very things, their star charts, right here in my briefcase if you want proof."

Correction, only a guy like Gottfried Kenton would wear a suit and carry a briefcase on a Devauray morning. He placed it on the table, opened it up, pulled the map of the night's sky out of it, shut it, and laid the star-chart atop it. His briefcase wasn't all he opened. Neither was his voice his anymore.

"Now let's scrap the pleasantries, shall we."

Oh, fuck!

========

"Cigar for your thoughts, Jordy?" So queried Janna St Peche-Montressor as she slinked into the empty chair across the table from him.

Smiling pleasantly she handed him an only partially smoked cigar. He ran it under his nose, recognizing the band he'd given her before he decided to come to the cafeteria-cum-bar.

"Ah, the scent of survival."

"Come on, the Fatman wants you. By the way, I didn't realize you signed autographs. Who was your fan?"

"Fan?"

Tethys regarded the half-drunk cup of coffee left on the table with a mixture of perplexity and panic. Then he looked at the blotch, unless it was a splotch, he'd made on the tablecloth. He calmed down almost immediately and smiled. Like the thankfully no longer irritatingly itchy scar in his forehead, which none of his 'incarnations' had before he came back inside them, it was a specifically Jordan Tethys smile.

"I have only two words for you, my dear, young, scrumptious, Lovely Lady Afrite."

"One of them better not begin with the letter 'f' and end with a 'k'."

"Security tapes!"

========

"Well?" asked Tethys, stubbing out the cigar as Janna emerged from the public elevator and entered the anteroom off Centauri's top-floor conservatory-cum-solarium.

He'd refused to go in to see the Fatman, and thereafter recommence his story of the Disunition of the Unities, until she'd had a chance to look at the security tapes he insisted she review. He hadn't been just idling smoking, though; he'd been doodling as well. Hadn't been idly doing that either; unless puzzling counted as idling.

A 'D' drawn at an angle of 90 degrees clockwise, the same design he'd splotched, or blotched, onto the tablecloth downstairs, had to have some significance, didn't it?

Janna wasn't in Lovely Lady mode; didn't look at all happy with him, sooth said. He just hoped she wasn't in War Witch mode. Although they considered themselves life-defenders more so than either life- or love-lovers, generally speaking Athenans had trigger tempers and she was alone. Hadn't brought an Althean Witch Healer with her, in other words.

"The corridor downstairs, there's you coming and going from your suite. Coming, no suitcase or rain slicker; going, you've both. You and the guards on duty in either case. The guards, we've talked. They still have a job."

"And the cafeteria?" Her look softened. Even better, most of her visible jewellery stopped glowing. That was a good sign, a very good sign. Most Inner Earth witches were materialists; very few of them ever materialized anything lethal. An exception were War Witches.

"You at a table, drinking a beer."

"But not a cup of coffee."

"It blipped, the cup. The devil was careless. Doesn't tell us who it was, though."

"Does this help?"

He showed her one of the many drawings he'd doodled up while waiting for her to return; doodled up in what some Outer Earthlings had been known to refer to as a near-unconscious 'Zen-like' state. She recognized the likeness. He already had.

"Gottfried Kenton, one of the Fatman's top-dog what-cha-ma-call-its?, his prips, his public relations professionals. Only I call them pricks, not prips."

"So do I – great minds and all that stench of codswallop."

"What of it?"

"You've always struck me as more sensible than sensitive, Janna. Tell me, you have any idea why I wrote this?" He flipped to another page. His Brainrock quill had a much better memory than he did. While he was in his Zen-state it had rewritten what he'd last used it to write, though he somehow sensed not so much in the sky as within it, if that made sense.

"Rendezvous here," she read. Carefully considered her response: "Nope. You?"

His sketchpad suddenly burst into flames. He hated it when that happened. Hated it even more when he had no idea why it happened. He dropped it with a yelp. They watched as it burnt into a cinder. Both registered the letter 'D', drawn at an angle of 90 degrees clockwise, linger glowingly before surrendering to ash's inevitable triumph.

"Not anymore. I like this life too much the way it is. How about APM, SPM?"

Janna looked shaken, not stirred. For a change she didn't say '*not possessed, Jordy*'; said instead: "Got a spare beer?"

She had his while he went to the infirmary.

=========

"Well, Smiler, was it worth it?" grumbled the twelve-foot, thickly-bearded devil-god of Fire Kings more so than Intuits.

"Look outside," responded his nowadays (on and off, as in up and down, since Antheal 5933) six-inch-tall wife, the unmasked devil-goddess of Intuits more so than even Fire Queens. "The stars of our lost children have never been brighter."

With one hand maintaining the beat he'd already set, their otherwise never-remembered guest tapped the two humanoid skulls — humanoid save for their third eyeholes — that depended from the chain around his neck as if they were bongos. He licked the pan-pipes he'd been playing with his other hand and, them thus prepped anew, beamed broadly.

"Care for another tune?"

****

7: Diabolical Conspirators

By the time he returned to the top floor after having his fingers attended to by a standard nurse, Jordan Tethys, the legendary 30-Year Man, had already forgotten what he was thinking when his sketchpad went up in flames. He put his lack of memory down to the fact he was also, very much justifiably, nicknamed 30-Beers.

Nonetheless, his inexplicably burnt fingertips bothered him. His only consolation was he still had his Brainrock quill and a functional splotch pad safely contained within it.

Burnt fingertips emphasized the need for handy-dandy emergency escape routes.

========

Spotting him enter her office, Janna St Peche-Montressor put down the phone. "Well," she said. "He's there all right."

"Didn't think he wouldn't be. Your father-in-law's a lot like Saladin Devason, the Master of Weir. He likes his bedtime stories; even when they're mid-afternoon tales."

"Not the Fatman, Jordy. God-afraid bloody-Kenton, future president of our fair land – albeit only if he has his way, it goes without saying."

Tethys had no idea what she was talking about. Then he did. Sort of. Time to wing it. "Best not to say it then. Still, I'm glad to hear it. And where might that be, pray tell?"

"Where he's supposed to be. Down south in Sedon's Beard trying to convince a bunch of fundamentalist, avian-human Ayres that Tangs aren't banquet material just because they've got fur instead of feathers. Seems to be doing all right as well. The Ayres are ready to give up on Tangs but draw the line at Babs and Pansies, of the non-Plantagenet genus."

Tethys recalled reading something about that in one of the local rags he'd been using as a blanket until Centauri set him up in such luxurious surroundings downstairs. He'd even been contemplating going to Djerridam-Goatwood to check out the situation for himself. After all, he was way better at winging things than whinging about them so he might even be able to help sort the situation out.

"Baboons I can see but Chimpanzees, no. Had a friend who married one once. Didn't realize how devoted they were to family. She had six brothers and five sisters, a mother, two fathers, and who knows how many aunts, uncles, cousins, nephews and nieces. Needless to say he left Goatwood and took a job in a pharmaceutical company specializing in birth control for Simian Sapiens."

Janna laughed amiably. "Did you just make that up?"

"Nope." He crossed his heart. "It's the god's truth; any god's truth. Upon my honour as an honest tail-teller."

"That about says it all, doesn't it. Anyhow, Kenton was quite shocked to hear from me. He's not used to dealing with one of the Fatman's personal bodyguards, especially one who's related to him. But he thanked me for my interest in ape abuse."

"Good thing you didn't tell him you were looking for a recipe for Orang-utan then. I've got one, by the way: Tang a-l'-Orange. It was a popular dish back in the bad old days of King Achigan and his predecessors. Which at least in part explains why the Tangs revolted."

"Sounds disgusting. Can I ask you a question?"

"Shoot. Wait, let me rephrase that."

"Don't bother. I gotcha."

"Not funny, Janna."

"It is if you're a War Witch. You have any idea why I was calling the prip?"

"To say hello?"

"Didn't think so. You better go in, the Fatman hates to be kept waiting."

"No more so than I hate being kept in the dark. You will tell me when you remember, won't you?"

"I might. Go on in. Your beer's in the fridge."

"Thanks. One last thing ..."

"I'm all ears."

"Do me a favour and requisition another sketchpad. See if you can find one made out of asbestos this time."

"I'll look into it." She flashed him a reassuring wink. A whole bagels-bunch, as opposed to brunch, of them. Wherever she'd been, APM All-Eyes was clearly back on the job.

And, flash though it was, he found that unaccountably comforting.

========

"Ah, Jordy. Come in. Have a beer." Alpha Centauri tossed the book he was looking at onto the settee. After grabbing a twist-top bottle, together with a chilled mug, out of the fridge, Tethys plopped down on the couch. Cracking the pilsner, he glanced at the book's cover. It was a copy of Homer's Odyssey.

"Great stuff that," said Centauri, indicating the book.

Forgetting his earlier vow to slow down lest he give away too much of his story too soon, Tethys slugged back half the bottle. The rest he poured into the stein. His excuse, if asked, which the Fatman wouldn't, was his fingers hurt. "The pill's just fine too. Hits the spotted spittoon." He took a settling sip then gave the book a deferential tip of the mug.

"For a guy who couldn't write, being blind, Homer's okay. Bit long-winded, what with all those genealogies and pedigrees, though. Not much in the way of sex either. I like a bit of the old in-out thrown in with the blood and guts myself. Of course it depends on the audience. I mean, Briseis and Achilles is one thing; it'd sell anytime, but Patroclus and Achilles, I doubt that'd go down too good these days. Risqué is always risky."

"*'A pornucopia of tits and slits'*, said a reviewer I read once. And he was talking about an opera. I prefer to paraphrase Pierre Trudeau, self-proclaimed godsend to Canadian culture: *'A poet has no business in the bedrooms of his subjects.'*" The Fatman was born in Toronto, back in '27 on both sides of Cathonia, the year, not the city.

"So what do you want me to do – backtrack to the Pied Piper of Hamelin or bash straight on to the Disunition of the Unities?"

"The Unities. I've read all about the Child Crusade. Terrible business that."

"The Pied Piper's got naught to do with the Child Crusade, or repopulating eastern Europe after the ravages of a particularly virulent plague, one of many, which is another theory I've heard bruited. Piper's how it started; rather, I suppose I should add, speculatively started, put better. And not against wiping out more than half of everyone alive on the Head, it wasn't. Because that's what culminated five hundred years ago."

"Pray continue then. I'm all ears."

"That's the second time today someone's said that to me." This time he had a brief flash that his host was all head. He shook that off and recommenced tale-telling.

"In 5487, Janna Somata's fourth pregnancy ended in her third stillbirth. Demanding blood paid, Unholy Abaddon single-handedly invaded Satanwyck, a Mithradite domain in case I haven't mentioned that already, and took over its misnamed capital city, Pandemonium – misnamed because it wasn't the domain of all demons, just a mightily slimy majority of them; a Mother Earth moraine of them, meaning not quite a mini-mountain but close.

"At any rate, this was an unheard of incursion. Devils were only allowed to enter other devils' protectorates with permission."

Still were, he thought but didn't say. Another thing he thought but didn't say was that he hoped Thrygragos Byron and his baby Byronics, faced with the burnt-fingers-evidence of an unwarranted incursion by at least one unknown devil into what was supposed to be their jointly shared sphere of influence – if not confederation of individualized thearchies, like those dotting predominantly Mithradite territories in the Upper Head – had the situation well in hand.

He doubted it, though. Hell's Teeth, Bodiless Byron didn't even have hands.

"Like the Forbidden Forest of Kala Tal north of here, which is pocked with time warps, Satanwyck is a multi-dimensional realm. A good many Master Devas have become lost in that bituminous bit of Hell on Earth; many more deliberately hide there. Yet, when the Chaos Unity came visiting, bedazzling Belialma was the only one to defend Pandemonium.

"Fittingly too, because in the still perplexing absence of Demon King Sedon, who hadn't been shining upstairs since the night or the Terrible Twins 18th birthday, it was more her realm now than her vice-regency. Stupidly dot-ditto, as it turned out. For all her troubles, for all devils were supposed to be accorded absolute authority in their own protectorates, Chaos beat her so badly he damn near – no pun intended – catasterized her.

"Possibly even worse, especially for the epitome of free love, though never anything-goes-libertinism in terms of sexual violence, he may also have raped her. For Lady Lust thus never again luscious, that must have been the ultimate humiliation. And it was only the start of Chaos's descent into stomach-churning cruelty."

"What, no graphic description?" said Centauri, harkening back to his '*pornucopia*' crack. It was pure Alpha. Had to be. The Byronics' unmoving all-father had no more of a sense of humour than he had a body.

"I said possibly," Tethys reiterated. "They were former lovers, recall. Besides, when you talk about Belialma, it's a hard line to draw, emphasis on hard. At the risk of repeating myself, she did have as her Tvasitar talisman the Ruby Red Apple of Concupiscence. As such, she had a much higher tolerance for perversion than most of us do."

The Fatman's glared disapprovingly. "Not that that's any excuse," Tethys stumble-mouthed, belatedly correctively.

"Nor should it be," Centauri said archly.

That remark may have been more Byron than Centauri. APM was the Great God's Venus, true, but there were certain otherwise peaceable refuges in Godbad so steeped in ancient tradition that rape amounted to an open and shut case of '*abuse it and loose it*'; in other words, a crime punishable by castration, not catasterization. As it happened, he'd lived in one such place as Sister Jordan.

Mostly temples dedicated to APM, as a result being under her aegis, they granted inviolate sanctuary to the mainly man-reviled clippers. In consideration of who was in the other room, Tethys wisely let the comment pass. He did get up and take out another beer before continuing, however. Talking to a Great God, even if he was only imagining his presence, was thirsty work.

========

A TETHYS TALE - JANNA FANGFINGERS: THE DISUNITION OF THE UNITIES OF LAZAREME – PART FOUR: ZALMAN'S GAMBLE; JANNA'S GAMBIT

========

The fact that Abe Chaos knocked hell out of Lady Lust in effect knocked her out of Hell, capitalized. Put better, harsh reality dictated that beguiling Belialma, Bouncing Belle as she was most endearingly known to her bedfellows, had all too literally lost too much face to continue on as the Domination of Satanwyck's Prime Sinistral.

Her pre-designated successor, that covetous little putto, sprite or cupid, Bobby Badboy, aka Robin Goodfellow, thereupon took a chance. He seized the opportunity to seize her. His ploy paid off. Her loss of face meant she'd lost the support, the howsoever begrudging worship, of her infernal minions, the demonic denizens of Sedon's Temple. Her mortification left her powerless to rebuke what amounted to Envy's palace revolt.

The new Prime Sinistral was, I believe, Number Six – though three or four of his predecessors, Lust among them, had repeated as the daemons-ruling regents over the multiple centuries since Dark Sedon ill-starred Number One, Domdaniel-Pride, circa 2500 YD. Duly acclaimed thusly, as skyborn top-cap of earthborn bottom-dwellers, he probably could have cathonitized her. However, presumably because Envy habitually took the aforementioned form of a cupid, as in the Classical Eros, and as such had, um, a soft spot for Lust, he merely sent her into exile.

The Unity had meanwhile returned to Kanin City. There he announced that, while Janna Somata could henceforth consider herself the Master of Kanin City, in title anyhow, he was now the de facto ruler of the Mastery of Marutia, the entirety of Sedon's Cheek. Which, him being Chaos, meant that there were no other rulers; even more precisely, that there were no longer any rules. Nor were there any enforceable laws, not even the quaint notion that *'Do as thou wilt shall be the whole of the law'.*

As for that other trite statement, *'Might makes right'*, feel free to try and prove it. You just better be absolutely certain you were mightier than Unholy Abaddon.

You must have surmised by now that Uncle Abe Chaos was spoiling for a fight. Sooth said, there were those who claimed he was suicidal; that he wanted to go out in a gung ho blaze of gory glory. Whatever the reality, fights he got; plenty of them. For the next three years he spent more time on the battlefield than he did at Janna's side. Sedon's Cheek was sorely beset.

It can and should be said that Chaos insisting rules were out the window constituted a rule unto itself. It follows that there had to be an exception to prove said rule. At least initially, Underlord Yama Nergal – the devils' Grim Reaper since he got rid of the Byronic, Vanthysces, during the expansion of the Empire of Lathakra centuries earlier – took it upon himself to be that exception.

Mindful of the unhinged Unity's previous promise to withdraw the Chaos Blade and render him one dead Death the next time they met, Yama himself never ventured beyond the vastly expanded boundaries of his de facto protectorate – de facto due to the near-total desertion of every other Master Deva way back in 4825 YD. His army, Death's Angels, the long Inglorious Dead, did, however.

For the record, Yama's original protectorate was merely part of Sedon's Forehead, which by then, as now, was deathly radioactive from the eyebrow and so-called sweat glands up to his crown, the Mystic Mountains. Once the Laughing Lands of so many pantheistic paradises, today's Ghostlands encompass such once notable, as well as noble, even desirous, destinations as the mighty Moloch's former cult centre, Grand Elysium (nowadays Yama's headquarters, Pettivisaya, the City of Wailing Souls or Unhappy Ghosts), the far-fabled Elysian Fields, and old Valhalla, the initial homeland of the Sangazur-animated Glorious Dead we're both so familiar with – me, as we'll soon sort of see, much more so than you.

Significantly, unlike the Underlord, their devic overlord, Death's Angels rarely ventured far from the Ghosts before Chaos went altogether mad dog on Marutia and then only in times of the severest droughts. The reason why they had stuck so close to home until then was because they were highly susceptible to fresh, falling rain – as opposed to the so-called Hard Rain they had become used to in the Ghosts.

Yet there was something about those days that emboldened them. While the Cheek was experiencing patches of uncharacteristic dryness, most of it wasn't adjacent to the Ghosts. Something else was just as odd. Previous times, when drought did allow them to invade Marutian territory, they found it so unpalatably full of life they ended up retreating back home.

There was no such impetus this time. It was as if the Living's force of will, their life-force if you will, had become palpable; that it was it, Life Itself, that drove them back to the Ghosts. Yet, most of five centuries ago, they met no such resistance; were as a result able to survive, even thrive, no matter how deep they ventured into the clean air of Marutia.

One plausible explanation for this phenomenon was the Ghostlands themselves were expanding. Another, one more likely in my book, and other books I've read on the subject, was that the land itself was dying; that something was draining it of its vitality. Could that some thing have been a some one, a devil by the name of Unholy Abaddon? That's what I thought back then and it may be I was right. Except, without getting too far ahead of myself, it wasn't just him, was it. Devils are really good at witching weather and no one's better at it than the missing Moloch.

Be that as it may, soon it wasn't just Ghostlanders who menaced Marutia. Enemies came from every direction. There were demons from Pandemonium, Saurs from the Floodlands, Lizarados from the Lake Lands, Sangazur-animated, not-just-humanoid warriors from the Bloodlands, Sedon's Inner Nose (what had become New Valhalla after the old Valhalla became the Ghostlands), red-capped and trouping feeorin from Crepuscule, Sedon's Outer Nose, the Land of Twilight, and – foreshadowing here – Iraches from the other side of the Diluvian Mountains, what's now Hadd but was then still Iraxas, Sedon's Mutton Chop.

They came by sea too. And not just from the east either, though the Mithrant legionnaires of Apple-Apis-etcetera Isle in the Gulf of Corona, Sedon's Human Eye, seeking to regain their ages-old hegemony of the Cheeks, formed by far the largest invasion force. From the other side, from across the Aural Sea, Sedon's Ear, came Dandset Typhon's Rajput warriors and similarly Mithradite-venerating, Ophidian snake-folk from Moorset, the Biblical Ophir some say. Nor was it only Mithradites who came to challenge Abe Chaos.

From the same direction, the west, slipping north through the Straits of Jaag from the Headworld's Interior Ocean of Akadan came adherent armies of Byron Spawn: Godbadians from the subcontinent; Panis from Krachla, the head of the Penile Peninsula, south of Iraxas proper; and Bandradins, the orange-skinned, as well as orange-textured, race of humanoids from the Cattail Peninsula, Chaos's traditional sphere of influence. It seemed everyone except Lazaremists wanted a piece of the once united, now fractured and foundering, effectively already ex-Mastery of Marutia.

The death toll was pathetic; made even more tragic when a Time Quake, what some of you Outer Earth mythology mavens like to call a Kronos Quake, rocked the central Cheek in the Year of the Dome 5489. Opposing armies were reduced to fighting in furs instead of armour, and with sticks and stones instead of forged blades and muskets. Which set things up nicely for the return, a year later, in 5490, of Janna's parents, Zalman and Melina born Tethys Somata.

Many of those with them were battle-hardened veterans of the same force of mostly mixed-blood Marutian-Utopians Zalman sailed to the Weirdom of Cabalarkon fourteen years earlier. Some of these included his brothers, Johann and George, and those who drowned with them just before the hybrid Marutians 'conquered', in quotation marks, Sedon's devic Eye-Land.

(Put better then, just before Quoits Tethys, Mel's Granny Jordy, as me, the never-so-tormented Legendarian, turned it over to them. Which should tell you all you need to know as to what side the Hellion Sisterhood, they with their Crystal Skulls full of life-restoring, personality-retaining Sangazurs, had taken.)

However, he hadn't returned with just them. He had returned with a large contingent of pureblood Utopians: white-as-light women and black-as-night men. These were the Trinondev Warriors of Weir, a few hundred of whose successors, under my friend for most of this century, Golgotha Nauroz (the admirable clone of none other than the famous Ubris, Saladin Devason and Morgianna Sarpedon's paternal grandfather), are currently in Hadd fighting alongside Godbad's own against the Ambulatory Dead.

(Mind you, today's Trinondevs are all-male; have been since Sal won the Challenge of Weir and replaced his great-grandmother as Cabalarkon's Master approaching thirty years ago.)

Zalman had always been extremely popular in Marutia. Known as a fair and judicious ruler, upon landing on the mainland, gulf coast of Corona he immediately reasserted his claim, officially never-relinquished, to the Weirdom of Kanin City and, with it, the centuries-old Mastery of Marutia.

The populace flocked to his banner. But his popularity, coupled with Chaos and hence Janna's corresponding infamy, was hardly the only reason for that. Not only hadn't aftershocks from the 4989 Time Quake hit his band of Trinondevs; being for the most part pre-Earth, their weaponry effectively made them immune to any subsequent Time Quakes.

Acquiring this weaponry, Kanin City's remnant versions of the same stuff having ceased functioning multiple hundreds of years earlier, was why Zalman had gone to Cabalarkon in the first place. Far more crucially, one particular aspect of their weaponry did much more than merely render Warriors of Weir immune to Time Quakes.

The eyeorbs that sat atop Trinondev eye-staves could capture Master Devas.

========

"Devils are hardly the only enemy they were designed to take out," Centauri felt obliged to point out, not precisely in passing.

========

The Legendarian nodded. "True enough, Al, though I'm not absolutely sure there are subtle matter daemons and suchlike chthonic critters anywhere except the Earth. Plus, earth-made eyeorbs don't work as prison pods on either Dark Sedon or his perpetual mate, Pyrame Silverstar. Didn't work, put better, since my providential pal ceased being a never-cathonitized, Perpetual Presence those selfsame thirty years ago.

"As for whether they work on Great Gods, I wouldn't want to speculate. Would you?"

The Fatman gave him a grin and a shrug. "Hey, you're the storyteller. I'm just the audience. But, leaving that aside for the moment, we agree they double as prison pods. When they open they can capture a devil's spirit self as well as his daemonic body and, I believe, his power focus, which suggests they were conceived from the get-go with Brainrock-Gypsium in mind. Which is even more interesting given they're partially composed of just that."

This was hardly surprising information. Tethys knew just about everything Utopians knew about their own weaponry due to the fact he'd reincarnated as a hybrid-Utopian more than a couple of times. He'd also been Cabalarkon's Master at least once.

"As you know, I've commissioned seemingly endless studies of the astonishing devices over the three decades I've been inside and in charge of Centauri Enterprises. One thing I've learned is that they funnel Utopian willpower. Another is that capturing devils, much more so than their azuras, fills them up on a one to one basis. That explains why eyeorbs are replaceable – they have to be. Full eyeorbs can't act as the pseudo-psionic batteries eye-staves need.

"And they don't work in devic protectorates. Which is why they're next-to-useless here in Godbad."

"The word I'd use is limited; as in their uses are limited in devic protectorates. Be that as it may, they're hardly useless anywhere. But you're right about their prison pod aspect. So long as Master Devas retain the adherence, as in worship or veneration, of their subjects they can't function as prison pods in a devil's own domain. And don't for a moment think Zalman wasn't aware of that. Sooth said, he was counting on it."

"What fools would worship Chaos?"

"Chaos gone crazy especially – precisely, Al. Except, what devil, Thrygragos Brother or Master Deva, had ever fathered a flesh and blood child, deviants that they are, in their now six thousand years plus on the Whole Earth, without first having to posses a sentient shell? And what devil keeps his power focus sheathed for fear of playing Shiva, Destroyer of Worlds. Or did keep his Black Blade sheathed, put equally precisely."

"Sorry for interrupting."

"So you should be." It was time for another beer. The Fatman had one too, the second of the day as far as Tethys knew. In fact Centauri had two, making three, in rapid succession.

Did that mean he was drinking for two? Could a Great God, especially one without a body of his own, get drunk? Other than on power, it went without saying; albeit only because the Legendarian didn't feel confident enough in his current position, sitting on a comfortable couch in a bright solarium on a chilly day, to voice such questions.

Bandages on fingers made wonderful mnemonics.

========

Perhaps as a consequence of not being worshipped by anyone, unless it was Janna Somata, non-King Chaos was faced with open revolt throughout the huge call-it-ex-Mastery.

========

Only the Weirdom of Kanin, the capital city, remained loyal, though its loyalty was more towards Janna – the brilliant-to-behold, silver-haired seductress who still nominally ruled them – than it was to him. (Was their affection for the Terrible

Twin a borderline-racial memory of their ancestors' onetime devotion to Pyrame Silverstar? That's something else I wouldn't want to speculate about.)

The Unity was summoned by his fellow Unities, Balance and Order, though significantly not their father, to the Gregarian Fields: a violence free zone by Sedonic Decree, recall. (Not that that stopped Thrygragos Varuna Mithras from bringing Thrygragon down upon himself. Truth told, yawn, they summoned him to the Medusa's Meadow, where the blood of Utopians more so than devic adherents soaked the ground on that very Mithramas, 4376 YD.)

There Abe was to face the censure of devazurs from all three tribes, including those of Thrygragos Byron, some of whom – notably the Great God's surviving first born, old pals Rufous Rudra and Umashakti Silvercloud – had journeyed north for the first time in nearly five centuries; since the days when Byronics held Kanin City as their effective satrapy. Cementing his reputation as well as his name, the Unity of Chaos flat out refused to attend the session. Other than Harmony and Yajur, no Lazaremists did either.

Of even more significance, their father remained asleep on Tympani, the Isle of Undying One, in the middle of the Aural Sea. (As for why Lazareme was called the Undying One rather than, say, the Rarely Awakening One, you'd have to ask ancient-time Illuminaries that; which would be difficult since resurrection is not part of their curricula vitae. Perhaps it was because, in Great Byron, they had an Unmoving One and, in Varuna Mithras, they had an Unliving One, as in an altogether dead one, and they were going for some sort of symmetry. Who can say?)

Their absence neither aborted the gathering nor silenced the Unity's critics. Anything but, in fact. However, as Abe Chaos must have appreciated, condemnatory attacks are useless when they're just words. No pen, not even my quill, is ever mightier than a sword at your throat and no tongue, no matter how forked, is a match for a Brainrock trident.

That said, generally speaking even devils like local favourite, APM All-Eyes, who rarely bothered to manifest one except – reportedly – in bed, were more mouth than teeth. So it was, without Abe, his father, nor any of his younger siblings around, they couldn't resist being even more voluble than usual.

Breaching another devil's territory, as he had when he entered Satanwyck and brutalized Lady Lust two years earlier, was a violation of a sacred trust, complained Sedona Spellbinder, then as now Byron's spokesperson. It sure as fuck was, confirmed the brutalized babe at issue, bedazzling Belialma, Bouncing Belle, the eldest Mithradite there. Yep, agreed Lord Order, a co-bed-bouncer of hers many times in the past.

Refusing to relinquish the Weirdom of Kanin City to we Mithradites come the end of the century is another unpardonable sin, put forward the Emperor Chameleon, he of the Lake Lands, Sedon's so-called Sweat Glands, the Lizarados' devic overlord. None of us are pardoning it, countered Balance.

Someone is, though, isn't he? Has to be, she added referring to the mightily missing eye-mouth self-evidently no longer mostly in the sky, if at all. Then what are you Lazaremists going to do about it, Chameleon challenged Abe's brood brother and sister, knowing full well it was only the Age of Panharmonium in Harmony's mind.

All there knew their father, the Undying One, Thrygragos Lazareme, was the only devil who could realistically expect to bring the Unholy One to toe, if not to boot. Yet he had refused to become involved, hadn't he. Nothing new about that, answered Order. Wasn't referring to him, said Balance, raising all three of her glorious eyes skyward, implying a Sedon-sanction.

Despite this, virtually every other Master Deva on the Headworld, every other non-Lazaremist anyhow, remained determined to see the defiant devil disciplined. Knew how as well. Yajur had a half-son and Harmony was once half his wife. Care to invite their return? Care to have me far-send them an invitation to return is what they really meant.

The Unities may have grunted begrudgingly. They may not have. Have I ever mentioned that I could never say no to Harmony? Well, I couldn't – and I didn't.

Not surprisingly, the Mithradite and Byronic Master Devas were too terrified to face eyeorbs themselves. They didn't just avoid them, though. They ordered their armies of adherents to stand aside and do nothing to impede the Trinondevs march on the Marutian Weirdom. Not that it was just a march: Zalman had brought functional vimanas, as ancient Outer Earthlings had them (cosmicars as Utopians did), with him from Cabalarkon.

Dozens of these vertical takeoff and landing, or VTOL, vessels landed on the outskirts of Kanin City. (Think of them as shuttle craft, because that was what they were, salvaged from Weir's otherwise mostly derelict, pre-Earth millennial ships and you've the gist of the grist.) Warily never stepping outside of the city himself, Uncle Abe promptly sent word to Kanin's former Master, and Cabalarkon's new one, that he was prepared to grant him an audience.

He promised no harm would come to him and that, so long as they left their eye-staves behind, Zalman could bring whomever he wished with him. Since devic oaths are inviolable, that should have been plenty. Nonetheless, mindful of how unpredictable – read plain crazy – Chaos had become, Order and Balance went a step beyond the customary. Distrustfully, even provocatively, risking Abe's wrath, they personally guaranteed Zal's protection.

They were living lightning, those two: Yajur via his unsheathed Lightning Blade; Harmony via her broken chains. (Call her living chain-lightning then.) Between them they had to be mightier than Chaos by mathematics alone: two equals equalled one more than solitary him in most anyone's ledger. Acting in unison, Abe's litter brother and sister should have more than ample raw power to bring him to his knees, if not outright cathonitize him; though they were likely quite capable of that as well.

Full of consequential confidence, Zalman agreed to all of Abe's conditions. He'd meet him and his disrespectful daughter, the Unity's unofficial coregent, in a land without rulers, minus his eye-stave, reputedly the oldest yet in existence. As an additional sign of goodwill, he further promised to leave his Trinondev Warriors Elite, they with their arguably equally extraterrestrial ones, outside the antediluvian City's walls.

(For the record, Daddy Zal and Mama Mel considered Janna unilaterally declaring herself Kanin City's Master more than just an act of disobedience; more than just disruptively usurpative. It was the unforgiveable act of a traitor to the shared

Utopian ideal of Panharmonium. As such, they'd already disowned her – albeit, as we'll soon see, only officially.)

Even though he was putting his life on the line, Zal did all this on his 114th birthday, the 30th of Antheal, precisely 14 years after leaving Kanin City to wife, life- and soul-mate, Melina born Tethys. He probably wasn't the only one who hoped Abaddon wouldn't be on his best behaviour either. The ever-irreconcilable animos- ity between the two male Unities, Order and Chaos, wasn't just the stuff of legend. It was the stuff of both friction and non-fiction, if not necessarily non-theoretical physics.

It truly was a sight never to be forgotten; a sight that became the subject of numerous paintings, including some of my own. I was there by the way, along with Janna's twin, and not just because it had the makings of a potentially monumental encounter. Since it was also going to be a family reunion for best buddy Sraddha, he'd prevailed on me to draw him hither from our outpost in the hinterland of south-central Marutia, where we'd been overseeing the re-dredging of ancient canals for a number of years by then.

Zalman strode into the great central hall, rotunda or megaron, of the Masters Palace hand-in-hand with his wife, the twins' distressingly throwback of a mother, Kanin's onetime Master-for-under-a-day. While neither was a pureblood, Zal's skin was by then far blacker than most hybrid males whereas Melina's was, if possible, even more the opposite, bordering on whiter than white.

(Must be the food up there – or what passes for food up there – I remember remarking to Shreds at the time. Remember cringing as I said it, dot-ditto. I'd never drunk myself to death before. Nor since, if you have to know.)

Both were simply garbed in unadorned, dyed-purple gowns, the colour of roy- alty on both sides of the Dome. Both wore boots of the finest patent leather and other than presumably underwear seemingly nothing else. As must have been pre- arranged, that means no crowns nor necklaces nor even jewellery, especially nothing that glowed. Indeed, except for the provocative purple, there was nothing showy about them; nothing showy about the indubitable Trinondevs and Illuminaries fol- lowing them either.

The women – unlike today some of whom were probably Trinondevs despite the lack of visible eye-staves – wore tan-coloured gowns. The men, some of whom were Illuminaries, which isn't quite as unheard of as female Trinondevs are these days, wore blue ones. I recognized a few of them from my miserable months as Quoits Tethys. Like their master and mistress, they were bare-headed, carried no obvious weapons, and wore no veils.

(Word to the wise: you see a Trinondev with his veil drawn you better hope he's on your side. He isn't, you better have some armour-piercing bullets in your gun and, even then, you better have some similarly equipped buddies blazing away at the same time from all sorts of angles. The force shields they project, usually in the form of gargoyles, are that strong.)

As guarantors of their safety, the other two Unities provided all the ostentation needed. Lord Yajur, in such a panoply of splashy Oriental splendour his trappings would make a proud Mogul potentate or Mongol khan look undressed by comparison, as-good-as-paraded to Mel's left. Harmony, as not-just-lips-smacking-gorgeous as always, flanked Zal, as you might imagine to his right.

The former had brown, make that bronze, skin. He wore a turban that looked like a thundercloud. Significantly, him being non-devilishly right-handed, he was carrying his sheathe, containing as it did his lightning blade, in his left hand, the quicker to withdraw. The latter, who, hair-wise and facially, had to my, as in Squiggly's, biased eyeballs something of the Outer Earth, gypsy-goddess wonderfulness about her, had a glowing torc about her neck.

From it depended, well, some said her entire body beautiful from the neck down, chain-link vestments and all, depended from her torc, her Brainrock power focus. She had all the requisite curves; to-die-for-magnificent they were too. She showed a fair amount of skin as well, no doubt deliberately. Sometimes her brothers were be-horned but they were always horny. Not that I'm implying she serviced them in any way, shape or form; all of which, if she did do, I'm sure would have been fantastic.

Her looks were subjective, even illusionary, as in described from Quill-Squiggly's perception alone, is all I am saying. Yajur's weren't; he was also all muscle. His, let's call it a short, as in cut off mid-thigh-length, sleeveless toga, covered very little of it, skin or muscle. So, while, given her born-beauteous attributes, everything about Harmony was unavoidably glamorous, in every shade of its meaning, everything about Yajur was threatening.

If Chaos came back to Kanin City spoiling for a fight, Order was presenting himself as just the entity, can't call him a person, to finish it. Only this time, for the first time ever, as his co-guarantor of Zal-Mel's safety, Balance was no longer betwixt and between the two bitterest of brotherly enemies. She was on Order's side, no question of it. If he was in his grave instead of his bed between-space off Tympani, Sedon's Eardrum, Thrygragos Lazareme would roll over.

And maybe he did, albeit between the sheets with whomever he was with, if anyone.

Awaiting them were Janna Somata and her paramour, Uncle Abe Chaos, albeit in anything except avuncular mode. Both had taken no small degree of care with their appearance. Like her Mother Melina, the younger Somata was porcelain pretty, if not ambulatory alabaster the same as her Mel. Today, though, her look was anything except white-as-light. I'd call her seraphic except she didn't have any wings. I'd call her sapphiric except I don't think that's a word, so how about cerulean or lazuline or even azure. (Not to be confused with azura.)

So, significantly, was his.

========

"Dare I say it – shades of your Outer Earth's J Robert Oppenheimer approaching 350 years later at Los Alamos, New Mexico? Guess I just did."

"Uh, oh," said Centauri, apprehending what quote was inevitably on its way.

========

Unless it was a glamour or a serpent splendour, a second skin in other words, hers had undoubtedly taken more time to prepare than his did. At least I assume dyeing one's skin a sky-blue and one's hair a leaf-green takes more time for a non-changeling than it does for an often moment-by-moment, metamorphic shape-shifter like Unholy Abaddon to grow an extra pair of arms. Which he had.

Janna was dressed a purple bodice, a violet skirt and a mauve waistband. Tucked into this last was the Stopstone scabbard that held the sword or long-knife she used to send her firstborn to the Outer Earth. In addition to all manner of jewellery, on all manner of appendages, including studs in one nostril, both ears and her bellybutton, which was visible because of her bared midriff, she had a tiara of ruby red bloodstones about her forehead and an egg-shaped, mirrored pendant dangling off a golden chain of her own around her neck.

Arguably like what was in the scabbard, I'm not persuaded Abe realized what they were in actuality. Except they weren't glowing either, so maybe he knew precisely what they were, no threat to anyone – if not what they were meant to represent, which is slightly different, as well as, in spirit, highly threatening.

Why weren't they glowing? Sooth said, as I'm about to sooth say, they weren't glowing because they weren't the genuine articles.

========

"They weren't the Trigregos Sisters' crown and mirror?"

"How could they be? Like I just said, and as I'm about to relate, given the opportunity, Zal and Mel, the Master and the High Illuminary of two Weirdoms simultaneously, had them."

"Oh," said Centauri.

"Aren't you supposed to say 'sorry for interrupting'?"

"Oh," the Fatman repeated.

========

Rightly or wrongly, in the past old-time Illuminaries often equated the three Unities of Lazareme with the Hindu Trimurti, as featured most notably in the Outer Earth's Vedas. Myself, since that triad was as male as the Christian Trinity, I was never quite sure which one was supposed to be Harmony: Brahma the Creator or Vishnu the Preserver. Whatever the case, this day in 5490 Abaddon was definitely in full Shiva the Destroyer mode, complete with ever-present trident, itself doubling as a sheathe for the Chaos Blade.

Besides sprouting two more arms than usual, he'd done his skin and hair to match Janna's, albeit perhaps a darker shade of blue; ultramarine perhaps. She didn't have a beard of course but he did. It was as long, as wild, and as stringy as his vine-green hair, but it was tree-bark brown. He wore no shirt, the better to show off his rivulets of old scar tissue, and a loose-fitting, multi-coloured sarong that was so splendidly made it probably cost the equivalent of a raja's ransom over in Ophir. It wasn't so much a Leprechaun's pot of gold at the end of the rainbow as it was the rainbow itself.

Janna Somata would have been 34 in 5490, her mother not quite twice that at 64 and her father would turn 114 on what, as we'll soon see, proved the most eventful day of his eventful life. Although title only – a title that, in a land whose only rule was there were no rules, nor any rulers, meant nothing – Janna was stubbornly clinging to Kanin's Mastery and, with it, that of Marutia, all the non-Mithradite territories of Sedon's Cheek.

She was doing thusly despite her father's proclamation that he was still the rightful Master of the nominal Weirdom of Kanin City. From his viewpoint, her mother only appointed her to what amounted to the role of little better than a temporary caretaker until he returned. She, like Mel a day before her, was supposed to take the advice of his left-behind ministers, not act of her own volition, as if a replacement plenipotentiary.

Furthermore, back in 5476, Mel resigned her own surrogate Mastery under duress, not in any way as an acknowledgement of guilt, and hence personal disgrace at getting caught, for a murder that allegedly took place not quite twenty years even earlier. No more than she did he, Zalman, the then High Illuminary did not – repeat, did not – set up Harmony to kill Quidnunc Tethys. Just as the doctors at time determined, the young swordsman died of a heart attack, plain and simple.

An upstanding future Sister Superior of the life-loving Sisterhood of Flowery Anthea could never condone let alone execute such a pernicious plan. By contrast, Abe Chaos wasn't called Unholy Abaddon because he was infused with an unswerving dedication to the truth to go along with unwavering righteousness. He'd put Mel up to not just accepting the blame for Quid's untimely death but believing it. He'd done so purely because he was Chaos, wickedness incarnate as well as incarnadine; albeit in this case bloody-brained, though manifestly not bloody-handed.

Perhaps he hoped that Harmony, retrospectively horrified by her dire deed, would cathonitize herself, thus leaving him free to tackle Lightning Lord Yajur without her intervention. Perhaps he was just feeling mischievous, like one of the fickle faeries or demented demons whose company he so enjoyed. Whatever his motivations, Zal, with Mel, and supported by the other two Unities, by now fully apprised of Chaos's malfeasance, had returned to make matters right again.

So, did Zalman's widely pre-broadcast slanders convince either of the thusly defamed debauchers that they should see the error of their evil ways and reform, let alone fall to their knees in front of the oncoming and beg forgiveness? Certainly, to judge immediately by their outfits, neither Janna nor Chaos – call them Parvati and Shiva if you prefer, for that was whom they were basing their physical presentations upon – appeared in any mood to turn the Weirdom back to Zalman.

Nonetheless, as soon as they entered Kanin's magnificent megaron – that wonderfully decorated, mirrored and statue-be-strewn snake's head extension of its antediluvian Great Hall – Janna approached her parents, as well as both her devic half-mother and half-paternal-grandfather, in what everyone there took to be a respectful, very much non-menacing manner.

Unholy Abaddon was right behind her. True, he was carrying his Brainrock trident but, unlike Lord Order's sheathe and the hilt of his Lightning Blade, it wasn't glowing. True as well, again like Yajur, he was holding his talisman in one hand, his lower right, him having four at the time. However, him suffering from what's sometimes called the sinister affliction, that was about as unintimidating as Chaos ever got.

Shockingly to many, Shreds and myself among them, Janna almost reverentially took a knee three steps in front of the quartet of father, mother, half-grandfather and half-mother. Abaddon would never stoop to that level, not even to his own father Lazareme, but he did nod at Zalman Somata. He also, perhaps for the first time in his endless existence as a solid entity, actually smiled at Melina born Tethys.

Whereupon Janna removed the scabbard from her waistband, pulled out the Susasword and proceeded to lay it atop the scabbard at the quartet's feet. You know the old image of eyes bulging out of their sockets in amazement at something they're seeing, well, for the three Unities of Lazareme all three of their eyes, each, bulged out of their sockets, all nine of them, the moment they recognized the Susasword.

"I believe this is yours," said Janna to her birth parents, ever-so-obsequiously. "Thanks for the loan but I don't need it anymore."

Whereupon Chaos exclaimed, didn't just say, though I suppose he did that as well, technically speaking, to quote him verbatim: "What the fuck's that, witch?"

Whereupon ...

========

The buzzer went off on Centauri's desk. He hit a button on the arm consol of his automated wheelchair, silencing it. Whereupon he smiled and said: "Whereupon?"

"Whereupon," said Tethys, "Zalman materialized his eye-stave."

"Trinondevs can do that sort of thing?"

"Not that I'm aware of, although Zal's was the oldest eye-stave in existence. In fact, to hear Demios Sarpedon tell it, it wasn't just pre-Earth. It was pre-Trinondevs. By which burst of boastful bombast he means it was manufactured on the First Weir World prior to the Devil, let alone the devils to follow, even existing. And I suppose he should know, since he's got it."

"I'll have to bear that in mind."

"You do that, Al." You too, Byron, thought but again didn't say the Legendarian.

========

Zalman's wife wasn't just the High Illuminary of two Weirs and Master of none. She was an Ant Nightingale, possibly the highest ranked Sister Superior of the Superior Sisterhood, that of Flowery Anthea, at the time, as well as, let's say this speculatively, the Hellion's Morrigan. So it's likely she was the one who materialized it. Materialized it with the eyeorb atop it already open. An eyeorb's membranous covering is akin to an eyelid. Only the eye inside a Trinondev's open eyeorb doesn't so much bulge out as it pokes out on tentacle-like tendrils.

It's an eye-eat-eye world out there when Trinondevs get close to devils. Trinondev eyeorbs capture devils by literally sucking out their third eyes. And it wasn't just Zal who suddenly had an open eyeorb in hand; most of the Utopians in the Somatas' retinue did too. Evidently Melina Somata had brought a whole coven of her fellow witches with her into the Masters Palace; a whole oven full of her fellow gingerbread bakers, as a famous Outer Earth fairytale-teller might put it.

Although Harmony and Yajur were closer to them than their litter brother, every one of the Trinondevs had focused their open eyeorbs exclusively upon Unholy Abaddon. The duplicitous Utopians didn't want to just suck out his spirit self; they wanted to irretrievably spaghetti-shred it into dozens of prison pods simultaneously. And in this they were clearly following the lead of the famous, to Hate-Sedonistas, Death's Head Hellion, who once sucked Sedon Himself into dozens, maybe even hundreds of recently evacuated, pre-Earth eyeorbs.

Didn't quite happen that way this time, though. Seemingly everyone in the Great Hall except the three Unities, the three Somatas and their fellow Utopians was prepossessed. Devils, Lazareme Spawn the sacrificial batch of them, spewed out of their shells. In short order they filled up all the prison pods in the palace. All save that of Zalman Somata, that is.

I was there, Al. Rather, if you want to get technical, an incarnation of me was there, recall – Shreds' second best pal Squiggles, second best after the original 'Q for Squiggly' Tethys. I, my then self, was prepossessed too. So much for me being a closet devil, eh? Being de-possessed didn't knock me for a loop either. I swear I was no more dazed than I was confused. I saw what happened next.

Abaddon's devic eye did visibly boggle outwards from his forehead. But it didn't detach. Instead a blast of devic eyefire came out of it; came out of it and went into Zal's eyeorb. Incinerated it, thoroughly scorching the top of the eye-stave upon which it was perched as well. Scorch-marks are still there, too. Get Demios to show them to you next time you see him.

Although Yajur would quibble, and a case could be made for Tantal Thanatos, King Cold of Lathakra, in his prime, in my view only the Great Gods were more individually powerful than Unholy Abaddon. Certainly Zal wasn't but, credit where credit is due, he was impressively resourceful for a mortal. Something else material-ized, about his neck. Something appeared about his wife's forehead as well. Zal had an egg-shaped, be-mirrored pendant dangling off a golden necklace of his own; Mel had a tiara of ruby red bloodstones about her forehead. And both of these were glowing, very brightly indeed. Then they weren't.

Taken aback, Zal nevertheless materialized another eyeorb atop his eye-stave. Maybe it's so old it makes its own. He'd learned his lesson, though. Manifested a force shield in the form of a be-winged griffin about himself and his stunned wife, who was gawking at their daughter, a look of absolute astonishment chiselled upon her ivory face. The griffin, a lion's body with an eagle's head and wings, sought to rise up, carrying them both with it. The two older Somatas were seeking to escape.

Without any further provocation, not that he needed any I suppose, Chaos flowed, yes flowed, over Janna. In one fluid motion, akin to one of Shiva's tsunamis perhaps, he grabbed the Susasword by its hilt, whirl-pooled upwards, not down-wards, and drove it into Zalman's force shield. Drove it through it, the griffin, and into his all-too-human heart, even if was still mostly a Utopian heart; all-too-mortal heart then. The old Utopian hero probably died more from the shock than the thrust.

Be that as it may, the griffin de-solidified upon his death and Melina found herself in the unenviable position of being about to gain some extra orifices courtesy of the three barb-ended prongs of his trident. It would have been a real pain in the neck, her gaining them, to pun it non-bluntly.

"Stop," yelled Janna.

That wasn't what stopped his trident, however. It was Harmony's golden-glow-ing torc. The Unity of Balance had repossessed her previous shell. Her chain-light-ning garment covering Melina Somata just as it had the Unity. It proved impervious to his trident. Commensurate contact didn't quite blunt their tips. That happened, in a manner of speaking, when Lord Yajur, lightning blade a blur of, well, lightning, sliced them off. Couldn't blunt what wasn't there anymore, this time to put it bluntly.

Then they were, sharper than ever. The two male Unities squared, ready to go at each other. "I said stop!"

Janna was on her feet. She had snatched the Susasword from her father's corpse. Her bloodstone tiara was glowing like it hadn't been mere seconds earlier. So was something Lord Yajur made the mistake of being the first to look at; look into, rather. It reflected him. Then he was inside it looking out; glaring out, more like. It was the egg-shaped, entirely mirror-surfaced pendant dangling from her chain necklace.

"Not him, you brainless bimbo," cried Harmony, albeit via Melina Somata's voice box. "Him!" She was using one of Mel's arms to point chains at Unholy Abaddon. "He's the one who killed your father. He's the one who thinks he can violate Sedonic decrees with impunity. Imprison him."

The bloodstone tiara she, both halves of her in their one, shared body, had wrapped around her forehead flared briefly. Simultaneously the one on Janna's head dulled. Then, before even Abaddon could react, the luminescence reversed, reverting exclusively to the tiara Janna was wearing.

So did Harmony, switch places, albeit only in so far as she was now inside her quarter-daughter's version of Crinsom's crown, as trapped as breed-brother Yajur was lower down, against Janna's chest. Melina fell to her knees, crawled to her husband's corpse, took him in her arms and began to rock silently, tears eroding her porcelain prettiness.

"That was well done, Janna." Chaos wasn't smiling. She was, however.

For the moment she, the now undisputed Master of the Weirdom of Kanin City, even dared to ignore the effectively now solitary Unity. Instead she addressed her liberated, as in unchained, birthmother. "Game over, mom. You lost. Have your Trinondev Elite release the Lazaremists. Then go, all of you go, while you still can. Take father's body with you, bury it up north, in his Weirdom, that of Cabalarkon, and never return to mine, that of Kanin.

"Do it now, High Illuminary, before I will everything you brought with you inoperable."

"I said that was well done," Abaddon repeated. "I did not say you were well-done. But you will be. Release my brother and sister this instant."

"I shall, my love. In due course, should you continue to insist on it. For I would have your children again, ones born alive and ones I don't have to send to the Outer Earth in order for them to stay alive. Bring me the head of Zuvem Nergalis, reunite it with his body, have him release the devic doom he placed upon me, on us, and there shall once again be three Unities of Lazareme."

Melina mutely signalled her warriors to let loose the Lazaremists. Which they did. Repossession neither deafened nor distracted me, though. I heard what Abe said next. Can't say I saw what happened just before that, however. Only its immediate result.

"I shall have to get 30-Beers there, wordsmith as well as fabulous sketch artist that he is, to explain to you the meaning of two simple words." By then, of course, seemingly suddenly sane again Uncle Abe Chaos already had hold of the not-to-devils, three Sacred Objects, the Trigregos Talismans. Janna no sooner realized it than she too fell to her knees, both of them this time, in appreciable concern for her life.

He'd been excessively indulgent. For him, *'this instant'* had seldom before meant as long as a tick-tock of a clock.

========

"And yours is signalling break."

========

"You're not going to end there, are you, Jordy? I turned off the buzzer and no one can get in here without my say-so. For one thing, other than being in the throne room presumably being possessed, dispossessed and then repossessed, you forgot to tell me what Janna's twin brother, Sraddha Somata, was doing during all this. Did he just stand there as Chaos killed one parent and the Crimson Corona took over the other one?"

"Been doing that a lot lately," remarked Tethys. "Forgetting, that is. Guess I've caught the CRAFT Syndrome, as in I *'can't remember a fucking thing'*. But I didn't forget, nor even neglect, to tell you about Shreds. Like I said, I don't want to get too quickly ahead of myself and his bit's mostly still to come.

"And, just by the bye, by signalling I meant the alert-light on your gewgaw over there on your desk." The Legendarian was referring to the Fatman's intercom. "It keeps winking."

"So? I told you, no one can ..."

"Sorry to interrupt, boss," said Janna St Peche-Montressor, the fullness of her physicality finally blinking into the solarium.

"You're fired," Centauri snapped.

========

Jordan 'Q for Quill' Tethys, recurring deviant that he was, was hardly the only taleteller on the Inner Earth, the Hidden Continent of Sedon's Head.

========

There was even a talking rodent, a tee-tee. Tee-tees were mostly indigenous to the Head's west coast, from the tip of Sedon's Beard, which is to say the south-west-ernmost regions of the subcontinent of Aka Godbad, all the way up to its far north. While they could no more survive in the Ghostlands than anyone mortal could, they were also found in Sedon's Crown, aka the Mystic Mountains, and beyond, in the Head's bald spot (better known as the Silent Sands of Cathune Bubastis, as ancient Illuminaries of Weir so named the Apocalyptic of Drought after a once highest echelon Egyptian Cat Goddess).

This yappy rodent would tell tales, albeit in exchange for its life's continuance. Its tail, should you be able to properly decipher its nodes and codes, its specks and flecks, had a tale to tell as well. So too did its chiropteran cousin. Only its tales weren't on its tail; they were on both sides of its wings. Tethys could decipher said sagas. He even kept a number of tee-tee-tails glued to his currently otherwise bald pate, beneath his checked cap, just in case he'd exhausted those stored in his head and needed some tactile reinforcements to pay for his beer or earn his supper.

Many a story, of any sort, told beneath the Cathonic Dome featured the two surviving, as in non-starry, Mithradite firstborn: namely, the Death Gods of La-thakra, Tantal and Methandra Thanatos. One Tethys tended to avoid retelling, due to the personally painful, as in fatally fiery, remembrances that necessarily began it, dove-tailed with that of the Death's Head Hellion and 4824/5's consequential end of the Era of Empires.

A few of the more recent ones even made mention the Thanatoids' terribly talented youngest, Sedunihas the Artist. He, an acclaimed-by-everyone sculptor, may have been a fourth generational devil. He may also have been just a mortal deviant, one with an external third eye and who aged only one year in five; strange forms of deviancy the pair of them. Whatever the case, this childlike-whatever didn't tell tales out loud, he signed them manually. He was deaf.

Something else he signed, albeit with a hammer-plus-chisel or etching rod, was his statuary. He was a tremendous craftsman. He liked to show off his stunningly lifelike masterpieces, too; to any and all who ventured, usually via between-space, high up into the partially hollowed-out, though sometimes-rumbling, so not quite extinct Lathakran volcano that served as the geological wonderment wherein he and not just his birthparents dwelled.

"What is it, boy?"

Sedunihas gestured at his latest accomplishments. Despite having never seen them in the flesh, let alone in action, the statues were of his elder siblings. (That he'd never met them was due to the fact he'd only been around for 25 years and they'd been gone for nearly twice that; gone from the Head's surface, if not its night's sky.)

There were ten of them. Seven had three eyes, two didn't, whilst the forehead of the tenth one sported only the bumpy, raised-skin-protrusion of a devic eye. It was as if his muse, if muse he had, hadn't been too clear how to render this last, a seemingly sheared bald, as opposed to born-hairless, female.

As perfectly rendered as they all were, only eight of the statues had one thing in common. Sedunihas had posed them with their thumbs-up.

========

Except he hadn't, had he, the ever-smiling viewer immediately apprehended. No wonder the boy, who wasn't altogether a boy, was so excited.

"So those ones got my message, got the message I had the taleteller send them. Good. It's a start anyhow. Tomorrow brings whatever tomorrow brings. May it be better."

****

8: New Iraxas Complications

And a purely pulchritudinous physicality it was too, as always admired the 30-Year Man.

========

"Fired?" repeated Janna St Peche-Montressor.

She appeared confused, somewhere between shaking and smirking. Of course, if APM All-Eyes was inside her, her uncertain-sounding response might be attributable to Byron's Venus. A devil's proper reaction when his or her Great God of a father says you're fired is to spontaneously combust. Which would be a terrible waste of all that pulchritude.

"You're supposed to have swept my solarium, and the whole fucking building with it, of witch-stones."

Both life-defending Athenans and love-loving Afrites could stepping-stone-step through between-space, the Weird, Samsara, the dark grey matter of the Universal Substance, on tiny, usually glowing gemstones. While neither War Witches nor Lovely Ladies called their particular stepping stones Anthean Agates, like Melina Somata would have hers and her fellow witches' centuries ago, a tomato was a tomato no matter how you pronounced it. Tethys had heard much the same about Chinese writing on the Outer Earth.

"We did," protested the Fatman's daughter-in-law. Implicitly therefore, she hadn't used one to come into the solarium. Ergo APM All-Eyes was indeed inside her; had come in, bringing this Janna with her, via her Tvasitar-talisman. Whatever that was; one of her multitude of eyeballs perhaps.

"Oh," said Alpha Centauri, who must have just realized the same thing Tethys had. Which suggested Great Byron wasn't inside of him.

"Does that mean I'm rehired?"

"Just get on with it, Janna."

"Ferdinand Niarchos is outside and he's brought word from his father."

Now this, thought the legendary 30-Year Man, was almost as interesting as the story he'd been telling the Fatman. Ferdinand's father, Gomez Niarchos, was dead. He had, however, survived death as a Dead Thing Walking. Fortunately for his friends and relatives, Gomez was a Sangazur-animated Dead Thing rather than a Haddazur-motivated, hence zombified, humanoid eating machine. (Omnivores, brains for Haddit zombies were only considered delicacies.)

There was a substantial difference, in all senses of the word '*substantial*'. Sangazurs were symbiotic. They actually preserved a corpse's living intelligence, their in-life individuality. In other words, in return for a body to call their home they as good as prolonged a person's lifetime. On top of that, there were on record occasions when they, Sangs, preserved a person's fertility as well as his dignity in terms of not smelling too terribly off.

His father being a fan of Outer Earth history, Ferdinand Niarchos was probably named after the Aragonese king that Squiggly Tethys died (for the first time) in the service of off Otranto in 1481 their time. Weird Ferd, as Tethys shamelessly, sometimes to his face, referred to him, wasn't the result Gomez's post-terminal tumescence, though. Couldn't be – he was in his late thirties or early forties and Gomez hadn't died until 5964, not much more than 16-years ago now.

Tethys wasn't so certain about Weirdo's own children; the ones he acknowledged as his. To the best of his recollection none of them were even in their midteens. Yet Ferdinand sure had a lot of them for a fellow who wasn't even married. Then again, since when had marriage, any more so than monogamy, been a precondition for propagation of the species, any species? For some women, though, more so than men, it was a prerequisite for becoming a parent.

Very much unreasonably, Tethys learned on more than a few occasions – to his severe imperilment, if thankfully not always the termination of his then latest lifetime – that those same women, and more than a few men when he wasn't one of them, often expected monogamy to go with marriage to go with having children. All of which was a major league annoyance for someone like him, someone afflicted with an unshakeable, procreative imperative.

The only thing besides ambulation a Haddit zombie prolonged was a body's ability to consume crap. And, cannibals excepted, the crap a zombie consumed was seldom the same stuff a living person willingly consumed, all the more so if it generally required cooking. His current incarnation having narrowly escaped a Lemurian soup-pot not much more than six years ago on Shenon, Witch Isle, Tethys doubly appreciated the distinction. He appreciated the effective extension of Gomez's existence trebly so.

After nearly two thousand years of living with his own life-extending form of deviancy, he had long ago got over any sense of guilt or regret he once might have had of coming back in his own offspring or their offspring, who were thereupon rendered irreconcilably dead. (Hey, they were dying anyhow.)

Still, when someone who knew about his serial re-currency, as he sometimes put it, someone like Niarchos Pater to be precise, died saving the life of one of his previous incarnations, a male at that, Tethys reckoned Sang-symbionts were worthy of being considered the Good Dead.

Other than common courtesy, albeit mostly in living memory of his father, Tethys was pretty sure he didn't owe Weird Ferd anything. He nevertheless welcomed the opportunity to hear word from Gomez, whom, living and dead, but not gone, Centauri had used as his ace factotum – his man for all seasons, including the down and dirty ones that didn't have standard dates – for much of his time on the Inner Earth.

It wasn't to be. Not immediately anyhow.

========

"Shall we have Janna order a pizza, Al?"

"Good idea. Better yet, why don't you and Janna go make one."

========

A TETHYS TALE - JANNA FANGFINGERS: THE DISUNITION OF THE UNITIES OF LAZAREME – PART FIVE: SEDON'S MIGRAINE

========

Zalman Somata's gamble had failed. Pudding proof of that, in the form of his corpse, lay splat on the floor. Daughter Janna's gambit, her attempt to disunite the three Unities of Lazareme, would have succeeded, however, had she been able to hold onto the Trigregos Talismans. Which, as I'm about to relate, she hadn't been able to do.

Faster than my eye could see, His Unholiness, non-King Chaos, snatched them from her: Crinsom's Crown, Susal's Sword and Amateram's Mirror. Whereupon, her still on both her knees, her therefore kneeling beside daddy's dead body and mommy's grief-wracked, prone one, he released his breed brother and sister via applied willpower, theirs probably as much as his.

Release didn't make them happy. You could tell by the way they were visibly igniting lightning bolts in the midst of their ever-darkening, subtle matter bodies; as magnificent as they both were in their own ways. Which is why I refrained from using the triteness of simmering angry. Their was nothing simmering about their anger. But they didn't dare release it, did they. Wouldn't be polite, would it.

Abaddon was visibly happy; at least he was visibly smiling. He had been doing an uncharacteristic lot of that this last day of Antheal 5490 Year of the Dome – the month I can never resist noting, just because I love irony, not ironing, that's named after and therefore dedicated to Flowery Anthea, the Lazaremist Goddess of Life's springtime renewal.

Bad brood bro and always scintillating, if not titillating, sister both owed him for their liberation from, her, the Crimson Corona and, him, the Amateramirror. Abe now wore them in the same places Janna had when she had them, ever so momentarily, around his forehead and dangling off a noose-like necklace not unlike Harmony's ditto. Which, as Al's pal Homer may have tale-told in his day, reputedly wrought ruination on anyone who put it on. At least it did in Classical Greek terms, though it never seemed to harm Harmony.

Chaos got rid of his two extra arms; grew noticeably larger when did so. He now held his trident in his right hand and the Susasword in his left one, his preferred one. Just in case his triplet brother and sister missed the significance of that, the consequential Unity of Insanity pointed the sword at the body of the dead Master of two Weirdoms.

"That's what I think of inviolable oaths and Sedonic decrees."

As you, the three of you, will know, by Sedonic decree devils are not allowed to kill lesser beings. Of course, as I've noted when it was just Al and I here, they're also genetically incapable of fathering flesh and blood children on flesh and blood women without possessing flesh and blood men first. Or vice versa. Mind you, they're not supposed to enter another devil's devic protectorate without permission either.

Then, though, it's left up to the Master Deva whose protectorate it is to punish the offending devil; if they're caught, I should add. As he or she sees fit, I should additionally qualify. There have been cases when said Master Devas have actually cathonitized equally said offending devils. However, in the past it has always fallen to the Moloch Sedon to punish wilful murder. And, as far as I've heard, he always has previously. Instantly.

Needless to say, he didn't this time. Was it because he wasn't upstairs anymore? Unlikely – how could there even be an upstairs, a Sedon Sphere, without a Moloch Sedon to keep it up let alone over under sideways down? So, did that mean Zalman Somata was not a lesser being? Let's say yes and leave it at that, if only because nothing happened, which makes it your elephant, Ferd, as in irrelevant if not irreverent.

Needs be I now flip to the obverse of that coin. Other devils were just as authorized to exact whatever punishments they deemed necessary. All they really needed was the wherewithal to do so. And in my estimation, as I mentioned to Al already, together Balance and Order were mightier than Chaos. Except they were now in his debt. For the time being. Not that that mattered a hill of hooters at a hamburger joint.

"I declare you rogue," pronounced Harmony sternly – thus, as was her wont as a rarely winged inspiration for Egyptian Isis or a never-blindfolded Lady Justice, rendering judgement.

"Let neither man nor devil give you succour."

Abe Chaos laughed in her even then fabulously fetching face. "Are we not the sons and daughters of the first born and greatest of the Great Gods, Thrygragos Lazareme? Is not complete liberty our birthright? By what laughable presumption of Almightiest Grinning Godhood have you to say otherwise? Should the Moloch Himself appear before me this moment, I shall deal no differently with him."

It wasn't bravado; it was provocation, a challenge. And no Grandfather Sedon, no howsoever-long-missing Deity of the Dome, either rose nor descended to accept it. "Be gone then, traitors to our own father," he commanded them. "You are no longer of my family." His breed sister whipped her chains around and obligingly went away.

Thunder & Lightning, he of the Sparking Azuras and the protozurs his Lightning Sword emitted like seeds on fallow ground – just like APM does her little angels when it strikes her fancy – removed just that, his Lightning Sword, from its scabbard. Just as lovely Harmony had just done, lordly Yajur didn't brandish it as if about to attack. On the contrary, he cut a gash through Samsara.

As he stepped through it, he warned his immediate brother: "We'll have a reckoning, you and I. And without Harmony around to balance us off against each other."

"So be it, Idiot Order. Just remember this. If you hadn't taken Gravedigger's head, none of this would have happened."

"Let the Lord above us all attend to that." That said, Yajur left the Weirdom of Kanin City for the last time.

"Lord above us all – ha! If he dared to he'd have already done so."

=========

With the death of Janna's blood-father, the First War Between the Living and the Dead commenced in earnest. Thereafter everyone who died in the struggle to unseat the Unholy One walked anew, as a dead thing. Zuvem Nergalis, Gravedigger, Devil Doom, the Planter to Vetala's Grower and Yama's Reaper, was having his revenge.

And Dark Sedon, wherever he was, was answering the challenge of Chaos in kind.

=========

Time Quakes had been plaguing Marutia, Sedon's Cheek, since Thrygragos Varuna Mithras played Chronoking Kronos on Thrygragon. Minor league mercifully, they only hit in the Cheek Lands. Also not to diminish the devastation they cause for those they hit, they often only strike in small, isolated segments of the Cheeks. I'm not sure how far-ranging the Time Quake of 5489 was – something else I mentioned to Al when you and our Janna weren't around earlier – but it was probably much larger than the one that apparently hit that selfsame baleful day, Zal's birth and death day both.

It was certainly much more normal, as in much more localized, than the previous year's massive quake. It definitely didn't strike Kanin City, where Sraddha and I were witnessing Zal's retaliatory, um, execution, for he didn't stand a chance against Abe Chaos, with or with out the Susasword coming into play. But, in our absence, it did hit the northern steppes of the Diluvia Mountain Range on down into the canal zone where we'd been toiling – he supervising, me sort of engineering in that I sketched what he wanted done – for a number of years by then.

Then as now Diluvia – after Diluvia Ran, the Mithradite Apocalyptic of, what else?, Flood – was the dreariest place on the Whole Earth. Legend had it rain had been falling non-stop there since the Genesea or Great Flood of Genesis. And in all my centuries on this or any other planet, not that I've been on any other planet, that's one of a very few legends I've never found cause to dispute.

The mountains themselves were thought impassable. That wasn't just because there weren't any passes either, though there weren't. Not over top them there weren't. Or so I understand, also without any cause to dispute. Too much water was forever falling. There was the concomitant, never-ending threat of landslides. Plus, and this is why I'll say what I will say, there was constant tectonic activity; not the threat thereof. It was easier to traverse the four oceans of Sedon's Head than to cross Diluvia.

More at sister Janna's insistence than his – he swore he'd go after Uncle Abe for killing his Zal-dad, which would only amount to a form of assisted suicide given Chaos's current temperament – I'd drawn Sraddha Somata back to his command post in charge of the canal-building, southernmost contingent of Kanin's still remarkably loyal army. (I'd stayed behind, albeit more at Abe's insistence than ex-darling Janna's – Chaos hated drinking alone.)

Shreds and his pre-assigned forces were bivouacked on the steppes Cheek-side of the mountain range when yet another Time Quake struck. And this one, having recounted this story any number of times, is why I said what I said seconds earlier. I reckon it was coupled with an actual earthquake or its aftershock.

At any rate, from what I understand dick-dildo, it was only a matter of hours more so than days before red-skinned Iraches from the other side of Diluvia began pouring almost literally out of the infra-mountains' cave-system; the very thing Shreds and his men, me once among them, were secretly searching for, as it happened. (Damn near anyone could re-dredge canals that were already damn near bottomless, hence why they still exist, let me tell you that for a non-coital quickie.)

Until then, at least in terms of verifiable history, the cave-system was more rumour than reality. In truth, Sraddha and his men had rarely ever seen an Irache before that night. Yet here they were, in their hundreds, perhaps even in their thousands. Although Shreds described it as a flight rather than an invasion, I think they were waiting for just such an opportunity. If so then they must have been massing in anticipation of the Time or Combination Quake. Which I grant you bespeaks of foreknowledge and neither before nor since have Time Quakes been predictable. Of course that doesn't negate the possibility of devil-doing. Hint, hint.

Whatever the case, flight or invasion, the Marutians under his command were at a decided disadvantage. They'd been used to metal, armour and, of late, primitive guns brought in from Apple Isle and the Head's occipital regions where Kronos Quakes didn't hit. Now, because one had, they were reduced to the same weaponry as the newcomers. And the Iraches had never used anything except sticks, stones, spears, atlatls, bows, and arrows.

If you'll permit an Outer Earth allusion, it was as if the American Indians invaded Spain, albeit on foot, with neither boats or horses to carry them, not the other way around.

Many of Sraddha's veteran elite, and not just his officers, had fought through Time Quakes previously. He'd hand-picked and indeed partially equipped many of them for just that eventuality. Much better disciplined than the Iraches, his troops managed to protect their position. They formed an enclave, a virtual island in the midst of red skins, and held it.

When he finally lay down in his tent, after two days without rest, Sraddha wanted only sleep. What he found instead were two female devils. Hence the hint, hint, earlier on. Their immediate need was sex, not conquest – though, hey, sometimes what's one without the other? When he stepped out of his tent, three days later, Sraddha was as sore and exhausted as he had been in his entire life.

Not surprisingly given the devils he made love to were bedazzling Belialma and Nergal Vetala. A Mithradite Moon Goddess devils addressed as Fecundity for reasons that shall shortly become paramount, the Nergalids' Grower was no slouch in the looks department either – so long as you don't mind greenish-tinged skin and thumbs on the wrong hands, if she'd gone that route. Which, Shreds later confided to Squiggly-me, she did a few times, albeit at his request. Janna's twin was almost as experimental as Janna herself, I'm reliably informed.

Due to Abe Chaos – her onetime lover, recall – his unconscionable assault on both her and Pandemonium, her Bastion of Bliss therein, Bouncing Belle had been deposed as Prime Sinistral of Satanwyck a couple of years earlier. Her replacement was the covetous Cupid, Sinistral Envy, Robin Goodfellow aka Bobby Badboy. However, he only exiled her.

While nobody, at least to my knowledge, ever bothered to learn what had become of her after her disgrace, she must have sought, and evidently found, refuge in what was then called Iraxas but began being called Hadd, as in *'had it'*, not all that long after the events I'm describing took place.

On a map of the Headworld, the likes of which your father, Ferd, has helped draw up over the years, the land beyond the Diluvian Mountain Range is generally noted as the Penile Peninsula. Iraxas is its shaft while Krachla is its tip. Betwixt and between Iraxas is the aptly named Circumcision Canal whereas the archipelago below it are called the Panic Isles.

Never one for rude or outré terms I usually refer to its totality as Sedon Mutton Chop, though for some that's a suggestive term in and of itself.

========

Tethys paused for a mouthful of pizza. It was good, too, all the more remarkably considering he helped prepare it. Although an accomplished artist in most media, he preferred praising the chef to being one. "Maybe, since there's a lady present, and a lovely one at that, perhaps I'd best refer to it as Sedon's Sideburn."

Predictably Janna St Peche-Montressor, the member third of his audience in the solarium besides the Fatman and Governor Niarchos, rose to the bait.

"Can the cracks, Jordy, and get on with it. Otherwise you'll be wearing that pizza."

"Your wish is my desire," he grinned.

"Not all of it, I'll wager," said Ferdinand, also predictably.

========

Since, circa 500 years ago, there were no such places as Free Iraxas, on the Cattail, nor New Iraxas, Godbad's north-easternmost province, which you so admirably administer, Ferd, what's now called Hadd was then the Iraches' sole homeland. Being in the southern parts of the Western Head, it lay in an area that traditionally belonged to Byron Spawn. However, as I'm sure none of you history buffs needs reminding, Nergal Vetala had taken it as her protectorate during the expansion of the Thanatoids' Lathakran empire in the Dome's 48th Century.

For many centuries, maybe even a few millennia before that, Vanthysces, Byron's Reaper, didn't so much rule Iraxas as administered it on behalf of the entire tribe. Rather than fleeing to Godbad like most of his brothers and sisters, he stood his ground and was cathonitized for his troubles. The Iraches, like the Lemurians who lived on its coasts, were never big on Byronics but they were big on Vetala, unless it was just the moon she personified. Then again, they may have adopted her for her beauty as much as in gratitude for their liberation.

To momentarily return to Sraddha Somata's observation that theirs was more flight than invasion, it could well have been a bit both. I allow that possibility because, at that time, crusading armies of Byronics were in the process of seeking to re-establish their claim to Sedon's, um, Sideburn. Certainly they'd already managed to wrest back control of Krachla, sending the now degenerate Lathakran Fire Kings scurrying homeward.

Neither were the Byronics just having their way on, all right, the Penile Peninsula. On the eastern side of the Internal Ocean of Akadan, on the Cattail Peninsula, the Bandradin race was seemingly converting to faith in Great Byron en masse. As I said to Al earlier, it was inarguably a bad time to be alive, especially if you were a peaceful sort like me. The whole Head was in such a state of constant turmoil I called a book I wrote about the era *'Sedon's Migraine'*.

So it could well be the two Mithradite Master Devas had been driven north at least in part to escape Byronic fanatics and the killing-efficiency of their war machine. Devils do need their worshippers after all and fanaticism breeds slaughter; always has, on both sides of the Dome. Hasn't been a war yet when God wasn't on the side of warriors on every side of the conflict. It's just a matter of which god, isn't it?

The loser's is the evil one; the winner's the great and good one. Whoever said Godbucks were the root of all-evil, and I know it wasn't you, Al, had it all wrong. Religion is the root of all-evil. It's also the route of all-evil. Put it another way: The god of the victors wins because there are more victims on all the other sides.

By that logic, therefore, it follows that so many of Nergal Vetala's chosen people followed them, the two Mithradites, into the Cheeks because, historically speaking, it was more the Iraches who chose her than the other way around, wasn't it? And the Byronics weren't going to forget that, were they?

As I tend to repeat sometimes ad nauseam, by Sedonic decree devils aren't allowed to kill lesser beings. Killing mortals, who by definition are lesser beings, is a waste of potential worshippers. At least so we mere mortals are instructed our devilgods are instructed. Devic adherents killing in the name of devils isn't the same as devils doing the killing themselves, is it? Couldn't be.

Otherwise the Sedon Sphere would be full of stars and the entire Head would be a devil-free zone. Which would sort of defeat the whole purpose of Cathonia.

========

"Hmm ..." said Tethys. It was a meaningful pause. Then he made it more than that. "Or should I say mm-good?" He meaningfully-eyed the last piece of pizza.

"Oh go ahead, Jordy," provided Janna. "I'm not much of a meat-eater anyways."

"Not you too, Janna," said Centauri, trying not to groan. "Bad enough I have to sit through double-entendres from Mr Tethys and Mr Niarchos without you joining in."

In formal settings, which this wasn't, the Fatman made a point of referring to his guests in just that way, formally. In informal settings, which this was, when he did so he was making a joke. No one ever laughed at his jokes. In fact, it was almost a joke no one ever did. Laughter did not ensue.

"Et tu, Mr Centauri," obligingly deadpanned Niarchos.

"Weirdo's right, Al," the Legendarian agreed. "That was brutal."

========

Bear in mind as well that Nergal Vetala was still Vulva-Vetala, a moon goddess who more like specialized in fertility, though her version off it was akin to being the devic goddess of fertilizer. Think of her as the middle part of the three Nergalids, ancient deities of cultivation. Zuvem Nergalis planted the seeds, Nergal Vetala had them, and Yama Nergal harvested them.

Fecundity, as they called her to her face, procreated profusely, giving birth up to 13 times a year. In other words, she waxed and waned with the moon on a hence more than monthly basis. But she didn't just mate at the time of the New Moon. Many, many, many times she took mortal lovers. Many, many, many more times she took over women who gave birth to her resultant half-children. Or quarter-children, if you prefer, since she was only ever half of one half-parent – the female half, to be absolutely precise.

Oddly, unusually for deviants they were often short-lived. Just as strangely, they almost invariably died in ignominy. In a similar, what?, downbeat way, when she was altogether herself and mating with devils, the Vetalazurs she consequently bore were beyond as next-to-useless as most azuras. The only things they could possess were dead things that rotted on their feet and/or fell apart in a steady drizzle.

The Nergalid may or may not have known who Sraddha Somata was but Lady Lust definitely did. Along with her brood sister and fellow Apple Goddess, Divine Coueranna or, to many devils, Kore-Concord, she was the eldest Mithradite left active. As such, she was behind the claims her lower-born brothers and sisters made on Zal-Mel's terrible twins at their birth and again later when they tried to make off with Janna's child, not half-child, by Uncle Abe Chaos.

Both devils harboured a shared desire for revenge. Belialma wanted to avenge herself against the Unity of Chaos for two main reasons. Firstly, his Unholiness jilted her in favour of a mere mortal, Sraddha's twin sister – Harmony, the Unity of Balance's quarter-daughter by half-father, Harm's own father, Thrygragos Every-man, as most everyone now realized. Secondly, he'd brutalized her so disgracefully she couldn't forestall Robby Brat-boy's seizure of her hellish throne. Or the footstool beside it, if rightful Demon King Sedon happened to come downstairs for a visit and felt like sitting in it.

By contrast, here we go with flight versus invasion again, Vetala wanted to get even with the Byron Spawn, and their adherents, for routing her and her Iraches from their homeland. Together they came up with a complicated scheme to wreak vengeance on all their enemies. Sraddha was the linchpin for both of them.

Which isn't to say they lynched him, just kept him busy not yet mirror-balling.

========

"Upon reflection, pun intended, they should never have let him loose long enough to return to Kanin City."

========

Throughout 5491 allegiances changed. It no longer became a matter of all against Unholy Abaddon and the Weirdom of Kanin City. Mithras's eponymous Primary Apocalyptics, War and Death in particular, though Disease and Disaster were never faraway, were in ascendancy. So too were the so-called Lesser Apocalyptics, Mithradites the lot – and there certainly were a lot of them. Still are, too; though, purely for storytelling purposes, allow me to double-underline I'm tongue-talking-totally of Mithradite Apocalyptics.

With the slain rising after every battle, after every food shortage, every plague, natural disaster, drought, pestilential infestation, flood, even after every death by accident or infirmity, it quickly became a matter of the Living against the Dead, hence the First War thereof. Clearly, Lazareme Spawn had to join in on behalf of the Living. Plus, to be successful they either had to re-conscript Chaos, their finest warrior, or work their way around him. They chose the latter and, for a time, were quite effective.

It seems their Grandfather Sedon's dictum that devils must never kill a lesser being didn't apply to Dead Things, including ones possessed by Sangazurs, like your yet-formidable father is today, Ferd. Even if it did, the Moloch Himself, the acknowledged king of devils and demons both, had done nothing to Abe Chaos for slaying Zalman Somata. Perhaps Sed's threats were meaningless after all.

Thinking themselves therefore immune from retribution, the Lazaremists took to the field and fought unrestrained by any compunctions. They became abominations of their former selves. But, and here I'd accept arguably, their cause was just. I mean really, when it comes right down to dust what use are things that should be dust, or heading that way, except to take up space and exhaust resources intended for keeping regular folks alive and praying to their god-devils?

No matter how complicit certain Utopians and near-Utopians were in any of this, in their view Mithradites had been behind much of what went wrong at first and was now growing worse exponentially. That determined not just by them, Lazareme extremists consequently banned worship of Mithras Spawn throughout the vast plains of Marutia. This made sense from a strategic point of view. Devils fed off the adulation of their adherents. It was also easy to enforce. What non-azura sentient would pray to a god who supported the forces of the Dead?

In order to secure more power for themselves, the Lazareme Spawn further banned the worship of Unmoving Byron and any of his offspring. On the surface, this was a little harder to understand but Lord Yajur, commander-in-chief of the Living, made it clear that he blamed Thrygragos Byron, not Unholy Abaddon, for the whole sorry mess Sedon's Head had become.

Which I have to admit sounds counterintuitive but there you have it.

========

"Let's pause for a few minutes," suggested Jordan Tethys, interrupting himself again, "In order to consider Yajur's perspective."

========

"From, roughly, YD 2000, until Abe decapitated their father, Thrygragos Varuna Mithras, on Thrygragon, the 25th of Tantalar 4376 YD, Mithradites pretty much had their own way. Not for nothing was the history of the Head between 2000 and 4400 Years of the Dome known as the Age of Mithras.

"Since then it had been the Age of Lazareme. No doubt the Mithradites were determined that there would be no Age of Byron. No doubt they were equally determined that the Age of Lazareme had to end. To do that, they had to disunite the Unities. More, to do that they had to destroy the Unities. Point being, on the other side of the coin, if there was to be an Age of Byron, the age of Lazareme still had to end and the Unities still had to be destroyed – and, since everyone here knows it, they were! Question is, who destroyed whom?

"Credit for the plot has been ascribed variously to Lady Lust, Divine Coueranna, Cruel Plathon, the three Nergalids, or even Mater Matare and the rest of the Apocalyptics. Coueranna, though, Kore of the Many Names, kept to herself, hiding away in her Hell. Plathon, the Bull of Mithras, was her link to the outside Head and is considered a candidate mostly because he is a member of the third or fourth litter born to Mithras. Then again, so is Zuvem Nergalis, an acknowledged fourth, not a disputable third, though most consider the Bull more intelligent.

"Other than his brief appearance, notable as it was, in the birth room of Johann-George, Plathon – Kind, Cruel or Indifferent, dependent on your perspective – had little to do with the events I've been describing. That isn't to say he and Kore weren't the guiding light behind-the-scenes; just to say there's no evidence they were.

"Certainly their Mithrant Legionnaires form the largest army on the Upper Head but, more and more, they fell back toward the Gulf of Corona, trying to hold onto their own. Similarly, I dismiss speculation that the Apocalyptics were the primary instigators of the conspiracy to unseat the non-rulers of Kanin City and its fast-fracturing, so-called Mastery.

"True, the Medusa, who named herself Mater Matare, Mother Murder, on Thrygragon, had a lot to gain if she realized the right to have children, she in her shells, by Abaddon's son, if he and Janna Somata had a son. However, once again, the same could be said of Zuvem Nergalis, who was due to mate with the Master of Kanin City if Abaddon and Janna had a daughter. Of course, too, or three, if any child Abe and Janna had proved susceptible to possession they could half-have the parentage of that son or daughter's children.

"However, due to the doom Devil Doom himself pronounced on Janna there wasn't much hope of any of that anymore. Janna's subsequent children were all stillborn. So, if only for his unmitigated stupidity, I can't credit the Nergalid Gravedigger for being anything more than an expendable component of a much grander design. Yajur atomized his body, his head was buried only Irisiel Mercherm knew where, and Ursine Bardol had turned over his power focus, his Brainrock spade, to Harmony for disposal and/or safekeeping.

"As for the two remaining Nergalids, Yama and Vetala, there is no question both of them played major roles in the Disunition of the Unities. Myself, I consider them functionaries; and perhaps, especially in the case of Vetala, unwitting ones. No, as important as the Nergalids were to the way things turned out, they were no more the masterminds than myrionymous Kore, Plathon, the Apocalyptics, or the devils of Satanwyck, Lust and Envy.

"Who then was the brains? Again, I can confidently state it wasn't Dream, Cold or Heat, Phantast or the Parents Thanatos, Tantal of Lathakra and Methandra still also of Mythland, the Jewel of Sedon's Crown. The three of them made up the first known litter of Varuna Mithras but they weren't even Headworld players anymore.

"As confirmed hundreds of years prior to the start of the First War between the Living and the Dead; as could be, as today, reconfirmed just by looking up at the night's sky; Dark Sedon cathonitized Phantast the Dreamweaver for his part in the debacle that became known as the Crimson Conspiracy. And that ended almost fifteen hundred years prior to the time of Sedon's Migraine, the sub-titular Disunition of the Unities.

"Since his encounter with the Idiot Twins, Tammuz and Osiraq, in 4825 YD, Tantal was in the midst of a thousand year sleep; eleven hundred year sleep, more like, as it turned out. His Scarlet Empress, Mithras's Virgin, was constantly at his side, albeit in a thousand-plus-year sleep of her own. At his side quite literally; at least they were reputedly, as in according to Abe Chaos.

"At the risk of repeating myself, he said he'd laid them together in the same bed; butt-naked, unless it's buck-naked, to boot, if only for a hoot. I shouldn't have to add '*reputedly*' but I will, and just did, in case Abe added lying to his obviously bottomless bucket of bents. I know I never ventured up into the heights of La-thakra's spine to verify who slept where and weren't wearing. I doubt anyone else did either. At any rate, neither Tantal nor Methandra return to the history of the Headworld until this very century.

"Although there is no satisfactory answer to this question, let's consider the evidence of the stars. If a devil is cathonitized – what Outer Earth mythologists call catasterized and most god-devils actually, and understandably, call ill-starring – his or her star would appear in the Cathonic Dome, the primary sky above, and indeed below, Sedon's Head. This, Cathonia, the Sedon Sphere, is, duh, because it's made up of his essence, Grandfather Sedon's zone to do with as he pleases. He treats it much like devils treat the Prison Beach of Incain, as a place where devils can be held indefinitely.

"Over the millennia, a large number of devils have been incarcerated within its Mandroid Monster Maker, the Gynosphinx who fancies herself All the Invincible but, as demonstrated on Thrygragon, is nothing of the sort. She nevertheless stores them, if you will, in a kind of enforced sleep of their own.

"A famous example is Abdullah Ziderite. Even though, when it comes to Mith-radites, not even Mithras was sure what order they were born in, I'll call him a sixth-born for the sake of simplicity. He was Mithras's highest born Persian or Earth Magician and, as near as I can make out, he has been inside All for roughly four thousand years.

"Another example is the Unnameable, so-called, though I've heard him or her or it given a bunch names. As a she, Lamia comes to mind; as a whatever, Demo-gorgon stands out. I'll stick to the Unnameable and say that, um, she or, rather, her power focus played a bordering on incalculably important role in Thrygragon's denouement. I'll also say that, no matter how many devils it can take out, as in im-mobilize, I hold it belonged to a solitary devil, one of Mithras's Twelfth, Vetala and Kala Tal's sexless, immediate sibling.

"After, according to more than a few tee-tee-tails I've read, Dark Sedon refused to accept the aforementioned Idiot Twins in Cathonia, they were stuck there too. And, if the rumours are accurate, their essence – that of Ziderite, whom devils also call Magnetism, the Unnameable and the Idiots, to name only a few of her more, um, permanent guests – currently power Incain's overseer, the aforementioned ages-old, pre-Flood Female Sphinx.

"For the record, not that it matters a fart of beans to my story, All can still be-come mobile; this despite Pyrame's cathonitization thirty years ago for attempting to re-conquer Cabalarkon, the Weirdom, and with it, Cabalarkon, the Undying Utopian Sedon regards as his father. In fact, Janna, I have it on good report Aortic Tsishah, the Mother Superior of the Anthean, Mariamnic and your own Athenan Sisterhoods, has been seen riding her."

On good report for Tethys meant Tethys himself. In 5974 he, in his current incarnation, was on Shenon, Witch Isle, when he saw Tsishah ride All, in her common, be-winged female sphinx form. It wasn't long thereafter that he and one of his companions, Saladin Devason, the current Master of Weir, was rescued from the Lemurian soup-pot; an experience he sometimes used as a non-Sedonic, tongue-in-cheek argument for vegetarianism. Recalling that ordeal still made him sneeze. The Lemurians spices were pungent to say the least.

"Byron Spawn use Incain as an alternative to cathonitizing their own kind. Pyrame Silverstar, the Pauper Priestess, the Mithraic half-mother of Sedon's sedons, the mortal-mystical foundations of the Sedon Sphere, considered it her protectorate until she was cathonitized thirty odd years ago. Which by the way, Pyrame being atomized for the second time this century, is a worrisome development. All the more so given how long it's lasted, but that's something else I don't intend to get into right now.

"It is often preferable to deal with rogue devils by imprisoning them in Incain where, if you've the mind's eye to see, their sleeping bodies can actually be seen. There, also, their fingerprint-like essences can be monitored in order to doubly demonstrate they're still present. Not that anyone has ever escaped from All's Incain. Probably no one ever will either. It's just not in the latter day Mother Machine's programming to allow escapes.

"Besides, how you'd ever come conscious long enough to even plan an escape is beyond me. Furthermore, as I understand it anyhow, even to attempt one automatically causes self-cathonitization. However, because of that programming, but also because all devils, not just the Libertine and the Unmoving One are genetically bound by their oaths, many devils have served time in Incain and been released accordingly.

"By contrast cathonitization is a much more permanent way of handling rogues. Again to the best of my knowledge, until he had to let the Pauper go in the mid-twenties, the Moloch Sedon has only ever released one devil he confined therein, a third-born Byron Spawn by the name of Nevair Neverknight.

"Like Phantast Thanatos, he was cathonitized as a direct consequence of the Crimson Conspiracy. Except, it turned out he was falsely accused by Kore-Eris, Kore-Discord, Marut Kanin, Fitna Marutia or just plain Strife, whose star many misidentified with what was actually Phantast's until Pyrame let it be known which one of them Sedon did cathonitize circa 4000 YD. As for Strife's ongoing fate, well, now's not the time to get into that either.

"Consider capital punishment, especially when we're talking about devils. A dead devil leaves no body. How could he or she leave a body when part of killing a devil involves atomizing that body? Then you have to bury the severed head, preferably without its extra eye, exactly a thousand miles away from where you atomized its body.

"As for the devil's power focus, his or hers Tvasitar-trinkets, the usual thing to do is melt it away in the lava lake of Sedon's Peak. Which is what Harmony did to Strife's Golden Apple of Discord when she tossed her into the molten Brainrock therein after the Crimson Conspiracy ended so badly for all concerned, including I might add Rumour of Lazareme, whose quill I inherit lifetime after lifetime. Either that or have someone like Harmony, or something like All, who doesn't think of herself as a thing, hold onto it just in case somebody else, doesn't have to be a devil, might find a use for it later.

"A variant method of dealing with rogue devils is what the Thanatoids of Lathakra did during the expansion of their empire. Many times they or their cronies, including Unholy Abaddon and Byron's firstborn Silverclouds, beat devils into submission. Occasionally, though, a no-matter-how-badly-beaten devil refused to submit to their will. This usually happened when the devil had a large and faithful following of his or her own. In that case, they carved his or her third eyes out of their skulls and secreted them in rings made by Tvasitar Smithmonger, the devic Prometheus, and according to some – though not me – ensorcelled by Methandra of Mythland.

"At the same time they filled transparent Tantaluses – named after Tantal naturally – specially prepared by the Anvil Artificer with the selfsame devils' talismans. At which point they squirreled both of them away, the Tantaluses and bags containing the rings, separately.

"The former, via the Wandering SAG Gap, which back then, as it still may, adhered to Methandra once a decade, they sent to the Outer Earth. There, you may recall one, two, or maybe even three of them were recovered some four decades ago, thus precipitating what Al here, who isn't supposed to know anything about it, calls the Secret War of Supranormals. As for the latter, the rings, well, that's yet another subject beyond the scope of this recitation.

"Suffice it to say that, first of all, that some devils left more than just a few of them with Tvasitar Smithmonger at his Prometheum atop Sedon's Peak. Anvil packed a kibisis full of the things that Harmony got hold of, howsoever painfully for both of them. She passed said kibisis or bottomless bag on to me, with instructions to bring it up to Pyrame Silverstar, who was then occupying the Master of the Weirdom of Cabalarkon. The long-terms results of that bitty bit of brilliancy were disastrous, as in Ghostlands disastrous.

"Second of all, as for presumably – because no one seem to have kept score – most of the rest that we know about to date, while the Scarlet Seeress has always been red-faced, she was shame-faced after she lost track of the two pan-dimensional Shangri-Las, Tivatimsa and Nikaya, where she hid them. Needless to say, this was sometime before the Idiot Twins blew themselves apart, rendering the Elysian Fields the Ghostlands, later on in 4825.

"Perhaps, however, what's needful to say, in all fairness to the War Witches' Great Goddess, is that she probably wouldn't have lost track of them if she, alongside King Cold, hadn't tried to absorb what the Atomic Idiots kept on putting out once they did blow. And, in all fairness to Abe Chaos, whom I don't want to slag either, he did pull both Thanatoids out of their way before they could follow Mithras into the great beyond unknown.

"In theory, not that they have as yet time-wise, all those death-dealing techniques might work for billions of years. With respect to the decapitation method that, with some assistance from his siblings, Ursine Bardol and the Angelus, Irisiel Mercherm, Yajur used to '*kill*' Zuvem Nergalis the day Johann-George was born, don't forget the natural forces of any planet. Earthquakes, volcanic eruptions, mountain-building, plate tectonics, and suchlike, that's what I mean by that.

"Bury the severed head of a slain devil a thousand miles away from where you atomized the body and it might stay dead; might being the operable word here. What if the dead person's head is removed from its exact location? Simple. The devil lives anew!" Jordan Tethys gulped back a pilsner in one extended glug. None of his three-person audience, Centauri, Niarchos and Janna St Peche-Montressor, who ordinarily didn't drink, followed suit. Nor did they interrupt him.

"Let's revisit Thrygragon, the feast-day as well as death-day of third-born Thrygragos Varuna Mithras – so far, so dead, I should qualify. Harmony, having got hold of the Unnameable's stone-staring neck-noodle, got Mr Myth's undivided attention. Thereby catching him in its gaze, she petrified him where he stood. Whereupon his Unholiness, Abaddon himself, quite literally wrenched Great Godly skull off Great Godly shoulders – thus pretty much putting paid to Truth, Light, Justice and so much more, if one can believe Mithras's own propaganda.

"The Medusa, just that day self-renamed Mater Matare, Mother Murder, attempted to devour Deva Daddy's shining soul; his essence or spirit-self, if you prefer. And, allowing for my suspicious nature, thus my above qualification, who can say whether she was successful or not? Had she thought of it perhaps she should have swallowed his third eye in order to be sure, just as Vladuca Fangfingers did Devil Zuvem Doom's on the day of Johann-George's birth.

"Other devils, prominently Abe's fellow Unities and Unmoving Byron, his firstborn Silverclouds together with all six of his commonest Nucleoids, APM therefore included, pulverized Myth's body on the spot it fell, in the midst of the henceforth Medusa's Meadows, deep within the Gregarian Fields, the Mole of Sedon's Cheek. Not satisfied with that, every devil there pebbles-pocketed – more like stones-secreted in their Tvasitar-trinkets or power foci – the leftover, Great Godly hunks and chunks.

"Which led, so I'm told, by him, Lazareme, to the firstborn Great God, aka almost as commonly Thrygragos Everyman, uttering the thereafter immortalized phrase: *'Everybody must get stones'*. (As an uncanny aside, those very words, albeit with a *'d'*, not an *'s'*, have been echoing ever so weirdly – sorry Ferd – on not just the western Outer Earth since the mid-Sixties. It's almost as if Lazareme was reciting them out of time, as it were: as if he first heard them then, in the Sixties, and afterwards repeated them way back when, on Thrygragon.)

"Be that as it may, that Great God didn't bury his baby brother's head a thousand miles from where they disintegrated his bodily balance. Instead, he laid it on his pallet, making a pillow out of it. That place, Tympani, in the Aural Sea, Sedon's Ear, is known to this day as the Isle of the Undying One and there, if you knew where to look between-space, you can still find the Libertine sleeping atop said severed, then shattered skull.

"I've no proof Mithras survived of course. Furthermore, I don't think Lazareme was behind the Disunition of his own firstborn. If I was to point a finger, I'd agree with Lord Order and blame Great Byron more so than Lady Lust and her younger sibs, the one who nevertheless catch most of the blame, particularly from Byronics. Which shouldn't surprise anyone. What tribe would acknowledge culpability for a war that, at its height, claimed the lives of well over half of those alive when it began?"

Tethys glanced at the copy of the Odyssey lying on the coffee table. His eyes suddenly brightened noticeably. "But," he blurted as if in an epiphany, "What if Mithras had a litter that predated Phantast, Methandra and Tantal; that came before Coueranna, Marut Kanin and Belialma; Zuvem-Gravedigger, Domdaniel-Pride and bullish Plathon; or any other Mithradites, such as Pyrame and her Ninth, the rest of the Nergalids, the Apocalyptics, and the devils of Pandemonium?"

That said, he seemed to reconsider this theory briefly. "Mind you, there is no firm evidence to suggest Mithras had a hidden litter. There are, I'm informed by the likes of pal Pyrame and, yes, Mithras himself, ample indicators that a malevolent force has been at work amongst the always disputatious Mithradites since well before devazurs came to Earth.

"That force has a name: Judge Druj or Ahriman, the original Prince of Darkness, the flip side of the Dualists' Deity."

The Fatman perked up at this. "You're talking Persian fire-faiths: that of the Magi and Zoroastrianism; then, much later on, that of the Heretical Christian, Mani or Manichaeus. You're equating Mithras with Ahura Mazda or Ormuzd, the Lord of Light. And why not? Ahura Mazda does sound a little like Varuna Mithras."

"That's what Mithras himself used to say, Al. I should know, too. For a mite more than a couple of centuries pre-Thrygragon, I used to spend hours drinking his surprisingly enjoyable beer up there atop Theopolis Hill, in his still-standing Mithradium, over on Apple Isle. To tongue-loosening effect, I might add. And, even though he did not imbibe anything containing alcohol, it often involved us tale-sharing as well as just me tale-telling."

"Didn't non-heretical Christians equate Mithras with St Michael?" contributed Janna St Peche-Montressor, not really looking for confirmation.

"The warrior angel," Tethys agreed. "Or Archangel, I guess, put more correctly. Ahriman was the dragon he's so often depicted slaying, like St George, hence Ahriman being associated with Satan, the Eternal Antagonist, out there. Of course, out there doesn't know anything about Sedon, who actually goes out of his way to look satanic."

"I seem to recall hearing something about a VAM Entity," said Niarchos.

"Then your hearing must be as weird as everything else about you," joked Tethys.

========

The Inner and the Outer Earth retained many commonalities from its Whole Earth days. One of them was language. Only here, on the Inner Earth, what some would call pre-Babel-Babble others, like Jordan Tethys, would call Sedon-Speak. Hence the ability for, say, a Mayan who came through the Dome to his particular Shadowland to understand, say, a Kyrgyz speaking his own language. In that respect Sedon's Head was a good place.

Then there was this never-remembered fellow who was so fond of making dramatic entrances out of the air itself. He currently called himself Daemonicus, hardly for the first time. Part of him did anyhow, the part of him currently on the Outer Earth. He was not a good thing. He did, however, have an engaging smile.

It had been a narrow thing but now it looked like the launching of the Cosmic Express would go ahead as planned. He said to those in his audience who were still conscious, most of whom would be scurrying off to change their pants as soon as he dematerialized: **"Tomorrow brings whatever tomorrow brings. May it be better, not bitter."**

This Daemonicus was hardly alone in expressing such a sentiment. Tethys was right about the Thanatoids of Lathakra. They had awakened not long after the turn of the 60ᵗʰ Century of the Dome. They had their way there wouldn't be a 61ˢᵗ Century because, within a decade or so of them getting their children back, there wouldn't be a Cathonic Dome anymore.

Wouldn't be a Moloch Sedon either, unless you counted the god-almightiest biggest statue on the reunited planet. That tomorrow come, things would indeed be infinitely better.

****

9: Fiendish Deductions

A Daemonicus on the outside linked to a certain just as never-remembered, ever-smiling fiend on the inside, how was that possible? As it happened it boiled down to an excess body. Just because you didn't need the one that kept you solid for multiple centuries anymore, why waste it? The subtle matter bodies of debrained demons were interchangeable, lots of people wore demons, and the formidable fellow wearing the one on the outside made good use of it.

Being re-formable it helped keep him together body and soul. Primarily because he kept blowing up the body with which he was born.

========

"That isn't fair, Jordy," Ferdinand Niarchos protested. "Gomez made sure I knew my external religiosity just in case I ever got to go outside. Ahura Mazda pretty much means Lord Light, dualism implies two and, when you're talking devils you're usually talking three, are you not? In this case, you're talking the three great spheres, Moon, Earth and Sun: Varuna Ahriman Mithras. That's the VAM Entity. And don't pretend you've never heard of it. Or forgotten it. Because that's what you told Gomez and he told me."

"I'm just messing with you, Ferd," said Jordan Tethys. "Except, to be absolutely accurate, Outer Earth legend has the VAM Entity slightly differently. I distinctly remember telling Mithras, if not Gomez damn near two thousand years later, that, in it, he was the sun of dawn and the day whereas Varuna was the moon and stars of night. As for Ahriman, he was the darkness of a starless, moonless night, of a total solar or lunar eclipse, of beneath the ground where plants root, minerals are found, and the dead are buried.

"But", the Legendarian continued, not quite back in tale-telling mode, "There's another ancient triumvirate. Looking at Homer just reminded me of it. Not the Father, Son and Holy Ghost, that's post-Homer. Long past Homer's post, I shouldn't add but just did. Not the Hindu Trimurti either – when we were talking earlier I said they were likely inspired by the Unities of Lazareme howsoever many thousand more years pre-Babe Ruth, as in homer, non-capitalized. No, I'm thinking Cretan then Greek Mythology. Does the name Rhadamanthys ring a bell?"

Niarchos gave him a blank look, but it seemed to Tethys gongs were going off in the heads of both the Fatman and his scrumptious daughter-in-law. "In terms of both Cretan and Greek mythology," 30-Beers carried on, more like 12-Beers (to the wind) by then, "He was one of the three sons of Phoenician Europa by Olympian Zeus, the other two being Minos and Sarpedon."

"Sarpedon?" grasped Janna, thankfully not reading minds – '*scrumptious*', referring to her, may have caused her to grasp something else, two some things else, and twist as she squeezed, very, very painfully. "As in Demios Sarpedon, wife Morgianna, whose maiden name was Somata, the same as your twins, Sraddha and Janna, and a different Melina, not that Janna's mother, Demios's twin sister, who's now Melina Zeross."

"Interesting, eh? Doubly and triply so because, as our Mel's Illuminaries will tell you, in the days of the Goddess Culture, most of four thousand years ago now, Crete was portioned into three distinct realms: one human, one Utopian and one devic. The human kings were always called Minos whereas the Utopians were ruled by a succession of Sarpedons. Indeed, time rendered '*Sarpedon*' more of a pejorative term for Utopian collaborationists beyond the Dome than the distinguished family name it began as and eventually became again.

"Sooth said, Sarpedons had fallen into such a decline, then such a perhaps unwarranted disgrace, long before they started finding their way to Sedon's Head sometime around the turn of the Dome's 40th Century. That'd make it centuries after most of the Outer Earth's Utopians were recalled inside in order to help revitalize the U-bloodline. For something like the 1500 years following their return, they were treated as Weir's underclass. But, except as background more for today than yesterday, that's sliding way off the topic.

"The devils, to force myself back in line, were ruled by someone named Rhadamanthys. And that's the only time they or anyone else, including me, has ever heard of a devil by that name. However, in exclusively Greek mythology, along with Minos and Aeacus, the Olympian top-dog top-god, Deus-Zeus, made Europa's son Rhadamanthys ..."

"Rhadamanthys?" leapt in Centauri, figuratively speaking. "Of course! He became one of the Judge-Kings of the Elysian Fields."

"The Druj-judge as a matter of fact."

"But," chimed in Weird Ferd, bells finally going off in his head, "According your own stories, Jordy, the Elysian Fields were in the Northern Head. Grand Elysium was Sedon's cult centre, the site of the largest pyramid ever built on the Whole Earth. It was bigger than even the biggest one in China, not Egypt, you're always saying."

"Saying sooth too, Ferd. It preceded Corona City as the equivalent of the Headworld's capital by two thousand years, maybe more. And, speaking of dualism, albeit in a much more fundamentally important manner than any philosophical good v/s evil gobbledygook, long before the Age of Mithras even began it was the centre of worship for both of the adult Perpetual Presences: the mighty Moloch when not altogether an eye-mouth in the sky and, lest we forget, none other than my providential pal, Pyrame Silverstar.

"It remained that for multiple centuries after devils became solid individuals and the Age of Mithras began in name as well as fact. It remained that after Thrygragon, during the ensuing Era of Empires more so than the Age of Lazareme, right up to a few months prior to the Laughing Lands of so many pantheistic paradises becoming the Ghostlands. There was even a time during the Era of Empires when Zuvem Nergalis presumed to set up headquarters in Grand Elysium, by far and away the Upper Head's largest conurbation."

"All of which means," the Fatman expounded, not that he could '*ex*', as in shed, any of his pounds, "Or might mean, if you're right about Rhadamanthys, then that's just another of Zuvem's myriad names, like Gravedigger and Devil Doom. Which suggests Nergalis was Lady Lust's confederate and consequential co-mastermind after all."

Tethys opened another of beer and promptly lost his train of thought. "Sorry, Al. What did you say?"

"Something about Homer, I think." Centauri sounded speculative, worriedly so. Janna looked blank and Niarchos simply shrugged, as if he hadn't been paying attention.

"And what was I saying?" had to ask the Legendarian, feeling stupid. Not quite halfway to his thirtieth beer of the day, he wasn't even close to slurring his words. His slightly burnt fingertips were throbbing again. Worse, the scar tissue in his forehead was feeling itchy. Which disturbed him even more than the just as inexplicable loss of his train of thought.

"Something about Great Byron being the brains behind the Disunition of the Unities," volunteered Janna. Her eyes brightened up expectantly, as if a spell had just passed.

"Precisely. In my opinion Yajur hit the nail bang on the Head there. Banning worship of Bodiless Byron and his children was a brilliant stroke. That ban spread across the continent. Just as no non-azura sentient would worship a god who supported the Dead, neither would they worship a god who had started such a devastating debacle in the first place."

"That didn't stop my forefathers worshipping Jehovah after the Genesea," said Centauri, referring to the Great Flood of Genesis.

"It hasn't stopped you either, Al," said Tethys. "Nor did it stop me, for awhile. But I've an excuse. I was a woman then."

Blindingly, very nearly breathtakingly fast, Janna Frisbee-flicked the empty pizza pie platter in his direction. So quick was she, he didn't have time to duck let alone catch it. Not with his fingers still attached, that was for sure. Fortunately, although her actions made it razor-sharp she was done docilely mincing good hostess for the sake of her father-in-law's amusement, she was less aiming at him than she was aiming to just miss him.

Fortunately also it was made of metal, so it didn't break any more than it stuck into the wall behind him. Didn't even crack the plaster; just clanged rather tinnily off it before, now badly bent, forlornly settling on the floor as if awaiting further instructions as much as any additional impetus.

"Hey," Tethys objected anyways. "I'm no John the Baptist. You want to hear the rest of my story or not?"

"Thanks to Salome," Janna retorted. "John the Baptist's head might have been on a platter but even he couldn't keep on speaking. You on the other hand ..."

"That's enough, Janna," Centauri sternly instructed her. "Mr Tethys is no devil."

"Not in the localized sense," she agreed, thereby chilling comparatively convivially if perhaps also obediently.

========

A Tethys Tale - JANNA FANGFINGERS: THE DISUNITION OF THE UNITIES OF LAZAREME – Part Six: BALANCE BETRAYED

========

YD 5492 is the pivotal year in the first war.

========

It began inauspiciously enough for the Mithras Spawn when Unholy Abaddon, acting entirely on his own, once again invaded Satanwyck singlehandedly, this time on Cupidam, its New Year's Day. (*"February the First on your part of the Outer Earth, Al; Lammas to your Christians; Imbolc in here and in Celtic lands out there."*) Like his predecessors in perfidy, that was when Bobby Badboy, Cupidity as, um, damned near everybody called him in those days even though his primary vice was envy, celebrated his birthday.

(*"We call it the First of Balam these days. That's when Cupidity's Number Seven successor, Baaloch Hellblob, Sinistral Sloth, celebrates his – all right, Janna – solidification more so than birthday. Domdaniel-Pride, Number One to us, Lucifer to you, Al, started the naming tradition once Demon King Sedon, to his eventual regret, and that of ravendeer everywhere, appointed him his plenipotentiary, or literal vice-regent, circa 2000 YD."*)

His Unholiness must have far-seen a great many Mithradites gathered in Pandemonium because he waded into them straightaway. He either left voluntarily or was driven away but, whichever it was, it was not before he captured Cathune Bubastis, Desiccated Drought, one of the lesser Apocalyptics I mentioned earlier.

One of the lesser ones, present company obliges me to qualify, by all of one litter down from the Male Apocalyptics (Carcinogen-Plague, War-Bellona and Ramazar-Catastrophe). As Pyrame and Tralalorn's brood sister, Cathune's also only one litter up from their original mates (Famish-Pestilence, Diluvia-Flood and Milady Malaise). She is, however, at least three superior to Bellona's main squeeze since Thrygragon, the Medusa, Mater Matare, the Sangazurs' primary mother, and the other two male Pocks' preferred, um, companion since then dot-ditto.

Nergalazurs are peculiarly vulnerable to clean, fresh, falling rain so Abe does this deliberately. Since he was hardly alone when it came to reckoning she had to be the one drying up the Upper Head, that must have made her his one and only target, the lone reason he went to Satanwyck. Certainly the moment he returns to Kanin City with her, he long-distance-summons Order and Balance to the Masters Palace.

He presents the Mithradite to them as a kind of peace offering. They accept the captive whereupon, howsoever-begrudgingly, they welcome his Unholiness back into the fold. Seems Chaos had decided to become a hero of the Living after all. As for whether Thrygragos Lazareme gave him no choice in the matter, well, I'll leave that implicit rather than explicit. Ask him yourself next time he pops round to visit his beloved brother, which I doubt he ever does and never will.

That night his Unholiness went to Janna Somata's bedroom to announce the news of his reinstatement into the ranks of Life's champions. Perhaps not so stunningly given her recent attitude towards procreative sex and their consequential avoidance of each other, he found her making love to another woman. Nonetheless aroused, he threw the interloper butt-naked into the hall and climbed into bed with Janna.

By her own admission, Janna had gone cold, distant, disinterested and disillusioned when it came to men in general and him in particular. Being back the good guys' good books, he didn't try to force himself on her. Even if she was wearing Crimson's Crown in bed, which for all I know she may have been, there was no point. Kanin's Master had steadfastly refused to make love to him until the doom Gravedigger placed on her was lifted and, as aroused as she presumably still was as well, wasn't about change her mind now.

Yet, despite Irisiel Mercherm, his younger sister in Lazareme, a heliodromus, sun-runner or messenger of the gods, telling him precisely where she'd buried it, he'd been unable to locate Zuvem's head. If he was to have any chance of resurrecting the Nergalid whatsoever, the first thing he had to do was find then unearth it. So, had someone else beat him to it? Irisiel swore she never told anyone other than him where she'd buried it; swore she'd have remembered if she had and devils never lied.

As interesting as I'm sure all that is, what I found even more interesting was what befell Janna's female lover. It seems the young beauty had a thing for Somata twins; also had her own arousal issues in need of immediate attention. No sooner had Abe tossed her out on her naked butt than she got up, dusted it off, went next door and crawled into bed with the ever-randy one, Sraddha Somata.

He'd been back in the still official Weirdom for a few months; was in the process of raising troops – and not just to replace the ones he'd lost to the Iraches on the Diluvian steppes a year or two gone by then. Had himself a notion, did our Shreds, one that reverberates to this day in Hadd, and one we'll assuredly return to in due course.

They diddled and dallied and diddled some more. Three days later they went outside to take the air and, under the glaring sun, she dropped dead on the spot. Whereupon her corpse stood up and attacked him, going straight for the jugular. While, after years of exploring the Upper Head and years more commanding troops loyal to his father's empire, Sraddha was much more than just a pretty face, he was having trouble holding her off.

Fortunately, myself and a few others were in the vicinity. Although the Squiggly-me was no more heroically inclined than most me's are, we'd learned how to deal with the ambulatory dead during the ongoing Irache wars. When it came, or comes, to Haddit zombies, who fought alongside Iraches on both sides of the Diluvian Mountain Range, the trick was, and is, as you all know, dismemberment. More, slicing and dicing then preferably firing the remains – ash blows away, it doesn't strike blows.

There she was kicking and screaming, yanking at his hair, but we got her off him, albeit with slightly more than just clumps of his hair in hand, which was why he started shaving his head again. We manly sorts proceeded to push her into the conveniently open courtyard. There we doused her down with a gluey but volatile liquid what passed for our scientists had been experimenting with recently.

We ignited her, it, stood back and watched as the corpse burned unto cinders. When there was nothing left to rise again we called in the dustmen and let them finish the clean up. From that moment on Sraddha knew he had a weapon in these flamethrowers of ours that maybe, just maybe, would allow the Living to defend themselves against the Dead without the aid of Lazareme Spawn nor any other devil.

Abaddon didn't learn about any of this right away. Having left Janna to her misery, if misery it was, he'd gone back to the border between the Lake Lands and the radioactive Ghostlands, where he was mopping up yet another incursion of the Inglorious Dead into the lands of the Living pretty much on his own. It was a time-consuming task. When your touch can kill, Death's Angels weren't so much on the offensive themselves as recruiting armies of Dead Things who would go on the offensive for them.

No sooner had he dealt with one batch than hundreds of miles away another batch would rise up. He desperately wanted to draw Underlord Yama out of his protectorate but the Nergalid wasn't feeling cooperative. Why should he? Everything was going his way. Sooner or later, his Unholiness would finally altogether flip out and enter the Ghosts on his own accord. Then he'd have him rather than the other way around.

Much to the delight of Byronics and their adherents in the Southern Head, which once again included much of reclaimed Hadd as well as – as I'm about to get to – parts of the Cattail's Pastures of Plenty and the Bandradin highlands behind them, the Lazaremists' Chaos and the Mithradites' Grim Reaper were too damn stubborn to break off their stalemate.

The months of Kamor, Hektoris, Rudar and Djerridam (July, August, September and October on the Outer Earth – the fifth, sixth, seventh and eighth months of the Sedonic Year) are known as the Byronic Ternary for the simple reason they make up the third of the year dedicated to Thrygragos Byron and his offspring.

In 5492, the re-subjugation of the Penile Peninsula mostly a fait accompli, Bodiless Byron's commanders chose the first of Kamor to send their armies across the Interior Ocean of Akadan in order to launch a full-scale invasion of the Cattail Peninsula, the last part of the Great God's former domain left in the hands of the decadent Empire of Lathakra.

At that time, the equivalent of devic protectorates on the Cattail, Sedon's Ponytail, largely belonged to Lazareme Spawn. As one might expect, the Cattail being Chaos's traditional power base, they were mostly in a state of, yes, chaos. There were a couple of nominally Mithradite protectorates there, though. One was the Frozen Isle of Lathakra itself, the domain of the Parents Thanatos, which lay off the far east-central coast of the peninsula.

While there was nothing nominal about Lathakra, there was about the only other protectorate a Mithras Spawn laid claim to: the Prison Beach of Incain. That was where the famous, or infamous if you prefer, Pyrame Silverstar resided when she wasn't elsewhere, on either side of the Dome, occupying female shells for the Moloch Sedon, he in his shells, to impregnate with his mortal-mystical sedons.

It was only her nominal protectorate because, unless you count the devils she imprisoned, Incain's She-Sphinx, All the self-proclaimed Invincible, was its only occupant besides my providential pal Pyrame. And while All may be many a man's master, and many a devil's jailer, she was no one's mistress.

In other words she, All, not she, Pyrame, reckoned herself subservient to no man, no woman, no devil and no demon.

========

"I don't want to get going on another rant but it's hard to resist. Just hear me out, before you interrupt. Okay?" Three nods. "Good."

========

In most cases on the Outer Earth, though exceptions might include officially atheistic nation-states such as the Soviet Union or Communist China, God is always on your side. Until you lose, that is. Whereupon it becomes God's Will. Here on the Head, though, the gods, devils that they are, are often quite literally that; visibly marching at your side.

Some eight weeks after the Byronics launched their full-scale invasion of the Cattail, the firstborn Silverclouds, Rufous Rudra and forever-mate Umashakti, Savage Storm and Moon's Gravity, were physically with Byron's forces, his army of adherents, when they reached the mountainside in the Whiplash Range overlooking Incain. As one might expect it was as empty of an army as it was of a population for an army to protect. The Pauper Priestess was the Prison Beach's sole devic defender; its sole defender, other than All, period. Nonetheless taking it away from her, from both hers, was not going to be an easy task.

Recall, if you need to, Pyrame is Sedon's forever-favourite; the Headworld's other adult Perpetual Presence – some say brood sister, some say demonic daughter, Tralalorn being its only other Perpetual Presence, albeit one who never appears as anything other than a spoilt brat. Without Pyrame to quarter-conceive his mortal-mystical sedons Cathonia, the Sedon Sphere that separates the Inner from the Outer Earth, would collapse.

Recall also that, as I've been saying, the official warden of Incain was All the Invincible. Mostly she hid out altogether between-space. However, when she did deign to appear, it was generally as a serpent-tailed, lion-bodied female androsphinx; that is to say she had the head and breasts of a woman, making her a gynosphinx. She also had eagle wings; wings being in sphinx-lore a sure sign of femininity I've been given to understand.

All was an antediluvian automaton left over from the days when the Head was the archipelago of Pacifica, the Places of Peace, or Lemuria, the Places of Pieces, as the joke goes. The First Patriarch, Alorus Ptah, who may have been an incarnation of the Male Entity, constructed her early to midway through the Golden Age of Humankind, the Whole Earth's successor civilization to that of Atlantis, what's more correctly referred to as Old Eden.

He did so such that she could assist the non-winged Androsphinx, he of the Giza Plateau in what's currently Egypt, in dealing with the first recorded incarnation of, I'll say, Demogorgon, the Conglomerate Devil, whom most devils still refer as the Unnameable. I'll also say, without any more elaboration, that Pyrame is, or was, hardly alone when it came to denying that this Demogorgon ever existed; that Heliosophos-Ptah constructed the sphinxes to take out the daemons' King Daemonicus and their Queen Lilith.

A tellurian half-life, albeit one with a high degree of intelligence, All was, and is, called the Mandroid Mother Machine because, first of all, no pun intended, she is a Mandroid half-life and, second of all, because she whelped Steltsar's Mandroids, which proved both deadly and so very nearly indestructible during Godbad's civil war. Fortunately for the subcontinent, heavy ordinance you managed to import from the Outer Earth, Al, and then, howsoever reluctantly, had your Centauri Enterprises begin manufacturing in here proved the *'very nearly'* bit.

All also manufactures Lemurian guard-bodies and, as a Mandroid herself, is akin to the Mantel half-lifers of Temporis as well as both earthborn faeries and chthonic demons, without the *'a'*. She's composed mostly of Stopstone, what Outer Earthlings most commonly call Solidium, a substance that accrues in manmade structures and one that most Master Devas, if not necessarily Great Gods, fear. For good reason too, though you'll have to add that to the list of things I won't be dealing with right now.

All of the above suggests that, at least theoretically, she's vulnerable to massive doses of Brainrock. Mandroids certainly are but just how much Brainrock it would take to destroy All, well, I'll leave that to your scientists and technicians. She probably wouldn't survive plummeting into the lava lake in the caldera of Sedon's Peak, I'll say that much. But if she crashed into the Brainrock Wall that separates the Cattail Peninsula from the Head's occipital regions she'd probably only be smarting for a few weeks. Tough stuff is our All. So is Pyrame Silverstar, but I doubt she's any tougher than almost any other highborn devil.

Called the Pauper for various reasons, almost all of them valid, you definitely can't call her powerless. Because of her affinity for All – the She-Sphinx actually did her bidding in the era of Sedon's Migraine – Pyrame could draw on the abilities of devils then incarcerated within her, All; could wield their power focuses and, yes, that would include the talismans of Magnetism, the Idiot Twins and even Demogorgon, had he or she had one. Which he or she did, assuming it was the gorgonian head Harmony used on Thrygragos Varuna Mithras came Thrygragon.

All in all then, especially if she was all in All, I'd say that together they made a formidable pair.

The Silverclouds, Byron's Beast and Byron's Bodice – please pardon the pun, SPM, but Lunar Uma does always present herself with ample bosoms – must have thought themselves equal to the challenge; otherwise they wouldn't have led their men against the Prison Beach. One thing in their favour was they were the two surviving members of the Unmoving One's first litter of three.

By contrast Pyrame came out of Mithras's ninth litter, the same as Drought and Tralalorn. Hardly an imposing origin, I'm sure they'd have agreed with you, while almost everything about Beast and Bodice was imposing, including said bosoms. Like his Hindu equivalent of the same name, Rufous Rudra was the devic God of Storm and an animal master to boot; hence the beast bit. Umashakti was the Byronic Moon Goddess. She also had the impressive ability to control gravity. As for the bodice bit, well, Rufous would tell you, and Lunar Uma would no doubt allow, laughingly, even her toenails were stacked.

The Priestess had no worshippers of her own; hadn't had since her days sitting alongside the Moloch Sedon in Grand Elysium. Evidently, unlike virtually every other Master Deva you'd care to mention, All and those incarcerated within her between-space off Incain were all she needed to keep herself together body and soul. Which, if you were to ask me, is just one more of the unsolvable mysteries surrounding Pyrame Silverstar.

(As I said earlier, I find it very worrisome her silver star's been shining out of the night's sky for thirty years now. How Sedon can hope to maintain the Dome with her in it escapes me.)

In the era of Sedon's Migraine, she'd thus far managed to keep herself aloof from all the mischief her brothers and sisters were responsible for in Marutia. In a way that's to be expected. Pyrame had never been your standard Mithradite. Her hatred for two of them, Divine Coueranna and Kind Plathon, predated Thrygragon by more than two millennia and, though she denies, denied, it vehemently, if ultimately unconvincingly, it had to be Pyrame who set up the Idiot Twins to put pay to the Thanatoids and the expansion of their Lathakran Empire in 4825.

Arguments could therefore be made that, if anything, Pyrame was more on Byron's side than she was on that of either her siblings or anyone else, possibly even including the Living. Mind you, as a multiple half-mother, conceptively speaking anyhow, were she here she might construe that as a slander. Certainly she had never caused Bodiless Byron any demonstrable trouble. In short, the Byronics had no compelling reason to go after her. Yet they did. Why?

Well, I could speculate it was because they wanted All, not her, and in order gain control of All they had to get her out of the way. Then again I could also speculate they wanted her submissive to them in order to gain a disproportionate influence over the Moloch Sedon Himself. Finally, I could speculate that her aloofness was a sham, that she was the real mastermind behind everything the Mithradites had done since even before Thrygragon, that Byron realized that and wanted her out of the way just because she was in the way. But now's not the time for speculation.

It being the Age of Lazareme, if no longer the Age of Panharmonium per se, Pyrame went to Isle of the Undying One in order to protest their incursion into her territory to that Great God directly. As usual, Thrygragos Libertine refused to intervene, though he did promise to send Datong Harmonia, the Unity of Balance, to check out the situation as soon as she was available.

Which, as it happened, was pretty much immediately. Not that, as it also happened, Harmony was necessarily there to take Pyrame's side against the Byronics. Quite the opposite in some respects, as it turned out, and this despite the previously alluded to, astonishingly enduring friendship between my two favourite devic goddesses – other than APM of course.

Rufous Rudra chose the first of Rudar, that month named after him, to launch an all-out assault on the Prison Beach. It was his chosen birth or solidification date so he reckoned that made it an auspicious day to attack. As the Pauper prepared herself to do or die defending Incain, figuratively speaking since devils rarely died as such, Harmony showed up. With her, entwined within her Brainrock chains, was Cathune Bubastis, Pyrame's generally cat-headed litter sister. The Apocalyptic of Drought had been a captive of the Lazaremists since Satanwyck's New Year's Day and looked sickened unto death from a lack of worshippers.

Incomparable Harmony gave providential pal Pyrame, also Sedon's Whore, a damned-if-you-do, damned-if-you-don't choice. Without worshippers Cathune would either die or self-cathonitize. She wouldn't be alone either; many a Mithradite Master Deva would suffer a similar fate. Grandfather never let anyone out of Cathonia and death was even more permanent, right?

So, if Pyrame turned control of All over to her exclusively then she, Harmony, would ensure that devil after devil, faced with a potentially fatal loss of worshippers, would be given the same option: namely, temporary incarceration within All. Of course she, Pyrame, could unleash All on the Silverclouds. Or she could take them on herself, relying on Sedon to come to her rescue if, um, all else failed.

But, before she did anything so rash, perhaps she should ask herself a few questions. For example, would the Silverclouds be here if they didn't think they'd win? Would All fight them or would she join them? Would Sedon care if the Byronics subjugated her? It wasn't as if she could refuse to occupy sentient shells for him, he in his, to impregnate. Devils can't refuse Dark Sedon, can they?

Sooth said, she, Harmony, might even be tempted to join with the Silverclouds. At least their followers were alive whereas Pyrame didn't have any anyhow. Unleash All, what could she hope to do against the Byronics' forces except start to kill them off? Only nowadays they'd just get up and keep on fighting, wouldn't they? Wouldn't it be more sensible for All, having just heard her offer of many a Master Deva to follow Cathune, to abandon Pyrame and opt into her plan instead? Shall we put it to her?

Pyrame relinquished her control of All. Harmony congratulated the Pauper Priestess on using her pointy head properly for a change then had All fully materialize. The She-Sphinx happily ate Cathune. The Balance Unity felt sorry for her, thought she still looked a tad peaked, so she had her eat Pyrame. Whereupon she waited for the invading army of Byronics to reach the beach. When they did, the Silverclouds at their head and All still fully materialized, fully frighteningly too, right behind her, she engaged in another brief discourse.

You Silverclouds, Harmony inquired, are aware of how debilitated Cathune became once she started losing her worshippers, aren't you? Even though you're at the head of an army of loyal fanatics, made even larger by the defection of the Bandradins from my brood brother's side of the ledger, how loyal do you think they'll remain once they find themselves fighting their dead fellows? We devils dare not kill lesser beings but All will defend her beach to the last drop of their blood. Fact is, it was the fanaticism of your followers that led you to think you could prevail against a Perpetual Presence, wasn't it?

You might even have a plan to overwhelm All. Probably do, a Brainrock asteroid Mama Moon there can haul down out of Outer Space perhaps. Of course we Lazaremists have plenty of adherents already, she added, semi-contradicting her statement re the Bandradins. But I'm not against gaining some more, especially since there's nothing wrong with destroying Dead Things.

Tell you what, I think I'll just let All defend away and mop up the Dead Things afterwards. For a price: namely, your loyalists' sensibly reconsidered loyalty. Which I'm sure they'll be delighted to provide once I decide to keep you two busy, about to become manifest losers, while All's defending her beach. Do you think I can catch a Brainrock asteroid with my chains? I've played a lot of ballgames with my brothers over the millennia, you know.

Oh, and speaking of the not-so-little devils, you do know what'll happen to the Head if you did somehow manage to prevail over me? I grant you that isn't too likely but, hey, you're a storm lord, beast bogey, my chains might rust; and you're a real heavyweight, lunar lunatic, maybe you'll sit on me until the end of time. Nothing ventured, nothing slain, and all that blot of rot.

And there'll be stacks of rot, most of it on its feet again, because we fight, your army gets caught in the middle, and that really would be a waste of not yet rotting flesh. There's a reason no devil has never challenged me. Or do you think there will be enough left of you to stand up against my brothers once I'm no longer around to, um, balance them off?

Here's how it works, she smiled reassuringly. Upon my inviolable oath as a Master Deva yours won't be a long imprisonment; just long enough for her and her fellow Lazareme Spawn to end the northern war between the Living and the Dead. When it was all over, she promised them, she would release them. And, it being low tide, they could take that to the sandbank.

It was almost in gratitude that Byron's Blustery Beast and his Bountiful Bodice accepted imprisonment in Incain. It definitely was in gratitude that their army retreated. Even with all the firepower they'd humped down the mountainside to her beach, what were they going to do against a mobile monstrosity like that? Hope she went as moribund as her male equivalent on the Outer Earth, then chip her to death?

Harmony was as good as her word, too. Though not, if you'll permit some irresistible foreshadowing, the bit about releasing them as soon as the war then underway in the Upper Head, more so than anywhere else, was over. Which isn't to say she wouldn't have, just that she was wildly off-base – to honour the Outer Earth's just concluded World Series – about what would happen once she was no longer around to balance off her two brothers.

The Silverclouds would survive, assuming someone else released them.

========

"Although," Tethys continued to extemporize, "For reasons that must be obvious from what I just said, I never got the chance to interview Harmony about her motivations for going to Incain, I expect gaining control of the Prison Beach was a deliberate strategy on the part of the Lazareme Spawn and their lord-laziest father.

"A short term goal would have been to get All to hand over Zuvem's Tvasitar-trinket, his Brainrock spade, which Abe would eventually need in order to resurrect the Nergalid should he ever locate and unearth his head. There's little doubt in my mind Harm would have known Ursine Bardol had given it to All for safekeeping. Fact is, if I know Harm, which I did, albeit never to the degree I desired, I expect she'd have been the one who told the Barrings' devic overlord to do just that in the first place.

"In the long term, though, All was a tried and true method of getting both Mithra-dite and Byronic Master Devas out of the way while they attended to resolving the First War between the Living and the Dead. Or, as certain personages to this day maintain was their real intention, usurping complete control of the Headworld for themselves.

"Cathonitization relied too much on Dark Sedon's whims whereas capital punish-ment, as we're about to see in the case of Zuvem Nergalis, just wasn't working out."

Tethys smiled suggestively. It was nowhere near Harmony's golden calibre – no one could smile like she could. It didn't have APM's, or the living Janna's, or the titular Janna's quality either, not even close. But it was appropriate given the circumstances. Taletellers, like comedians, always smiled when a punch-line was approaching.

It was a cue to their audience, no matter how small, in this case three in a solarium, that applause was shortly to be expected. Just be patient a moment or two longer.

========

Throughout the Lazareme Ternary, which make up the first four months of the Sedonic Year, and well into the third month of Great Byron's four months, His Unholiness, non-King Chaos, Abaddon the 1st, worst and hopefully the last, kept returning to the borderlands separating the Lakes and the Ghosts. For some reason – might that reason be Janna Somata once again had the Crimson Corona? – he couldn't get it out of his mind that he should invade Yama Nergal's protectorate just as he had Belialma's then Robin Goodfellow's Satanwyck.

He knew the dangers of the Ghostlands. Quite apart from the fact they were the Nergalid's territory, the area was thoroughly irradiated with what we, now on both sides of the Dome, recognize as Atomic Energy. Even if he was a god of death – of the underworld, put more precisely – it was a wonderment Yama could survive in such a place. Yet survive he had, laudably if not necessarily laughing loudly, in what had formerly been the Laughing Lands.

Then, in the middle of 5492's Rudar, a mere fortnight, if that, after Harmony, the Unity of Balance, had All of Incain eat the Silverclouds, Desiccated Drought, and scintillant Silverstar – so much for Pyrame being the Mithradites' mastermind, eh? – Abe Chaos was, after a fashion, rewarded for his persistent headaches. The Reaper appeared before him. They met, were within sight of each other anyhow, on either side of the presumably Sedon-demarcated line between where the Ghosts' radiation finally petered out and the Lakes' altogether healthy air began.

Although I wasn't there, I've heard it was raining. On Abe's side the falling rain was fresh, liquid sunshine, lively and warm for the time of year (*"Rudar being your September, Al"*); on Yama's side it was, to use an Outer Earth term, a hard rain a-falling, deathly glowing. The Nergalid broke out in a broad grin. An odd sight that, you'll agree; almost as odd as glowing rain. He thereupon played his trump card. Zuvem Nergalis materialized beside the Underlord.

"Here he is, Unholy One," taunted Yama, still smiling as best a skinless skull in a raiment of cloaking darkness could smile. "A lot the worse for wear but Devil Doom in the daemonic flesh."

Abaddon looked and sounded astonished. "How?"

"Your quicksilver sister, Thrygragos Lazareme's hotdog heliodromus, Irisiel Mercherm as Cabalarkon's Utopian Illuminaries named her centuries ago, won't re-member telling me where she buried his head but she did. Amazing how forthcoming a devil becomes when you've her head in your hands and the rest of her body's lying some distance away. You should try it sometime; with me doing the holding, needles to slay.

"As for how I got All of Incain to turn over his Tvasitar talisman, well, let's just say the Pauper Priestess and I are old buddies from pre-Peak days and leave it at that."

"It's her I'll leave without a head – after you."

"Be my guest. Whatever you do to her, though, Grandfather Sedon will just as quickly undo. He needs her. I don't particularly need this washed-up old twerp, but did you really believe I was going to let a fellow Nergalid die? Even if he got what was coming to him for cursing your Janna the way he did, he's still my elder brother."

"I want him," demanded Abaddon.

"Then come and get him."

"Oh, I will," promised the Unity. "But not today. Maybe tomorrow. Or haven't you heard? All of Incain's become the property of my ever-so-clever sister Unity. She can free the Idiot Twins and, just as they caused it, they can expunge all that precious radiation you're hiding behind from the Ghosts. Once that's done, I'll come for Gravedigger. He'll be as no longer laughing as his Laughing Lands laugh no longer. And I won't stop with him. Turn him over to me now and maybe, just maybe, I'll forget your part in all this."

If it was possible for a shadow-hooded skull to frown then Yama Nergal did. Still, he nevertheless projected a defiant attitude, whereupon he was once again doing his best imitation of a Death's Head beam. "Let's save us both the trouble. I'll step outside the Ghostlands and we can duel for Devil Doom."

His Unholiness was flabbergasted at the offer. "Name the place and the time."

"The Gregarian Fields. In the Medusa's Meadow. On Harmony's Feast Day. Next week."

"Done."

========

Abe Chaos returned to the Weirdom of Kanin City forthwith. In that way most devils have of communicating over extraordinarily long distances, he contacted the Harm in harmony, if sadly not the harem. Yes, she told him, so sorry to say but it's too terribly true. All no longer has the elder Nergalid's power focus. She'd given it to the Egyptian – Pyrame Silverstar, not Cathune Bubastis ...

(Just to clarify, Pyrame wasn't named after the Great Pyramid of Giza. On account of she was so hot-headed, her name came from 'pyre'. Most everyone thought otherwise, which was why 'Egyptian' became one of her commonest nicknames.)

'Only when I woke her up,' she further imparted, *'Pyrame claimed she had no recollection of whom she gave it to afterwards. You still want me to release the Idiot Twins?'*

He said no; told her additionally that the Reaper had agreed to come out and fight him in the Gregarian Fields. Winner gets Gravedigger. Harmony snorted at that. Abe Chaos does not appreciate being snorted at. It makes him mad. Then again he still had the Susasword, so he was most of the way mad already.

'You do realize he's trying to provoke the Moloch Sedon. Mithras allowing violence to the occur in the Gregarian Fields when it was his responsibility, like it is ours now, to

prevent that very thing happening is the reason Grandfather did nothing to thwart us doing what we did to his favourite son.'

'So what? Haven't I already told you what I think of Sedonic decrees? You think the Dead could rise without Grandfather's acquiescence? He's the Living's real enemy.'

'No, you are – have been all along!'

It wasn't just an incendiary thing to say, it was an incredibly stupid thing to say. (Which sometimes make me think it wasn't her who transmitted it; that it was some sort of mental mind-fuck courtesy of a psychic ventriloquist of sinister providence, one playing both the Unities as the dummies.)

At any rate, if Abe wasn't already incensed enough, he was truly pissed now. He demanded Harmony take it back. This time she outright laughed at him, howsoever safely from afar. Which was another really, really dumb thing to do. (See above.) He said he'd make her take it back. He'd make her eat her words, served on the tri-tined fork-ends of his trident.

She telepathically retorted directly, to quote him quoting her: *'Go fuck yourself!'* Then she cut off communication.

While devils can speak to each other long distance that doesn't necessarily mean they know where the devil they're speaking with is at the moment of their chat. There's a solution to that, albeit not in terms of winding back the clock. He came to see me. Which is how I came to hear everything that went down between Abe and both Yama then Harmony.

That'd be the Squiggly-me. For the record, I've been rehabilitated – as Abe's drinking buddy if not Janna's, um, most handsome and desirous of men. (*"Sorry, Al, but I couldn't resist, Besides, Ferd and Janna weren't here last time I used it."*)

That means I'm re-ensconced in the same residence I'd been occupying for something like half of that century. When I wasn't off dancing the legless limbo or being the Quoits-me up in Cabalarkon or else globetrotting alongside Sraddha Somata, that is to say; since the time of the Quibble then the Quidnunc me's, that is also to say.

========

"And before any of you say I could've just said no, allow me to repeat a few words for you: 'tri-tined', 'fork-ends', 'eat'. I wasn't hungry."

========

A week shy of the Autumnal Equinox, her regular feast day, I drew Chaos to Balance. He found her, his immediate sibling, lying on a rock in a cave beside Janna Somata, her own half- or quarter-daughter, however you want to slice it. While a rock isn't the sack – and, for all I know, they were completely clothed – for him it was bye-bye brain-birdie big-time. Put more melodramatically, if not so entertainingly, what Abe saw must have finally tipped him over the brimstone brink into the broiling breach of irredeemable insanity.

A massive man at the best of times, and a massively maddened one at the worst of times, which this was, he was so enraged he bodily hauled his ever-enchanting sister Unity up by her golden neck-torc, her 3500-hundred-year-old power focus. (Other than for himself Harmony was the first Master Deva for whom Tvasitar Smithmonger ever fashioned a Brainrock talisman.)

To my everlasting dismay, she didn't instantly go all Nemesis on his ass. Sooth said, from the sounds of things at any rate, she didn't seem overly perturbed that he had found her, first of all; that he had found her with Janna, second of all; and that, third of all, he was in a decidedly nasty mood.

"She's sick," Balance defended herself, presumably playing on his perceived love for the terrible twin. "I was just trying to make her well again. We devils are good at that; the best there are in that regard and Brainrock makes us even better. Or," she added, still seeking to reason with him, "Failing wellness, to comfort her. Haven't you seen what's been happening to her lovers? They wake up dead."

She smiled reassuringly; smiling was part of her arsenal of charms. She'd smooth-talked the Silverclouds into All at the beginning of Rudar, don't forget, and she hadn't done it with unassailable logic, that was for sure. Who could resist a smile like hers? His Unholiness was, and is, today's answer to that.

Had she lost something of her seductiveness securing Incain for the Lazaremists? I don't think so. I suspect that, had either of them bothered to look upon Kanin's Master, they'd have detected – with their third eyes if she was keeping it hidden from ordinary sight – that Janna was wearing Crinsom's Crown, the Crimson Corona, the Mind of Sapiendev; that she was using it to give her half-mother cranial cramps and her half-uncle an apotheosis of animosity, to pull an old chestnut out of my word-chest of fay-sayings.

Then again, if she was wearing the Crimson Corona, then most likely she wasn't thinking at all. The three Sacred Objects are anything but sacred to everyone or, in my view, should be to anyone. Indeed, it may well be that, through Janna and using Harmony's telepathic voice-print, it had far-goaded Chaos so recklessly. Or does that give an inanimate object too much credit for the dire deeds of its wielder?

(*"Don't be too quick to jump on that bandwagon is my best advice to ye and thee tempted to think that way."*)

Still, say it was Janna herself. It's not an altogether groundless ocean – make that notion – so let's not dismiss it out of hand; out of fang-fingered glove, put more entertainingly. Great God Lazareme's half-daughter had, like her twin brother, inherited a truly masterful ability to control devils possessing her, rather than the other way round, the way it usually went. Might she not be able to master the Trigregos Talismans just as comparatively easily?

(*"A scary thought, I know, but what isn't scary about Janna Fangfingers?"*)

Maybe she thought she was getting back at the Unities for what she'd been forced to do to her only live-born child; for the doom Zuvem Nergalis thereafter placed on her; for all her subsequent stillbirths; for what happened to her father; the humiliation of the mother; for all that had gone wrong in her life since my last day as the Quibble-Quill, my first day as the Quidnunc-Quill and, simultaneously, Shreds and hers day one out of the womb.

In truth, he'd tell me later, at the same time Uncle Abe told me what he did next, Janna's promiscuity had been bothering him. It wasn't that she was going to bed with dozens of different partners, men and women, at times in combinations, often three or four a night. It wasn't that her appetite for sex had, all of a relative sudden, become unquenchable.

It wasn't that she denied him her affections. Neither of them wanted another nine month pregnancy with a dead-end-issue. It wasn't that she slept every day from dawn to dusk. It was not even that her lovers woke up dead three nights later. What infuriated him the most was that her dead lovers woke up at all. If you are dead, you should do like Mithras did and have the common decency to stay dead.

As for what he did next, he, his Unholiness, Abe Chaos, he of the Biblical Bottomless Pit, his was no jilted lover's temper tantrum as Harmony must have thought so innocently unlike her. He remembered having the Solidium Sheathe that held the Susasword in his right hand, his bad hand. He'd kept it on him, or secreted in his trident, ever since the day he used it to kill that Janna's birthfather, Zalman Somata.

Then suddenly he wasn't only Chaos Incarnate. Once again he was Chaos Incarnadine. Pulling out the curved blade with his good hand, his left, he did a bordering on impossibly bad thing. He drove the cursed blade through her chains, through her, his immediate sister, drove her backwards and pinned her to the boulder of Brainrock off of which he'd only moments earlier yanked her away from his bedazzled beloved, who wasn't on it anymore either.

He thereupon grabbed Janna and cut them both back to Kanin City. Harmony has, as far as I've heard, been stuck to that boulder, in whichever cave it is wherever, ever since.

========

"A boulder of Brainrock you say," the Fatman ruminated out loud. "And you've no idea where it is?"

========

"I've tried drawing myself to Harmony any number of times over the centuries. I even tried drawing her with the Susasword pinning her to a slab of the ungodly Godstuff. I had the cave's background, you see. It drew itself, just before I drew Abe to it. He had me draw it again, truth told, within a day of the madness leaving him.

"He couldn't remember where it was either. How could he? It was just a cave that was somewhere I drew him to and somewhere dot-ditto he sliced himself away from, between-space, when he returned to Kanin City's Masters Palace. It might not even have been on the Head, though that's proven impossible whenever I try to do that from in here. You want to know what happened?"

"He killed you in frustration."

"No, that was later. The Squiggly-me of the moment had always been a randy old fucker so, according to a certain some, he could even have deserved it. What did happen, every time I tried to draw myself or anyone else there, the pad of paper, the pad of parchment, the pad of whatever I was using to draw on, burst into flames. The plain fact of the matter is Dark Sedon just doesn't want Harmony found."

"Sedon?"

"Who else? He wasn't in the night's sky because he didn't want to have ill-star devils who killed lesser beings. Yet that's exactly what needed to be done in order to re-purify the Head after Quoits Tethys and her contagion collectors soiled it so awfully over the course of the previous two centuries."

"He countenanced the culling and to do that he had to figure out a way to neutralize more so than altogether abolish Harmony? Colour me highly sceptical."

"All right, someone approximating his power doesn't, didn't, want her found if that makes you feel less, um, colourful. Nonetheless, short of a Great God, who can even come close to approximating the Moloch Sedon's power?"

"Who indeed?" Centauri ruminated the more. "Let's call it your elephant then."

"Let's do just that," Tethys picked up, "Notwithstanding the nonetheless, though, let me also tell you something almost as interesting while it's still on my mind. Harmony told Abe that Janna was sick. There could be another reason she hoped to cure her by lying on a slab of Brainrock with her besides the one she gave him."

"She thought she was possessed by a demon," appreciated Janna St Peche-Montressor, the Janna in the solarium with them, though it could have been APM All-Eyes, the devil occupying her doing the talking. "Not every demon is highly inflammable. Salamanders thrive in flames, for example. But every demon is as vulnerable to excess amounts of Brainrock as most devils are to too much Stopstone, the stuff of Mandroids."

"Was she?" wondered Niarchos. "Possessed of a demon, I mean?"

"Technically demons don't possess anyone so much as they overcoat them, howsoever-transparently. Still," Tethys added, pleasantly enough. "You can always ask her yourself the next time you sit down to negotiate the terms of her vampires' supervisory duties in New Iraxas."

"I'll try to remember to do just that," Niarchos snorted, or scoffed, more so than chortled an agreement. "Though I have to tell you I'm just like my old man used to be when he was in my shoes all those years ago. I'd only be caught dead negotiating with them or especially her. That's why Gomez, when he's around, does it nowadays."

Weird Ferd had a twinkle in his eye but at least he wasn't grinning.

========

Pyrame Silverstar was hardly the only devil who could wield another devil's power focus.

========

Indeed, any sentient being could do so, which was what made them so precious to well-moneyed collectors or treasure hunters. In that regard, the Death Goddess of the Thanatoids (Methandra also of Mythland, once Mithras's Virgin, once maybe Mediterranean Athena, the Olympian goddess of – contrarily in most folks' estimation – war and wisdom, but always Heat to her triplet-brother-husband's Cold) was no different.

The Anvil Artificer, Tvasitar Smithmonger, initially fashioned the cauldron whose scarlet vapours she was using to spy upon Fatman and friends for a second-born Lazaremist, one Metisophia by Illuminary-given name: Titanic Metis, by Olympian Zeus mother of the Muses according to some classical mythologists.

According to almost anyone who came across her, she deserved her devic appellation, Wisdom of Lazareme – as opposed to Methandra's Wisdom of Mithras. (As everybody who knew much of anything about her, the latter hadn't been Mithras's Virgin in any way shape or form since she woke up in 5908 with her immediate brother all over her. She was still Hot Stuff, though – especially, as said brother and thence hubby Tantal would confirm, were it as recently as 50 years ago, in bed.)

Titanic Metis was Quill Tethys's devic half-mother. (Prior to being eaten by faeries, and thereafter, arguably, regurgitated as Tomcat Tattletail, Rumour of Lazareme was his half-father.) Metis was still around and as wise as ever. Much like Faustus Vladuca became after Abe Chaos handed Janna Somata his fang-fingered glove, hand still in it, during Sedon's Migraine, she'd been a mere spirit being since the Era of Empires.

Even though it was no secret Miss Myth had her cauldron, Metis made no effort to regain it during the Thanatoid's thousand-plus-years asleep. Despite having had it for so long, when it came to using what was effectively a between-space camera, the Scarlet Empress – as King Cold's Crimson Queen became known during the expansion of the Lathakran empire in the 48th Century of the Dome – wasn't as accomplished as one might expect she should be by now.

For one thing, she could only tune in visuals, not audio, but she was good at reading lips. So was one of the two with her.

========

"One of these days the tail-teller's going to remember you, Smiler."

"Him? Not a chance. One of these days that fat fool friend of his is going to remember to turn on his tape-recorder again, though."

****

10: Labour Squabbles

Weird Ferd, Ferdinand Niarchos, governor of New Iraxas, Great Godbad's filthy, oil-producing, north-easternmost state, only had a twinkle in one of his eyes, but at least he only had two. As did Alpha Centauri and Janna St Peche-Montressor. Jordan Tethys had a scar in the middle of his forehead, where a third eye would have shone out had he had one, which he didn't. Thankfully its itching had subsided slightly in the last few seconds.

That still suggested devils were around somewhere. Then again, they would never be far away from the Fatman, Unmoving Byron's only known, albeit only occasional, shell. It did not signify they were possessing any of his companions or himself; not beyond a shadow of doubt, it didn't. It was impossible to tell that. Still, his scar's scratchiness was a fair indicator how close they were and it wasn't very.

Popping another beer as a reward for their rectitude – he'd lost count as to how many he was up to already – the Legendarian pressed on.

========

A Tethys Tale - JANNA FANGFINGERS: THE DISUNITION OF THE UNITIES OF LAZAREME – Part Seven: THE THOUSAND DAYS' DAZE

========

In terms of the Disunition of the Unities, it was a matter of one down, two to go.

========

A week later, on the by-now-late Harmony's feast day, the Autumnal Equinox of 5492, Unholy Abaddon met Yama Nergal in the Medusa's Meadow. The entire encounter consisted of his Unholiness striking at his Under-Lordship with his trident and the Nergalid blocking the blow with his scythe. Which, in case I haven't mentioned it previously, was Vanthysces the Byronic Reaper's power focus fused with Yama's own miner's pickaxe.

That solitary clang of Tvasitar talismans was enough to violate Grandfather Sedon's dictate that no violence ever be done in the Gregarian Fields, Sedon's Mole. King Harvest, the Mithradite Reaper, didn't hang around to see if the Mighty Moloch appeared in order to exact divine retribution. He sliced himself elsewhere, presumably back to the Ghostlands, his radioactive wasteland. Chaos was so enraged by the Nergalid's cowardly retreat he may have actually cut himself between-space to the Ghosts himself and taken his chances tangling with a highborn in his own protectorate.

Whatever his intentions were, Abe was in the process of cutting himself somewhere when his passage through Samsara was obstructed by Lord Yajur, lightning blade already drawn. "I told you we'd have a reckoning," the Unity of Order challenged him. "A reckoning without Harmony around to balance us off."

"Suits me fine. I knew there had to be a reason I got her out of our way."

As if by unspoken, yet entirely mutual agreement, the two immediate brothers quit the Gregarian Fields. A few seconds later they both reappeared, unimaginably huge, towering over the vast plains of Marutia. Yajur was Grandfather Sedon's paladin. Abaddon was, as always, himself, Chaos Incarnate.

They fought for three years.

========

On Djerridam the 12th, 5492, the twelfth of October on the Outer Earth, Sraddha Somata and a number of scouts attached to his recently bolstered army *'discovered'* the land of Iraxas. As he carried on with the fullness of his army, his men freshly outfitted, again, with scads of state-of-the-times' weaponry they'd imported from Twilight, Ap Isle, Ophir-Moorset and the rest of the Head's Occipital regions, none of which were plagued by Time Quakes, his emissaries returned to Marutia and proclaimed Iraxas ripe for the plucking.

By the end of that year, the Spring Equinox on both sides of the Cathonic Dome, mostly closet, Mithradite-venerating Marutians were flooding through the infra-Diluvia cave-system in tsunami numbers. Although their historians might tell you differently, they weren't looking for a land of golden opportunity. While that's what they eventually, howsoever briefly, came to call what they did find, they came there fleeing the lands of the trampled Dead.

There's a quirky congruity here. Their nominal allies, the similarly equipped, equally anti-Byronic Iraches – who still swore by Nergal Vetala, even carried her banner, a contrarily green stone-sickle with a brownish, hardwood handle against a dirt-dark background – had a long history of ancestor worship. Did that make Iraxas already a land of the Dead? I suppose it did.

Still, there's no denying that, among other things, what the duelling Unities of Lazareme were making of the Marutians' traditional homeland, Sedon's Cheek, was just that: a Land of Dead Things Walking. What I find so paradoxically self-fulfilling is that before too long the actions of its Marutian invaders guaranteed that, to this day, Iraxas shows up on Godbadian maps as Hadd, the land of you know what.

Deva-devastation, the ruination of the Head, was at hand.

========

"As I've already hinted at, though now seems an appropriate moment to confirm it, more foreboding here, long before he returned to the Diluvian Mountain Range his twin sister had given Sraddha the Amateramirror to wear."

========

The Years of the Dome, 5492 to 5495, are quite properly known as the Thousand Days of Disbelief. The Unities of Order and Chaos were locked in perpetual combat, with no winner in sight. Neither devil showed any sign of faltering. Far worse, neither devil seemed remotely concerned about the damage they were doing to the Upper Head. It could be their forces-of-nature hatred for each other was so extreme, so all-engrossing, they weren't even conscious of the approaching incalculable ramifications of their actions, but that excuses nothing.

While the trampled Dead couldn't always get up, they usually could at least keep crawling and, thereafter, killing those the Unities hadn't altogether trampled to death. And, don't forget, Yama's Inglorious Dead, Death's Angels, were so radioactive their touch could kill. All in all, then, is it any wonder fully alive, non-azura sentient beings lost all faith in devils. And that now included Lazareme Spawn as well as Master Devas from the other two tribes.

Consequently, devils grew weaker and weaker. Yajur and Abaddon were exceptions of course. Their faith in themselves was enough to sustain them throughout their never-ending clash of titans. So it was that other devils took to their own protectorates and strove to defend them as never before. Many failed. As to what happened to them, well, it's said that not even Sedon Himself knows the names of all the stars shining out of the night's sky beside him. Be that as it may, myself I reckon they may have perished, the same as so many other, never properly named, devic Spirit Beings perished during the Great Flood of Genesis.

Of the Primary Apocalyptics, Carcinogen and Bellona managed to hold onto at least a tiny percentage of their domains, the Pristine Isles and the Bloodlands respectively. The Medusa, Mater Matare, and Headless Ramazar lost their protectorates. Presumably after possessing living shells, they nonetheless somehow found their way to Incain. There, even though Harmony was no longer around to guarantee their eventually release, they voluntarily submitted themselves to the She-Sphinx for open-ended imprisonment as the only option to cathonitization, or the possibility of a final death, left to them.

A great many Lazareme Spawn made the same choice. In truth, it's also said, and I'll repeat it now if only because I'll be taking you there myself shortly, figuratively speaking of course, that All of Incain had never been so sated, or so consequentially powerful, as she was during the Thousand Days of Disbelief. Never forgetting the debasement of Thrygragon, she might actually have finally been approaching invincible.

A few of the most powerful Mithras Spawn joined Divine Coueranna and Cruel Plathon on Apple Isle, the pupil of the Headworld's Human Eye, the Gulf of Corona. Many more, including a certain highly significant Nergalid, joined Bobby Badboy and hid out in the multi-dimensional realm of Satanwyck. En masse, Byron Spawn fled from any territories they had only relatively recently re-secured on the Cattail Peninsula or Iraxas-Krachla. They made the subcontinent of Aka Godbad their stronghold and for a time successfully drove away Yajur and Abaddon, once the two behemoths carried their travelling slaughterhouse their way there.

Saving Godbad was one of the reasons faith in devils began returning to the Hidden Headworld, albeit in the form of the yet-enduring Age of Byron. Memory of those days is also one of the main reasons, your best efforts notwithstanding, Al, your monotheistic leanings have never really taken hold here. What really finished the Age of Lazareme, though, occurred in 5495 YD. That was when, as advertised, devazurs of all three tribes came together in defence of All the Invincible, the ante-diluvian, Sphinx-like warden of Incain.

Before that a number of things happened, all of which contributed not only to the Disunition of the Unities but to the unofficial conclusion to the First War Between the Living and the Dead. In other words Sedon's Migraine was about to get a whole lot worse before it got even marginally better.

========

"Next question is, how are the three of you doing in terms of headaches? I know I could do with a pill, as in another pilsner."

========

Janna St Peche-Montressor did her best to get her father-in-law and boss to go to bed. However, given the alternatives of more beer and the no doubt stirring climax of a Tethys Tale, the Fatman wasn't interested. So she curled herself in the couch, the copy of Homer's Iliad on a coffee table, along with another pot of coffee, her second favourite stimulant, and joined Centauri and Ferdinand Niarchos as they listened to the Legendarian wind down his saga.

"Pivotal to the events of 5492-5495 are three devils, ones perhaps not very important in their own rites but indispensable to the end-result of this writing, *'Sedon's Migraine'*, not that it's been reprinted for awhile. Although I'm sure you and Centauri Enterprises could help me out in that regard, Al. I do own the rights, you know." No response. Still, he supposed mute was preferable to moot.

The Legendarian had never quite understand how legalistic crap, like rules regarding an author's death, expiration of the rights of inheritors to an estate, even if it was just a cardboard box in an alleyway, and the consequential *'reversion'* of literary masterpieces he, and no one else, had written to the public domain, affected fine folks like him. Was this not the Headworld? Did deviants have no rights?

Tethys soldiered on. "They are: 1) Fecundity, Vulva-Vetala, a 12th born Mithra-dite fertility goddess, she whose aforementioned banner the Iraches hoisted proudly aloft; 2) bedazzling as well as beguiling Belialma, Bouncing Belle, she long-no-long-er Sinistral Lust of Satanwyck, whose icon, the Ruby Red Apple of Concupiscence, certain of the Marutians' camp-followers stencilled onto religiously pre-starched, female knickers and thereupon hung from their tent-poles; they and 3) one other.

"Prepare yourselves for the death-defying return of First Fangs, Faustus Vla-duca, to our evidently non-dopey, as in sleep-inducing, drama. That and the sad episode of yet another time I didn't make it to my latest lifetime's allotment of 30 years." He emitted an exaggerated groan of faux-anguish. "That was an emphatic ouch, by the way."

========

He scratched his forehead, gone way itchy again.

========

Many have tried to list the greatest fighters of devazurkind in terms of prowess, which by my definition encompasses strength, skill and courage, in terms of dogged determinedness or indefatigability, in terms of intelligence, and in terms of simple victories. It is, like most lists, a meaningless exercise but fun nevertheless.

Except for intelligence, Abaddon would place first in all of the above categor-ies. In terms of intelligence, he would place second behind Lord Yajur. By the same token, Order would place second to Chaos in the other categories. Every other devil, including the three Great Gods, takes a back seat to these two.

If it all came down to dust, Abaddon would defeat Yajur nine times out of ten. If he had a weak-point, it was emotionalism. But emotionalism is mandatory for anyone, man or devil, who wins consistently, is it not. If Yajur had an advantage, it was his ability to plan a fight. Of course it didn't hurt that Abaddon was clearly crazed and could care less what madness he unleashed. Order, though, was fighting for the survival of the Whole Earth.

Consequently, given time, Yajur would attract powerful allies whereas Abe Chaos would battle on as a sort of one man army corps. Knowing that time was on his side, Order would engage his brother then retreat; as little as possible, but retreat nonetheless. When Abaddon got too close he would cut himself through Samsara. Sometimes it took days for Chaos to track him through the universal substance. And, when he did, Yajur would simply repeat the pattern. Ultimately it might not do him any good but, Order knew, the longer he prolonged the fight, the more chance other devils had of influencing events towards his end.

It was during one of these lulls in their deadly duel that Abe returned to the Weirdom of Kanin City, which still proclaimed itself the capital of Marutia. It was the last day of the Year of the Dome 5493, as time is counted in much of the Headworld. On the Outer Earth therefore that made it the night before the Spring Equinox in the Year 1493.

To mark the occasion Janna Somata, still the official Mastery's nominal Master, vowed to make love to every citizen of Kanin City who could reach her specially built, very much oversized bed between dusk and the dawn of New Years Day 5494. In a scene reminiscent of the decadent Roman Empire on the Outer Earth fifteen hundred years earlier, she did precisely as she promised as well.

How many men, how many male and changeling devils, how many women either/or, for Janna had long since ceased to be gender-specific, and post-pubescent children entered her bedroom – which for that night was the Masters Palace's lavishly decorated rotunda, megaron or Great Hall, the same place Abe killed Zalman in 5490 – preparatory to entering Janna, no one has ever been able to say.

I was the inaugural entry, I can say that, and so I should have been. Was not Squiggly Tethys, pre-me, betrothed to her on her 18th birthday? And was not Quidnunc Tethys, 18 years the then me, her first lover? The answer to both is a resounding yes. Which, yes, was also the cheer I let out ever-so-resoundingly after I got off, so to speak, seconds before I got out of the bed Number Two was already piling into; piling into Janna's welcoming arms dot-ditto.

One of which ended in Vladuca's fang-fingered glove, I'll add just because it's as non-elephantine-relevant as I'm longwinded, if not deprecatingly long-trunked.

========

"Stifle thy hilarity, Ferd."
"Then lead us not into it, Jordy."

========

Along with Number Two and a privileged few of our fellow, early-on honourees I was in a tavern drinking to her health, and the realization of her ambitious agenda, when Unholy Abaddon popped in for a few belts of his own. To say the least, the ensuing stampede towards, and through, the exits had nothing to do with anyone rushing back to the Masters Palace in order to get in line for seconds.

I caught a knock; said knock knocked my cap off my head before I could pluck my quill from it and thereafter draw myself elsewhere, on a napkin or whatever. Abe must have spotted Squiggly-me right away – tee-tee-tails stuck to one's head tend to make one stand out – because he had me in a bear hug before I could even pull out any of the non-pre-secreted splotches I'd already prepared of my typical escape outlets.

So that was how, me blurting, he learned what his just as crazed consort was up to that night. He didn't kill me yet, though he did drag me to the Great Hall to prove to himself that I wasn't lying. Which I never do, upon my troth as a truth-telling storyteller – and not due to the calumnious cant that I was once a devil and therefore couldn't lie even if I tried.

You and I know I retain the memories of all of my previous incarnations. While I often suffer from a deficiency of just that, memory, and sometimes put it down to too much beer, like Al says it's a poor workman who blames his lubricant. Neither do I lose my memory because I'm losing my mind.

Sooth said, soothsayer that I am as a necessary consequence of whom I am, and how I make my living, my livings, I lose memories because my mind's full and old ones have to go before I can accumulate new ones. Some things are indelibly etched upon it, though, my mind and memory, and that's why I can tell you the gory details of what happened next without any risk of contradiction.

Should preface said sadness-upcoming with notational downloading that, well, you've realized by now that he hadn't kept all three of the thrice-cursed Godly Glories on him after murdering Zalman Somata on his 114th birthday. Should perhaps have made that clear when the opportunity presented itself, but I've an excuse. I may have been suffering from a late night fluid deficiency when I failed to do so.

Failure hereby corrected, he tossed me aside and was both bulling and bullying his way through the line toward Janna's bed when the Crimson Corona suddenly appeared around his forehead. Far from having the effect she must have expected it would, he thereupon, quite literally, began chopping through everyone and anyone between him and her. Reaching her bed, he drove his trident into Janna's chest.

She clawed at it, with the fang-fingered glove she'd been wearing for howsoever long by then, but he held it there, in her. Kept holding it there, ignoring her shrieks and all the assaults launched against him from behind by her both foolish and fearless protectors, not to mention ignoring all the pointy objects they managed to lodge in his back, until the devil possessing Janna revealed herself.

It was bedazzling Belialma, Bouncing Belle, having returned to familiar territory for another roller-coaster ride in the human-Utopian, hybrid hay.

Chaos kept her pinned until she cathonitized.

========

"I know she cathonitized because there was a new star in the Mithradic Quadrant of the Sedon Sphere that night. Big deal, eh. What's the whoop about a new star shining out of the night's sky during the Thousand Days of Disbelief? Only, a couple of nights later, I was able to confirm it by looking through one of those at-the-time-newfangled telescopes Yati had in Godbad City and it looked like a ruby red apple."

Tethys held up a warning hand. It meant there was another punch-line coming. His audience braced themselves.

"Of course I was dead by then again."

========

Lady Lust gone, you'd have thought Janna Somata would die. If you were a dispossessed mortal with a Brainrock trident driven through your chest you'd die, too. Would have already, I'd have thought. I know I did. But I'm still alive and watching in sick fascination as Janna writhes about like a skewered dolphin at the end of a harpoon; dolphins being Shiva as well as Apollo's pet psychopomps, you mythology duffs, unless it's buffs, might recall.

The Crimson Corona was still wrapped around his forehead. I've never seen it, before nor since, and I've seen it a few times since, glow so brightly. Something came out of it. Abe was free to finish the job at hand. Janna burst into flames. Leaving only the fang-fingered glove smouldering on the oversized bed to mark her passage, she blew away into so much smoke in the breeze of his brutality.

That was enough for me. My boy, my Squiggly incarnation of the day, may not have been the swashbuckling sort, not in comparison to his, then mine, best buddy, Janna's Sraddha of a twin bro, but he was relatively fit for his years and liabilities, meaning me. Even though I lived there, in keeping with our procreative imperative, he, me, we, had a secret way into and out of the palace, an upper floor window.

Unfortunately, the vines broke and so did my leg when I landed. I wasn't done yet, though; not half. I knew I had to get away, no dummy me, and I knew both how and where to get away to, so long as I could first get to the tavern where – through no fault of my own, you'll no doubt recall since I just described how Uncle Abe hauled my most desirous ass to the Masters Palace – I'd left my cap, quill stuck in it.

I was in unbelievable pain. It was so bad I couldn't concentrate enough to will it back to me. Dying always hurts, but I'd died lots of burial plots over the centuries, so pain and I went way back. I persevered. At the point of exhaustion and at times beyond it – I kept passing out, only to have the incessant if not quite incandescent throbbing in my leg jolt me back to consciousness – I hopped and hobbled and, in the end, crawled and slithered toward my getaway.

I made it too, to boot, albeit what must have been hours later. Whereupon I discovered firsthand what Janna had just experienced.

========

"How could you feel firsthand what that Janna felt," Governor Niarchos quibbled. "You weren't possessed."

"For one thing," said Tethys, more than a mite annoyed at the interruption. "Sinistral Lust's star, the one I saw through Yati's telescope once I made it to Godbad City, didn't just dazzle. It dazzled distinctively. For another, it wasn't the only new star in the night's sky. It was just the newest star in the Mithradic Quadrant."

"That tells me nothing."

"Maybe nothing's what you deserve, Ferd. Patience isn't a virtue, it's a necessity. Especially when I'm telling the story. So, you staying or you going?"

"I, um, I'm staying."

"Then shut the fuck up!" This last came from Centauri's daughter-in-law.

This Janna was as tart of tongue as the Janna of nearly half a millennia ago had been, admired Tethys. *Then again, Yataghan raised Montressor was far more brawn than brains. So, other than her choice in husbands, and her sprouting more than the regulation two eyes once in a while, there wasn't much he didn't admire about her.*

Be still, procreative imperative!

========

Abe Chaos wasn't done yet either.

While I'm trying to reach my quill he's turned on his Janna's would-be and earlier-on lovers. Not only does he slaughter every last living one of them in the palace; he eyefire-crisps every last recently dead one, too. And not just those who'd reflexively tried to get up and get away again either. The actions of his Unholiness were not so much madness incarnadine as madness incendiary.

The Masters Palace is aflame by the time I make it to the tavern. So is a good percentage of the Weirdom. Or at least it's as ablaze as a mostly stone city-state can be, blaze-wise. I'm having a lot of trouble breathing but there it is, on the floor, my favourite cap of the day and my one and only quill of any day. I'm in slither-mode by now. I extend my hand. I grab for it. I have it; the quill's mine again.

Then the hand grabbing it is wearing the fang-fingered glove and First Fangs has me.

========

"The Crimson Corona didn't work on Abe Chaos because it was already occupied," twigged Centauri's daughter-in-law. *"By Faustus Vladuca."*

"Shut the fuck up, Janna!" This latest came from Ferdinand Niarchos.

Tit for tat that, supposed Tethys.

========

Faustus Vladuca was what, who, came out of the Crimson Corona. The fang-fingered glove was his power focus and he didn't approve of anyone else having it. Call him jealous or selfish, if you want to tow the Illuminaries' line about Sinistral Envy – Cupidity, the perpetual putto – being the mastermind behind his actions, but there's no denying regaining it would make him whole again.

He'd have come to Kanin City possessing one of Satanwyck's demonic vampires. Vamps are tremendous mesmerists. That's well known. They also have tremendous appetites. So maybe he simply couldn't resist putting the bite on her. That said, and other than to reacquire his Tvasitar-trinket, which he did, I've no way of knowing for sure what motivated him.

Don't forget he was still in love with Janna Somata so, howsoever-perversely, that's how I'm leaning. Possibly reasoning that neither Abe nor anyone else, other than him, would want to have anything to do with a bloodsucking bat, I think he put the bite on her deliberately. Theirs wouldn't be the first marriage remade in hell.

Be that as it may, he should have been satisfied with just getting his fang-fingered glove back and gone away, never to return. He didn't. Kept pestering her. Regardless of what vamps tell you about never forcing anyone to become one of them against their will, he had violated her and so, in my opinion, only got what he deserved.

Sometime after Abe Chaos and Lord Order got so devastatingly unbalanced, Janna finally became so fed up with his unwanted attentions she nabbed him within

Crinsom's Crown, the same as she had Harmony the day Abe killed her father months before. He was still inside it when Belialma got hold of her, possibly to try to cure her of vampirism. And, ironically, that's what saved her life as an undead bloodsucker; her existence, put better.

Abe expelled him just before Janna burst into flame and blew away; which, turning to smoke, is another of a vamp's tremendous knacks. He had enough time to get hold of his glove but not enough to get altogether away. He was body-bouncing, trying to hide in one shell after another shell, living and dead, but a killing frenzy was on Abe by then and when First Fangs got hold of me, I got what he deserved.

========

"And the first person who says I also got what I deserved gets a personally signed drawing of them sky-diving from the balcony without a parachute."

It was an empty threat, made in jest. Everyone there knew that Jordan Tethys couldn't draw anyone conscious anywhere without their expressed permission. He nevertheless looked around for any takers. No one took him up on his offer. But he still wasn't done venting.

"So, yes, Ferd. You're right in that I didn't quite experience firsthand what Janna had. I was devil-possessed when Abe Chaos drove his trident into me but I was on my stomach, on the tavern floor; not on my back, in a no matter how oversized but, until then, comfy bed.

"And I no more burst into flames than I writhed about in agony the moment First Fangs body-bounced onto his next victim. Fact is, my death-throes were limited to a loud but not particularly lengthy yowl."

========

Their cat and mouse game continued throughout New Years Day of 5494 and well into its evening. As I eventually learn – from a tee-tee-tail I read lifetimes later, if you have to know – before night fully fell his Unholiness had obliterated, then burnt unto ash, most of the people, living and dead, in the Weirdom of Kanin. It's only after dark that he stops.

"You finally nail him, Uncle Abe?" I ask, after he signals me to approach.

Which I do, me being dead by then, a crispy critter, and using a pair of charred but not-quite-yet, altogether ashen beams I salvaged from the ruined tavern as crutches. I figured it was a safe thing to do. He, all singed and bloody, looked so calm, so serene, staring as he was into the night's sky. Besides, he was holding my quill. Wasn't wearing the Crinsom Corona, though, I couldn't help notice.

"Must have missed you," he said by way of response. "Too bad about the tee-tee-tails but I suppose they'll grow back, on some other tee-tee somewhere. So will you, eventually. Want me to put you out of your misery?"

"It's a temptation. I'll grant you that. Going to answer me?"

"Yeah, I nailed him all right. Or all wrong, as I'm sure you'd have it. He ran me a merry chase but eventually there was no one else left to possess. He had the audacity to fully manifest himself and plead, brother to brother, for me to incarcerate him within All of Incain rather than ill-star him. I declined."

"And cathonitized him."

"Look for yourself, Jordy." His Unholiness indicated a new star in the Lazaremist quarter of the night's sky. "That's him, not far from Lady Luck and her stellar Triskelion."

(His Orderliness, Lord Yajur, took out Squiggly's devic half-mother, Fata Fortuna, Wintry Moira, whose power focus was indeed a Triskelion, or three-pronged Wheel of – what else? – Fortune, when he thought he was taking out Gravedigger, Devil Doom, Zuvem Nergalis, on the Terrible Twins' 18th birthday, among other events.)

"And that's her, Bouncing Belle, Lady Lust, over there in the Mithradic Quadrant. Not a bad day's work, even if I do say so myself. Fancy yourself shining up there?"

"Not an option, Abe," I said to him. "I'm a deviant, not a devil." He gave me another once-over visually.

"Who's acquired a Guardian Angel Sangazur, I see. He why you keep coming back, lifetime after lifetime?"

"It's not even twenty years since you and yours, riding psychopomp steeds, did your imitation of the Four Horsemen of the Apocalypse over in Dand Sraddha's protectorate for a depilated deviant. Even if you don't remember Deadnunk, ex-me-Quidnunc, I do. So I doubt a Sang got hold of me. One did, I'd revert to Squiggly's persona, wouldn't I, and I'm still me."

"Yet you're so mobile your tongue's wagging even if your tee-tee-tails aren't."

"Like you said, you missed altogether immolating me by fractions of degrees worth of combustion. You didn't miss too many others, though; if any. The dead are rising everywhere these days but azuras need largely intact shells to reanimate and I reckon mine's no different. Except, I've a stronger, not to mention far more practised, will to live than most. A regular azura of whatever persuasion got me up again bodily is how I figure it. But I managed to keep its personality Squiggles-me, not Squiggles-him."

"Not a bad theory, as theories go."

"Thanks. Can I have my quill back now? I can draw anything. Even skin."

"Sorry about that, Jordy," Abe apologized as he handed me my Brainrock quill. "I need another power focus like I need another hole in my head."

"Speaking of which …"

"The Crimson Corona? I gave it back to her."

"So I'm not the only one you missed."

"Oh, I didn't miss her. Just what she'd become. She misted."

"I see. And the fang-fingered glove?"

"It, too. That's where I finally got smart. Fangfingers was popping from one shell to another, had been all day. He had his talisman with him. That meant he was whole. I cut it off him; cut his hand off him ditto, like I did before. Only this time I didn't let him go. I held on until I cathonitized him. The sun had gone down by then."

"Ah, that explains that then."

"I suppose it does. I've always found it difficult to say no to her."

"Must be a load off your mind."

"You could say that."

"I just did. Where is she now?"

"I have no idea."

Neither did I. Not until after the Deflection of the Unities anyhow.

========

"Here's the scoop on Sangazurs, though I'm sure you know it already."

========

By that time, as they had been during the early years of the so-called Goddess Culture on the Outer Earth, they're mostly the azura offspring of the Medusa, Mater Matare, Mother Murder. Being polyandrous, her main mates were the all-male members of Mithras's Eighth: War, Plague and Catastrophe, as in Sudden Disaster. Or, to name them as itinerant Illuminaries of Weir did in ancient times: Mars Bellona, Carcinogen the Leper and Nakba Ramazar.

However, even after Thrygragon the male Apocalyptics didn't confine their attentions to just the Medusa. Celibacy is no more a devic trait than monogamy. That's why so few Master Devas consider themselves inseparable, as a standard husband and wife pairing. Besides, she wasn't around for most of the millennia between the halcyon days of the mad goddesses' man-hating matriarchate and Mithras's Death Day, so Sangs had plenty of other mothers.

Among the male three's other mates include the female Apocalyptics and Baby, Badhbh, one of Lazareme's three Battle Goddesses, aka the Morrigu. Which should not be confused with the Hellion's Morrigan, though that's easy to do. Baby's power focus is of course the famous Sabre Rattle and while she retained, retains I should say, and as Gomez would happily confirm since he hangs with her, non-literally, a soft spot for me, she didn't assign one of her Sangs to be my guardian angel.

If I was to guess, the azura that reanimated me belonged to either my devic half-mother, owlish Metisophia, or her younger sister, Rumour's preferred squeeze, Fata Fortuna, Wintry Moira, but I can't say one or the other for sure. I'm not averse to calling him, or it, Guardian Angel Jordan, though; have done, for storytelling purposes, for going on five hundred years.

That said, I told Al the era of Sedon's Migraine was a bad time to be alive. The converse of that is that it was good time to be dead. So now I'm dead but, for whatever reason, I'm no damn zombie. Lucky that, eh? Afraid not. While I had no problem drawing myself a second set of skin to crawl into, I exaggerated somewhat when I told Abe I could draw anything.

I could no more draw my leg unbroken than I could draw myself non-dead. And, by gosh and by golliwogs, boy, does it hurt. Which was why I drew myself to Godbad City. All the more so with Kanin City in ruins, then as now the subcontinent has the highest standards of medical care on the Inner Earth.

Unfortunately, the Godbadians' 55th Century standards weren't quite as high as their surgeons' saws were sharp. I spent the rest of that, can't call it a proper lifetime anymore but I will anyhow, as a Pegleg Pete named Jordan or, as I came to prefer, Pegleg Squigs.

End digression.

========

Throughout the Year of the Dome 5494 the Unities of Order and Chaos continued to battle each other; reengaging over and over again; one would find the other or the other would find the one. They fought south and east from Marutia to the Bloodlands and Twilight, Sedon's Inner and Outer Noses, into the western ocean and back, over the Forbidden Forest of Kala Tal, and, finally, into the Subcontinent of Aka-Godbad, the last refuge of Thrygragos Byron and his offspring. The last refuge of Jordan Tethys, too, in a manner of speaking.

Guardian Angel Jordan or no Guardian Angel Jordan, one-legged Squigs-me stinks. I've been adopted, though, again in a manner of speaking, by a devil who stinks even worse. That'd be Yati, the smoke-belching Dragon of Byron. He's the nonetheless erudite fellow Great Byron has always assigned to keep his eye, all three of them, on events occurring on the Outer Earth.

Yati recognized me immediately. Quill in cap tends to be something of a dead giveaway, pardon the pun, though he'd met Squiggly briefly up in Kanin City the night Sedon disappeared from the night's sky coming up to twenty years earlier. He, in his human form, was the fellow who had the telescope I mentioned earlier, the one he used to focus in on Lady Lust's star.

He'd built it; didn't build the sawbones' saw used to saw off my leg. That was just a standard accoutrement of warzones like the ones he frequented, as a kind of hobby, albeit usually for purposes hygienic, in order to keep down the dead, also quite literally. Perhaps because he stank worse than I was starting to – azuras being far more preservative than curative, especially when compared to their devic forbearers – he took to carrying me around, in his dragon form, from one battlefield to another.

It seems dragons like pictures and, in later lifetimes, I turned many of the rough drawings I made then into full-fledged paintings.

(*"You've a few of them, Al. There's many more in galleries and museums found throughout Godbad and elsewhere. Sooth said seriously, wherever you go on the Hidden Headworld, the very best collections have samples of my signature on all their better pieces. Mind you, granted, I didn't finish that many of them myself but, hey, that's something else we'll have to talk about someday, remuneratively speaking."*)

So it was I was there, serendipitously on the ground, in Petrograd – the seriously stinky city you call home, Ferd – sketching not at all merrily away, very painfully away, sooth said, when the Unmoving One, Bodiless Byron, force-formed by far his biggest Nucleus to that date. And, indeed, to this one dick-dildo, though I sit prepared to be corrected on that.

Desperate times, desperate measures, the firstborn pair of Silverclouds already inside All of Incain, that Great God amalgamated his second-born three, his third-born three, his remaining Zodiacals, the likes of Qosgod, Sexy Woman, Yati, and Petrogod himself, along with virtually every other member of his then not so much surviving as still available tribal offspring to do so. And, credit due, the consequential Byronhead deflected the Unities from Godbad.

Call it synchronicity if you must but, by not just my calculations, it was 669 years to the day after the date that the Idiot Twins became the Atomic Twins and thus catastrophically brought into existence the thereafter radioactively uninhabitable Ghostlands. That would make it the 1st of Maruta, 5494 Year of the Dome, 1 November on the Outer Earth.

Out there, beyond the Cathonic Zone, the same date is, and was, All Saints Day, not that there's anything saintly about devils. Here on the Hidden Headworld, there's naught anywhere near so general. It's All Death Day, the one and thereafter, hopefully, only. And it, that date in 5494, has gone down as such, in absolute infamy, because the mobile Dead thereon outnumbered the yet Living.

As for what finally tipped the balance from one to the other – not that the Unity of Balance is around any longer, I shouldn't have to remind you – I'd call it a double-bummer.

========

"Although I gather 'bummer' is one their favourite sayings, why I call it that, times two, has nothing to do with the Outer Earth's intriguing hippy sorts Al's told me so much about over the last decade or so. The yearly celebrated, particularly here in Godbad, Deflection of the Unities, as opposed to my tale's titular Disunition of same, resulted in a pair of bums, those of the last two Unities, coming down upon the biggest battle then raging between forces of the Still Breathing but Badly Bleeding.

"The Gleaming City of Manoa, flattened as it was, on both sides of it, the besieged Iraches as well as the besieging Sraddhites, has never been the same. And, oh yes, lest I forget, neither has the rest of the Irache Nation. Then again they, the Iraches, have always enjoyed having tea and buttered scones with their ancestors, no matter how crushed they were or are."

"Until Fangs unionized them," said Niarchos, sounding disgruntled. "Now they call them scabs."

"Do they really? I wonder why?"

"All part of the negotiation process, Jordy."

"Sounds like an unfolding story; one I'll have to check out one of these days. Let's finish this one first."

****

11: The Nous Has It

With enough stimulants sleep could be put off. When the stimulants of choice are liquid, however, certain other bodily functions cannot be.

Once they reconvened, Jordan Tethys had a brain-teaser for them: "Riddle me this: Everyone knows vampires are infertile so how is it a vamp can give birth?"

========

"Answer is this: With practised ease. So long as the vampire's already a multiple mom by the name of Nergal Vetala and she's a devil who was multiply pregnant before she became a bat."

"I knew that," said Centauri.

"Then you probably know this too. On All Death Day, Nergal Vetala – Vulva-Vetala, as some devils called her, though never to her face – gave birth to a multitude of azuras. Those azuras have become known as Haddazurs because they were born on the day Iraxas became known as Hadd. All of which explains how the Iraches managed to turn the tide and drive the double-dealing Sraddhites back to Lake Sedona, where they've been pretty much isolated ever since."

"It does not," Niarchos objected.

"Of course it does, Ferd. Iraches have tea and buttered scones with their ancestors, Sraddhites incinerate theirs. While they're as thick as a brick-bucks-bank, Haddazur zombies know which side their scones are buttered on, even if they're burnt. Better to be fed and dead than cinders dulling from red."

"Oh," said Niarchos, no doubt making a mental note for his next set of negotiations.

========

A Tethys Tale - JANNA FANGFINGERS: THE DISUNITION OF THE UNITIES OF LAZAREME – Part Eight: ALL DEATH DAY

========

Since 'discovering' Iraxas two years earlier, Sraddha Somata has become known as the Emperor in Exile.

========

Although sentimentally, rather than realistically, they persistently referred to it as a Mastery, the empire at issue was really only a gutted, barely floundering insult to the memory of the serene domination his father and their ancestors – hybrid Utopians for the most part – built, as if to mark the start of the Dome's Sixth Millennium, and thereafter maintained, in the spirit if not the name, per se, of Panharmonium.

The vast plains of Marutia, Sedon's Cheek, had been in a state of constant turmoil since its much larger, nearly Headworld-wide larger, predecessor powerhouse, the Empire of Lathakra, began dissolving in the 49th Century of the Dome. Time quakes or no time quakes, in terms of ease of agriculture the Cheek Lands doubled as Sedon's Bread Basket. Their decay couldn't be allowed to continue. Which was part of the reason these hybrids, once they marched out of their base in Kanin City and the nearby Gregarian Fields, met so little resistance.

Of course, in this, the ongoing Age of Lazareme, they would never have got very far without the support of Datong Harmonia, the much admired, even beloved Unity of Balance as well as, yes, Panharmonium. So, notwithstanding their own atheistic leanings and the very visible backing of Lazaremist extremists, their efforts to gradually stabilize so many formerly Mithradite territories were close to universally embraced.

So, succeed these mixed U-bloods, along with their Marutian and/or Lazaremist allies did, for hundreds of years. Now, though, thanks to the literal devastation caused by the two Unities, the Mastery was expelling its last gasps barely two years after Harmony did hers in whichever cave it was wherever.

Marutia and, with it, the hybrid Utopians' Mastery already lay in wreckage. But, rather than mourn its passing, Sraddha had gone on to establish a new Mastery, or resuscitate the old one, as he'd have had it; a brave new world for Marutians to populate at any rate.

To do so he initially formed a cynical alliance with the Vetala-worshipping Iraches. Since his own forces were mostly still closet Mithradites that wasn't too hard. It was, after all, adherents of Great Byron and his tribe who had been driving the Iraches northwards in the first place. However, once the Byronics unwisely divided their forces, sending some to retake the Southern Cattail, the Iraches rose up and joined with the invaders and their returning brethren en masse.

Events up north, though, displaced more and more Marutians southwards. So it was, in a matter of months, the Iraches were being squeezed in on all sides. Some clans left Iraxas altogether. Many fled to the northern Cattail, where they formed the very loosely knit confederation of Free Iraxas. Others headed into Godbad, specifically to the foul-smelling, petroleum-rich but, largely because of that, only sparsely populated territory of what Godbadians now call New Iraxas. By far and away the majority of Iraches fought backwards to the Gleaming City of Manoa, where they prepared to make their last stand.

We're well into the Thousand Days of Disbelief by now. Other than the Godbadians' Byronics and the Iraches' Nergal Vetala, virtually no one alive is worshipping devils anymore. And, when it all comes down to dust, what good is worshipping her doing the Iraches? I mean, where is she in this, their most desperate hour?

Mark me, though, there's something about sentient beings that makes them want to worship some higher power; a God Gene, maybe, or some such mechanism wired into their blustery brainpans. Sraddha – who is so far beyond childhood nicknames I promise not to call him Shreds anymore – realizes this. With what was for him previously uncharacteristic brutality, he's leading a disciplined, superbly equipped, professionally trained and numerically superior Marutian military in triumph after triumph against his former allies. But he wants more than paltry victories over disheartened foes.

So he concocts an entirely new religion, with himself not only as pontiff but as Living God. Rather, he re-concocts it – which kind of negates the previous sentence, doesn't it. Except, this time Faustus Vladuca isn't occupying him. Neither is any other devil-god. Which means he isn't controlling any paranormal power save his own considerable savvy. Which in turn means there's nothing outwardly supernatural or superstitious about his religion. And that makes it new in my book; makes it welcome as well.

He does not claim immortality; though, since his forbearers on one bedside or the other, or both in his case, had long been possessed by devils, he does anticipate a long life. He does not claim omnipotence nor ubiquity; nor divinity in the sense of being beautiful or infallible. What he does claim is being the only real chance the living have against either devils or the ambulatory dead. Furthermore, he teaches that he's no less than the embodiment of the three supernatural virtues: Faith, Hope and Charity; and of the four natural virtues: Justice, Fortitude, Prudence and Temperance. Modest he wasn't.

Sraddha establishes a rigid code of ethics for himself and his Marutian followers. His message is much the same Xuthros Hor gave to his followers before and immediately after the Great Flood: *'Have faith in yourself because there is no one else deserving it.'* Understand, even though he and Squiggly, pre-me, came across them during our sojourn on the Outer Earth, I'm not suggesting he was a closet member of the always secretive Xuthrodite Brotherhood – aka the Horrites, as they're disparaged in here – but he wasn't far off.

Those who can't or won't match his ideals, his devotion to the cause of life, his rigorous pursuit of Man's higher instincts in the face of the baseness that's everywhere else around them, are denounced as heathen and either enslaved or put to the torch. (After all, as I may have mentioned on more than a few occasions already, ash is about the only thing Dead Things can't reanimate.)

In this, he and his fanatical followers echo the attitudes of so many religious supremacists found throughout history, on both sides of the Whole Earth. It makes no natural sense; never has and never will. In the name of devotion to the cause of Life, your life is forfeit because you dare to demand the freedom to live it as you please? Don't give me a break, give yourself one; preferably fatal. Religion, thy name is intolerance.

In his honour the faithful, men and women both, took to imitating Sraddha Somata by shaving the hair off their heads and wearing brown robes – under their armour, as needed. Consequently calling themselves Sraddhites they go so far as to hunt down Iraches just because they still worship Vetala. Those that convert are disarmed and, even then only begrudgingly, forced to perform the most menial of tasks.

For what? The most meagre rewards: food, clothing, tents or shacks wherein they could lay their heads. That and, oh yes, the opportunity to keep breathing, not to mention bleeding. The cause of Life? What kind of life? There is the mockery. (And if all this sounds like what the Sarpedons, to hear Demios tell it, were put through in the Weirdom of Cabalarkon for thousands of years, well, the piss-poorness of their beer isn't the only reason I sometimes refer to Utopians as Dsytopians.)

Who could believe Iraches would ever seriously convert to anything? Leopards and spots that, any sensible Marutian would tell you. Once a Vetala-venerating infidel always a Vetala-venerating infidel. Plainly, Iraches were inferior beings. So, as I said, many Iraches flee westwards to Godbad or eastwards, across the Sea of Akadan, to the Cattail Peninsula.

Many, many more don't; though for some, I'll accept, it's mostly because they missed the boats and have lived to regret it. Yet look what conversion got their brethren, the relative few who opted for it? About the same as their veneration of Vetala has, to be blunt, which isn't much of anything.

So here they are, in the Gleaming City, the ages-old capital of Iraxas, where the streets are paved with gold and the roofs inlaid with precious stones. And here they're going to fight and die, then get up and fight some more, until there's no more left of either them or their city than there is of Kanin City and its inhabitants.

Desperation hasn't made them suicidal. The Sraddhites have.

========

The Gleaming City had always been known as Manoa. By this time, though, Marutians had stopped referring to the country containing it as Iraxas. Rather, they were once again referring to the huge, verdant, tear-dropped shaped peninsula, some 250,000 square miles in size, by an old, Byronic term: namely, El Dorado, the aforementioned land of golden opportunity.

Although to the indigent, initially animistic, non-devil-worshipping Iraches it had always been Iraxas, in the centuries before the Empire of Lathakra took root there circa 4800 Year of the Dome, much of the Penile Peninsula was spotted with the Byronic equivalent of up north's devic protectorates; spaces generously allocated to individual Byron Spawn by their Great God of a father, who nevertheless reserved the right to remove or relocate them at his whim.

The dominant devil-god overruling Manoa in those days was a third-born, APM and Nevair Neverknight's brood brother: Damon Goldenrod, Byron's Apollo, hence the El Dorado reference. Manoa itself was his designated sphere of influence while the plains beyond belonged to Chimaera Glimmenmare and his alien Centaurs, who terrorized Iraches just for sport.

Even earlier, meaning pre 2000 YD, Manoa was a Weirdom, the same as most of the other long-standing, megalithic metropolises on the Head. Somewhat ironically, Sraddha ran his new religion out of yet another formerly Utopian edifice, the monastery built atop a multilevel ziggurat in the middle of one of the dozens of islands within Lake Sedona. That'd be, then as now, Sraddha Isle.

I say ironically because Sraddhites were largely materialistic, reliant upon science and discovery, whereas Smokey Sedona was Byron's goddess of magic, sorcery and arcane witchery; hence her Spellbinder surname. Like Chimaera and Vayu Maelstrom, likely the *'Hurican'* or hurricane Mayan peoples worshipped until comparatively recent times beyond the Dome, Sedona is a second-born Byronic, one of that Great God's Primary Nucleoids.

I said somewhat because, hey, I can't be absolutely certain it wasn't one of her spells that caused the Unities to deflect where they deflected. However, if it was then it backfired.

========

"And, no, I'm not making a fart joke. I'll leave them to you, Ferd."

========

"After all, you live in a land of flatulence. That's why about the only people who can safely work there for any length of time are Dead Things."

"Which is one reason they've gone on strike," the governor countered, with a straight face but a sardonic tone. "They're striking for more unsafe working conditions whereas we're heading the opposite direction. Never underestimate the lure of filthy lucre in an Outer-Earth-modern economy such as the one Centauri Enterprises is foisting upon ROG, the rest of Godbad. It was only a matter of time before it reached Petrograd."

"It won't be filthy much longer, Mr Niarchos," said the Fatman, switching into formal mode, as he always did when discussing business. "In fact, I'm thinking of changing the name of our currency from Godbucks to Greenbacks." Tethys was about to laugh at that. Then he caught himself. He never laughed at Centauri's jokes so it'd be positively rude to laugh when he wasn't making one.

Godbad's Green Movement was no longer nascent. (He knew this because he read its mostly CE-controlled press. Truth told, which he always did, even if he occasionally exaggerated, he used some of the better rags as blankets some nights.) The Fatman enjoyed being popular and, while he was hardly above manipulating the media, had a passion for it actually, he wouldn't do so to make himself unpopular. So something was up.

"Greenbacks, green spaces," Tethys considered. "I'm to gather the underground economy of New Iraxas is switching to an over-ground economy."

"We're working on it, Mr Tethys," said Centauri.

Yes indeed. Something was definitely up; in the air itself, it seemed. One good thing about worshipping devils was they had to give as good as they got. And who's to say Bodiless Byron couldn't clean up the regularly non-breathable air in New Iraxas. When one of your sons, the Primary Nucleoid old-time Illuminaries named Vayu Maelstrom, was best known among his fellow devazurs as Devil Wind, it had to be within the realm of possibility.

His scar wasn't itching – much – but his nose was twitching. He rubbed it. "Let's stick with Jordy for now, Al."

Scratch Goatwood. Good reporter that he was, the next stop for him had to be New Iraxas.

========

"Even though Sedon's Cheek Lands were plagued by Time Quakes, the Marutians never forgot how to forge sharp-edged weapons or firearms."

========

By contrast, Iraches never learned proper metallurgic techniques. They were, in terms of the Outer Earth's historical reckoning, barely into the Bronze Age whereas Marutians were well-advanced into the Iron Age. Byronic god-devils fleet in flight, their soldiers less so, on their feet and in their rescue boats, duplicitous Sraddhites cut off their source of advanced weaponry from Upper Head realms peripheral to the Cheek. For the Iraches' present it was back to the past.

Manoa was surrounded. It should have fallen as easily as the Outer Earth's Tenochtitlan, the future Mexico City, fell to Hernan Cortez's Spaniards a few decades later in your 16th Century, Al. Easier, I'd say. Conquistadors were minuscule in number but overwhelming in terms of weaponry. On the other hand, Sraddhites were overwhelming in terms of both.

For their part, the besieged Iraches acknowledge the invaders as their superiors in every way but one; two actually. As I said, the Marutians, men and women, fighters and followers, shaved their skulls bald, like their Living God, whereas the Iraches, whose men did most of the fighting, wore their dark hair long and proud, as did their missing devil-queen. So that's one.

More importantly, the Iraches still had faith in their devil-god, Fecundity, Nergal Vetala. One of these days she'd return to the Gleaming City, her power base for so many centuries. She wouldn't return just to protect its denizens, either. She was going to turn their misfortunes into fortunes; their bad times altogether around, back into their best times. So that's two.

Except, where the hell was she? Exactly.

Well, not exactly, not on All Death Day, but that's where she ended up after the Godbadians chased her and her most fervid followers out of Iraxas in the Spring of 5490; rather, chased them as far as somewhere in the southernmost heights of Diluvia, where they got away into the cave-system undermining the mountain range.

Leaving her faithful semi-safely on the northern side, she took herself through between-space all the way to Pandemonium, the capital of Satanwyck: Sedon's Temple, Hell on Earth, paradise for the damned and homeland to demons, mostly without the '*a*'. Thereafter, until his Unholiness, the Unity of Chaos, busted the place up at the beginning of Cupidam 5492, she spent most of her time inputting spermatozoon donations from male Mithradite Master Devas and outputting their azuras.

Although her circumstances had drastically changed by the time Chaos came by to collect Cathune Bubastis, the Apocalyptic of Drought, he raised enough hell, sorry; caused enough pure Pandemonium, sorry again; provided enough of a distraction, for her to evade said impregnating males' imposed, um, layover, unless you prefer layabout, and altogether escape Satanwyck, again via between-space. And by drastically I also mean toothily.

You'll have deduced, if I didn't state it explicitly, that she was outraged the Byronics of Godbad drove her out of Iraxas in the first place. After all, for many centuries she felt it her protectorate. Yet how could that be when she'd failed to hold onto it in the face of their impressive offensive?

So what if the Godbadians had state-of-the-killing-art's guns and metallic weaponry as well as both a tactical and numerical superiority over the primitive Iraches who worshipped her? What truly militated against her, besides a lack of Lathakrans, were Grandfather Sedon's dictates against devils taking to the battlefield and killing anyone on behalf of their adherents. Was that what made her decide to hie herself to Satanwyck and thereafter go toothy? Wouldn't want to speculate, would I.

She was on her way to Hell, accompanied by her just as displaced guest of, what?, three years earlier, something like that, the always beguiling Belialma, when the two devils had their marathon tryst with Sraddha Somata. That'd be the afore-mentioned three-day free-for-all they enjoyed on the Marutian side of the Diluvia Range sometime after the combination Time Quake and earthquake hit the area on, I understand, the same day Chaos killed Zalman in 5490.

(Despite what he may have believed, she didn't gravitate back to him, once she got out of Satanwyck, because he was such a stud. At least that wasn't all of it.)

As I said, she'd been dutifully churning out azuras to reanimate Dead Things for most of her months and years in Pandemonium. While I'm no expert when it comes to the reproductive systems of female Master Devas, I do know they have comparatively short gestation periods and, in addition to being able to carry multiple foeti, if I can use that term when referring to unborn azura spirit beings, they can carry multiple foeti from multiple fathers with no need for any sort of simultaneous insemination.

In other words, they can hoard them inside themselves for months, even years at a time. Furthermore, so long as they stay sexually active they can add more and more to the unborn miasma, as it were. And they can keep doing that until nature simply can't be denied any longer or – and this is key – the devic mother-to-be decides to be an azura-mother-letting-free. Talk about being Pro-Choice, that being the case, the devic dame breaks her own devic dam and lets loose all the baby bundles of spiritual joy she's been holding back in one big burst of birth.

So that explains the first part of the devic delivery system. Other than saying she earned the designation as much as nickname of Fecundity, it does not explain Vulva-Vetala's unique capaciousness; if that isn't putting it too indelicately for sensitive ears hereabouts. It nevertheless seems that it was a non-lunar aspect of her attribute; one her elders, the two remaining Apple Goddesses I'm guessing, perhaps slanderously, discovered and happily exploited.

(With or without Vetala's permission, I'll footnote for the sake of clarity. Lower born can't disobey higher born, especially not without their father around to rule differently.)

As Al here will tell you, after its Second World War ended in 1945, large areas of the Outer Earth experienced what he calls a 'baby boom'. Well, I'm here to tell you that the higher born Mithradites, via Vetala, devised a particularly potent form of 'baby bomb'. Of course there was no point letting it go off in Satanwyck, where there's only demons for her azuras to occupy, but devils are self-psychopomps so nay probs, eh.

The trickier part is getting her to deny nature – the need to give birth when due, if not before – such that she can hold onto them long enough to transport herself to corpses-choked killing fields where they could actually do some good; something useful for the Mithradite higher-ups, put better. Or something particularly bad if you were alive in those days, which I still am, if not for much longer.

Perhaps in a valiant, if misguided, demonstration that she was boss of her own body, Vetala went along with this nonsense for the longest time. Put insensitively but accurately, Fecundity found a way to keep her dam-busters, her not-yet-newly-born azuras, together inside her as a cohesive unit, a bomb if you will, until she simply couldn't hold onto them anymore.

At which point she, or more likely they, carrying her, materialized overtop some aforesaid corpses-choked killing field left behind by the duelling Unities and she let it, her baby bomb, or them, her accumulation of finally aborning azuras, drop. Whereupon, as you'll have anticipated, the corpses rose up ready to choke the more. And need I tell you who azuras defer to? Didn't think so – their fathers, not their mothers.

Then one day she just stops.

Without presuming to read her mind, I'll speculate she grew sick and tired of being used in such a degrading manner, as if she was some sort of seed receptacle, an automated reproduction machine. Just as speculatively, she went into bewitching mode. Belialma was still around, so she hadn't inherited Lady Lust's mantle as a sex-crazed nymph-node, but Moon Goddesses are almost by definition seductive so no surprise there.

She wouldn't have had any trouble enticing Faustus Vladuca into putting the bite on her. (Mind you, he may have been dominating a vampiric shell – and, if so, possibly the very one he later used to turn Janna Somata after she refused to give him back his fang-fingered glove. Then again, he may have gone toothy himself.) For that matter, Vetala being Vetala, she wouldn't have had trouble persuading any other vamp to do it to her, either.

Then again, again, we've already touched on a vampire's innate mesmeric abilities so who's to say it was her idea? As I said, not me. And I'm not about to ask her, am I. Besides, regardless of responsibility, becoming a vamp of the truly toothy, non-shoe variety isn't such an awful move on her part, all things considered.

As a devil she could probably cure herself of vampirism any time she felt like it. As a vampire, though, she isn't just beyond the interest of male Master Devas. She's beyond the Moloch Sedon's ability to cathonitize. Can't cathonitize a devil when she's mostly something else. Devic suicides know that; which is why they cut out their third eyes in order to commit just that.

The only problem with that is it makes them eminently killable. Provided you can catch and thereupon nail them, I shouldn't have to add. Vetala figures she's got it both ways, though. She hasn't cut out her third eye and, as a batty bloodsucker, she's rendered herself pretty much unkillable to hoot, if not to stake.

So long as she stays away from pointy sticks, and only attends battles after dark, she's gone from the devic reproduction line – with her as the breeding machine in the middle of the seed-to-egg-to-newborn conveyer belt – to an infertile killer who can't be ill-starred.

And if the thought of a killer devil isn't bloodcurdling then your blood's already curdled.

There's more, though. No more fertility, she's no more use to male Master Devas. But, as I foreboded, she's full up when she escapes Satanwyck. There's no telling how many unborn azuras she's massing inside her but, practised Baby Bomber that she is by now, she knows she has to maximize the effectiveness of her last chance at damned damsel dam-bursting, to fay-say some buns in the oven.

A big, bloody battlefield in Iraxas full of fresh, preferably non-Irache corpses will be ideal, she reckons. So she cuts herself to former lover Sraddha's side and, by gosh and by golliwogs, they come to an accommodation. It isn't a matter of she'll show him hers if he shows her his because they're already beyond that. But she does show him the infra-mountain cave-way through Diluvia into the Penile Peninsula that he and his men have been searching for; the one she and her then fleeing forces used in 5490.

Either that or she cuts him a new one. Again, I wasn't there so couldn't possibly say one way or the other. But I can say that on the 12ᵗʰ of Djerridam, Year on the Dome 5492, Sraddha *'discovered'*, in quotes, Iraxas. Coincidentally, it's the same day, albeit the 12ᵗʰ of October 1492, that Columbus lands in the Bahamas and *'discovers'*, also in quotes, the Americas.

But that's neither here nor there. What is here, on the Head, and there, in Iraxas, is that Shredder – my new nickname for him – and his strengthened army, packed as it mostly is with stacks of raw recruits whose ancestors were Mithradite-worshippers, join up with her just as Byronics-hating Iraches-in-waiting and head south.

Over the next few months their combined forces trounce the Godbadians whenever and wherever they meet in battle. As its non-devic leadership is by now taking a telltale as well as tables-turning amount of fatalities after dark, these encounters, bloody as they are, quickly become few and far between.

Faced, as they only belatedly realize, with all-night assaults by a vanguard of hungry vamps, an increasing number of whom were once these very leaders, the Godbadians may or may not realize they're also up against a killer devil. Yet they are – Nergal Vetala, henceforth the Vampire Queen of the Dead.

What resistance they do mount is mostly rearguard, delaying action intended to facilitate a full-blown retreat to the safety of the subcontinent. There – should the terrible alliance of Iraches and Sraddhites, with their marching Dead Things and nightly bat-whacks, get that far – they reason their devil-gods would find it much easier to push back without fear of violating the Moloch Sedon's dictates against killing lesser beings; not that that, obviously. includes vampires.

As a result, no doubt disappointingly to her, there's no big battlefield choked with hundreds of dead, onetime Byronic worshippers over which Vetala can deliver her come-to-term-terminal, hence fully-bloomed *'boom'*. She nonetheless manfully, if I dare use the word in such a context, holds onto those she contains until one presents itself.

Except, one doesn't, does it. Indeed, things go so well for Sraddha-Vetala's joint forces that, within the same matter of months, his Marutians – who by now worship him alone, not any Great God or devil from any tribe – are turning on their former allies, her Iraches. Far, far worse, as far she's concerned anyhow, he's letting them run amok. And the first folks, if you can call them that, he targets are her prized bloodsuckers.

Much to Vetala's discredit, not to mention everlasting shame and humiliation, they, her greatest assets, chose to make their daily lairs within fortified encampments close to the allies' always advancing frontlines. No matter how well-guarded they are, given they're so vulnerable during the day – sunlight roasts them irretrievably – that has to be the height of arrogance. To me it remains a wonderment that Sraddha capitalized on their sheer brainlessness before Bodiless Byron and his most militant offspring, the likes of Sedona Spellbinder, Nevair Neverknight and Heroic Hektoris, thought to do so.

As if that wasn't devastating enough, the Marutians make a pyrotic, not pyrrhic, point of thoroughly incinerating, with their fire canisters and hoses, the Iraches out of whom they've already made mincemeat. Horror of horrors, this now devic horror is horrified by such a horrendous development within her former pseudo-protectorate. Which is about when that tremendous appetite I noted previously with respect to toothsome bloodsuckers kicks in.

She changes her diet. Marutians, not Godbadians, become her favourite meal. So do her vamps, the ones who smartly slept in her vicinity, away from the armies' backlines during the day. Vampires follow their makers as slavishly as devazurs do their fathers but she reserves Sraddha for herself. Which Shredder – see mincemeat above – must have expected. Thus, when it comes time for her to add him to her plate, the Emperor in Exile makes a measured response. Make that makes a mirrored response.

All of which tells you where Vetala's been until All Death Day.

========

Jordan Tethys paused again. "Are there any questions?"

It was getting late and they hadn't got around to ordering in more pilsners. Bordering on worse, while his nose had stopped twitching, the scar tissue in the centre of his forehead, where a devil would have a third eye, had recommenced itching badly. Ergo, devils were much closer than they had been prior to darkness falling.

Itches required scratching. He scratched his itch.

========

"I realize that's the history of the Upper Head," volunteered Janna, taking advantage of the invitation. "There probably would never have been an Era of Empires, or the need for Taurus Chrysaor Attis and his Mithrant Legionnaires before Thrygragon, if resident devils could kill to defend their declared territories. But former? Wouldn't Iraxas have reverted back to her the moment the Godbadians and their devil-gods fled back here?"

"Iraches are animists at heart, Janna," Niarchos lectured her indulgently, as if jumping at the opportunity to show her he knew something besides how to be obnoxious. "Devic worship doesn't come naturally to them. Plus, it's faith in a devil, not the devil's mere presence, that makes for a protectorate or, in the Byronic terms I'm used to, a sphere of influence.

"But there's another reason Jordy intentionally added pseudo. It wasn't hers to start with, was it? Vastness-wise, pun intended, if not population-wise, pollution not intended, it originally belonged to Vanthysces Vastness, the Byronic Grim Reaper. Ask me, the Iraches were never too chuffed with him. Otherwise Vetala couldn't have taken it over so comparatively easily during the expansion of the Empire of Lathakra six or seven hundred years earlier."

"Not bad, Ferd," Tethys allowed, having attended to scratching of itching if not the beery dilution of dehydration. "Although I personally veer to the perhaps blasphemous view that it's more a matter of Byronic Master Devas having no choice except to share their nominal domains with their father. A faith divided is no faith at all, they say. That's the reason Outer Earth Protestants don't revere the Virgin Mary anywhere near as much as they do her son. There's term for that, but I can't remember it."

"Mariolatry," provided the Fatman. "That's why we secular Catholics are more broad-minded than Outer Earth Protestants or evangelicals." He regarded those with him apparently expectantly. "That's a joke by the way." Three blank looks continued to greet him. "Women's rights, broad-minded, broad ... Forget it."

"I'm sure we are all duly appreciative of the illumination, Al," said Tethys, having no difficulty not laughing this time.

"Maybe I better get us – get you, Jordy – some more beer," said Janna, evidently needing something to do other than smacking her father-in-law across the old cauliflower earhole.

"I can wait," said Tethys, not wanting to hold off until she returned.

"So can we," said Niarchos, whom Janna had cut off a while back.

"I never got a chance to ask him for confirmation one way or the other," Tethys carried on, "But I suspect Sraddha always intended to turn on the Iraches. From the reports I gathered particularly later on, he'd grown cruel and callous since Squiggly-him or Squiggly-me spent so much time travelling together with him-he, Shreds-then, Shredder-now, on either side of the Dome. Proximity to one of the Trigregos Talismans does that to man and devil both."

(He'd already told them that he'd stayed behind in Kanin City after Zalman's murder because his murderer demanded a drinking buddy and one didn't say no to homicidal maniacs.)

"The mirror being transmutable, like all devic power foci, including mine, it's likely the Vampire Queen didn't even realize he had it on him. He wouldn't have been quaking in his boots when she came for him, fangs bared, that's for sure. He'd been with me in Kanin City when Janna used it on whichever one it was, Yajur or Harmony, the day Abe killed their father, so he definitely knew what it could do when charged by enough willpower.

"Similarly withstanding firsthand verification, as opposed to vilification, I'm prepared to go further and impugn that he planned to use it against her the moment she'd, um, out-batted rather than outlived her worth to him. As for mental might, he was just as capable of putting a stop to her as his twin sister was First Fangs, whether or not he was bodily a vampire by then, when he kept pestering her after he came back to Kanin City hoping to regain his power focus."

"The Crimson Corona didn't work the way Janna wanted it to on Abe Chaos because First Fangs was already in it," Janna repeated, in case Ferd or the Fatman had missed its import earlier on. "And, sometime before then he'd used the other one, the Susasword, to dispose of his triplet sister. That's how the Unities became so unbalanced in the first place."

Tethys glanced around the solarium. Mrs Yataghan had cleared away the dirtied dishes over the course of their last few breaks. So it looked safe for him to echo her father-in-law and congratulate her non-inimitably, without fear of personal injury let alone loss of the wherewithal for procreative imperatives.

"Always said you were a bright broad."

Damnation, he'd forgotten she was a materialist. How could he have forgotten such a salient, even life-preserving fact? Most fully trained Afrites or Athenans were and she was both. Was it too late to blame his lubricant, or momentary lack thereof? Whereupon, much to his immense relief as well as dickish delight, what she materialized was a kumquat. It was certainly preferable to a prickly pear.

He flinched anyways. War Witches could kill with anything.

========

"The morning of All Death Day," he resumed once Janna had gone and come back, nibbles and, happily, another six-pack of cool pills in hand. "Sraddha Somata was still asleep in his tent some distance from where the main Marutian forces were already back battering at the Gates of Manoa."

========

Sraddhites believed the Gleaming City's nonetheless still gleaming walls would finally topple today; emphasis on *'finally'.* They weren't wrong – but when the double-whammy of the double-bummer came crashing down upon its outermost ramparts, gleaming consequently no longer, they weren't anywhere near so numerous either, on either side of the walls.

While he was one of the lucky ones to survive the asshole-Unities' initial impact, his survival had no more to do with Lady Luck than mine did in Kanin City a month or so previously. Not unless she could influence events from her perch in the Sedon Sphere, it didn't. No fool he, and no doubt mindful of the disunited brothers' seemingly unified efforts to depopulate the Head, he took himself physically into the Amateramirror – and, no, you don't have to be a spirit being or have a subtle matter body to accomplish that.

His desperate move had the, perhaps-to-him, unanticipated effect of releasing Vetala from it. Whereupon, apparently shocked into action after such an extended period of enforced inaction, the equivalent of my legless limbo for anyone dead-head-internalized in its emptiness, she thereupon began, howsoever involuntarily, having birth-pangs.

She proceeded to birth-burst-forth, more painfully than bundles of joyfully, multiple hundreds of Haddazurs. Whereupon virtually all of that day's Freshly Dead, on both sides of Manoa's now shattered walls, got up and began pursuing Shredder's Sraddhites, those until then spared, back toward Sraddha Island, hundreds of miles to the northeast.

About the only thing that saved the majority's piss-pants-panicked, still-wannabe-imperialist bacon was, aside from some revisionist, Outer Earth zombie movies, Dead Things plod awfully slowly.

========

"In the absence of fathers, azuras do as their mothers command."

"That they do, Ferd. And, let me tell you, Vetala was mightily miffed."

"Permission granted," said Centauri, which actually brought a snicker or three from his surprisingly appreciative audience.

========

Re-enter Pegleg Squigs – that'd be me.

I was, as I may have neglected to note, in Petrogod's Petrograd when the Byronic Nucleus deflected both Unity-bums from above it across the Gulf of Aka to over top Manoa. Whereupon they dumped upon the Gleaming City big-ass plops-time. The deflection fragmented the Nucleus. Dozens of Byronics had made it up and, to a Jack and Jill one of them, even their fabled far-sight was discombobulated as a result. They had no idea where they'd sent them; no idea if they'd even knocked them out of Aka Godbad proper between-space.

Reeling, but nevertheless remarkably remembering that he'd brought me there, adoptive-dad Yati, Byron's Dragon, sought out and found me. Not the most reassuring sight, a reeling dragon, permission granted to assure you. He wanted me to draw myself to wherever they'd landed and report back what damage Order and Chaos had done, or were doing, in case there was anything they, he and his fellow Byronics, could do salvation-wise – as in saving face at the same time they were saving worshippers.

And who, except me, could tell where they'd gone? Unless you were there, where the Byronics weren't, no one answers that. Ah, but how was I to know where that was, you might ask, and I might tell you, for another pilsner; all the more so when Godbad's god-devils didn't? Trial and error, hit and miss – and thank you, miss. Please don't hit me, missus.

Only, every time I drew either Uncle Abe Chaos or Thunder & Lightning Lord Order, the background filled in different places. Possibly as badly affected as the Byronics who deflected them elsewhere, they'd reflexively reverted to type; were back to their old tricks. His Unholiness and His Orderliness were having another recuperative break away from each other.

But that didn't answer Yati's question. Where had they deflected to first? My quill doesn't come with a built-in instruction manual so you can call it divine inspiration if you feel you must. I did as tasked as well as asked. I did what the Byronic Nucleus and its fractured components couldn't do. I drew the two remaining Unities backwards.

I can do that. And that's how I ended up in Manoa that night.

========

"Whereupon?" Niarchos prodded.

"Whereupon … Okay, Ferd, you've got me here. Call it Crimson-Corona-inspirational, if you like. Just be sure you give me all due credit when it comes to the endgame."

"Not to mention when it all comes down to dust. Or sand. On Incain."

"Not to mention that either. Sure you don't want to tell the story yourself?"

"That'd be nonsensical, not commonsensical."

"The nous has it then."

"Better than the noose."

"Shut up, Ferd," said Centauri, very much informally.

"Guess who's still cut off, governor?" Janna St Peche-Montressor tit-for-tatted.

"Carry on, Jordy," Niarchos encouraged, cracking a bottle of pills anyhow.

========

Shortly after arriving in what's left of Manoa I'm in place to witness Janna Fangfingers, silver-haired, pale as the proverbial Ghast-handkerchief, big sharp teeth, particularly her canines, bloody red lips and eyeballs, one of which is in her forehead, picking up the broken shards of the Amateramirror. Or should I call them shreds?

Regardless of that, she's in an opulent but deliberately kept darkened tent. Unless I missed my guess, it was precisely the kind of travelling canvas palace where you'd expect a top-of-the-command-structure general might sleep. Which, since it was Sraddha's until that morning – hence my shards versus shreds debate – it turned out I didn't. My guess, I mean, not my debate. And it's Shredder, not Shreds, isn't it. So shards it is.

She's wearing a black gown slit up the sides of her legs and down both the front and back of her chest to midriff level. Very fetching, for a fetch, as in wraith, one who would obviously never be seeing the downhill side of forty. Never be seeing the sunnier side of the day either, I dare say now, though I refrained then.

As you will have taken from the third eye, some devil or other had taken her over. By the mere fact she's wearing clothes I didn't think it was Bouncing Belle. Besides, like I said, I'd spotted Lady Lust's ruby red star shining out of the night's sky. I'd also spotted First Fangs' star up there, beside that other alliterative lady – Luck, not Lust – Squigs' half-mom, Dame Chance, so the observable truth she was wearing his fang-figured glove only confirmed it was Janna born Somata and I'd already figured that out.

While she wasn't porcelain pretty anymore, she'd almost always been a very pale white, skin and hair-wise, and now she was only more so. Bloodless, you might call her. Except she was hardly that, was she. Even if the blood mostly wasn't hers by then. Moreover, who else would go about so blatantly with the Crimson Crown draped around her forehead?

Since I'm already dead, with nary a trickle of anybody's blood, let alone my own, running through my veins, I'm not overly concerned about approaching a viral if not virulent, as in unfriendly, vamp; not even one wearing one of the three Sacred Objects and trying to piece another of them together. Of course, as I may have failed to mention, I'm not exactly in a position to do anything about the approaching bit.

I am kind of stinky, and while that alone is suggestive of my current state of non-living, I'm nevertheless a non-combatant. I haven't joined the vast army of the shambling dead then currently chasing the surviving Sraddhites away from the ruined gates of Manoa. Which further suggests I'm my own man; or corpse, if that suits your need for morbid precision. Plus, I've this here telltale scar in my forehead, there's a couple of spanking new tee-tee-tails pinned to my skull, underneath my cap, and there's a glowing quill attached to it, the cap.

Being black, like many a Marutian with residual U-blood, the live Iraches who capture me must have been tempted to tear me asunder; a wonderfully evocative word that I rarely get to use. Instead, they bring me to their shaman, one Koatyl by name. We knew each other from my last incarnation save one. That'd be Quidnunc, pre-Deadnunk; not Quoits, post Mel's Granny Jordy (making her Janna's great-granny Jordy), if you're keeping count.

He's the High Priest of Nergal Vetala from the days, as well as nights, when she was the Iraches' Fertility Goddess. He snatches off my cap, quill with it, and takes satchel, my pads of parchment containing drawings of preferred getaways inside it, and has me escorted, arms-locked, into Janna's presence.

He addresses her as *'Mistress'*, not *'Master'*, so it's starting to dawn on me which devil has hold of her. Then dear-heart, become dear-heartless, Janna figures out who I am, goes all pale-greenish, skin-wise, and dirty haired, tresses-wise, and any lingering uncertainty's duly dispelled.

I'd come across Vetala lots of times before, and in lots of previous incarnations, only never quite like this. You see, she smiles. A lot of devils smile when they see me; my tales are as popular with most of them as they are with most of you. And she had a very a pretty smile. Then again any devil can be very pretty, in lots of ways, if he or she so chooses.

It's just that the way the Nergalid is smiling at me – extremely toothily, shall we say – makes me think she fancies a nip at, unless it's of, my jugular. She's as vampire vicious as Janna's become since I last saw her during the day. Which, now that I think about it, has been quite awhile. Had I bagged a vamp on New Years Eve? Must have.

"He's dead, mistress," says Koatyl, who isn't, but doesn't seem too worried about his jugular, more fool he. "He isn't one of yours, though. Apparently a different sort of azura got hold of him in Kanin City. Not a Sang, he tells me, though he calls it Guardian Angel Jordan and does seem himself, except for the breathing bit. These bucks here don't trust him and they might be right.

"I had a look at some of the sketches he had in his bag. I've been in Godbad City and Petrograd. Plus, I've seen Unmoving Byron and more than a few of his devils before, including the Dragon, in both his forms. So he's obviously been in Godbad for the last few months. That makes him a spy in my books. There isn't much meat left on him and, what there is, is probably rancid but, say the word, and we'll stew him up for supper."

"I may be a spy," I brave, blustery sort that I am, always have been and always will be no matter what kind of azura's animating me. "But, as ever, I am a spy for posterity. There's a tale here to tell and, with your permission, your, um, Ladyship, I'd be happy to learn it firsthand, from you, rather than wait for it to show up on a tee-tee-tail."

"There's more than one tale to learn today, Jordy," says Vetala. "But you shall have mine in return for one of your sketches. Of me, as I am, without this thrice-cursed thing on my head." Then she does a shiver, and goes *'arrgh'*, or at least emits a sound-effect to that effect, and then it's Janna, minus the third eye, but back to being all woefully wan and despicably dental again, who's talking.

"You'd be better off with mine, Tethys, if only in return for all the favours I bestowed upon you and your father, the Quidnunc Legendarian – who's you now, not my Squiggly – in Kanin City. Just draw the Amateramirror whole again, with all its pieces in one piece, just as it was just before Vetala smashed it so I couldn't use it on her like my brother did."

Talk about your pickle of a conundrum. As if being dead isn't bad enough, on the one hand Koatyl, who still has my quill and satchel full of drawings, wants to stew me up for his men, probably using pickles as spicing. Meanwhile, on the other hand, which has a fang-fingered glove on it, the only woman he'll obey is a devil additionally turned vamp; a vampire, mind, and him like his men still alive, with all that tasty blood coursing in their veins.

She – Vulva-Vetala, Fecundity – is evidently stuck in a similarly vampiric shell of a hybrid Utopian with truly extraordinary half-parents; my ex-lover no less, now twice over. And that-she is controlling the same confounded, crimson confabulation they're both simultaneously wearing. Except, the Terrible-Twin-she probably doesn't need it to control her infernal internal because that's just what she and her just as terrible bro do to devils dumb enough to occupy them.

Hardly for the first time I wish a different somatic Master of, eventually, two Weirdoms, my ex long-pre-Thrygragon – meaning, what?, more than 1100 years earlier – hadn't taken all six of the Great Godly Glories up to Cabalarkon when the Pauper Priestess expelled her from Kanin City years post-it. But that's my way out of the pickle jar, isn't it. It isn't so much staring me in the face as I'm staring at it on Janna-cum-Vetala's forehead.

"Perhaps I could accommodate you both," I venture, testing the waters. "I can draw you as you are, Janna, with that thing on your head, that other thing on your hand, and that third thing, the Amateramirror, whole again, all in the same place. I'd recommend Daddy Cabby's Weirdom, if only because your Mama Melina must be its Master by now.

"I'm not sure how she'll react to her patricidal daughter becoming a bat but, you never know, she might be in a forgiving mood. Plus, amidst all that bad beer and extraterrestrial gadgetry up there she might be able to find a cure for vampirism. Mind you, she's a Sister Superior of the Superior Sisterhood, a life-loving Ant Nightingale – among other things, Abe told me during one of our drinking sessions pre you vamping out on us – and maybe they already have one.

"Of course I couldn't chance drawing myself up there. Azuras come from devils and eyeorbs don't even partially fill up taking them out of folks. Not that that matters a fart of beans. I'd already be dancing the legless limbo by then. You'd have to let Vetala loose first, dot-ditto. But I'm sure she'd agree not to come after you, especially up there. Vampire or no vampire, devils don't last long in Cabby's Weirdom.

"Oh, and Koatyl here would have to give me back my quill and swear on a stack of whatever – peyote pods, maybe – to let me go after I milk his mistress for her-story. I may be dead but I can still drink beer and right now I'm more parched than desiccated. All in all, without All of Incain around, that seems the most sensible solution for all concerned."

Janna glared at me silently, no doubt having inner converse with herself. And not just herself either. Then she went all greenish and third-eyed again. "That is satisfactory to us, Jordy. High Priest, give him back his quill and parchment. And don't worry about him being a spy. He's a storyteller first and foremost and I've quite the story to tell him."

Koatyl hesitated, then nodded at his men to let me go. They did so, albeit reluctantly. After he handed me back my wherewithal – just as distrustfully, I don't doubt – I set down to work. I was having trouble with the Amateramirror but Vetala, once Janna let her go and she was there with us, in the subtle matter flesh, them both separately, said it wasn't a mirrored orb anymore. Nor was it a glass bauble on a cheap ring that didn't even glow when Sraddha nabbed her the better part of two years earlier.

It was as it commonly appeared when Taurus Chrysaor Attis, the Universal Soldier, had it on Thrygragon: a circular, shield-like object. In that respect, even if he had declared himself a Living God, I was happy to hear Sraddha was a traditionalist. Which gave me a thought. There were indeed a couple of other stories here and I might as well glean them while I could.

"By the way," I said to Second Fangs, "I draw the Amateramirror whole again, who'll be in it – your brother?"

"And he better come out of it wholly alive, too, Tethys. Or I'll put off taking any cure my mother might come up with and start looking for you; your next you and the one after that, as long as it takes. Vamps are undying. I'll outlast you if I have to – and I'm relentless. You're a vamp, though, you're infertile. I'll keep you like that until all your children and grandchildren are dead and buried."

"You'll feed me steak until it's time for the stake."

"You're better at words than me. Big whoop. I'm better at biting."

"I'll have to take up wearing garlic necklaces then. How'd you get here? As you'll probably appreciate I'm particular about who I go drinking with, all the more so when I might become the lubricant. But I think I'd have heard if bats can bat about in the Weird like devils, witches or psychopomps."

"Or you," Vetala contributed.

"Or me," I allowed.

"You've your quill," Janna reminded me, making a fist out of the fang-fingered glove. "I've this and we're both deviants. Except I'm no good with it, not even for getting around. Fact is, I don't even know what I can do with it. I only took it back from Abe on the night I did a Sedona and smoked free of his trident because, well, I'd grown attached to it."

"It does make for a nice fashion accessory," I said to her. If a vampire can have a sense of humour then so can an azura-animated Dead Thing. "As a conversation piece if nothing else."

"Still, since you asked, we are. At least I am. *'Only the best bat for my baby',* First Fangs promised me. *'And I brought you the best bat in Satanwyck. He's a regular psycho if ever there was one.'* I figured that since I was already verging on suicidal after having nothing but stillborns for fifteen years, or thereabouts, I might as well be a psychopomp bat. So I let him put the bite on me. One thing about wearing Crinsom's Crown, visibly or invisibly, all that time, it sure does make you crazy."

"Tell me about it," Vetala commiserated. "Your brother having the Amateramirror for so long certainly made him just as crazy. Why else would he stick me inside it?"

"Because you were going to eat him?" Second Fangs suggested snarkily, if not sharkily. (Unlike our fine fishy friend Fisherwoman, fangs on her fingers and in her mouth, no matter how shark-sharp they were, did not make her an ingredient for shark-fin soup.)

"Not eat him, turn him. That boy's attitude to the Ambulatory Dead was sickening and the way he was treating Living Iraches was even worse. We are talking food for the ages here, don't forget. Don't want all the blood sacrifices-to-come wasted, do you. Besides, when you're mortal, how can you claim to be a god? Gods don't die. Not proper gods anyhow. I'd have only been ensuring the longevity of his contemptible cult."

I'd had enough. I finished my drawing and signed it with my usual flourish. Endgame Somata Twins? Don't I just wish.

========

"Shall we pause here for the obligatory yowl?"
****

12: Telltale Titanism

"Just to recapitulate," said Jordan 'Q for Quill' Tethys, the legendary 30-Year Man.

========

"First Fangs, Faustus Vladuca, conspired to turn both Nergal Vetala and Janna Somata into vampires: the former in Pandemonium, Sedon's Temple; the latter in Kanin City, where she's also controlling Satanwyck's ex Prime Sinistral as of mid-to-late 5492. His Unholiness, Uncle Abe Chaos, rewards him appropriately, with a star, albeit in the night's sky.

"He'd done a ditto with said-Sinistral, Lady Lust, a couple of hours earlier, if that. Who should not be confused with Lady Luck, the half-mother of many a Quill Tethys, whom His Orderliness, Thunder & Lightning Lord Yajur, sent upstairs on the Summer Solstice of 5474. Which is where, my thereafter lucky star, it's been shining ever since in terms of our storyline. Coincidentally, if perhaps not so consequently, Star Sedon has simultaneously not shone on – except, that is, doubly darkly, as in night to go along with day."

"I heard," said Ferdinand Niarchos, the Governor of New Iraxas, wherein unionized Dead Things worked, supervised by vampires, because the oil fields were too polluted for ordinary flesh and blood Godbadians to breathe properly, "That the mighty Eye-Mouth in the sky took himself out of it in order to avoid her constant nattering."

"That's one theory, Ferd. Another is that he was already downstairs having a lark. At my expense I might add, since I was the one he occupied, fatally as it happened."

"Because that Janna," said their Janna, Mrs Yataghan, Janna St Peche-Montressor, who didn't, "Had gorgeous silvery hair and thus reminded him of Pyrame Silverstar."

"And he chose to look like Zuvem Nergalis," inserted the Fatman, "Because Planter, or Gravedigger, or Devil Doom, had the temerity to sit on his Hell-throne next to his appointed or anointed vice-regent, bedazzling Belialma, the aforementioned Lady Lust, then Satanwyck's Prime Sinistral. In other words, everything that thereafter ensued was a Sedonplay and we all know who always wins those."

"So we do, Al," said Tethys, rubbing his forehead not so much contemplatively as irritably. He'd just had a flash, which he didn't vocalize. It was shaped like the letter 'D', capitalized and at a 90° angle clockwise. A faceless grin? Why would he flash a faceless grin? Yet, he suddenly apprehended, juddering involuntarily, it was hardly the first time he done so lately – and not just lately either.

Janna shot him a worried glance. Had she just experienced something similar? He shook it off, proceeded apace, tongue-wise as well as, hopefully, both unshaken and not stirred.

"There's also the competing theory that what culminates in the First War between the Living and Dead boils down to a particularly brutal game of chance. In short, that it isn't a Sedonplay so much as Lady Luck's settling stellar scores for Yajur ill-starring her, not to mention slaying me in the form of her half-son Quidnunc, on the twin's 18th birthday.

"This theory has it that Dame Chance, Fata Fortuna, Wintry Moira, call her what you will, deliberately rolled the dice such that the Unities, Harmony first among them, paid for favourite son Quid's first death back on the day of their birth via a poisoned pinprick. And there's something to that theory, it has to be said, especially when you consider how Chaos cathonitized beguiling Belialma all those years later.

"Devils aren't known for their imagination. By driving his trident through Janna Somata, chest downwards, Unholy Abaddon should have killed her. That he hadn't was a fairly strong indication that Hell's Belle must have come to the forefront, thereby rendering his Janna-killing thrust her catasterizing one instead.

"That's probably precisely what happened to Lady Luck, too. It was just that no one put two and two together and thus figured out the extent of the twins' deviancy years before she took over the Skinless Rasp and he did a ditto with First Fangs; not that either of those episodes figure overly much in this sagacious saga.

"Be that as it may, let's move on."

========

A TETHYS TALE - JANNA FANGFINGERS: THE DISUNITION OF THE UNITIES OF LAZAREME – PART NINE: ALL INCAIN DAY

========

Unholy Abaddon reinvades Satanwyck on Imbolc-Lammas Day 5492 (the 1st of Cupidam there then; the 1st of Balam there now). Nergal Vetala seizes the opportunity to escape Sedon's Temple, presumably with First Fangs, via between-space. Harmony's history – or, as she'd have preferred, her-story – as of mid-Rudar 5492. With Vetala's help, Shredder discovers the cave-way to Iraxas in the second week of Djerridam that year, October 1492.

Months later, on New Years Eve 5492/3 and with Belialma inside her, Janna answers her own challenge to take on all-comers sexually. Uncle Abe overreacts ridiculously, cathonitizes Bouncing Belle then goes seriously crazy. I'm a casualty – only Guardian Angel Jordy keeps me going.

(BTW, I'm nowadays inclined to believe he was a Fatazur – that's with a hard 'a', not a soft one, for anyone taking notes later. Fatazurs are the azura offspring of Fata Fortuna and Rumour of Lazareme from just before faeries ate the latter circa

4000 YD. I mean, if Battle Babe, she with her silly Sabre Rattle, can have symbiotic Sangazurs why can't Dame Chance have similarly endowed offspring?)

Abe ill-stars First Fangs then returns the fang-fingered glove she's had for damn near a decade now to Janna, Second Fangs by then. He also gives her back the Crimson Corona, where she'd been holding First Fangs ever since he returned to Kanin City, inside a psycho bat, and either turned her or had her turned. But the damage is done.

If the First War between the Living and the Dead began with the birth of Johann-George Somata-Faust on Halloween 5480 and the Thousand Days of Disbelief got underway when His Orderliness prevented His Unholiness ill-starring his Under-Lordship Yama Nergal, he of the grinning death's head, on the Autumnal Equinox of 5492, both accelerated unstoppably on this date, the Spring Equinox of what was already 1493 on the Outer Earth.

There is no doubt that dead things continued to line up at Janna's bed, from dusk to dawn, all during the Lazareme and Byron ternaries of that year. I say no doubt because this isn't just what Vetala told me, having gleaned as much from her brief occupancy of Janna Fangfingers on All-Death Day, but what Janna herself subsequently confirmed. And if that isn't a chilling image, well, best go polish up an ice cube, Ferd.

There is considerable doubt as to what form of azura animated the things. Vetala couldn't help me there. But it's also one of those your elephant moments in that it scarcely matters, does it. Fatazurs, like Sangazurs, Vetalazurs and Nergalazurs such as those sired on her by either Zuvem Nergalis or Yama Nergal, are just types of azuras. There are as many varieties of azuras as there are their just as immortal parents, Great Gods and Master Devas alike.

What is relevant is that on Maruta the First 5494, All Souls Day 1494, Vetala gave birth to an absolutely amazing amount of azuras; the Headworld's last Vetalazurs, I've been given to understand. This massive infusion tipped the balance, apologies to Harmony, in terms of ambulatory beings of the sentient sort. In other words, there were now more dead things walking than there were live men and women talking, generically speaking.

They've become known as Haddazurs because they were simultaneously born on the day Iraxas became known as Hadd, as in "Iraxas has had it, hasn't it?" Which is what I asked her on All-Death Day. To which Vetala replied: "Hardly, the domination of the Ambulatory Dead has just begun. But I like it so I'll use it. It's past time Iraxas got a new name to go along with its renewed status as my hereafter inviolable protectorate."

She promptly proved it too, most emphatically and as only a god-devil could. Rain hasn't fallen within its borders since Iraxas became Hadd.

========

"So you can blame me for Hadd and Haddit Zombies; the designations, not the grim reality of a forever cloud-shrouded, but hence not-so-miraculously rainless land of abhorrent abominations. Thanks to Guardian Angel Jordy – the azura offspring of, if I'm right about him, my devic half-father and my favourite-ever devic stalker – dead-me, Pegleg Squigs, instantly felt right at home there."

"*May she shine on brightly,*" *mock-prayed Janna, who couldn't have known Lady Luck, though APM All-Eyes definitely had.*

"*Ear, hear,*" *said Tethys, wiping a faux-tear from his eye in memory of Dame Chance and their many nights together in the now distant past,* "*One thing I've always said is that, even if they aren't around anymore, devils are really, really good at witching weather. If Vetala hadn't made Hadd indisputably hers, Haddit Zombies would have had it a long, long time ago.*"

"*A long time does not equal forever,*" *said Centauri.*

"*Here, here,*" *cheered Governor Niarchos, happy to please the boss even if he was echoing 3-Beers' vocalization re the half-mother of so many earlier Legendarians.*

========

The Year of the Dome 5494 saw the Unities of Order and Chaos battle each other more on than off, yet always indecisively. They fought south all over the facial Head, capitalized, from Cheek Lands to Sweat Glands then into the western ocean, over the forbidden forest of Kala Tal, and throughout the subcontinent of Aka-Godbad, the last refuge of Thrygragos Byron and his offspring, before autumn became winter.

Give the Byron Spawn credit. The Unmoving One had to meld with virtually all his still loose offspring in order to form his most grandiose Nucleus ever. But they successfully '*deflected*' the Unities, to use their terminology, away from Godbad and across the Gulf of Aka into the Iraches' adjacent territory.

A lovely, verdant peninsula shaped like an upside-down teardrop or, um, something else, when viewed from the Sedon Sphere, I'm reliably informed it's roughly 250,000 square miles in size; hence, according to Ferd, who's weird, one reason why Vanthysces, its onetime overseer, embraced '*Vastness*' as his surname.

(Initially, antique Illuminaries meant it as an admittedly obscure euphemism for the Reaper, the Scarecrow, in other words '*death*' — the vastness thereof, as opposed to the sad shortness of life even for long-lived like the idiots of Weir. This would be the same death devils rendered not quite universally inevitable; rendered it instead merely vastly unavoidable.)

Marutians called the area El Dorado but its natives had it as Iraxas, after themselves, since time immemorial. Due to a not-at-all-smartass crack I made, Vetala renamed it Hadd later on the same day the Unities landed atop Manoa, bums foremost. And that's the name that's stuck even though it's as verdant as ever (because waters spilling down the southern slopes of the Diluvia Mountain Range keep it that way), if nowhere near as brightly so (due to a dearth of sunshine to match an absence of falling rain).

There are those who say the Unities did not fight each other like other duellists would, to the death, if Master Devas can truly die. Certainly, Abaddon did not unsheathe the Chaos Blade until the very last moment when, to do anything else, would have guaranteed his defeat and, if not his death per se, then likely his ill-starring, catasterization or cathonitization, which usually results in much the same thing for devils.

However, on a more subtle level, there's a good deal to be said for a conspiracy theory we've yet to touch upon to the degree it's worth. Which, as we'll eventually see, is quite a lot in not just my view, but their Father Lazareme's as well, to name but one who felt the same way. It says that the Unities fought each other along a mutually prearranged corridor.

First they took out Marutia, Sedon's Cheek. Then they fought through the northlands, shaving Sedon's Eyebrow, Forehead and Skull save for the Ghostlands, which they initially avoided – thereby nearly confirming my hypothesis that they started out crazy like foxes; as in were only feigning madness. After that they trimmed the Head short-back and to the sides, keeping things militarily tight around the Aural Sea, the Ear of the Head, though not Tympani, Eardrum Isle, perhaps for fear of waking their notoriously laissez-faire father.

Two devic razors, they sliced the cheek up again and again then moved into the inner and outer noses: the Bloodlands, Crepuscule, and the Pristine Isles, Sedon's Snot sneezed out. They fought through the moustache and teeth, Dukkha, Tal, Sedon's Bight, Achigan, Crimson and Nonsynchron, the lips and mouth areas of the Hidden Headworld (minus Yati's already centuries' displaced tongue). As already noted in considerable detail, they brought their duel to the subcontinent of Aka Godbad during the late Summer and early Autumn of 5494.

If they had an agreement to wreak deathly devastation throughout the Headworld, wiping out previously inviolable protectorates along the way, they were doing a pretty good job of it until Godbad. Yet, when they resumed going at it hammer and tong, or sword and trident, after the Byronic Nucleus deflected them onto Manoa, they didn't immediately return for another crack at the subcontinent. No, they took their travelling, two-devil war party to the Cattail Peninsula, once Chaos's de facto realm, and started fighting up its coast northwards.

And why would they do that? Because they'd done enough elsewhere, at least they had for the time being. What they were really doing, according to this strain of conspiratorial chattering, was culling, both maximally and randomly, the continent of contagion carriers left over from the 200-year-long efforts of Quoits Tethys, preme, to wipe out the Inner Earth's devil worshippers. (Which started accidentally, I learned from her post-me, with the panpipe-playing Rat Catcher of Hamelin in 1284, Al's time.)

In this they acted much like the industrialized, bottom-trawling fisheries of the Outer Earth that so appal Godbad's aforementioned, ever-fishifying former queen, wherever she is, and our most noble host sitting right here with us. And, no, without me having to tell that story too, the insidious efforts of Quoits, et al, didn't end with Lazareme dethroning, quite literally, with a boot to the butt, the deviant-god of Twilight's Hoodoo Hamlet back in 5476.

And who was the so-called depilated Dand? Put it this way, if you reckoned we'd seen the last of the Terrible Twins, you reckoned wrongly.

========

"Spare us the attitude, Jordy," Centauri objected.

========

"For one thing, no matter how much you'd like to pretend otherwise, Fish and I only agree on a few things; a few of our mutual enemies, to be absolutely accurate.

"We definitely disagree on how Godbad should be run. She's a monarchist, not a democrat like me. Much more tellingly, she reckons she should be monarch – without King Achigan Auranja, her faeries-compromised hubby, Godbad's supposedly rightful ruler, even if he and his predecessors were Bandradin imports, slowing her down.

"For another, everyone knows the twins both came back to what was Hadd by then – came back as bats."

"Spoilsport," complained Janna.

"And that's why it's so preposterous Brown Robes still think of Sraddha Somata as the greatest hero the living ever had."

"So they do, Al. And so he is, or was, as I'm about to relate." Tethys took only a sip, not a glug, of pilsner – a sure sign he was closing in on his thirty beer max for the day. "Recall, Second Fangs told me Sraddha better come out of the mirror whole and alive? Well, he got the alive part right, but the whole part? Not half!

"Mel – not Harry Zeross's Mel, Melina born Sarpedon, Demios's twin sister and current High Illuminary of Weir; the Terrible Twins' mother, Melina Somata – was the Master of Weir by then, as I'd anticipated. As to whether she could find in her recipe files a cure for vampirism, she didn't even try. The reason for that was son Sraddha came out of the mirror not so much as shattered, as it had been, as cut to pieces by its shatters, its glassy shards or slivers.

"You might say Shredder had been shredded – but I wouldn't as it's too obvious and besides, you know me, I hate puns.

"He'd have bled out but Mama Mel used her witch-wiles on him as best she could in order to stop his exsanguination, keep his heart pumping, his blood coursing if not curdling. But, not long thereafter, funny thing, funny things start happening in the Hills or Slopes of the Sleepers; funny things that, as we'll soon see, undercut to the point of demolishing Mel's growing reputation as the Trigregos Titaness.

"Should append that by saying that I don't mean 'titan', 'titanic' or 'titaness' – which I'm sure Janna here would consider sexist – in terms of gigantism. I mean it the same sense as when I refer to Metisophia, my devic half-mother, as Titanic Metis. I mean it as in 'Titanism', capitalized, a fancy word for rebelliousness.

"Her Mastery honoured the spirit of Zalman Somata, her dead and never risen hubby, who began remaking Cabalarkon's status quo, or established order, as of its Independence Day. Which, you probably know, is celebrated on the 4th of Kamor up there; the same day, albeit with a 300-year head start, the American colonies mark their breaking away from Great Britain.

"What you may or may not know is that the Slopes of the Sleepers demarcate the Weirdom's inland boundary with, nowadays, the Ghostlands. They're where ancient Utopians buried their huge, sometimes asteroid-sized, millennial or generational ships after arriving on the planet a decade or so before Dark Sedon was forced to raise the Cathonic Zone, out of his own essence, in order to escape the Genesea or Great Flood of Genesis. That's not all they buried there either.

"Trapped more like inside than beneath Cathonia, age obstinately creeps up on them. Put better, time does what time generally does to even long-lived mortals like these Utopians of Weir. The vast majority don't drop dead, though. Instead, on the verge of it, they're placed in tubs or sarcophagi full of animation-suspending Cathonic Fluid until such time as the survivors, or their descendants, find a cure for whatever ailed them. Let's call it Imminent Death because that's the catch-all phrase Utopians actually use.

"Remarkably, Utopians are still laying their not-quite-dead fellows in such-like tubs some 5,500 years later. Of course celebrity sleepers – as I call them – like Daddy Cabby are usually deposited in the Catacombs of the Sleepers. That'd be beneath the Citadel of the Thinkers and Cabalarkon's main square or zocala, its massive 'People's Plaza'. Grateful pal Zal, you may also recall, accorded me, the Quoits Tethys Legendarian, just such a privileged resting place until she, um, drowned Sedon-somehow.

"Yet another thing you may recall from earlier in our little tell-no-lies session is that I can draw myself semi-substantially elsewhere. I believe the correct term for that is ectoplasmically but, um, hard as it might be for you to fathom, I could actually be incorrect about that. Anyhow, I did that when Janna, through Sraddha, who was then still friend Shreds, asked me to invite her parents to her wedding to First Fangs on Hymeneal Day – in whatever year that was? 5481, if memory serves.

"Although, as Al rubbed in tongue-saltily a few hours ago, I buggered up when it came to discovering the unconscionable depths to which Quoits Tethys and her Contagion Collectors had been descending for decades and decades, I'm also by nature cat-curious. Finally non-fatally – though it's too late for me in that respect now – being 30-Beers, I am prone to following up what I've gone and no doubt good-intentionally done, if only to remind myself what I did.

"As I'd told Second Fangs on All-Death Day, I didn't want to go up there personally, due to aforementioned stinky as opposed to sticky situation in term of occupancy. But I do like to occasionally check in with some old, U-blooded friends of mine; my buds in tubs, including Daddy Cabby himself. So I do. And, guess what? Other than Cabby, they're not old anymore.

"Their sarcophagi are dry and they're irretrievably desiccated; so much dust potentially in the wind. Which is where they're left to waft shortly after peg-legged, not-quite-substantial, yet mouthy-as-ever me starts visiting Quoits' hard-ass, collusive killers; veterans from the Contagion Collectors catastrophe who're still around.

"Azuras can do no more about dust than they can about ashes and, even if she was born a Tethys, I've had just about enough of the throwback. (Despite her reprehensible deeds, Utopian annals still refer to her as the Trigregos Titaness, which puts her in the same company as another mass-murderous Master, Morgan Abyss, the one they immortalized as the Death's Head Hellion.) For my part, I blame the twins' Mama Mel for everything that's gone wrong since she masterminded Quidnunc's unforgiveable first death all those decades ago.

"With, as I say, Pegleg-me too insubstantial to draw blood myself, I'm nevertheless there in Cabby's crypt beneath the Citadel of the Thinkers when Quoits' hard-asses squeeze some of their own venal juice into his sarcophagus. We proceed to have ourselves a wee chinwag, do the Undying Utopian and this here more-than-merely-apparitional, still-beyond-dying deviant.

"Soon, another funny thing this, things stop working the way they should up in Cabby's Weirdom. When things stop working up there, Masters don't last much longer. Melina Somata, the now suddenly short term – very short term – former Master of two Weirdoms, exited, as I tend to say, stage exile. She also exited stage electric.

"To put it officially, she involuntarily retired; took herself, as I later learned, to a Witch Shelter somewhere in the Forever Forest of Wildwyck. A Hellion stronghold, you won't be surprised to hear, that's where – another spoiler alert, punchline coming – she began dying of an appropriately incurable, poetically just, blood disorder.

"The exit stage electric plug above? That referred to this mortal electrode; as in coil."

"Someone blew a transfusion," Centauri interpreted. "As opposed to a transformer."

"By giving her bad blood, in contrast to a wire wound up and used to introduce induction into a circuit, to quote your father, Ferd, who was always something of a techie. I must've told you this part of the story before, Al. Sorry about that. Must be the memory-full, compression-versus-repression beeswax I was telling you about awhile ago."

"Actually you haven't; not in so many words anyhow. But it's a proven method to cure vampirism. So I applied a little deductive reasoning of my own. As Mr Niarchos will tell you, if you're nice to him, the problem is getting a vamp to lie still for it." Tethys took note of the formality – more business obviously – but chose to conclude his story instead of commenting.

"Except we're talking 55th Century of the Dome. Even woodland Nightingales, with all their wily witch-ways and wondrous training, couldn't have had the best conditions, sanitarily speaking. Anyhow again, Abe Chaos and Lord Order came both battling by, and battling in, between-space, which is where witches hide their shelters.

"A few of the Hellions got away. They told me later on, in a near-lifetime, when I was nosing about doing some research of the cat-curious, truth-will-out variety, that they thought it was deliberate. They figured Mel had guided them inside just because, well … She was the Trigregos Titaness, the cure was killing her, and she'd already been dead once by then; didn't like it either."

"That Mel-witch was some Somata-bitch," contributed Ferdinand Niarchos. He sounded a lot like his well-travelled, not exactly altogether late father – the domicile of, presumably, a Sangazur naturally named Guardian Angel Gomez. Tethys gave him in a checkmark in the air more for his fay-saying than his erudition.

"Nonetheless, Ferd, however so much so she was bodily a hybrid, Melina Somata was a Utopian at heart. Utopians exist to obliterate devils. She must have figured: *'Why waste the incurable Sleepers in a perpetual state of Imminent Death when their Immediate Death can serve to feed my bloodsucking children?'*

"Need I mention that the throwback had retaken possession of both the Amateramirror and the Crimson Corona by then? Thought not. That's where the Trigregos Titaness epithet came from – Illuminaries, like she was, as well as everything else, are big on making up aptonyms. Still, no matter how insane the Godly Glories made her, she reckoned she was just doing her duty as a true daughter of Weir."

"Yet," said the Janna in the solarium with them, "It was a line pureblood Utopians, imbeciles that most of them are, and were then, were unprepared to let her cross."

"Something like that anyways. She might have got away with it as well. And there were rug-rats worth of non-imbeciles up there by then; young, born and raised rebellious ones, the offspring of Kanin's hybrids and Cabalarkon's purebloods, so she had plenty of supporters. Plus, she had the two Trigregos Talismans to help keep her in power.

"But, back to the staccato, then and then and then narrative, just as things were starting to malfunction up there, the Unities staggered out of the Ghostlands. By their presence alone, they were threatening the Weirdom. She had no choice except to use them to get rid of them. She did so by transferring them to them, if I haven't lost you by now."

"The Hellions told you Titanic Mel lured them into their Wildwyck Witch Shelter," Janna pieced together. "She didn't have the Trigregos Talismans anymore, the Unities had, but she could still control them. She was their puppeteer. She remained the Trigregos, um, Titaness until the bitterest of her end."

"The Lovely Lady gets one, too." Tethys made another air-check. "Yajur had the Amateramirror whilst Abe had the Crimson Corona, again. Myself, though, I think what proved Titanic Mel's ultimate undoing was she decided to go after Cabalarkon, the undying Utopian Sedon regards as his father. I've no proof of that but being struck by lightning whilst strolling in the People's Plaza of Cabalarkon, the city, is suggestive, wouldn't you say?"

It was a rhetorical question. He didn't bother to add that that's how the aptonymous Death's Head Hellion, another Master who'd trifled with Daddy Cabby, met her electrifying extinction centuries gone bye-bye by then. "So," he carried on, not waiting for a response, "Just as she had to do for Sraddha, when he emerged from the Amateramirror so seriously slashed apart, Janna turns their mother, who's still ticking, albeit only sporadically, into a vamp.

"As psychopomp-bats, the three of them flee the Weirdom. The twins, munching on whomever along the way, eventually return to Sraddha Isle; to the monastery complex that still stands not far off the shore of Lake Sedona. Meanwhile, mom goes off to Wildwyck in quest of a successful cure that, instead, successfully starts killing her again. Or at least starts killing her psychologically since, as a nevertheless life-loving Ant Superior, she must have hated having to drain wholly alive people in order to stay, um, undead, to use the common parlance.

"That they could fly through the Weird was because, as Janna told me in Manoa, Vladuca had used the '*best bat for First Fangs' best babe*' to turn her. Or words to that effect. So she, the second-best-bat, passed on to her momentarily baby brother and mommy dearest what she'd received from first-best-bat. So it is to this day those Second Fangs turns can travel at will between-space."

"Forgive me for anticipating you, Jordy," Niarchos, clearly tiring, apologized in advance. "But All Death Day only marked a median between the ascendancy of the Ambulatory Dead and the corresponding decline of the Living, if that's the right way of putting it."

"It might be, numerically speaking, if you mean the midpoint of the Thousand Days of Disbelief. What I suspect you're really trying to say is that, with more and more Dead Things walking, and less and less Living Folks fighting them, and with the Unities by now rampaging through the Head's occipital and Cattail regions, the Lazaremists' traditional territories, something had to give."

"How about what I'm really trying to say is that an alarm clock finally went off on Eardrum Isle."

"Unfortunately much too late for the exquisite Harmony and an unknown bundle of much lesser Master Devas, but you're right, Ferd. No more checkmarks, though. I've run out."

========

Even Vetala isn't that prodigious in terms of begetting azuras. The Mithradites haven't had a *'baby bomb'* since she escaped Satanwyck, a couple of years ago by now, and no other female Master Deva has volunteered to step up, then lay down or bend over, in an effort to fill the ovular void, as it were. Likely no one could – but it may also be that, due to an increasing lack of worshippers, devils are becoming infertile in terms of azuras.

(It isn't until this century that any of them manage to produce a fourth generation of devakind. But now's hardly the time to start speculating as to how the reawakened Thanatoids of Lathakra began doing so. Other than saying Mama Methandra was resolutely Mithras's Virgin until the Atomic Twins knocked both the Frozen Isle's Death Gods out of action for over a thousand years, it isn't. Maybe abstinence truly does make the ovaries grow sounder.)

Yet, back to storyville, while there's a limited number of Haddazurs, there's no limit to fresh corpses. Fact is there's so many of their shells dropping dead that, for quite some time now, what the Ambulant Dead themselves don't store away for future use, azuras of any description, save those of the Byronics in Godbad, are what's been getting them up and going again.

That's why Abe Chaos capturing Cathune, the Apocalyptic of Drought, and Harmony sticking her in All of Incain, failed to stem the Dead Things' advancement. Fresh, falling rain only works against Nergalazurs such as Yamazurs, Vetalazurs and Haddazurs. (Don't recall what Zuvem's azuras, the ones born without Vetala as their intermediary, are called. Might be Zuvazurs or, maybe, since he's the eldest of the three, Nergalazurs refer to his azuras exclusively.)

Great Byron realizes it. So too does Thrygragos Lazareme. And, once his firstborn sons, irrevocably driven insane by the Trigregos Talismans, trash Tympani, Sedon's Eardrum, in the middle of the Aural Sea, where he's been sleeping more off than on since Thrygragon, he wakes up. Time for another confab in the Gregarian Fields, wouldn't you think? They did.

Time for the Unnameable, too, you might also think. Its power focus had worked on Mithras, after all, pun put as yet without reward. The Great Gods didn't, though, probably for that very reason – didn't want it turned on them, did they? However, I don't doubt that's what the fox-crazed Unities were thinking: that Harmony had left its head within All on Incain after Thrygragon. (Which, by the way, is by no means certain. What Harmony did with it went to the grave with her; or boulder of Brainrock, put as per reality.)

That was probably why they were smashing and crashing their way towards the Prison Beach, which they'd skipped on their first bash through the Cattail after All-Death Day. What it was time for was devils to rein in their azuras. And they did.

Azuras are no more capable of disobeying their fathers than devils are their three sires.

Lazareme apprehends there's no point trying to order his Unities to cease their senseless carnage. They're so far gone they'd just turn on him. They'd already attacked the Weirdom of Cabalarkon, hadn't they. And it amounts to Sedon's protectorate, you'll have heard, though not from the current Mel's Illuminaries. But he does command his offspring to start marshalling the Dead Things their azuras are animating into pre-prepared burning fields, where they're systematically incinerated by their Living adherents.

When that works, a few Mithradites start doing the same thing. And, with the full cooperation of most members of the two other tribes, Great Byron begins to bring Byronic azuras into areas outside Godbad, where corpses are just rotting away due to not enough azuras to occupy them. A massive, time-consuming and horrifically smoke-generating cleanup has begun. It's ugly and it's sickening but, hey, Mother Earth has always had a knack for renewing herself so why shouldn't the Hidden Headworld? It's the same planet after all.

Two highborn, definite Mithradites aren't onboard. They'd be the two male Nergalids. They need to get to their female third, their middleman as it were, even if she's a woman, convince her to cure herself of vampirism and get back to the business of being Fecundity, the formerly no longer just lunar-monthly-fertile mother of their Nergalazurs.

So they march obscene numbers of their Nergalazur-animated dead men and dead women, they with their scavenged materiel, through the infra-Diluvia cave-system into what's already Hadd. There they join forces with Vetala's Iraches and their Dead Things against the mostly Marutian Sraddhites.

Their target? Sraddha Isle, where the two Somata twins, psycho-bats that they are, have by now joined their living compatriots and the whomever they've been munching on since leaving Cabalarkon. So it is both sides have vampires fighting alongside them. And if that isn't the single most paradoxical aspect of the First War, then the fact that Life's Champions – as the anti-zombie Sraddhites styled themselves – didn't have any devils on their side might be.

In hindsight, perhaps their then altogether alive man-god should never have declared himself the only chance the Living had against either devils or the Dead and thus alienate both.

========

"Thanks for the beer, Janna. Imported from the Outer Earth, eh. Czechoslovakia, I see. Only the best beer for our best busker, you say, Al? I appreciate the thought but you really don't want to hear me sing. We artistic types have to know our limitations and I can't carry a tune any more than I can a full head of hair, at least not in my male incarnations.

"Cheese and olives? Thanks again, Janna. Don't mind if I do. No, you can hold onto the kumquats. And I mean that literally. Until you eat them anyways."

========

By this time of course Iraxas, the land that had it all, and still does in many respects, has had the buns. The relentless Dead outnumber the Living so egregiously they're threatening to overwhelm not just Iraxas but the entire Headworld. Not so oddly – not after the Unities landed atop the walls and near extremities of Manoa – there are more ex-Marutian Sraddhites among the Dead in Iraxas than there are her loyalists: ex-Iraches in terms of breath, not death.

Virtually all of them are animated by azuras she gave birth to on All-Death Day. That makes them hers regardless of birthplaces, so she's at least moderately pleased. So much so, inspired by one of my wisecracks, pale-pal-Vetala has decided to rename it Hadd. The name qualifies as an aptonym and it sticks. It also makes said azuras Haddazurs as well as Vetalazurs. Quibble if you must about its appropriateness but there's no denying the term '*Haddit Zombies*' gongs a noteworthy chord.

Not much else has changed, though, and we're well into 5495 by now: mid-Azky, June on the Outer Earth. Her now nearly nine months' minted Haddazurs are as vulnerable to clean, fresh rainfall as her offspring by strictly Gravedigger and the Underlord, their Nergalazurs, had always been. Something about her peculiar genetic makeup, I suppose. So it's still perpetually cloud-covered and has yet to rain there. Still hasn't, sooth said, half a millennium later.

Sad to say that means Zuvem and Yama's newly arrived battalions of the Dead couldn't find a safer haven than Hadd. But there's something else about her genetic makeup that really pisses her off. Let me rephrase that. There's something about the genetic makeup of devazurs in general that really pisses her off. That's the paternity issue we keep coming back to: namely, that devazurs are incapable of disobeying their sires.

What with Zuvem and Yama up north in the Upper Head for so many centuries, except for their brief, bi-lunar visits for purposes purely procreative, Vetala's had it pretty much her own way down here in Iraxas. Without their fathers around to boss more so than bash them about, azuras default to a devic form of Mariolatry.

Sinistral Cupidity had himself quite the party going in Satanwyck – until she finally convinced First Fangs to turn her, if he did – so, while her Haddazurs have multiple fathers, her Nergalazurs have only the two. And they're both in Hadd, sucking her dry of worshippers. (Which is an apropos metaphor when you consider what's she's been doing to Sraddhite prisoners her Iraches bring her for supper.)

But what's she to do? Both Zuvem and Yama are her seniors. Which brings up another interesting aspect of the genetic makeup of devazurs, of Master Devas anyhow, and then usually only so long as they're outside the boundaries of their own protectorates. When their fathers aren't around, their genes tend to make them default to their older brothers and sisters.

Should she let it rain in Hadd? That would only wipe out the zombies their azuras were animating, if they didn't find cover quickly enough. No, she wasn't going to let Bodiless Byron back in; Byronics and their army of adherents were the ones who drove her north in the first place, what?, howsoever many years earlier by now. And she wasn't going to run away to another devil's protectorate; to, say, Kala Tal's northerly, then sharp westerly, neighbouring Forbidden Forest, which is my suggestion.

As she pointed out, quite rightly, while the arachnid devil was her immediate sibling in Mithras's Twelfth – her definite immediate sister since neither of them was too sure the Medusa, Mater Matare, was their third triplet or a lowborn gorgon like

I believed – the Unities had ravaged her woodland protectorate, Sedon's Moustache, on their way to Godbad a few months before All-Death Day.

As a consequence, best buds that they were, even she couldn't be certain Kala wasn't one of the new stars that had been popping out in the Sedon Sphere since the Thousand Days of Disbelief had begun most of a thousand days earlier. She certainly wasn't responding to any of her far-cries for help. Although, to be fair, what good could she do if she did? The male Nergalids were as much the Spider Goddess's elders as they were hers.

Vetala wanted Yama and Zuvem out of Hadd one way or another. Or, better yet, two ways or another, as in bifurcated. As already alluded to, she isn't the only one. She's just the most selfish one – assuming you can call the Terrible Twins, vamps that they are, altruistic. Besides freeing up their food supplies, they want the Nergalids gone such that their Marutian acolytes can complete the takeover of El Dorado at the expense of the native Iraches and their ambulatory ancestors as well as, more and more, recently zombified contemporaries.

I no more know they're back than I do what's happened up in Cabalarkon, the place, after I informed Cabalarkon, the Undying Utopian, of what'd become of his fellow Sleepers. Or, as far that goes, how Mama Mel had met her fate over in Wildwyck. Presumably neither does Vetala but, re ridding herself of her much-more-than-pesky brothers, she put to me … Except, I remonstrate, what about my built-in, not-at-all-petty consciousness qualifier? I can't draw the Unities to Hadd against their will.

"But you could let them know where they were, couldn't you, Jordy?"

"And where might that be?" I inquire, knowing vampires, like devils, have hard to beat attributes when it comes to mesmerism and she was both.

"Massing their forces on the mainland opposite Sraddha Isle," she said. "Most of the Sraddhites have fled to Diluvia, where it's always raining. Our Dead Things can't go after them in the mountains. But they've kept a heavily fortified bastion on Sraddha Isle and we can get to them there. It'll be a vicious battle, my Living Iraches will be slaughtered, and that would be a waste of future nourishment.

"I'll send word to the Planter and Reaper that, the moment they take the island, I'll join them there. Whereupon they can have me as they want me, as a non-vampire. Which I will do, since I still can't tell any lies. Except, with your help, the Unities won't be far behind. Sraddha Isle won't automatically become part of our devic domain just because the Marutians have surrendered; not that there's anything inviolate about protectorates to those two anymore, if there ever was."

"You can cure yourself?" I query, though I've long ago figured she was still enough of a devil to pull it off.

"I've been practising," she smiles toothily.

"But," I start to protest … She anticipates the question.

"And what can be unmade once can be remade again, as in any number of times. Been practising that, too."

I'd been wondering why I'd only been seeing chortling chum Koatyl after dark of late.

So I get a date and start to draw these huge posters, properly called cartoons, done on the backside of Manoan drapery too damaged to be of any other use. Possibly because he's the elder, I do Zuvem Nergalis first: big, black and bad, just like he always enjoyed being portrayed, with powerful arms and his Brainrock spade pointy and poised like a pig-sticking spear rather than a utilitarian shovel. Only I draw him against an archery target.

(Regardless of the, to me, unwelcome arrival of guns and firearms of non-hose diversity, despicable levellers that they may be for unskilled simpletons everywhere, bows and arrows remain very popular – and not just among Iraches and Marutians plagued by Time Quakes. They do on the Outer Earth around this time, 500 years ago, too.)

Then I draw the reversely redecorated drapes, which would probably be worth a small fortune these days, in Godbucks or Greenbacks, to where I've predetermined the Unities are fighting, which is southward along the Cattail's Bandradin Plateau towards and thence into the Whiplash Range. A few days later I start sending them similar posters of Underlord Yama, in full Death's Head Grinning mode, and do a dot-ditto. Or dick-dildo in their headcases.

After that I draw them together, Deadhead alongside Gravedigger, except now they're with Sraddha Isle in the background, instead of a dartboard, and with the date on it. I'm running out of damaged drapes so I even try drawing a blaringly loudmouth version of my skull screaming, not grinning, to them insubstantially. But, no matter how ear-piercingly loud I make it, they pay my spectral bonehead no more heed than they did my non-cacophonous cartoons.

I'm sure as hell not going to draw myself to them, am I? I'm Pegleg Squigs. I've only the one leg left and I could do without a broken back to go with it. Angels they weren't; they really didn't care where they were treading, or falling. Hadn't done, other than when they were taking breaks, which was about the only time they weren't breaking anything, and anyone, in their path since they began their duel on Harmony's Feast Day, the Autumnal Equinox of 5492.

The date's the 22nd of Azky, by the way – the Summer Solstice of 5495; also the 39th birthday of the Terrible Twins, if you're into bizarre synchronicities – but nothing I try gets through. Or they're so busy trampling everything else they trample everything I send them. Someone else does, though; clever girl. But I shouldn't get ahead of myself yet again. So, what else happens beforehand?

Right, Lazareme's Angelus – or Angela, if you're a stickler and not a stinker like me – hasn't been so distracted. We've met Thrygragos Lazareme's quicksilver-quick heliodromus before in this narrative, you'll recall. She's who Lord Yajur assigned to dispose of Zuvem's body after he decapitated him; the one who didn't remember telling Death's Head Grinning, the Nergalid Underlord, where she'd buried it.

The devic sun-runner's been dogging the Unities steps; dodging them as well – Irisiel Mercherm is really, really fast, which is why devils call her Speedy. She spotted some of my sendings and thereby discovered Vetala's designated date for the fall of Sraddha Isle. Messages being her stock and trade, she gets word of it to her Daddy Dearest. Whereupon sunny-he and full-mooning Unmoving, his brother biggest in terms of size, not primogeniture, put their sometimes substantial craniums together and devil-devise what they consider a workable endgame stratagem.

First, they combine forces to collapse the infra-Diluvia cave-system. In doing so they effectively trap both the Haddazur- and Nergalazur-animated Dead Things in Hadd. They still can't make it rain there, though. To do that they'd have to oust all three Nergalids; Hadd being by then, as I've explained, their protectorate due to an empowering blend of shared azuras and Irache faithful. So Irisiel still has some more running around to do; additional missives rather than missiles to deliver.

I'm with Vetala in Manoa when everyone's favourite Vampire Queen of the Dead gets hers. No way is she abandoning Hadd. Faced with incurring the wrath of the Head's last two remaining Great Gods, Yama isn't so stupid. He cuts himself – and as many of Death's Angels, his Inglorious Dead, as he has time to – back to the radioactive Ghostlands, where they still make their home, such as it is.

And believe me the two Unities made even more of a wasteland of the place when they tore through it on the way to Cabby's Weirdom back in Yamana.

(If you'll allow me a late night whiff of whimsy, since it's named after Yama Nergal maybe it was just their way of saying Happy Birthday, Bleeper Reaper. They didn't tarry there long, that I don't have to imagine. Even a pair of Unities maddened by mutual hatred, though not yet by the two still extant Trigregos Talismans, aren't altogether immune to radiation of that intensity.)

Already ensconced near Lake Sedona, the Planter, Gravedigger, Devil Doom, isn't so easily spooked, if you'll pardon the play on verbs. He reckons he's got it laid in Hadd's shade. It's an even better situation than he had in Satanwyck, sitting beside Hell's Belle for so long. His own protectorate having gone the way of the Ghostlands, Hadd's as good as its replacement now that his barely younger baby brother has fled the scene.

Of course, should Speedy deliver him Order's severed head, to be buried in Hadd, next time she was in the area, he might reconsider. 'Want a guarantee?' he asked her. 'Bring me the heads of both Unities and I'll leave for sure.' He and Fecundity would be much happier in Cupidity's Satanwyck. Its demons deserved a better or badder Prime Sinistral than that envious little sprite, didn't they? Instead of Sinistral Spiteful, they could have Sinistral Shovelful.

Fatuous chance of that, says our speedster. If, in order to save the Head, either one or both of the Great Gods could have decapitated, and thereafter finished killing either one or both of the Unities, they'd have done so already, she tells the cocksure Nergalid. Still, devils don't generally shoot the messenger – though less considerate sorts might – and, since that's what she does, delivers stuff, she promises to pass on his generous offer to the two Great Gods.

Which she does, in under a day, there and not quite back. As Irisiel-Angelus reminds me pointlessly, Master Devas can no more disavow their promises than they can lie. Except, she further assures me – she on her way back to Lake Sedona with their risible response – she isn't so much distracted as diverted. On daddy's instructions, not those of Uncle Unmoving, she additionally advises, she's obliged to stop off in Manoa. Only this time it's me to see, not my toothy hostess.

She finds me, too, alone – Vetala having gone up to join her older brothers in the battle for Sraddha Isle the night before. (She probably wouldn't have realized it was brother-singular until she got there. I know I didn't until Irisiel tells me the next day that Yama's already bad-bogey-buggered off.)

It's a seething furnace of fury, she let's me know by way of a warm-up as to why she's come so comparatively far out of her way to see me before returning to it.

Ferocious fighting has been going on for days and days. And it only gets worse after dark, when the Sraddhites bring out their vampires to counter the long-serving ones loyal to Vetala and the Nergalids' Iraches.

(Which is how I learn the Terrible Twins have come back and that Janna had to turn Shredder on account of him being shredded coming out of the Amateramirror the year before in Cabalarkon. It's also how I learn their Mama Mel forced the Trigregos Talismans onto the two Unities in order to drive them away from the Weirdom.)

Bats fly, have gripping paws, they drop incendiaries on Dead Things waiting to cross over the lake to the island; drop them where the Sraddhites' still primitive, only approximately targeted, armaments can't reach. Gravedigger's trying to deal with their batty leadership with his third eye. Reckons he can burn them up with devic eyefire. Which of course he can, if he hits them. Bats move awfully fast, though not as fast as cousin Speedy.

"The Nergalid nicked one last night. She must have recognized him from years earlier, when Thunder & Lightning cut off his head and had me bury it down in Diluvia. She's brave, but has to be dumb as they come because she went after him. What good's a vamp, even one wearing a Tvasitar Talisman, against a Master Deva, let alone a highborn Mithradite?

"I saw where she fell and, even if I personally detest bloodsuckers, they're capable of worship so I risked rescuing her. Besides, she's always had a way with Chaos, might be the only who still does, so there's a chance she might yet prove worth the effort. She'll be all right, in a manner of speaking, once she drinks enough blood. Yuck. But right now she can't fly in her bat-form. That means she can't get anywhere via between-space either.

"You know who I'm talking about. I can take her to him. Only I'm not as dumb as they come, am I?"

I agree with her there, albeit without picking up on the implications of everything she just said, unintentionally indicatively. I guess, being dead, I've developed a deadhead to go along with a peg leg and a dread of bathing out of fear I'll dissolve. Janna was arrogant, yes. And while that might make her reckless, she never was as dumb as they come. So, other than she despised him for cursing her with two decades of stillborns, why would she seek out Devil Doom?

Think Luck and Lust, both capitalized; think Rasp and, for Sraddha, think First Fangs. That's my best advice to you today. Too bad I didn't give it to myself back then.

"Father's this notion," she carries on blithely, not realizing she'd almost given away the tooth fairy's farm. "You can't draw anyone conscious anywhere against their will but you're good with inanimate objects. I'm not saying you can draw their power foci away from them. They're too intertwined for that. I am saying, and so is dad, you could draw the Trigregos Talismans away from them. Draw them here and I'll take over from there."

"They'd poison you the same as they would anyone else."

"I'm quicker than anyone else, Jordy. I can scoot over to the caldera of Sedon's Peak in the blink of two eyes, three for me. Then I'll do a Harmony to Strife, 1500 hundred years ago, and dad to Harmony's tawdry Tattletail back in 5476. I'll dispose of them in Brother Smithy's lava lake, from whence he forged them in the first place. You can do that, can't you?"

"It's a thought," I allow. "But what makes you and Grandfather Everyman so sure Order and Chaos will stop doing whatever they're doing, which is mostly trying to kill each other, as well as everyone caught underneath them, the moment they're no longer under the influence of the thrice-cursed Godly Glories? They didn't need them to get going, did they?"

"We don't know that, do we? Sooth, as you're forever saying, arguably is they're why the Head's in this horrific state today. I mean, what got them going in the first place was Abe Chaos eliminating her Harmoniousness, the balance between his Un-holiness and his Orderliness. By his own admission, he would never have done that if he didn't have the Susasword. By his own admission according to you, I shouldn't have to add."

"Then I shouldn't have to subtract," I countered, "That, once he was out of its range, Uncle Abe immediately regretted what he did to her. Besides being beauty in the eyes of any beholder, legend had his incomparable brood sister as the first Master Deva ever born, albeit by only a matter of seconds before her triplet bros saw whatever passed for the light of day in the first Weir System.

"Not at all legendarily, let alone arguably, Harmony was certainly the most popular devic goddess on the entire Hidden Headworld when he did her in, sword and Brainrock-boulder-wise. There's no question that, if it were anyone else, pinning her to a slab of Godstuff might prove fatal. But she was also mostly Gypsium herself, wasn't she.

"Desperate as it sounds, he reasoned his actions might therefore be reversible. So he asked me draw him to her. And if you don't know what happened then, well, put it this way: I'm dead; I wasn't a thousand odd days ago. The Dead burn much easier than the Living. My sketchpad goes up now then I might as well."

"Dad's been busy cogitating, Jordy. It's hideously hard work sleeping, particularly when you're using Mithras's head for your pillow. Imagine the nightmares. So now that he's awake again he finds it a refreshing change. Sanity has its rewards, as they say; obedience first and foremost. You pull this off, they no longer suffer from too-proximate, motherly overrides, we'll find a way to make that forehead-scar of yours start to blink again. You don't, well, like you just said, you're already dead, aren't you?"

"Gravedigger?" I enquire. Being dead myself, I'd rather not become involved in any more death-dealing. Hell's teeth, I only eat what's already too far gone to be reanimated.

"He promised to vacate Hadd, as you've so mischievously persuaded Fecundity to rename Iraxas, once I bring him the two Unities' heads. You know about devic genetics. We're as incapable of violating our oaths as we are of disobeying our fathers. So that's precisely what he'll have to do, isn't it."

"If you bring him their heads."

"Nay probs, Jordy. Once I dispose of the Trigregos Talismans, dad will make sure, as in divine-rightly-demand, that the Unities' heads no longer connect to their shoulders. And they'll stay detached until I deliver them to the Nergalid. For about two more seconds. When it comes to devic oaths, you have to be very, very specific."

"Gravedigger?" I repeat, underpinning my concern re unnecessary complicity.

"I left him an option, the same deal I offered Vetala and his brood-younger sibling, the Ghosts' Under-Lordship. He wants to stay in Hadd, fine. He wants to get away, fine as well. He balks; he doesn't leave Hadd right that minute, to wherever he chooses to go, well, every remaining devil, of every tribe, will be between-space when I present him with dad's ultimatum. That'll not only persuade him, it'll leave him only one way through the Weird. That'll be to Incain and into All.

"Same deal holds if formerly Fecundity, Vulva-Vetala, doesn't smarten up. Except, for her, it'll needs be stake-in-the-heart time first. That said, given how many she's already killed, or turned – and how many they've subsequently done away with – we'll be hard-pressed to prevent Grandfather Mighty Eye-Mouth in the Sky cathonitizing her as soon as he returns from wherever he's been hiding. Sooth also said, very few of us would object if the Great Gods beat him to it."

I'm still not convinced. Then I am. Irisiel has a third eye. Third eyes are far more useful than even Trinondev eyeorbs. She didn't have to unleash any eyefire. An eye-lock robbed me of my freewill just as assuredly as if she'd possessed me. Which she couldn't very well do, could she? Not given her present, um, compromised condition, which you'll have figured out by now.

And that's what happened. Or near enough.

Thus ends the Tethys Tale entitled: *'Janna Fangfingers'* or *'The Disunition of the Three Unities of Lazareme.'*

========

"It better not," said Centauri.

****

13: Finale Finally – If Not Finally Fatally

"What's the matter, haven't I been effusively allusive enough for you?"
Alpha Centauri and Ferdinand Niarchos exchanged glances. They weren't getting it. Janna St Peche-Montressor did.

========

She smiled borderline angelically. "Zuvem Nergalis scorched Janna Somata. Angelus-Irisiel had to get into her in order to use her devic healing talents and thereby ensure she was okay. So she, that Janna, seized the opportunity and took hold of her, Irisiel, instead. Over the course of the previous twenty-odd-years she'd done the same thing to Dame Chance, the Skinless Rasp and Hell's Belle."

"Also Nergal Vetala, on All-Death Day." Tethys trumped her. "Except that time our vampy Vet was so weak, after surviving however many months immobilized inside the thrice-cursed Amateramirror, and then giving birth so explosively to hundreds of Haddazurs, Janna possessed her, not the other way around. That's why she attacked Gravedigger. She figured she could get into him just as effortlessly. She thereafter anticipated no difficulty dominating him, through inborn force of will, like she had so many other Master Devas."

"And the hot-eyed Nergalid wasn't feeling cooperative. He was feeling homicidal. Unless *'vampircidal'* is a word, which I doubt."

"You're cheating," said the governor. "You gleaned him."

"Why would I bother?" their Janna objected. "I'd have thought it obvious."

"Oh, hold on, you two," said Tethys, before Centauri could get peremptorily declarative on his underlings. "I'm only teasing. Want some epilogues, Al? Jolly-jim-dandy. More beer? Thanks, Janna. Oh dear, running low on the precious thinking fluid, eh? No matter. I'll survive. Vampircidal's good too. May have to steal it.

"Out of olives already? Too bad. Cheese and crackers will be fine, though I can sort of provide the latter. Because they're firecrackers – the epilogues, I mean, even if I can't personally testify as to their accuracy 100%. With that proviso in mind, here goes."

========

A Tethys Tale - JANNA FANGFINGERS: THE DISUNIT-ION OF THE UNITIES OF LAZAREME – Part Ten: PHAN-

TOM PIPING

========

The two triplet brothers rumbled out of between-space grappling, as if bad boys wrestling for fun in a Marutian schoolyard. Both were bloodied, never bowed. Springing onto their feet well away from each other, they paused as if to take in their surroundings. For a change they'd landed in an area of pristine delight: a long, perfectly glorious stretch of, given the season, hot-to-the-touch but soft, smooth, fine-grain sand.

There was no one in sight either alive or ambulatory deceased, as was as often the case in these terrible times, and that included seabirds of either variety. Wrack and sams-free, as in no jetsam nor any flotsam visible anywhere, the seashore wasn't windswept. It was All-swept. That made it the Prison Beach of Incain.

To describe the Unities, other than as equally enormous and equally enraged, with either red-skin and shaggy, unkempt dark hair or as butterscotch-brown with luminous, very much electric hair, serves no purpose. They hadn't groomed for this latest encounter and, when it all comes down to dust, or sand, probably could care less what they looked like or who perceived them however.

What was more noticeable than their predictable weaponry, the shapes of which they rarely altered, was what the former had round his neck and the latter had strapped to his left arm as a shield: respectively, the Crimson Corona and the Amateramirror. Both of which, the Mind of Sapiendev and the Soul of Devaura, unless I've mixed them up, suddenly erupt into flames and promptly weren't there anymore.

Crispy Unities anyone? Get them while they're hot. Which they're not for long. They heal themselves with a thought just as All of Incain manifests itself-her-self out of the Weird and into the Blue. The She-Sphinx was as she usually appeared: a lioness's massive body, legs, paws and claws; the outstretched wings of a just as disproportionately huge hawk, eagle or garuda; the whip-snap-wagging tail-end of an impossible serpent; and both the distinctive head and bared breasts of a beautiful woman.

For a change the woman wasn't either 3-eyed or Pyrame Silverstar. Not inexplicably she closely resembled a dark-haired, tanned or Mediterranean-skinned version of their unfailingly feminine third, Datong Harmonia, the Unity of just that, as well as lost Panharmonium. Actually, since Harmony always appeared as beauty in the eyes of the beholder, and both Lord Yajur and Unholy Abaddon had slightly different perceptions of what constituted loveliness idealized, neither would have reckoned her Harmony somehow found and thence devoured by All.

They'd have seen All's head as how it was originally fashioned: as reminiscent of Trishtar Thrae's neck-nut. She'd be the Biblical Eve (one of them), apocryphally the second wife of Alorus Ptah, Golden Age Humanity's Number One Patriarch. (He'd be the golden-apple-eater that deliberately sank old Eden easily in excess of a thousand years prior to his just as malignant descendant, Number Ten, Xuthros Hor, causing the Genesea.)

Their other claim to fame, besides Ptah being the Biblical Adam (one of them), and she supplanting Primeval Lilith as his forever-mate, is that they were, in all likelihood, the time-tumbling Male and Female Entities in, I've heard, their 61st lifetimes together. Which, if so, suggests they committed their detestable maleficence many multiple millennia after accessing First Weir's technology in order to become the joint creators of none other than the Moloch Sedon himself.

(Along with a certain scientocratic geneticist by the name of Cabalarkon, long before he became the Undying Utopian, if said-Sed is to be believed. Which of course we all do.)

Put better, and much less long-windedly, that's how the Unities would have perceived All's face at first, because she abruptly began growing dozens of plesiosaur-like necks, all of which had emergent heads with different faces. Significantly, as previously noted save for the Female Entity's, every one of them had three eyes. Every one of them also had readily identifiable features.

Rather, they would have had if either Unity could recollect, let alone care, what the likes of Abdullah Ziderite (Magnetism) and the 700-years-gone Idiot-cum-Atomic Twins looked like in their commonest forms. They would have spotted the familiar faces of Byron's Silverclouds, the snake-haired Medusa (Mother Murder), Cathune Bubastis (the Apocalyptic of Drought), and many others, most of whom had only comparatively recently taken themselves into the She-Sphinx of their own accord.

One exception to that was Pyrame Silverstar, who hadn't so much volunteered to be swallowed as Harmony concluded All was still hungry after the Pauper Priest-ess relinquished control of the Mandroid Monster Maker to her on, recall, the 1st of Rudar 5494. She was among the snaky heads, though; in one of her typically idiosyncratic phases, too. A tetrahedron with three triangular upper sides, each with a solitary eye peering out of it, makes for an unmistakable manifestation, I'm sure you'll confer concurrence.

As for the bodiless, yet nevertheless full-mooning fellow who appeared above and behind the now-rearing, suddenly tentacle-necked She-Sphinx, in broad daylight, there was no doubt as to his identity either. There might have been about the main hydra-head, though, the one that grew even longer and thicker than that reminiscent of All's maker, aka Milady Memory or, every now and then, the Mnemosyne Machine.

Were it not for the third eye, he might have passed for the Male Entity – if aka Heliosophos had sky-blue skin, sea-green eyes and radiating, sun-blonde hair. Which he may have as Alorus Ptah, again if anyone there could go back that far in terms of reliable memory, non-capitalized.

The mystery head wasn't so much so when one recalls how Harmony perceived her father, Thrygragos Everyman. Or for that matter how her tawdry Tattletail, as Irisiel-Janna had characterized Tatty Tom not so long ago their time, looked back in 5476. Who, now that I drink about it, figured in one aspect of a story – one aspect of a series of stories, more like – that I said I wasn't going to get into today.

(Tomcat Tattletail, just for the record, was the somehow recurring faerie fart I maintain was what was left of my devic half-dad, Rumour of Lazareme. If I haven't already, remind me to tell you about him sometime. If you don't mind me pausing to puke every little while, that is. Unlike Harmony, I always found Trillion-Timing Tommy insufferable: a truculent, stomach-churning shithead, truth told.)

This, though, was no approximation of Thrygragos Lazareme. The moment said-hydra-head spoke, the Unities knew it couldn't have been just anyone; not the way his voice resonated in their own headcases. It could only have been their Lord Laziest sire. As for what he was doing inside of All, given the countless atrocities his sons had committed over the previous three years and more, especially when it came to Abe Chaos, he probably felt it the safest place to be.

"Hear me, Sedon Pawns. I am your father, aggrieved and grieving. Cease this depravity this instant. Get to your knees and pray my forgiveness."

Before the Great God reached *'aggrieved and grieving'* the Crimson Corona reappeared on Uncle Abe. It did so around his forehead this time, not around his neck – like a crown of thorns, I've heard it said, and him already charcoal-crusted, burnt-barely-bearded and doubly bloody due to it having unexpectedly ignited moments earlier.

Abe vanished before their appreciably inconsolable, great godly daddy got as far as the, for him, atypically insistent *'to your knees'* nonsense. Yajur didn't. Neither did he pay any attention to his father's command. He might have, assuming it really was Lazareme, had not Demogorgon chosen that moment fire up all its devic eyes.

For that had to be who was actually controlling All.

========

"Demogorgon?"

========

"The Conglomerate Deva, Ferd," Tethys responded. "Aka the Unnameable, on both sides of the Dome, a version of it reportedly came together on Thrygragon. Only then, well, Al and Janna will remember Volsanga's Nut from yesterday. In other words, I wasn't consciously there at that instant. And virtually everyone who was there was otherwise occupied trying to live through it, so no one was sure what precise form it took."

"Roman Catholics had a superstitious dread about the Unnameable," Centauri contributed, as if to demonstrate that he occasionally recalled tales Tethys told him. "If you ever said his actual name, so it went, evil in the form of death or disaster would visit the speaker and his or her family, their friends or cronies, for three generations.

"Then a religious philosopher by the name of Lactantius wrote a still extant treatise – the name of which I've forgotten – at the request of his patron, Constantine the Great, the Roman Emperor son of Helena Augusta, whom Jordy says was depicted in the mosaic we watched being mounted in the Headworld Museum yesterday, before the Molech Xibalba or his ghostly-ghastly doppelganger interrupted proceedings. And there it was for all to see."

"Sounds like this Lactantius fellow was you," said Niarchos.

"A son, maybe," Tethys allowed. "As for the form the no longer unnameable horror took on Thrygragon, tee-tee-tails I've read describe it as a monstrous arm, severed yet perversely mobile. It grew out of a mound of daemonic crud, walked on its fingertips then sprouted, out of its shoulder-ball, tall thick stems ending in repugnant, as much as refulgent, sunflowers with devic heads for hearts, as in the centres of the feckless florae themselves."

"Close enough," Centauri considered. "Presumably the devils glaring out of the petaliferous limb-thing on Thrygragon were similar, if not always identical, to the snakeheads on Incain in your story." His confirmatory statement extracted double and triple takes from those with him in the solarium.

"What?" he retorted, as if in answer to their evident astonishment. "I said presumably."

"Before that, Al. As in *'close enough'.*" Had Great Byron just spoken through his host? Tethys shot Janna St Peche-Montressor a quick glance. She shrugged.

"APM was there," she acknowledged, albeit without admitting she was occupied any more than her father-in-law just had. "As was Thrygragos Byron. Plus, we've both heard multiple renditions of that theomachy's ultimately fatal encounters and they all agree it didn't last long. So maybe it's one of your elephants, like the plesiosaur necks."

"What's irrelevant about them?"

"Other than your florid language, nothing. It just that they sound like elephant trunks."

"Plesiosaur necks do not trumpet."

"You know what I mean, Jordy."

========

Call them elephant trunks if you prefer, Janna, but the devic eyes atop the heads at the end of them opened up full-bore, with cathonitizing energy to boot. Or at least to ill-star. How Yajur withstood the barrage was a measure of his magnificence, not to mention his sheer obstinacy. That and the fact that neither his father nor Great Byron, full-mooning above and beyond All as he was, joined in. Oh, yes, all of the above, non-capitalized, and the fact that he willed the Amateramirror back onto his arm in time to duck behind it.

I'd been looking into it; not out of it, note. Both of us were: Angelus-Irisiel and me, Pegleg Squigs. I'd drawn it to Manoa, just like she wanted. If only to show off how, um, masterful she was with it, she suspended it in the air – on nothing that I could see – whereupon she twiddled some nonexistent knobs mentally and tuned into Incain such that we could use it to far-see what was going on there.

Like a glassine yoyo on an interspatial string it vanished at virtually the same second we long-distance-witnessed the Crimson Corona rewrap itself around Chaos's forehead. It disappearing like that made me think someone else, an unknown interloper, had done a me, returned the favour, as it were, or righted a wrong and drawn it away from us. It also made me think that the same unknown someone was now controlling Chaos's behaviour.

Angelus-Irisiel wasted nary a second panicking; took off between-space after it. To do so she necessarily had to break the eye-lock she had me in all this time; not that I'd realized I'd been acting as her unwitting thrall until then. I hadn't realized it was Yajur who had called the mirror back to him either. That'd come later, albeit with an odd twist.

At the time I reckoned it was the same someone who'd made the Amateramirror act like a circular television set, 500 years before there was such a device on the Outer Earth, or a telescopic porthole on a boat or plane, which I assume there still isn't unless you count satellite surveillance systems. That unknown someone had to be really, really good with Trigregos Talismans.

That unknown someone also had to be in control of Chaos by now because that's what one did with Crinsom's Crown. In short, that someone wasn't unknown at all. I called her masterful for a reason. A Master of Weir was my tilt, though it turned out I was leaning towards the wrong Master.

I drew Chaos as I'd last seen him, with the Crimson Corona around his forehead, not his neck. Much to my shock, the background didn't fill in with Incain. Notwithstanding my ongoing malodorous circumstances, the reporter in me took over. You might call that double death-wish curious of me but I nevertheless took myself up to wherever Chaos went after we lost our visuals. I reappeared in time to see him atomize Zuvem Nergalis firsthand. But I did miss much of the simultaneous action on Incain; hence the cautionary nature of my prefatory remark.

Yes, I missed the neck, or trunk, out of which Grandfather Lazareme's head had been poking, rocket off this latest Demogorgon like a non-missive missile that landed far out into Tempestuous Psychron, the Hidden Headworld's eastern ocean. (Which, now that I drink about it, is the wrong word. It didn't land; it watered.)

Yes, I missed Yajur conjuring the Amateramirror back to him, massively enlarged, in time to reflect all that cathonic energy back at hydra-headed All. Missed him growing even more magnificently insane, toss off the mirror and start zapping the remaining, by now thoroughly horrified heads with his lightning blade.

How many more Master Devas did he blast into the Headworld's heavens before All retracted those necks left exposed and vanished back between-space? I don't know but I bet it was at least a dozen. One I know Yajur didn't send into the Sedon Sphere. I know because – like I didn't allude to effusively; like I alluded to just once, sooth profusely alleged – I arrived in time to witness Abe Chaos do it.

Before I got there, to what had been Sedona Spellbinder's lakeshore for a couple of thousand years prior to the 48th Century expansion of the Lathakran Empire, it must have looked like two Sunday afternoon gardeners going at each other over who had the better compost heap. Unholy Abaddon had his pitchfork-like trident while Gravedigger had his Brainrock shovel. In the end, as he'd done to both beguiling Belialma, Bouncing Belle, and First Fangs, Faustus Vladuca, months earlier in Kanin City, his Unholiness prevails.

He pins the Nergalid to the ground, yanks his talisman out of his grip, reverses it and cleaves it into his skull, caving it in. Never releasing his hold on his trident he's not done yet – not until, ka-boom!, he devil-dooms the Planter, Gravedigger, Zuvem Nergalis. Bye-bye, Cruel Earth; hidey-ho, High Night's Sky.

Uncle Abe spots me standing nearby gawping incredulously. Amazingly he nods as if in dazed recognition. He smiles but I swear there are tears in his eyes. Then he yanks the Crimson Corona off his head and gives it a flip, like a kid would a glowing hula hoop. Just as its mirrored, just as cursed cousin had in Manoa – or like one of Harry Zeross's teleportive rings does today – it turns in the air on nothingness.

He jumps through it; vanishes between-space; a circus lion returning to the fray, as it also were, albeit well beyond Hadd's Big Tent. It, Crinsom's Crown, doesn't do an Abe, though. It's still there, hovering beckoningly, as if silently singing *'Can I get a Witness?'*. I'm still dead. So far, so good. What the hey. I follow suit, pegleg-leap after him.

So, to end this epilogue, I'm beached not unlike an undead whale, blubbering but without any blubber. It's a sunny day and the sand is sizzling. But the moon is out – no, I'm wrong. It's the Byronhead way up there. Thunder & Lightning Lord Yajur is finally on his knees; in all probability out of exhaustion, not obedience. His hair's barely sparking. He's barely Sparky.

The Amateramirror is over there, discarded. His Orderliness has not suddenly become his Disorderliness; just done for the day, I further reckon. Then he spots his triplet brother striding resolutely towards him and must realize he isn't. Suddenly the Crimson Corona is around Chaos's head again. I look over there. His Unholiness, my Uncle Abe, does too. It's seventh-born Angelus-Irisiel, my devil-dad Rumour's brood sister. Except in a way it isn't.

She's not a big dresser, isn't my therefore immediate aunt. I don't know if what she has on is a chiton or a himation or even a sari, so I won't call it any of the above. How about a mini-tunic, like one of those oddball, Sixties' fashion statements out there; albeit one suitable for a sprinter, not a hippy? I'll go for that so you'll have to too; at least until you have a chance to make me sit corrected.

I do know she had on her famous power focus, her wings-of-Mercury sandals. Unless they're Hermes' sandals or Egyptian Thoth's. Then her skin goes transparent and by that I don't mean she goes skinless, like the Rasp, Rastha Aragon. That'd be the flagellating White Godling who probably wasn't Janna Fangfingers' first foil after all, if I'm right about the luscious Lady Luck's unlucky ill-starring in 5474. That'd also be one of All's now reabsorbed or Yajur-cathonitized heads.

As one might expect from her Illuminary-given name, Irisiel Mercherm tends towards the prismatic, hair- and skin-wise; albeit leaning more blondish and more bluish in the same order. Who's looking out of her – the ghost within, if you will, or even if you won't – is silver-haired and alabastrine white. We know who she is right away: the love of both Abe and Squiggly's lives, pre-me, and in many respects the bane of all three of us, Yajur being the third, though as the Legendarian I haven't been doing too well by her either.

Only now does it occur to me that my masterful apprehensions of a few minutes ago were erroneous. It wasn't Master Mama, it was Master Daughter. Janna had become a junior Trigregos Titaness; what I'm tempted to call a mini-Mel, as opposed to a miniskirt. Or a mini-flirt, as far as that goes, because she hadn't shrunk, just grown fangs

Like I said, while it is getting late, it's still sunny so, being a vamp, she can't come out to play, let alone say goodbye. But that's what it amounts to since Abe once again rips the Crimson Corona off his head and contemptuously tosses it over there, very near to the Amateramirror. Neither of the talismans are glowing anymore. It's as if both have been power-drained; rendered inconsequential trinkets, little more than cheap, costume jewellery.

Yajur hauls himself to his feet wearily but determinedly. I chance a glance upstairs. The Byronhead is glowing like I haven't seen it glow since the Deflection of the Unities last Samhain, your Halloween. It's a cathonitizer, recall, and I can guess what's it's preparing to do. So can Abe, I suspect. I also suspect, knowing him as well as I did, that Yajur egocentrically reckons it'll only target his brother. Abe's the bad guy, not Sparky.

True or not, for Abe Chaos that would never do. His Unholiness unsheathes the Chaos Blade. (The tines of his trident are its hilt, recall as well.) Does Yajur – sorry, his Orderliness – go all Sparky again and scream *'Nooo!'* as he charges his brother. I'll say yes. He certainly screams something really, really loudly.

Does someone else scream it too? Might it be Great Byron? I'll say you'd have to ask him. I know I do; scream as I'm hitting the turf, not the surf. And probably so does Irisiel-Janna, before she speeds off. Call it a chorus of angels, devils that they are, if you must, but, whomever, whatever if it was All echoing between-space, the screams come too late.

Is it the end of everything? Self-evidently the answer's everywhere you look, then and now. When the smoke clears, and there's plenty of it, Yajur's gone upstairs, as ill-starred as he remains today. And there's Abe – impaled, through his third eye, with his re-sheathed trident's central prong. His head dissolves into it, body follows flowingly, whereupon his trident dissolves, or turns to dust, sand if you'd prefer. A gust of wind blows it out to sea, where it could well have subsequently drifted forevermore.

Thus, save for a couple of peculiar particulars, ends one epilogue.

========

"Just a couple?" semi-scoffed Centauri, significantly not volunteering confirmation that Tethys, as Pegleg Squiggly, could have heard Unmoving Byron scream 'Nooo!' really, really loudly. Or even that he could've heard his regular mouthpiece, Sedona Spellbinder, scream it on his behalf.

"Only the one beer left. How could there be more?"

========

Grandfather Lazareme helps me to my feet. And he is wearing a chiton or a himation or whatever's the East Indian equivalent of a toga. "You're a mess," he understates, remarkably pleasantly given everything that had occurred not just that same solstice day, Year of the Dome 5495, but over the course of last three plus years. "It'd be a mercy to finish you off."

"It might, indeed. Except I'm never sure I'll come back, am I."

"There is that."

"Where've you been? You're all wet."

"I'll take that literally, not figuratively, and point out there. Psychron's called the ocean of madness, you know. And it's true. Except I'm angry-mad, not insane-mad."

"Not even with grief?"

"Why do you think I never got out of bed when Abe destroyed the world?"

"World seems to be still here, granddad."

"Your world, Jordy. Mine was Harmony. She was my world."

"That's so sad."

"It's pathetic. But it's what happens when you get caught up in a Sedonplay. Want to bet whose star will be back tonight?"

"Only if I'm still around to collect." (It was; I wasn't.)

"Fine. Collect those two first. You know what to do afterwards."

"Answer me one thing first. Are you who drew the Amateramirror back to Sparky? I know you're good with my quill." (He'd proved that on Thrygragon, once he got hold of it. Which he did some time after a certain deadly dryad named Barbara Tethys acorn-ate, as in soul-sunk, a legendary, 30-Year-mainly-manly spirit-self before I could make the leap to limbo.)

"Don't you mean Rumour's Quill?"

"That too."

"Didn't you?"

"You can't answer a question with another question."

"Why not?" I glared at him; may have stomped my foot as well. "What's that?"

He wasn't being evasive. I heard it too – the phantom piping.

========

"Phantom piping," grasped Janna. "Like yesterday?"

"It certainly wasn't plumbing," said Tethys, suddenly scratching the scar in his forehead urgently. "Except yesterday wasn't phantom piping; it was a phantom piping."

"And on Incain?"

"It stopped after a couple of minutes, if that. No source, just sound."

"Did Lazareme ever answer you?"

"No, he turned into an elephant and tromped off northwards, leaving really, really big paw prints on All's no longer anywhere near paradisiacal beach."

"Jordy ..."

"He said if it wasn't me then it had to be Yajur. And we can't ask him, can we."

"Why'd he go swimming?"

"All ejected him. Rather, all the devils in All ejected him as if by consensus. He was trying to stop them ill-starring Order."

"What's wrong with your forehead?"

"Nothing that a prefrontal lobotomy won't cure."

========

Compelled or not, I'm brilliant. I knew that already of course. Should have thought of it long before Rumour's howsoever-compromised, immediate sister put the notion to me. They cause my pad to burn or they don't. It's a simple as that, always has been, albeit mostly in retrospective pain.

So, there they are, the two leftover Trigregos Talismans, power-drained or not. Next, Manoan drawing rapidly redone with a different destination, there they go – much to my happily unburned astonishment and assuming, also in retrospect, they are the real Crimson Corona and Amateramirror. Only this time I skip the middle man, or woman, or women, two in one. This time I draw them straight into the caldera of Sedon's Peak.

I expect them to melt down into nothingness. And maybe they do; into so much Brainrock slag. Only they're still around, aren't they? Or were – again assuming Second Fangs, employing Aunt Speedy's blinding speed, didn't whip the originals and leave sleight-of-handy-dandy facsimiles behind. Which I imagine she'd deny, unless pressed; with a wooden stake against the chest above her heart, I shouldn't have to add.

Even if I can't show you where they are now, because my pad of paper would definitely ignite if I tried, I have seen them, the mirror and the crown, since Incain

Day. I can't say the same thing about the Susasword. Still have no idea where it's been, or is, have I. Want to see my freshly supplied pad of paper ignite? Good. Neither do I.

Too bad there's no such thing as asbestos sheets. At least, so Janna tells me, there isn't pocket-sized and for purposes purely pictorial in terms of artful scribbling. As for the one she did give me, my fingertips still tingle with burning sensations of the literal variety. So I haven't bothered to try it out yet.

========

"Are those enough peculiar particulars for tonight?

"My namesake?" Janna St Peche-Montressor wanted to know.

"Oh, she survived; with or without the Trigregos Talismans — though I reckon it much more likely it's without or she would never have been able to resist using them. Survives to this day, as Ferd will tell you. Additional pudding proof's yesterday's note: the one signed with a 'j' dotted with an eyeball. That and a dreadfully used and abused tee-tee since deceased."

"I meant in terms of your story."

"Of course you did. But, ah, that's another epilogue. Want to beer it?" Janna took the hint this time; looked to her father-in-law, who nodded, no doubt reluctantly. No matter how deviated he may be in terms of multiple births and thus far endless recurrences, a guy like Tethys would always prefer a bottle in front of him than a prefrontal lobotomy.

Said Legendarian gratefully accepted the proffered pill, the pilsner, the last of the Fatman's presumably hard-to-come-by Czechoslovakian stash. It was still cold. He laid it against his forehead; worked too. Like the phantom piping did after a mournful few minutes that fraught, ever-so-eventful evening on Incain, his inexplicable itching stopped.

"I've long ago forgiven her for finishing me off by the way. Not so sure about Guardian Angel Jordan. Fortunately or unfortunately, he's someone else you can't ask."

========

Bat-Koatyl's to blame. Alongside his succulent sister, Bat-Sraddha's been rallying the Sraddhite troops night after night. Life-loving hypocrites that they were by then, the shave-skulled Brown Robes weren't doing much to return the favour. What with no devils on their side, they were wimps compared to their vamps. The latter, though, can only mystify away from ordinary mortals. They can't mystify away from their fellow bats.

On that selfsame night, the night Star Sedon finally reappeared upstairs after a 20-year absence, Koatyl tracked him down and held him up. Nergal Vetala came out of the Weird and caught him in an immobilizing eye-lock. (Which is yet another indication she retained some degree of devic might.) She thereupon took, for her, a modest measure of both personal and impersonal revenge.

The latter's on behalf of her faithful followers — alive, dead, and those never given the opportunity to reanimate due to flame-belching arm-hoses and suchlike pyrotechnics — whereas the former's on account of the male of the Somata twins confining her within the Amateramirror for all those many months.

That he did so, at least arguably, to prevent her having him for supper didn't enter into her non-mirrored reflections. That's just what vampires did, eat folks, so forget any dissembling re the righteousness of her actions. Survival of the fittest, as well as the battiest, that's all there is to that, don't you know.

I'm there watching as Bat-Koatyl carves him up; with his claws, not a boning or scaling knife. It isn't a pleasant sight, let me tell you. But, Vetala being my pale-pal, not to mention my adopted mom, I'm inured to unpleasant sights by then. I dutifully register it for posterity's sake as they flay his hide. Take some of the choicest raw flesh to chew on for myself, sooth said. I'm far beyond redemption by then.

He's all but skinless when Vetala makes the mistake of bending over to give him a last kiss goodbye. As I may have mentioned a few minutes ago, vamps aren't anything unless it's hard to kill other than properly. He sticks up about all that left of him and rams it through her heart right properly. It's one of his shin-splints. She mystifies but it's not good enough to get away. And that's why he's rightfully considered the Living's greatest hero to this day. Without Vetala around anymore she'll never again help whelp Haddazurs.

Janna Somata reappears about then, though she may have been there before, between-space, for all I know. Regardless of her psycho-bat talents, her Mama Mel was a witch, so she probably was and is as well. Maybe even a natural born one like nowadays' friend Fish's sister Wilderwitch was prior to everlasting death claiming her on the Outer Earth's Damnation Isle, up in the Aleutians, a quarter century ago.

There's no smile; no wave goodbye, not even for Squiggly, her never-requited truelove from their carefree childhood – when, she'll tell you, she was last happy; the last time all three of them probably were, the third being Shreds this time. A devic eye opens in her forehead and the next thing I know it's years later. I'm a female plant-person. Something to do with tree-ticks, I'm given to understand by the Forbidden Forest's local, Plantagenet royalty.

What really happened? I've asked Second Fangs that myself, me with my garlic necklace on – I told you about being partial about who I drink with, not wanting to become the drink myself. She just tells me I stank; that I offended her, olfactory-wise. So she eyefire-blasted me not so much into perdition as into my next incarnation.

I suppose, in some ways, Grandfather Lazareme was right. He usually is. It was the merciful thing to do. No matter how fanatically healthy I managed to draw myself looking, skin-wise; no matter how well I kept myself smelling, externally; I was, internally, slowly rotting away anyways.

And I did recur; have kept recurring, knock wooden head. I'm still never sure if this is my last one, but the burden of uncertainty's just something I bear gracefully. Keeps me on my toes, thanks Al. Keeps me cowardly, thanks Ferd. Sympathy card's in the mail, thanks Janna. Couldn't make it on the back of a postcard with you in a bikini? Didn't think so.

So, did Second Fangs acquire Vetala or was she still holding onto Auntie Angelus, Irisiel Mercherm? Well, the Vampire Queen's been back a few times since the First War; albeit never again as the mother of any azuras. I could tell you a few of them some other time, should you so desire. So could Thartarre Holgatson, the Sraddhites' one-armed, current High Priest, who's the altogether mortal, as in non-deviated, son of the last one I know about. Which is a story I shouldn't have to tell you about as it's so well-known hereabouts.

But Hadd's as perpetually cloud-covered as ever, it still doesn't rain there, Second Fangs persists and living Iraches – the ones in Hadd and the ones in New Iraxas anyhow – still accord her a tremendous amount of deference, even devotion. Which is simultaneously curious and bordering on remarkable, given she's a non-Irache.

Also, while there's no doubt she's had, over the centuries, more trouble keeping her Irache vamps in line than she has her Marutian ones, the mere fact she's still around attests to her staying power. Iraches still worship Vetala, too, so I can't say yay or nay as to whether Second Fangs has kept a part of her ever since Incain Day.

She's something in that Crystal Skull of hers, though. That's for certain.

========

"End epilogues."

****

14: Pregame Prelude

"Oh, I don't know about that, Mr Tethys," said Alpha Centauri, disturbingly re-verting to business formality. "The fact of the matter is one's being written as we speak, in deed as well as in pen and ink; not to mention for television and the movies. And in Free Iraxas as well as both New Iraxas and Hadd proper. It may even be you'll be suggesting I rename it Haas soon."

"Haas?"

"As in 'has it all again'. With the exception of bats and Dead Things Walking."

========

"How so, Mr Centauri?"

"Tell him, Mr Niarchos."

"Be glad to, sir. Be glad to show you too, Mr Tethys. If you'd care to accompany me to Petrograd tomorrow. It'll mean missing the official reopening of the Headworld Museum on Sedonda but, from what I understand, you've seen the Kanin City mosaic plenty of times before. It is a Tethys, isn't it?"

"A Gordon *'G for Glee'* Tethys, not a Jordan *'Q for Quill'* Tethys, at least not initially, but, yes, I have. Seen Petrograd too. Or weren't you paying attention?"

"Not like this you haven't; at least not like this in most of a century. For one thing, in case *you* weren't paying attention, there's no need for a respirator anymore, though many of our recent arrivals, altogether living workers from Godbad proper, still wear simple air-filtration masks, like a surgeon does in a hospital. Given this new-to-me, nifty knack of yours for drawing backwards, you might even be able to help me solve a minor technical glitch we've been having of late."

"Technical glitches are hardly my specialty, weirdo. Sorry, Mr Niarchos. But now that you've deliberately twigged my interest, what is it?"

"Ever since Centauri Enterprises accepted my recommendations and put a bounty on vamps, we've been having problems verifying the, um, kills, I guess you could call them. I mean it's not like they leave scalps behind when my vampire-hunters stake them."

"Scalps!" Centauri castigated the governor, very sternly for him. "I have warned you against using such an inciting term previously, Mr Niarchos. Where I come from, from the arctic tip of North America to the toe of South America, aboriginal Americans regard the very word *'scalps'* very, very negatively.

"Nor should I need to remind you, especially not after the many references we've had to genetics over the course of today alone, that, as varied as they are, Iraches are genetically identical to American aboriginals, as varied as they are too. Or close enough to it that their differences aren't statistically significant.

"These Second Chancers you occasionally hear about – not to be confused with either cankers or chancres – where do you think they were First Chancers? Old Iraxas is the Outer Earthlings' Shadowland, where their spirits go to await entry to wherever they go next; even if it's back to where they came from, as a few believe.

"You need only to look at some of the place names – there's a Tulum on the outside for example – or some of their personal names: Koatyl, Xibalba, Tsishah and that Mani-Balam fellow who runs Free Iraxas. And don't get me going on about Night Owl. Everyone's heard of vamps turning into bats. I've heard of them turning into rats and wolves, too. But owls? Come on! That's lamiae territory."

Tethys knew all of them; the first two from previous incarnations, the last two from his current one as well as a couple of recent ones. Tsishah Twilight was the senior, non-Lemurian, Quarter Queen of Shenon, Witch Isle. Although scheduled to retire come the Spring Equinox, as the public face of a number of Witch Sisterhoods, including Janna's own Athenan Sisterhood, she wielded significant influence on Headworld affairs.

Mani-Balam, whose honorific was Jester Jaguar, was the Aortic's estranged husband, the father of her four children. Even though he'd have been a central character in a couple of the Vetala-focused her-stories Tethys could have related, if he'd had time, Koatyl was long ago dust. As for Xibalba, well, he'd been Second Fangs' mortal enemy, emphasis on mortal. He'd also been the twin son of Night Owl, who was still around from the sounds of things, and an eventual Lamia or Night Hag, from before either/or joined the ranks of the Head's undead.

Lamiae did indeed transmogrify into hoot-owls but, having died giving birth, they were also always women. Obviously that wasn't the case with Night Owl. What was, how he'd gained the, um, wisdom to shape shift to an owl of all things, well, when you're a deviant it wasn't just your procreations that made bizarre choices.

"And don't get me started on some of their social customs either," Centauri continued motor-mouthing. "The Spaniards in South and Central America were right to try to convert the Iraches' cousins to Catholicism. As for the French and Brits who mostly populated the States and Canada, at least initially, any form of Christianity is preferable to whatever faiths, or lack thereof, the natives were practising at the time of their conquest."

That said, that vented, the Fatman returned to the subject at hand, addressing Niarchos directly. "If microscopic analyses of the dust these dusted vamps of yours leave behind remains insufficient to identify which specific bloodsuckers have been dusted, then the bounty must be paid generically. Dust from a dusted vamp is dust from a dusted vamp and one more dusted vamp means one less bloodsucker, regardless of whether he or she is Irache or non-Irache."

"I'm sorry, sir," Governor Ferdinand Niarchos responded, though perhaps not as abjectly as Tethys might have expected. "But I'm also sorry that there's no scientific way of proving how much dust constitutes one dusted vamp." And that, Tethys had to admit to himself, was something even he, in all his lifetimes, had never thought of before.

"While I grant you Marutian vamps are, generally speaking, better off than Irache vamps, I have no way of demonstrating to CE's bean-counters that my grain-counters, the vast majority of whom are living Iraches, aren't claiming two or three Irache vamps as certifiable kills when all they've, um, scored is one Marutian fat bat; as opposed to fat cat, to use an Outer Earth term for wealthy bastard.

"We are talking Outer Earth capitalism here, sir, and, as a shareholder, I must ensure fair value for vamp-dust delivered."

"Whoa," said 30-Beers. "What are you up to, Al?"

"If I may," interposed Janna.

"May away," all-but-begged the Legendarian.

Both the Fatman and his handpicked, then elected, administrator acquiesced wordlessly, as if she didn't need verbal permission. Which, to judge by the way she responsively *'made-away'*, she didn't. Devils could read minds next-to-effortlessly; hence Niarchos accusing her of gleaning him, Tethys, mere minutes earlier.

"The Corporate State of Greater Godbad already encompasses the subcontinent, the Penile Peninsula's glans or head, more politely known as Krachla, and large swaths of territory on the Cattail Peninsula. Due to tradition, not to mention devic interference, and their objections, it has little room to expand northwards. Neither, perhaps, should it seek to do so. Centauri Enterprises offers benefits to everyone of course. But that is for the long term. For the immediate term El Dorado beckons.

"Dead Things Walking are an abomination, Mr Tethys. So are their vampiric overseers, albeit somewhat less so, if only because, like you said the heliodromus of Lazareme remarked about Janna Fangfingers, they're still capable of worship. Which in turn indicates they retain most of their intelligence, like your Guardian Angel Jordan – whatever he was; your brother if you're right about him being Rumour's son by Wintry Moira – helped you retain yours.

"I am an Athenan War Witch as well as, as you often refer to me sniggeringly, a Lovely Lady Afrite. We have ever-strived against unnatural Dead Things. So too have any sensible devils. As has Grandfather Sedon. You have eloquently reminded us that devils may not need their adherents alive. But it's certainly preferable they are that and, yes, reproductively so. Outer Earth military technology may be messy but it is effective."

"Thank you for that, APM," said Tethys. Janna winked at him, multiply, briefly. Weird Ferd didn't seem to notice.

"Our plan is simplicity in itself, Mr Tethys," the governor of New Iraxas, Godbad's north-easternmost province, elaborated. "Armed properly, with mostly Outer Earth weaponry that myself, my father and Godbad's General Quentin Anvil, among others, have already vetted and authorized CE to purchase, we'll incinerate or otherwise destroy all of Vetala's Haddazur- or Nergalazur-animated zombies.

"Godbad's unsurpassed armed forces will swoop in from the west. And not just on their feet or in armoured vehicles either. Anvil assures us that his airborne regiments lack only blooding to prove they're second to none. The Sraddhites, in great number – and even you might be surprised how many they number nowadays – will come off of Lake Sedona's islets and out of Diluvia to the north. Meanwhile, ordinarily strictly seafaring Krachlans have massed marines on their side of the Circumcision Canal. So they'll approach from the south.

"But here's a new crunch-factor: the forces of Free Iraxas, under the unifying leadership of Mani-Balam, this remarkably capable Jester Jaguar of theirs, have rethought their isolationism and embraced progress. As a result, they too are already disembarking from across the Internal Ocean of Akadan to the east."

"They're not the only new crunch-factor, Mr Niarchos," said Centauri's daughter-in-law.

"Didn't say they were, Janna. But, as you've just reminded us, you in your War Witch Sisterhood have always been life-defenders. What is new, I'll grant you, is your Mother Superior is the year-younger sister of the Master of Weir – of Daddy Cabby's Weirdom, as Jordy so quaintly refers to it – and she's finally convinced him to send to our side a contingent of Weir's Warrior Elite, his famously formidable Trinondevs, albeit under the command of a clone, Golgotha Nauroz."

"A clone with a very distinguished template," objected Tethys, who knew them both, the template and the clone. "His name was Ubris Nauroz. He was the current Master of Weir's grandfather. I'd have said '*is*' except he had a falling out with Second Fangs and I had to stake him, years ago now, him in the heart, me in another incarnation."

"Be that as it may," Niarchos persisted, both confidently and seemingly proudly, as if victory was a done deal, "Coming in from every coast we've got the Dead Things in a classical pincer movement. We'll eventually catch them in the middle of Hadd; around the vicinity of Dustmound, if you have to know. Haddazur zombies cannot abide running water of any kind, your turn to recall. They'll go down like lemmings over a cliff."

"Mixed up your metaphors there, weirdo," smirked Legendarian. It was so late he felt a smirk was an allowable facial response. "Dustmound's in the middle of Hadd, not on any of its seaside cliffs." Ferdinand Niarchos looked to Alpha Centauri and his daughter-in-law. The Fatman was first to come to the governor's rescue.

"You might not always need an umbrella in New Iraxas, Mr Tethys, but you'd best bring one to Petrograd anyhow. Because the Godbadian Air Force is going to make it rain in Hadd!"

========

Even for Jordan 'Quill' Tethys, it wasn't 'what the hey' anymore. It was time to hit the hay.

Janna St Peche-Montressor wheeled Alpha Centauri across the solarium toward its internal elevator. It would take them to the just-as-well-fortified, sleeping side of the Fatman's Aka Godbad stronghold and, therefore, Centauri Enterprises' unofficial headquarters – the official one being in Godbad City, the currently corporate state's ancient capital.

She paused at his signal. "Go off with Governor Niarchos, Jordy," he said to his guests for the night, as if only now having made up his mind. "And do try to get along for a few days, won't you. When you come back, it'll be my turn to tell you a story. I've already got its title. It'll be called: 'The Launching of the Cosmic Express'!"

========

Niarchos and the Legendarian took the comparative commoners' elevator opening onto Janna's waiting room and office. They agreed on transportation arrangements for late morning and parted ways at the nevertheless heavily guarded VIP level. Less immune than inured to the effects of drinking upwards to thirty beers a day, once he reached his own only moderately less secure floor Tethys more like staggered than walked down the hallway to his spiffy suite.

Someone was waiting for him in its living room. He recognized her right away. Even if he hadn't just been talking about her for howsoever many hours in nearly a row, he would have. Bloodless beauty coupled with a fang-fingered glove and a crystal skull depended off a ruby-inlaid necklace tended to minimize misidentification.

What she was doing in a living room would have been the first question he asked if he didn't hate punning so much. Or hadn't downed close to thirty beers already.

"How'd you get in?"

"Public spaces, Jordy."

"Like fuck it is. I locked the door when I left and it was still locked when I came back."

"Doors don't affect me; not much does. You should know that. And I only need an invite to enter private spaces. You should know that, too."

It was never too late to panic, but even he wouldn't be able to produce his quill, splotch out a pre-drawn destination onto whatever, and dot his way to safety before she was on him. Besides, who's to say she couldn't pull a Pusan Wanderlust and follow him through the Weird?

Like Grandfather Lazareme used to say, it was never too late to procrastinate either. Plus, *'always better to kill time than get killed'* was one of his most heartfelt mottos: "What can I do for you?"

"I need help and you're going to draw him to me."

"Consciousness qualifier, Fangs."

"Since when has dust been conscious?"

"Why should I?"

"Infertility, Tethys. What was it you said to me once – raw, human steak until it's time for the stake? Something like that. And three generations betwixt and between for me to make your children and grandchildren my favourite meals; yours too. First generation's you and your siblings, however many of them you can remember from your last life. And believe me, you'll have plenty of time to tell me all about them."

"What's that?"

Then she heard it too – the phantom piping.

========

Hoot-owls have very good hearing so he must have heard it as well.

========

Clearly doors didn't affect this particular hoot-owl either. And it was see-through-clear when it first shrieked out of between-space. Janna Fangfingers mystified into the Weird just in time to avoid going the way any number of order Rodentia, big or small, had previously, including reanimated ones. And bats, not that they were rodents as such, particularly Marutian bats, were reputedly at the top of this owl's list of favourite meals.

"Hello, mom," said Tethys, as the hoot-owl transmogrified first into a male Irache then went as transparent as, albeit oppositely, Angelus-Irisiel did on the Prison Beach of Incain five hundred years earlier. "How long have you been around?"

"Night Owl's my howsoever hostile host, Jordy. He hates it when you call him '*mom*'; thinks it's rude."

To say the least, the speaker, who chose to manifest what he could see of her as a matronly Mother Goddess of Chinese or Oriental descent, had quite the her-story. Rebellious, free-thinking sort that she – Metisophia, Titanic Metis, Wisdom of Lazareme – had always been, she'd lost her own body during the expansion of the Empire of Lathakra; lost her power focus, a Brainrock cauldron, at the same time.

The Frozen Isle's Death Goddess – Hot-Stuff, Mithras's Virgin, Methandra Thanatos as antique Illuminaries had her – confiscated and kept it after she stuck her in a ringot during the Dome's 48th Century. For some reason Metis never sought to regain either/or. As for how she got out of the ringot, that was another story he could have told the Fatman, the galling governor and Mrs Yataghan had he had the time or inclination.

"Tough tiddlywinks. You doing the piping?"

"I cause your scar to itch?"

"All devils cause my scar to itch."

"Not true. Is it, cousin?"

"Not if you say it isn't, smart ass," said APM All-Eyes protectively, as she wafted out of mind and into sight beside the Legendarian.

She didn't solidify as Janna St Peche-Montressor, though being a practised ethrealist – as in '*make ether real*' – she could have. Being a master illusionist like all devils, she may not have altogether solidified either, though she certainly looked it. Looked, as well, to be a Janna-sized, feminine form composed entirely of blinking eyeballs.

She wasn't, nowhere near. Past experience suggested she was, most likely, only a solitary eyeball with invisible wings to go along with pulchritudinous proportions.

As per usual, he'd had no idea he'd been possessed, albeit by one of her little angels, let alone for how long – though it had probably been since shortly after his lunchtime encounter with whomever had been masquerading as the absent prip, Gottfried Kenton, who was actually in Djerridam-Goatwood.

Aphropsyche Morningstar was about the only devil who could approximate being in two, or two dozen, places at once. While her little angels were little more than glorified azuras, with nary a knack of their own, that she'd stuck one inside of him – to go along with one she presumably kept inside of Mrs Yataghan on a nearly fulltime basis – explained why Janna and he kept exchanging trepidatious looks as the afternoon progressed into evening, progressed into a very late night.

The little angels were looking at each other.

As for the rest of APM, she'd no doubt be along shortly. In the meantime, the aspect here could still speak for the completeness coming: "You've a lot of nerve bringing Night Owl here."

"We're unkind of inseparable these days, *eye-bomination*. And I wouldn't have had to if you'd been doing your job instead of pretty peahen-preening at every man you come across while your husband's outside being other-body bodyguard. What Great Byron, through the Fatman, is seeking to do in Hadd is intolerable."

"Hate to interrupt a pair of big brains like you but what about the goddamned piping?"

"He's warning you off; has been for two days now. And so am I. Cease and desist. Persist and finally die; all of you. Your precious Headworld with you."

"Who's he?" APM's little angel demanded.

"So many eyes and so little eyesight – the Smiling Fiend of course."

Metisophia was once, sort of, Morgianna Sarpedon's *'towel'*. She was also, once, the Legendarian's half-mother. She was gone before APM All-Eyes was all there physically; as in debrained demonically, not Janna St Peche-Montressor corporeally. Night Owl went with her – though given their longstanding, extremely perverse, relationship it was more like Night Owl took them both away between-space, two in one.

"The Smiling Fiend?" one said to the other.

The piping stopped.

"What did you say?" the other responded.

========

The Legendarian had a hot shower, alone. He was non-Metowl-towelling himself off when he chanced to look into the bathroom mirror. What was that streaked into its steaminess? No bout a-doubt-it. Undeniably, that was the letter 'D', done at an angle of 90° clockwise.

As for why it looked like it was smiling, well, wasn't that what the letter 'D' done at that angle would do?

That determined, that then instantly forgotten, he had a remarkably good night's sleep.

****

Goddess Gambit

- Year of the Dome 5980 -

Jim McPherson

"For the Dead to thrive, the Living must die!" So proclaims Nergal Vetala, the Blood Queen of Hadd.

Mercy is a capital **Offense**

Jim McPherson

A **PHANTACEA** **Mythos** Mosaic Novel

published by James H McPherson

ISBN 978-0-9781342-2-8

The launching of the Cosmic Express occurred on Sunday, the 30th of November 1980. On the Hidden Continent of Sedon's Head it was Sedonda, the 30th of Maruta 5980.

The Cosmic Express never reached the Whole Earth's Outer Space. It did, however, reach an aspect of its Inner Space.

Briefly.

1: The Deviant Dead

Sedonda, Maruta 30, 5980

Cosmicaptain Dmetri Diomad and the six cosmicompanions with him inside Cosmicar Four writhed under the stress of takeoff. So did the 60-odd other crewmembers aboard the Cosmic Express proper, its hub-craft, control capsule and six cosmicars.

Something happened.

========

Diomad had seen some peculiar sights in his twenty-seven years. Nothing matched this; not even the disappearance of an entire island, Trigon, his foster father's tri-peaked, ancestral home in the Aegean Sea, a dozen years earlier. The spacecraft was somehow still intact. Whatever hit it managed to inject it into some sort of black space. The Cosmicaptain felt a strange sense of deep joy, almost of accomplishment. Hundreds of pinpoints of light approached the Express. Stars, faeries, angels? Devils!

As the smaller pinpoints kept coming, the largest, the brightest, resolved itself. It was at least ten times the size of the Cosmic Express, which was close to twenty storeys high if you included its firing rockets, what were only now detaching themselves. What it was – what it appeared to be – was a single, impossibly huge, disembodied eye. Its pupil had lips and teeth and a tongue. A mouth. It spoke.

"YOU PIG-WHUMPING, MECHANICAL LOLLIPOP, LOOK WHAT YOU'VE DONE.

"NOT ONLY HAVE YOU RIPPED MY HOLY HALO AND PIERCED THE FORBIDDEN ZONE, YOU'VE FREED SOME OF MY JACKASS OFFSPRING AS WELL."

Over his headphones he heard the Cosmic Express's Cosmicommander shout to one his technicians: "Fire second stage. Let's get the hell out of here."

"Second stage fired, sir!" That'd be its Gypsium fuel-stage. Gypsium was teleportive.

"AND AFTER ALL THAT, YOU'RE TRYING TO GET AWAY. WELL, PUKE ON YOU. A LITTLE GOD-SUCK'LL TEACH YOU SOME MANNERS."

Pursing its lips, the eye-mouth slurped the Express into its mass. Began to chew it.

RRRUURP!

"BLOODY HELL! YOU OUTER EARTHLINGS TASTE AS LOUSY AS YOU DID SIX THOUSAND YEARS AGO."

The eye-mouth spat them not just out of its craw but out of wherever they were in the first place.

"YUK!"

========

He knew they were after him. They'd been after him for days and endless days. Ever since they'd ambushed his patrol. In the jungle. He'd only freshly arrived. Was barely old enough to join them. His patrol, what they ambushed. But, whoa. Not this jungle. At least it didn't look like this jungle. Yet it had to be this jungle. What other jungle could it be?

Couldn't think. No time to think. Days and endless days. Run. They were after him. Running. Always running. For days. They weren't going to catch him. Not alive at least.

He'd kill himself first.

========

And so he ran. And staggered and tripped and fell and crawled and slithered. Through the jungle. The reeking jungle. Must be the same. Days and endless days. The jungle. The slime. The swamp muck. They weren't going to catch him. Aren't going to catch me. I'll kill them first. Kill myself first. Kill myself. Run. Jungle. Stagger. Slime. Fall. Swamp Muck. Leeches. Worms. Skulls. Crawl. They aren't kill myself. Catch them first. Slither. Serpent. Bite off head. Suck blood. Eat. Save ammo.

Heard what they do. In jungle. Muck the fuck. Must be same. Duck! Ambush. Move. Through swamp fuck. Stop laughing. Kill something.

He passes out. Face down. In the swamp muck. Above him monstrous vultures are already circling. He'd forgotten to kill himself.

Better to have remembered.

========

He awoke. Became aware of two strong hands gripping him by the arms, dragging him through the mud. So, they've caught me. He flops his hands at his side. Possum. Dare not open eyes. Yes, possum. Pogo-possum. Must think. Feel. Still there. Fools forgot to take my hand-Gatling. Battle-hardened. Trained never to panic in face of enemy. Feigns unconsciousness. Bides time. Collects thoughts. Concentrates. Steels his nerve. Waits. It's the only way. Should have tried it long ago. NOW!

Twists his body. Yanks free. Rolls. Draw gun-Gatling. Fires. "Fucking kill me. So? Take some of you yellow fuckers with me." Gasps. Incredulity. Stops firing. Missed! Captors? Captor! One. Female. Yellow? White as Aegean whitewash. Resumes firing. Empties automatic handgun into ancient crone. "Impossible. Couldn't have missed. Never missed before. Not so close!"

"Hold, mortal!" chortles hideous hag. "Cease this idiocy. I am the Goddess of Life Eternal. None dare defy my will."

He knows it's a trick; knows they've got him; knows this hateful old woman isn't really there. Hallucination. Result of some foul experiment gooks performed. Heard what they do to captives. Sick fucks. Remembers vow. Hold Gatling to eye. Must be full of bloody blanks. Couldn't have missed. Impossible. Blank in eye's as good as bullet, right?

"Hold, damn you to Satanwyck!" commands the crone, no longer amused. "I've not dragged you all this way just to let you kill yourself."

Fingers tense. Knows it's a trick. Knows there's no old woman standing in front of him. Heard what they can do to men's minds. They, them, slants, captors, raptors, enemy. Knows it's a trick. Must pull trigger. Now, while time still has.

"Hold I say!" The etching of a third eye appears in her forehead. From it shoots a faint beam of light. He pulls trigger. Nothing. Empty. Fumbles for ammunition pouch. "Raise your eyes, soldier. Behold." He obeys. Lifts head. There, perched on a hill cleared of the grasping jungle stands an emerald and gold pagoda, a reminder of heaven in the hell of this Eden.

"You please me, soldier. Live."

========

Jordan Tethys, the legendary 30-Year Man, disliked wearing a garlic necklace.

========

A scruffy looking fellow with a stubble beard and thinning, reddish-blond hair, Tethys made his living telling stories; hence one of his nicknames: the Legendarian. He was wearing his favourite tweed jacket and a checked cap. Like him, both jacket and cap had seen better days. Underneath the cap, stuck to his scalp by their own gluey ichors, were a half-dozen tee-tee tails.

Tee-tees were talking rodents. He could also read the ridges and nodules of their tails, which constituted tales. Pierced into his cap was what appeared to be an ordinary feathered quill. Appearances were deceiving. It was made of Brainrock-

Gypsium, the miraculous Godstuff, the post Big Bang remnants of the Primordial Godhead, that, besides being teleportive and transmutable, composed devic power focuses.

The Legendarian looked to be of an indeterminate age, anywhere from his early thirties to his mid forties. Physically his body was only 32-years old. He lived rough, often in the streets; treated his bodies disrespectfully. At the most he could only hold onto them for 30 years; hence another of his nicknames: the 30-Year Man. At the earliest he could only get into them when they'd been around for 20 years.

This particular body had been, more so than belonged to, George Taurson. George had always been sickly; had died young, barely out of his teens. Tethys had taken it over when he did; made it healthy again. That was an oddity of his deviancy, one of a number. George was his son. He'd been doing that sort of thing for going on 2,000 years.

Tethys claimed he was born of an ordinary man and woman around the start of the Outer Earth's Christian era. The one that he knew of for sure was possessed by a Master Deva, a third generational devil, when he'd been conceived as well as born. He said his devic half-mother was Metisophia, Titanic Metis, she whose Brainrock cauldron Methandra Thanatos, Heat to her husband and breed-brother's Cold, now owned by right of possession. He denied he was a devil, although he did have a scar in his forehead about where a devil's third eye would be. Significantly none of his offspring, or their offspring, had a scar in their forehead until he incarnated within them.

Two incarnations ago he was a woman. She was a nun. She was also a tippler. He, even as a she, drank a lot of beer. Hence his third major nickname: 30-Beers.

He was doing that now.

========

After a short nap, and a shorter flight from Aka Godbad City, he was in Petrograd, the coastal capital of New Iraxas, the subcontinent of Godbad's north-easternmost province. Across the Gulf of Aka from New Iraxas was Old Iraxas, Hadd, the Land of the Ambulant Dead as well as living Iraches. He was in Petrograd as a guest of Ferdinand Niarchos, the provincial governor as well as one of most influential figures within Centauri Enterprises, the Corporate State of Greater Godbad's real power. CE, Centauri Enterprises, was named after its founder, Alpha Centauri. Alpha Centauri was not the Fatman's real name.

So-called, often to his face, because he was well-north of 400 pounds, the Fatman was Tethys's patron in Aka Godbad. They often drank together. Indeed, they'd been drinking together most of yesterday, the 29th of Maruta. Centauri liked his stories. And, if only in terms of length, Tethys had told him a whopper: 'The Disunition of the Unities'.

It wasn't a whopper in terms of verisimilitude, however. Even though the events he told him about took place five centuries ago, some of its characters were still around. One of them often used the Fatman as his shell. That was Thrygragos Byron, one of the Three Great Gods, the second generational devils who sired the entirety of devazurkind's third generation.

Another was Tethys himself. A third and a fourth were the Terrible Twins, Janna and Sraddha Somata. Well, the male of the two may not be around anymore. However, the female of the two still had a Crystal Skull attached to the torc she perpetually wore around her neck and it might contain Sraddha's soul.

Tethys wasn't the only one who referred to the governor as Weird Ferd. The largely CE-owned media-paparazzi often did as well. Even though he never bothered to get married, Ferd had lots of children. Some of them probably belonged to his father Gomez. When the subcontinent was still a monarchy, one ruled by an aristocracy, which it hadn't been for most of three decades, Gomez was the hereditary Duke of the Duchy of Aka Godbad.

Thanks in large measure to Alpha Centauri, and the Great God who sometimes used the Fatman as his shell, the subcontinent was nowadays a nominal democracy, the Corporate State of Greater Godbad. Thanks mostly to Tethys himself, Gomez was now dead and possessed of a Sangazur Spirit Being, Guardian Angel Gomez.

Father and son still talked, usually via Crystal Skull-sets. Gomez was still fertile. His children were fully alive. The pollution of New Iraxas was nonetheless preferable to trying to raise kids in the Bloodlands, where Gomez currently resided. Sedon's Inner Nose wasn't called New Valhalla for nothing. In New Valhalla sibling rivalry was a blood sport.

Although Weird Ferd hadn't required of him any Tethys Tales as partial payment for his room and board, he had required of him some backward drawing. Backward-drawing was one of Tethys's talents. With it the Legendarian had thereby confirmed Ferd's suspicions re Irache capitalism. Yes indeed, as well as in deed, folks cheated. Living Irache vampire-hunters had been gathering the powdered remains of freshly dusted Marutian or Sraddhite fat-cat-bats and passing them off as two or three dusted, oppressed underclass, Irache vamps in order to collect a triple bounty from Centauri Enterprises.

Somewhat disquietingly, though it turned out Ferd had suspected this as well, the Irache bounty-hunters got their information as to the whereabouts of non-Irache fat-cat-bats from scrawny Irache bats. Niarchos had been particularly displeased when one of Tethys's backward-drawings filled in with the familiar face and form of Night Owl, the chief Irache vampire in New Iraxas. While Night Owl was hardly the most imaginative of names, Night Owl was a very hardy vamp. He'd been around since the Simultaneous Summonings of 19/5920 and, as Tethys himself was fond of saying, he had his-stories.

He also had a pair of twin sons, both of whom were now dead and non-risen, a wife who died having them, whereupon she became a Lamia, which meant she had to be dealt with more terminally later on, and a deviant heritage. Which meant he was very difficult to deal with himself, though both Ferd and Tethys thought he had been. Until yesterday, that is, when he and Mama Metis jointly showed up in Tethys's public-spaces-suite in the Fatman's Aka Godbad fortress. In doing so, he-they drove away the vampire who'd turned him, pre-Metis.

Something else about Night Owl was he chewed garlic. He did so because said vamp, Second Fangs, Janna Fangfingers, found the smell of garlic appalling and when one of your sons was her mortal enemy, emphasis on 'was', his own discomfort was a small price to pay to keep her off his back. Or at least keep her too distant to rip out his backbone with her fang-fingered glove.

Born Janna Somata, in 5456 Year of the Dome, Second Fangs and her twin brother, Sraddha, were two of the non-devic, main characters in his rendition of *'The Disunition of the Unities'*. The Terrible Twins were deviants. Their birth parents were hybrid Utopians: Zalman and Melina Somata.

Paternally their devic half-grandfather was Lord Yajur, the Unity of Order, while their half-father was none other than Thrygragos Lazareme himself, whom everybody who saw him seemed to think was their idea of god, albeit non-capitalized; hence Thrygragos Everyman. Maternally their devic half-mother was Datong Harmonia, the Unity of Harmony or Balance, everybody's ideal of female beauty.

Most believed the third Unity, Unholy Abaddon, Abe Chaos, using a Trigregos Talisman, the Susasword, had killed Harmony in 5492. Certainly neither the Female Unity nor the curved, Brainrock blade had been seen since then. Chaos cathonitized Order, rendered him a star in the night's sky, on the Prison Beach of Incain in 5495.

He thereafter committed devic suicide by cutting out his third eye. Actually it was far more brutal than even that. He drove the central prong of his trident, the hilt and sheathe of his Chaos Blade, through his third eye. His debrained daemonic body dissolved, Brainrock trident with it; his remains blowing out to sea. Tethys was there, saw it happen. More than just chances were he was still around somewhere, though. No one knew where; probably no one cared where either.

Tethys, though, was glad Ferd gave him a garlic necklace when he decided to leave the governor's staid domicile in order take a walk and taste the remarkably breathable night air of Petrograd. It wasn't just the night air he wanted to taste either. Now that a majority of altogether alive workers, mostly from Godbad proper, were living here on a daily basis there were some great public bars in Petrograd. Too bad he'd chosen one that didn't have garlic garlands strung around its doors and windows. Vamps were public, too.

Garlic wouldn't do any good against Night Owl but right now it was certainly keeping Second Fangs far enough away for him to finish his getaway drawing. Which he did. It wasn't perfect but it'd be good enough.

"Oh, don't be in such a rush to flush, Tethys," she fay-said, sauntering up to his table. "At least have another beer; for old times' sake if nothing else."

"Sorry, Fangs, but I'm particular about who I drink with. I hate being the person who's drunk. Or haven't I mentioned that to you before?"

"I expect you have." She sat down unbidden. "Waitress, another beer for my friend here."

The bar had become noticeably emptier the moment she walked in, all in white. Sleeveless cloak, stylish crewneck blouse and pleated skirt cut just below the knee, hose or leggings, stiletto-heeled boots, even the strip of cloth she wore about her throat, like the Brainrock torc her devic half-mother wore about her neck, was white. The cameo attached to it wasn't, however. Cameo might not be the right word for the ornament but he knew what it looked like: a crystalline skull. Very charming. And ever so appropriate for a vampire.

One thing he'd never quite figured out, despite nearly twenty centuries worth of incarnations, was how vamps could shape-shift clothes or jewellery out of their bat-forms. He supposed it had something to do with them being soulless demons. Not that most demons wore clothes they manufactured. Those that didn't go naked tended to wear the clothes of those they ate. Still, one of these nights he hoped to see a bat, in bat form, wearing a dress, tux or cape as if it was about to attend the opera.

Second Fangs was all white herself. Being originally a Utopian hybrid, she always had been, hair and flesh; though the former was, technically speaking, more silvery than whitish. Her lips and teeth were red, however, while her furry, fang-fingered glove was dripping. "Nothing for me, I've already had my fill for the night."

"So I noticed," he said. Her Brainrock glove was drenched with blood.

The glove was once the power focus of First Fangs, a foppish Master Deva prone to wearing, yes, opera capes. A lowborn Lazaremist antique Illuminaries named Faustus Vladuca after some obscure figures from East European folklore, at one point in time Janna married him; something mortals rarely did devils. (Except, that is, when the latter were possessing the spouse they did marry.)

Her actual lover, Abe Chaos, first acquired it for her – the Fop's hand still inside it – when she was altogether alive.

"Been meaning to ask what happened to your third eye?" he asked, friendly like.

During the First War between the Living and the Dead, which Illuminaries dated from the birth of Janna's lone offspring in 5480 until his death in 5538, Tethys had the misfortune of being killed then possessed by a symbiotic Fatazur, Guardian Angel Jordan. In 5495 Janna Somata, by then Second Fangs, was possessed of Nergal Vetala, the Vampire Queen of the Dead. Janna-Vetala had, he believed for a number of subsequent incarnations, eyefire-burned Guardian Angel Jordan out of existence, thus ending that particular incarnation.

"Oh, I haven't had one for years and years. That an Illuminary star-chart sticking out of your satchel?" She didn't expect an answer. She knew what it was and that was what it was, an Illuminary star-chart. "Not much use tonight, is it? I'm pretty sure Star Belialma's still up there but there's some big ones missing." Belialma was Lady Lust, a onetime Prime Sinistral of Satanwyck, which was where demonic vampires originated.

"So there is," he agreed, finishing his beer. He hated to drink and run; not that he'd be running as such. "Lord Order's the biggest one in the Lazaremist Quadrant but there's an equally significant one over in the Mithradic Quadrant. Star Phantast is no piker either." Star Phantast had been in the Night's Sky for going on 2,000 years. Tethys blamed him for his first death. "The entire Constellation Thanatos has vanished, so that's got me in conspiracy theory mode. Non-Lazaremist firstborns tend to stick together."

Phantast Thanatos, aka the Dreamweaver, along with Methandra and Tantal, the Death Gods of Lathakra, were firstborn Mithradites. By contrast the two Silverclouds, who were as married as Heat and Cold, were Great Byron's firstborn, the only two who made it to the Whole Earth pre-Genesea. For most of their existence the Lazaremists had stuck together. So long as Harmony, the Unity of Balance, Second Fangs' devic half-mother, was around to stick herself between her two brothers, the Unities of Order and Chaos, that is to say. Only then they forgot the togetherness part and started trying to stick it to each other; Unholy Abaddon being more successful in that department than other two.

The waitress was bringing him another pilsner. He eyeballed her. It was a different waitress than the one who'd been serving him earlier. This one wasn't wearing a garlic necklace whereas the previous one had been. She also had black skin whereas her predecessor was an Irache redskin. Her skin colour didn't mean much; there were plenty of women with black skin in Godbad. Mind you, he thought to himself, tapping the tip of his Brainrock quill against his drawing, there were plenty of women from Marutia who had black skin, too.

That her head was shaven did mean something. Only Sraddhites shaved the hair off their heads and, because they abolished ambulatory Dead Things, Sraddhites weren't very popular in New Iraxas. That she put the beer down in front of Fangs, skewing her nose as she did so, meant something as well. He squiggled his name on the bottom of the drawing but held off doing his getaway dot. He could as easily drink one-handed as he could dot his drawing with the other one.

"Really, Tethys," Fangfingers, who knew him for the deviant he was, reproached him for readying his getaway. "I'm disappointed in you. We're old pals, you and I. Besides, I haven't turned everyone left in this room. Some of the Iraches Night Owl turned are no more offended at the smell of garlic than he is, which is to say not so much so as mine. And enough of them are as pissed off at him as I am. Bats shouldn't rat on bats, even fat-cat-bats."

Using her blood-crusted, faintly glowing Brainrock glove she shoved the beer mug across the table to within his easy reach. He was tempted. She was tempting him; mesmerizing him, put better. "In other words," he appreciated, taking it by its handle, "I was as dead as you wanted me to be. Which isn't at all, right? Not right away anyways." He took a sip. Beer would be the death of him yet. Again, make that.

"Why'd you come here, Fangs? What is it you really want – a drawing of Night Owl? Ferd did too: Where he was during the daytime; then where he was after dark. Except, well, as much as the Wily Owl's as much my old pal as you are, albeit not so much so old, I'll grant you, and as much as, you know, I'm such a big bat-lover, it seems he's his spies just as you've your spies. Only his spies got word to him during the daytime. Furthermore, it seems he's become more of a shape-shifter than most of you bats are already. Sorry to disappoint, Janna."

"Janna's nice, Jordy. No one's called me that for, well, centuries. I'm perfectly capable of fighting my own battles; always have been, as you should recall. I'll find Wily Old eventually, no matter what shapes he can take nowadays. Those stars you mentioned, I didn't realize Phantast and Constellation Thanatos were missing. I did, however, realize three others were, one in each of the Great Gods' quadrant: Star Straw-Man, Star Shovel-Nose and Star First Fangs. Even I can't fight them all at once, can I? So, yes, I want a drawing from you; one of a certain Tvasitar Talisman."

Tethys pretended to mishear her meaning. He flipped some pages back on the sketchpad he'd been working on all day. Most of them needed their backgrounds filling in, then his signature and dotting, but otherwise they were finished products. He ripped off three of the sheets, the ones where he'd done drawings of the Trigregos

Talismans: the Amateramirror, the Crimson Corona and the Susasword. Reputedly any of one of them could kill a devil. He poised his quill to dot whichever one she chose.

"You're hardly the only one. Which one do you want?"

She scowled at him. Then she smiled, too toothily for his taste, unfinished beer or no unfinished beer. "Nice try, dickhead. You reckon you can get away that easily? In a puff of smoke no less. That's my trick. One of them anyhow. I know what'll happen if you dot any one of those things. The sheet will burst into flames. No, my lad. I'm quicker than that. And so are they."

The beer hall had always been smoke-filled. Most taverns were; except in Aka-Godbad City, that is. Smokeless bars were another of the Fatman's recent innovations in the name of *greening*' Godbad. So distracted was he, though, he hadn't realized the smoke in the bar, particularly around his table, had become a whole lot thicker than it had been before Second Fangs walked into the bar.

Which was something else he'd always wondered about vampires. How could they travel about as mist? A decent fart would blow them away, wouldn't it?

Then they had him, her vamps, demystifying out of all that smoke. Had him, arms pinned back against the chair, his quill shaken out of his grip onto the table-top, his garlic necklace torn off and tossed against the wall, before he could dot a ditto to any of his getaway pages. Second Fangs leaned forward. Her breath was fetid. Nothing new about that. She licked her lips then bared her fangs. Nothing new about either of that either.

"Maybe I'm still thirsty, dearest, latest, incarnation of one of my first and last living lovers. Maybe I'm not. But they are, my bats. Then again, another of your howsoever recent pals, CE's Fatman, has been providing us, day by day, with fresh food, night by night. So, here's what you can do for me, 30-Years, if you want your 30 beers. You can draw me a Tvasitar Talisman, a trident, you know the one, and I won't have to fight all of my battles all by myself. Abe Chaos could never say no to me."

The nib of his Brainrock quill no longer just perceptibly glowed. It ignited instead, began to glow as brightly as a miniature sunburst. About time too, thought Tethys, having had enough sense to close his eyes, both of them, just before it did so. When he opened them again, the smoke in the barroom was even thicker and Athenan War Witches were all about the place, gathering up dust. They were bounty-hunters, too, although unlike capitalistic Iraches they'd have done it for free.

One of them was Morgianna Sarpedon, the Athenans' so-called Grandmother Superior, the Hellions' Morrigan as well. Her birth name was Nauroz but when Morg's great-grandmother, Kyprian Somata, the then Master of Weir, adopted her, she changed her maiden name to her own – Somata also being Janna Fangfingers' birth name. They were in fact directly, via Kyprian's daughter (Morg's grandmother) Chryseis therefore born Somata, if distantly, by a few centuries, related.

She was just as white-as-light, only she wore a pantsuit rather a blouse and skirt. There was also nothing dead about her. Probably was something daemonic about her, though. The Morrigan may have been an honorific but it came with certain horrific perks, one of which was an invisible, debrained demon. Of course she'd had to earn it and part of earning it meant de-braining it.

Morg congratulated him. "Well done, Jordy, though I have to wonder why you were so slow on the dotting. Good thing Sister Scylla here doesn't trust anyone. Otherwise you would have been well-done-for."

"Things are missing, mother," said Morg's daughter, the eldest of two, Tsishah Twilight, Shenon's non-Lemurian Aortic.

She was another one wearing a demon. Her demon wasn't invisible. It made her look like a red-skinned Irache, not a pureblood Utopian. (Which Morgianna very nearly was; it was only her mother, Pandora Mannering, who had mixed blood. Her father, Augustus Nauroz, was as pure as the driven snow; if there was such a thing as pure black snow, driven or otherwise.)

"Her Crystal Skull and the fang-figured glove, where are they?"

"She got away," said one of the other Athenans there, Janna St Peche-Montressor, Alpha Centauri's daughter-in-law, who'd also been on hand last night when Janna Fangfingers sought to get him to draw Abe Chaos to her the first time. Rather, she'd been in the same building, father-in-law Fatman's residence-cum-fortress in Aka Godbad City.

This Janna's maiden name sounded French because it was; albeit Inner Earth French. She hailed from Dukkha, on the Coast of Fearsome Fobbiat, on the edge of Sedon's Moustache, his hairy Upper Lip, the same place Tsishah's father, Tammuz Rhymer, was born and raised before he became Tom-Tiddly Taddletale, a recurring faerie-type.

The second half of her surname sort of did too, but that was because, during the Godbadian Civil War, Centauri had to foster out his son, whose first name was Yataghan, to a family whose last name was Montressor. She'd married him some years back; was the mother of Yat's (thus far) lone child, a girl by the decidedly non-French-sounding name of Gudrun.

Other than many of the Mantel replicas of Subcranial Temporis, only Dukkhans had as their birth-tongue a language different from Sedon Speak; pre-Babel Babble as Tethys called it. How that came about was one of the post-Disunition stories he'd have told the Fatman, Governor Niarchos and this Janna last night, had he had the time.

"And you know that because you're named after her?" queried Witch Isle's other Aortic, the amphibious, Lemurian Frog Woman of the two.

Aortic Amphitrite was being sarcastic. She was also wearing a Mandroid guard-body as opposed to a debrained demon; was more squished into it than wearing it, sooth said; was akin to a humanoid frog preserved in amber. It kept her sprayed with ordinary, as in non-vampiric, mist. Like Morgianna she was a Summoning Child, which meant she was approaching her sixtieth birthday. That was old for a Lemurian. Soon she'd have to submerge herself beneath the Head's Interior Ocean of Akadan permanently.

The only reason she hadn't done so already, she'd told him at the governor's mansion this afternoon, was because her deviant daughter Lakshmi, who lived way up north in Subcranial Temporis, beneath Sedon's Cranium, was turning eighteen this Lazam, Friday on the Outer Earth. That wasn't all of it either. The very next day, Devauray or Saturday, Lakshmi was getting married to a much older man, one

Centurion Sophiscient by name, and Amphitrite wanted to be there for that as well. Jordy was of course invited.

Since Temporis was one of his favourite places on the Whole Head, even if the Thousand Caverns of Tariqartha were actually in its underside, and since he knew all the parties involved, he said he wouldn't miss it for the world. Then he'd agreed to this hair-brained scheme Ferd and the Athenans put to him and his world very nearly ended, at least for the time being.

Which was why he whirled to rail at the eldest witch there.

She was Amphitrite's slightly older step-sister, the one the others, her-stories all of them, deferred to even though she wasn't in any position of authority over them. She'd once been the Queen of Godbad, though, and still was the Duchess of Achigan, the dukedom at the tip of Sedon's Lower Lip. Like Amphitrite she was amphibious, albeit with her gills discretely placed behind her ears instead of in her neck.

That meant she was Piscine rather than Lemurian; made her akin to a Melusine Piscine like the fabled Death's Head Hellion of so many centuries ago; the Master of Weir who caused both the Ghostlands and the Thanatoids of Lathakra to sink into their thousand year sleep – although, strictly speaking, it was more like an 1100-year sleep.

Melusine Piscines being the probable inspiration for mermaids, one of them, it also made her an exotic form of human being; exotic in every sense of the word, including erotic. As much as he found Living Janna as irresistible, albeit in a living way, as he had been finding the Undead Janna irresistible in a potentially deathly way, this witch was still by far the best looking of the lovely lot who'd come to his rescue.

That she was a deviant, like him and Amphitrite's Lakshmi, only partially explained how she managed to hold onto her looks. Her human forbearers were very good looking as well. Not that he got any of them. Then again, once he incarnated in them, the boys much more so than girls, who didn't lose their hair, started to look more like him than they looked liked themselves.

That she wielded three Brainrock power foci, one of which, what she called her soul-net, had extremely coercive qualities to it, had nothing to do with how she'd convinced him to go along with tonight's idiocy. Like Abe Chaos to Janna Somata, in all the incarnations he'd known her, which was all of the incarnations he'd had this century, he'd never been able to say no to her.

He couldn't say no to her even when she was just a little girl digging large, disturbingly penile geoducks on Shenon, Witch Isle, for Merthetis, her adoptive mother – who eventually became the heart-shaped island's Lemurian Aortic, a position now held by her Summoning Child daughter, nearing sixty Amphitrite.

Neither had his current incarnation George Taurson, he sort of remembered, when he was just a little boy and she – by then a beauty fully grown, including the sharpness of her incisors, which matched her wit – came by Apple Isle for one of her infrequent visits there.

(Fisherwoman and the Korant Corn Queens' Miracle Maenad George Taurson called mom may not have been bosom buddies but they shared the same bosom, albeit almost a decade apart and with a different Master Deva lactating said breast milk behind the scenes, as it were.)

After what he just been through, he could envisage saying no to her now. He felt sure of that; told her as much as well. "That's the last time I let you use me as bat-bait, Fish-Witch."

"Oh, do clam the oyster-shuck up, Jordan River," the exotic retorted. "At least you're still altogether alluvial alive. And that's albacore-more than I can say about my nephew."

He hated it when she called him that but she was right. Auntie Fish didn't just have fish-stories, she had bilge buckets brimming over with them. And in a convoluted way his current incarnation did indeed live out his life as her nephew. He might live out his death as well, if a Sangazur or Fatazur or some such symbiotic spirit being got hold of this body after he, the Legendarian, passed on to his next 30-year lifetime.

He flipped a page, dotted a getaway-drawing, took himself elsewhere.

=========

The Ice Palace was carved out of a glacier high up in the Labrys Mountain Range that gave the Frozen Isle of Lathakra its geographical backbone. Largely composed of active volcanoes, the Labrys Range effectively divided Lathakra into two distinct realms. Those were that of the Fire Kings on the west, Sea of Clouds side, where lava rivers flowed; and that of the Intuits on the east, Ocean of Psychron side, where the sun rose but where there was little besides Intuit settlements on ice floes.

Here banged the Piper.

"Well, Smiler, was it worth it?" grumbled the twelve-foot tall, blue-skinned, snow-haired, hoar-bearded god-devil of Lathakra.

"Look upstairs," responded his fiery, red-faced and red-haired, six-inch tall sister-wife, Heat to his Cold. "The stars of our lost children, never shining more brilliantly than they were last night, are no longer in Sedon's heavens."

Maintaining the bongo-beat he'd already set, their never-remembered guest continued to tap the two humanoid skulls depending from the Brainrock chain around his neck. He did so with pinkish fingers that were too long by at least a joint. Small mercy, he'd stopped tooting on his panpipes. Instead he licked their nibs with a forked tongue to keep them moist.

"Care for another tune?"

****